CHAPTER ONE

Lorcan

"I'll tear you into fucking scraps for this. Then, I'll feed you to my demons," I hiss as I prowl toward Ezra, glittering shards of glass crunching under my boots.

"I'd love to see you try," Ezra challenges. "Besides, all I did was tell her the truth."

My fingers dig into my kneecaps as I pant through the onslaught of torturous reflection ricocheting inside my mind. I yearn for my Evie with every godsdamn breath. The ache to have her safely back in my arms suffocates the oxygen in my blood as effectively as a pillow pressed tightly against an enemy's face.

"You wanted her to leave me."

"Of course," Ezra says with a shrug, "but it's not like I could've guessed she would pull a magic mirror out of her ass. Not to mention, you clearly have feelings for the witch and no relationship should start on a bed of lies."

"I *despise* you."

Ezra grins. "Like wise."

I think back to when my hatred for Evie morphed into something else. The moment I placed one foot in the Human Realm, I was done for. Naturally, I didn't realize my feelings until it was too late, and Evie left me. It was my fault. I should have known she'd find out the truth in that grimoire, not that it was the whole truth.

Trust for Evie's great aunt Evangeline to warp the truth, even in the pages of her own journals.

I grab the sides of my head. I would claw the flesh from my skull if it would stop the vile thoughts of worry spreading like the plague in my mind.

Where has Edward, and therefore The Order, taken her? What are they doing to her?

I stand in front of the shattered portal mirror. It's been days and I still haven't been able to track her. The memory of Evie's blood soaking into the carpet burns across my vision, and I stumble back a step.

My shadows coil in my chest, then explode from every pore. "Fuck!"

A warm emotion tightens around my loathing like a thick, gray storm cloud picking away at my hatred and need for revenge like a corrosive. The full strength of her aura rocked the foundation

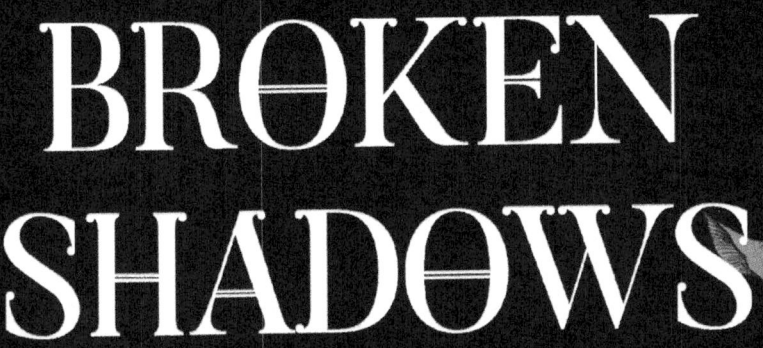

BROKEN SHADOWS

REBECCA L. GARCIA
CM HUTTON

Proofread by Kerri at Dark Bear Edits
Cover design by Jay at Simply Defined Art

PLAYLIST

Animal- Magnolia Park, Ethan Ross, PLVTINUM

NO FACE- Arankai

Closer- Nine Inch Nails

The Dark of You- Breaking Benjamin

CONTORTIONIST Arankai

Habitual Decline- Like Moths To Flames

Like A Villain- Bad Omens

Dance With The Devil- Breaking Benjamin

Hello- Evanescence

House of Memories- Panic! At The Disco

Rapture- Pedro The Lion

POLTERGEIST!- CORPSE, OmenXIII

The In-Between- In This Moment

Voices- Motionless In White

For Yarilys, Iris, Ruby Sutton, Elise Crowley, and Hannah.
Fly those red flags high!

For those who suffered through our epic cliffhanger, this one's for you!

CONTENT WARNINGS

This is a work of fiction and any BDSM references are not meant as a guide, nor are they accurately portrayed. Please see a full list of content warnings below. Broken Shadows is a dark paranormal romance, with scenes of non-consent and other topics that can be triggering.

BDSM

Breath Play

Blood Play

Body Modification

Clowns (very short scene within a chapter)

Death of a Minor Character

Degradation

Demons

Domestic Violence

Dormaphilia

Drug Use/Abuse

Dub-Con

Erotic Asphyxiation

Expressionism

Foul Language

Grief

Gore

Genital mutilation and removal (villain)

Knife Play

Masks

Mental Illness

Murder

Non-Con

Orgasm Denial

Parental Abuse

Religious Occult

Religious Trauma

Sex Without a Condom

Sexual Abuse (briefly depicted)

Sexual Violence

Sleep Paralysis

Smoking

Somnophilia

Stalking

Strangulation

Suicidal ideation

Violence

PRONUNCIATION

Evie- (E-vee)
Lorcan- (Lore-can)
Gomez- (Go-mehz)
Ezra- (Ez-rah)
Rosa- (Row-sa)
Aiden- (Ay-den)
Gideon- (Gid-ee-on)
Samuel- (Sam-u-el)
Asher- (Ash-er)
Lazarus- (L-az-are-us)
Silus- (Sigh-luss)
Lucifer- (Lou-si-fur)
Evangeline- (Ee-van-gel-een)

BROKEN SHADOWS

of my sanity, and some part of me knew I couldn't ever let her go. I should have told her when my feelings changed, when I knew I couldn't keep to my original plan to have her take my place here. Maybe then she wouldn't have left.

Ezra clears his throat, dragging me from the what ifs plaguing my mind. "All hostility aside, telling her the truth was the only sure way I had to drive you two apart."

"The truth? You mean half-truths and barely veiled manipulations. Whatever you want to call our relationship, it's a moot point." Mental claws shred through my psyche, the scant amount of sanity left dangles by a thin thread. My organs catch fire, then turn to ash as my rage boils me alive from the inside out. "She left me."

Ezra snorts. "I'd be happy about that, if it wasn't for the fact that she trapped me in here too. At least I'm in *great* company."

I throw my hands up. "What's another few centuries of solitude? Except I'm trapped with my egomaniac of a brother who plotted against me and trapped me in a cage for decades."

"Or maybe you never left the cage and *this*," Ezra proclaims, with laughter in his voice. "Is all a grand, twisted illusion." He throws his arms out to his sides and spins slowly.

"I won't let you fuck with my head again. Not that it matters. I feel nothing without my little witch."

"Pathetic," my brother declares, shaking his head.

"What the fuck did you just say?"

I said you're fucking pathetic. Ezra's voice sounds in my mind as he pushes the thought through my mental shields.

"Get out of my head!" A shiver races up my spine, dragging memories of the cage and every barbed mental taunt from Ezra and Lazarus. The carpet shreds and the pine baseboards crack underneath our feet as my shadows swirl into a cyclone and into the ground, thrashing and demolishing everything in my path as I sprint from the servant's quarters, powdery snow clouding the yard.

A shadow connects with the doors of the manor's grand entrance, slamming them open. My footsteps echo off the marble flooring as I pace between the two staircases. Ezra's arms fold over his chest, snow flurries drifting around him. I rub the nape of my neck and glare at him.

"Are you done?" he asks and steps forward, his shadows closing the doors behind him.

I squeeze my eyes shut and breathe through my clenched teeth. "No."

I reach for his throat, but his fist smashes into my face, sending streaks of agony through my cheekbone. My eyes blink several times, then warm, heavy hands land on my shoulders as my vision finally clears.

I lift my fingers to my lips. Crimson stains my skin when I make contact, and I laugh maniacally. "I'm going to kill you," I growl, each word I utter drips with the promise of violence as they rush off my tongue.

I launch myself at him, claws first, the muscles in his neck tensing as my nails penetrate the flesh of his chest. Demon blood, in a shade of blue so deep that it appears nearly black, blossoms across his shirt. The jagged slashes of fabric now resembling the innards of a Hell beast.

Fury blinds me as my shadows lash across his face, leaving paper cut like wounds in their wake. His eyes burn into mine, black fire rising in their depths. Good. Let the wrath rise, then I can dispose of him and retrieve my witch. I grin and curl two fingers toward me, but Ezra moves faster than I expect as my madness distorts reality.

My breathing hitches, then cuts off entirely as Ezra cinches my windpipe with a shadow. He moves me a safe distance away from him and coils another length of shadow around my torso and calves, pinning my arms to my sides. My boots scrape across the marble floor as his shadows drag me through the foyer to the dining room, depositing me into a velvet upholstered chair, his shadows continuing to render me immobile.

"You motherfucker," I mouth, but no sound escapes to form the words.

Ezra smirks, obsidian flames dancing in his irises. "Now, you can fucking listen for once." He grunts as he runs his fingers through his hair and encounters the tangled knot of his bun. A purple hair tie snaps against his wrist, then he continues unknotting his dark hair with his tattooed fingers. "You always were so intense when you were upset."

The words flow off his tongue so flippantly, as if losing the one thing in my life that I give a shit about means absolutely nothing. Besides, he's one to talk. He's fucking Wrath, the embodiment of anger. I've never come close to the fits he throws.

I press my arms and legs into his shadows while shifting my torso as much as possible. My muscles bulge and strain against their binds, but Ezra only tightens his shadow ropes. Blackness seeps into the edges of my vision as my lungs starve for oxygen.

"This is pitiful, Brother." Ezra sighs as his demonic body slowly fades into his human-like one. "If you don't get a handle on your madness, or whatever it is you call this," Ezra states, motioning up and down with a hand, "you'll be no use to me."

I freeze, ice quenching the fire in my blood so thoroughly I swear it hisses.

My brother's gaze flicks back and forth over my face. He nods slowly as he acknowledges the weariness settling over my features. With one fluid movement, his shadows dissipate. I pant and grip my knees for support as my trachea and lungs burn, their membranes flooding with precious air.

Ezra plucks at his ruined clothes, the gore drenched, slashed fabric clinging to his skin, then plants his ass on the mahogany table. "We have bigger things to worry about, like getting the fuck out of here," he states, his upper lip curling, "but you still owe me a new shirt, dick."

"I agree and plan to find a way out *by myself.*"

Ezra scoffs. "You need my help. As much as it pains me to admit, we need to work together on this one." He shakes his head and blows out a tense breath. "If your witch hadn't smashed the damn mirror—"

"It's your own fault. You followed us into the Shadow Realm of your own free will."

He rolls his eyes. "Yes, but she wouldn't have been in the Shadow Realm to begin with if you didn't stalk her through mirrors for months and make it easy for us to find her."

My eyelid twitches as I struggle to keep my composure intact. "Why were you looking for her, anyway? We both know The Order means nothing to you."

"It doesn't, but we needed the extra hands."

"What is it you want with Evie?" I ask again, knowing I won't ask a third damned time.

"To unleash her magic," he admits, and fury laces my veins as my fingers flex with the urge to destroy him. "I knew you'd try to use her so you could leave the Shadow Realm. I didn't want you out. In fact, I wanted you dead. But things changed recently."

Of course, the fucker wanted me gone. "What things?"

He doesn't answer as he paces around the room. The usual snark in his tone returns when he opens his mouth. "Do you know what the advantage of skulking around in the shadows is?" He pauses, rubbing his jaw thoughtfully. "I witnessed so much more between the two of you than you realize. It was both intriguing and disgusting watching you pant at the witch's heels like a well-trained dog."

"Fucking lech."

Ezra continues as if I haven't spoken. "I don't even want to get into the psychological fuckity-fuck that was. How do you think she found her aunt's grimoire and knew what was under your mask?"

A growl rumbles in my chest, but Ezra continues to speak over it.

"Look, if I hadn't interfered, I would have been stuck here for the rest of my damn days with only the sound of you two fucking all over the manor for company."

"Again, you're a godsdamn pervert."

"Have I ever denied it? Although, I'll admit it was fucking hilarious seeing that cute little bat piss you off so thoroughly. I think you're officially bronamies. What was it you called him?" He taps a finger against his chin, then chuckles. "Oh right, Fluffy Fucker. Classic Lorcan, an emotional wreck."

I march up to him, snarling in his face. "The only thing your interference accomplished was scaring her into destroying the portal, the very one you needed to leave here too." I draw away, my claw not so accidentally cutting the hair tie from his wrist, then blow out a slow, wistful breath. "Maybe if you behaved, your plan would have succeeded, and she would have left me and wouldn't have been terrified enough to ruin your only way out of here."

Ezra snorts and shoves his hair out of his face. "Perhaps you're right."

"I usually am." I rub my temples. "Let's be done with this conversation. I'm tired of looking at your godsdamn face."

Ezra meanders to the windows, then pushes aside the purple, black, and gray layered drapes. He sighs and leans his ass on the sill. "I, too, am sick of looking at *your* face." He smirks. "So, in the spirit of that goal, perhaps we should form a truce."

The dining room chair creaks as I drop my weight onto its velvet cushion, my anger retreating into a slow burn in my gut. I rub my temples and contemplate his suggestion. "You have been keeping secrets from me for hundreds of years. In order to have a truce, there must be some level of trust between us. How in the fuck can I trust you?"

Ezra grins, then shrugs. "Maybe you can't, but you'll have to take the risk if you want to save your witch's skin."

"Tell me why your motives changed," I demand, reflecting on our earlier conversation. "Your goal was to keep me trapped in here and get Evie out so you could unleash her magic to what? Kill me?"

He smirks. "Isn't someone clever?"

I roll my eyes. "So, what could have possibly happened that made you change your mind about destroying me? It must have been something big."

Miraculous silence descends as Ezra taps his lips with a tattooed index finger before taking the seat next to me, the legs of his chair scraping along the stone floor.

"There is a lot you don't know, but I'll start with the most fuckity-fucked one."

I dip my chin in acknowledgement as I wait for Ezra to reveal why he's really here and possibly drop any hints to what Evie might be subjected to by The Order.

Ezra leans forward and bites his lip. "I think that Evangeline, you know the *other* Fallenmore witch, is in Hell doing her damned best to manipulate our father," he confesses and my jaw drops. "She's the reason all our brothers, including myself, allied against you initially. Well, Samuel told us you were after Dad's throne. However, after spending time in the oh so lovely Shadow Realm—"

"And stalking me."

"Yep, that too. I find it hard to believe that you give a shit about ruling Hell. You have zero ambition to return there."

I shout, "Samuel is a fucking liar. I've never desired to rule Hell. How could you believe anything that cunt said?"

My brother's hands clench into fists as they rest on the table. "Well, I deduced when you didn't seem to know anything about the throne, that Samuel lied. I never actually verified anything our brother said with Lucifer. None of us, except for Eva and Samuel, are allowed to see Dad. But I'm observant, more than our other brothers, who still believe his bullshit. Samuel is obviously in love with Evangeline, even though she's supposed to be with Lucifer. You know what she's like, and I bet she's manipulating them both."

My eyes roll so far into my skull I swear I see brain matter. "Of course, she is. So, I guess now we're both fucked."

Ezra clears his throat. "*Some* more than others. But the fact remains that all the shit our family continues to put up with from that bitch Evangeline is because of *your* actions," he proclaims, accusation heavy in his voice. "Come now, Brother, I remember the way she clung to you, even if Samuel and the others pretend that didn't happen. She was always *my love* this, *my love* that."

I drum my fingers on my jean clad thigh, then freeze. Something about those specific words seems familiar. A locked box buried deep in my subconscious creaks open, oppressed memories flying out like a swarm of locusts. Shit. I grab the sides of my head as the information overloads my mind.

"Lor?" Ezra calls, but it's as if I'm miles under the ocean's waves. My thoughts come to a trickle, then cease all together as the pressure inside my skull threatens to crack it open like an egg.

I gasp as memory after memory detonates across my mind's eye. Fuck, I've forgotten so much. Too much.

The memory unfolds, her voice echoing into my mind from decades before.

"Love." Evangeline cackles as she sashays across an unfamiliar room, her jade robe swishing around her bare legs. *Her image blurs as the next memory threatens to take its place. I dig mental claws into the scene playing out, enraged fury lashing through my bloodstream.*

"I love you, Lorcan. No one will ever take you away from me. I'll make sure of it," Evangeline says, hovering over me.

Frost coats my ribs. My eyes burn like they've been scrubbed with sand. Fuck. I can't close my eyes. What the Hell has this bitch done to me? I try to shove her away, but something is cutting off the circulation in my wrists and binding me to the bed. Metal clinks, and I whip my head to the side.

"Get the fuck away from me, Eva. Did you not hear a word I said last night? I want nothing to do with you," I growl, my eyes landing on the glowing chains attached to my wrist. "Fuck!" I roar, flinching as agony screams into my bones.

"That's not very nice, Love," she pouts. Pulses of liquid agony throb throughout my wrist as the witch twists a metal eyehook deeper into the bone. "Let's just tighten these chains a little, shall we? I certainly can't have you escaping me again."

My vision swims as the memory dissolves. Ezra's crouched form comes into focus. "That was creepy as shit, Brother."

"What?" I mumble, the coherent thought still struggling to resurface.

"Your eyes rolled back in your head, the whites showing and everything. Your shadows made this swirling cocoon around you a second later," Ezra explains, patting my knee.

Two words burn into my brain matter. *Unrequited love.*

Godsfuckingdammit. I stare at my brother. "Evangeline must be doing all of this for revenge. She could never accept that I didn't love her," I growl, my claws sinking into my knees. "But that still doesn't explain everything. Why didn't you verify with our father that it was all his orders?"

"Samuel was very convincing," Ezra expounds, then shrugs. "I thought you were a threat to our dad and I just… I didn't think."

The breath whooshes past my lips as I huff, stabbing a hand through my hair. "You've always been a fucking daddy's boy."

"And damn proud of it." Ezra grins so widely the chandelier above glints off his teeth. "Now, tell me more about this unlocked memory."

I sigh. Damn him to Hell's torture fields. "I never had a relationship with Evangeline. She forced me into one through magic. I befriended her. That was it." The memories rush back one by one, and I grip the sides of my head until they subside. "I manipulated her," I admit. "Through friendship. She was an outcast, and I made her feel seen. She was so powerful, Brother, and I wanted to ensure you and Lazarus and Samuel wouldn't hurt me again. I never thought she'd go all crazy on my ass and trap me in the Shadow Realm."

Ezra's face flows through a series of emotions; it would be comical if I wasn't ripping my fucking heart open and bearing its bleeding core.

"I just find it unbelievable that she somehow controlled you. You're, well, you. King of Demons, Lucifer's eldest son and all that shit. A witch cannot fuck the memories of royal demons, no matter how powerful."

I rub my temples. "Oh, but she can. We both know she was the most powerful witch in existence. She always had her nose in a spell book and dedicated her life to her craft, more so than the rest of her family. Eva was practicing the most complex rituals since she was a kid. That entire family was powerful on their own, but practiced? That's why I knew Evie could get me out. With her family dead, she holds the power of her entire coven. She's stronger than even Evangeline. If she ever embraces her magic, that is."

Shadows wrap around my legs and spread across the floor like obsidian fog. Ezra's shadows join mine, swirling together in a chaotic dance as he penetrates my mind for the truth.

"Fuck. You really are telling the truth," Ezra affirms, his jaw falling open.

"Yes, imbecile. Close your fucking mouth or I'll shove my boot down your throat."

Ezra laughs. "Just like the good old days, eh?" His feet clomp against the floor as he stands and bounces on the balls of his feet.

My back cracks as I lean against the carved back of the chair. "So, are we going to work together to get out of here and stop the bitch? Or would you like to continue to taunt me instead?"

Ezra nods, a smile spreading across his face, then thrusts his hand toward me. "Both."

"Evie is off limits."

Finally, he smiles. "After what you just told me, I doubt I'd survive her, anyway. So, truce?"

Everything within me recoils, reluctant to trust anyone but myself and my little witch, even if she's the weapon my brothers and The Order plan to use against me.

"Fuck." I grasp his tattooed hand with mine and squeeze his knuckles harder than necessary. "Truce."

CHAPTER TWO

Evie

I should have stayed with my demon. The thought trickles into my mind unbidden. The grimoire, the truth of his history with my family, suddenly seems insignificant compared to the evil I face now. Memories of my final days in the Shadow Realm offer some comfort as I lay strapped to the hospital bed in the basement at The Order's Headquarters.

I close my eyes and my stomach flutters when I recall how Lorcan's arms tightened around me when we'd danced in the library. He'd removed his mask that night, unveiling his true name inked into the skin blow his right eye.. I'd never seen him so vulnerable, laid bare for me in the physical and mental sense. Until that moment, any intimacy was fleeting between us, lost somewhere between hate and lust.

The moment plays repeatedly in my mind as the soundtrack to *Blossom in the Dark* plays like an eerie backtrack, Lorcan's voice deep and smooth, as if he were still singing the lyrics in my ear. My lips curve when I recall how his dimples deepened when I giggled as he spun me around.

It was the first time things felt easy between us, and it was cut so damned short. I didn't even get a chance to kiss him without his mask before he found the grimoire pages and then Ezra came, punctuating our time together.

I knew it had to end. He loved my great aunt. I shudder as thoughts of them together make me cringe. I shouldn't care. I'd left him behind and now it was over. Everything Lorcan said was a lie. He never cared for me. It was pretend. So why can't I stop thinking about him?

The wooden steps creak, disrupting my mental torture. Edward's loud footsteps protrude into the basement of the church.

Thinking about all the depraved things I plan on doing to my father once I get free keeps me from succumbing to the relief that death promises.

Tears line my lashes as the word *father* echoes along my brainwaves. Rosa never understood why I continue to call Edward that, but only a parent can inflict the brand of pain that burrows deep in my bones.

Despite the hatred fueling my desire to stay awake and not give them the satisfaction of knowing they've broken me, I continue to toe the line of sanity. At times I stumble, pinwheeling my arms to regain balance as I fight the dangerously weak hold on my lucidity.

Exhaustion coats my entire body with unbearable heaviness. I inflate my lungs with an inhale, the abhorrent scent of ammonia and ethanol lingering inside my nose.

I take in my surroundings through slitted eyes as I wait for whatever new suffering Edward has come up with in his attempts to exhume my magic. Candlelight flickers around the room, casting shadows over blood splatters, chunks of muscle, and pieces of flesh coating the walls.

How many more will die before my father is satisfied? *It's for the greater good*, he said when he realized murder was the key to enhancing my magic.

I plan on spitting those words back at him when I bury him alive.

With every surge of death magic that left my body, there was a new person dragged from the streets to take the blast of my magic until I was depleted. I tried to control my power, but here my death magic is too unsteady and reactive to my emotions and the living, and unfortunately Edward knows exactly how to provoke it. Through torture and hurt, he pulls out the fatal power and uses innocent people to absorb the shocks of it. After all, my death magic requires sacrifice in blood to grow stronger.

The victims are so-called godless people living on the fringes of society—the people no one would miss, as he justified it, when he went with the demon brothers to bury what was left of another one.

I wonder if my *self-proclaimed* saint of a father realizes he's also a damned serial killer.

I wish more than anything that I could use my powers on him. I'd do anything to feel that deadly hum buzz through my veins, then watch him explode and splatter against the walls. Unfortunately, the damn cross hanging around his neck—gilded, and upside down—is his protection against me. Against *all* magic.

My father comes into view as he stands over me. "Are you ready to succumb and release your magic?"

"Never," I spit between clenched teeth. My gaze drifts to the remnants of dirt clinging to his fingernails, and his eyes follow my trail. "Does burying the bodies yourself bring you some peace?" I question, lifting my stare back to meet his. "Does it make you feel better about killing them?"

The muscle in his jaw twitches. "You murdered them, not me."

"We'll see what your God has to say about that," I spit.

"You will not bait me with your words, whore of Satan!" he yells, losing the scrap of composure he dons like a second skin. His hands—once used to tuck me into bed and hold me when I cried— wrap around my throat, his fingers constricting. His wide, blue eyes fray into a smoky gray, as if my defiance has sucked the life out of him. The lines around his mouth deepen with each twitch as a battle of wills plays out in his expression.

His grip tightens, blocking any air from reaching my lungs. I squirm against the cheap foam mattress, wondering if I've pushed him too far this time. His fingers loosen when I attempt a dry scream, and he lets out a heavy sigh before releasing me. Spluttering a little as the pressure against my clavicle eases, I struggle in a shaky lungful of air.

His eyes drift to my chest, transfixed by the visible swells exposed by my poorly fitting hospital gown, realization filtering into his hard stare as his gaze shifts to the word tattooed there. His throat bobs before he turns away.

Lorcan's claiming tattoo remains unblemished, the shadow ink a rich onyx despite Edwards' many attempts to flay it from my skin. I hold on to that miniscule spot of light in the darkness. It's one of the few things this asshole can't take from me.

I clear my throat, swallowing a few times before spluttering, "Nothing's changed in all these years. You still covet my body with your eyes like a fucking pervert."

He spins to face me, cheeks red as spittle flies in my direction when he shouts, "I don't covet you. Everything I do is *only* to punish you!"

I grit my teeth. "I'm your daughter, you sicko."

"You were *never* my daughter."

An unhinged, muted chuckle rolls from my lips as he turns his back to me. "I am, and your denial doesn't change that."

"Enough," he commands before grabbing a scalpel from a metal tray. "You will learn to obey. I'll pull this evil out of you until you serve your greater purpose. I won't kill you, no matter how much you try to bait me into doing so."

I'm sure the words are intended for him more than me. I've lost count on how many times he's come close to killing me during the time he's kept me captive. After the fourth time, I stopped trying to keep count. The nights easily bleed together without sunlight or clocks.

He brings the scalpel to my fingers, facing the sharp edge into my palm. "Squeeze the blade, Evie. It's time to serve your penance." My father scowls at me. "Unless you want me to bring you another victim?"

I crack open my eyes as best I can as I slowly squeeze the blade tightly in my palm while glaring at Edward.

The steel bites into my skin, a sharp sting that blossoms into searing pain radiating down my wrist. Hot blood trickles down my fingers. Each thick drop lands audibly as it feeds the steady pool of blood on the stone floor beneath the bed. His lips purse, exaggerating his wrinkles, as he glowers down at me, anticipation tugging at the corner of his thin lips.

I force my gaze away from his face, allowing them to linger on anything other than the pain as agony slashes through me. The iron deeply embedded into the stone wall grabs my attention, each piece evenly spaced apart, likely part of the original foundation.

The pain sharpens my focus as tears flow freely, streaming down my temples and saturating my hair.

Burning prickles over my palm, the sensation heightening with each throb of my heartbeat. I repress the scream building at the back of my throat as my skin yields to the blade. A whimper escapes my lips, barely audible as I fight the urge to let go, knowing if I do, my father will drag another innocent in for my death magic to tear apart.

Another sharp intake of breath follows as I hiss through clenched teeth, the metallic tang of blood filling my nose.

"Good," he says. My fingers uncoil slowly one by one as I release and drop the blade with a shuddering exhale. Every shiver running down my spine, jolting my body, strengthens my resolve not to scream. I refuse to let him see how much pain I'm in.

My death magic stirs weakly in my chest, then falls silent. I've lost track of time, utterly trapped in the abyss of all too familiar torture.

Edward plucks a pair of medical scissors from the tray and cuts a clean line down my gown to my naval. "Do you repent your evil ways, Evie?"

"Not to you."

"You will learn," he spits, placated by my act of squeezing the scalpel. "Do you remember what I used to tell you when you were a child? How we must bear all to God."

"How could I forget? I wonder, though, if it's God who wishes to bear witness to my body or if it's you."

Edward's eyes spark with fury. "It's an age-old punishment."

"You can't humiliate me," I say, moisture pooling in the corner of my eyes. Dammit. Why the fuck won't my tear ducts listen to my command not to cry right now?

He focuses on my glossy eyes and smiles weakly. "Another lie."

The final snick of the scissors severs the gown, unveiling my breasts. My nipples harden as the cold air circulating the room explores my skin with icy fingers. Panic swarms through my body and I gasp.

I squeeze my eyes shut. Not this. Please Gods, not this. I can barely catch my breath when his fingertips graze my cleavage. My lips tremble and I want to cry, regressing to my childlike want to tantrum and panic, to scream for help until someone comes.

But there's no one here to save me.

Goosebumps prickle over my arms as nausea swarms with every press of his hand against the swell of my chest.

"This is for your own good," he states, excitement pinching his words.

His mouth moves, but I can't hear beyond my stammering heartbeat. My pulse pounds like a little hammer drumming against my eardrums as everything falls into slow motion. His hands are on me again, the cut gown trapped beneath me trembling with my shaking body.

My eyes flutter open to the ceiling as the room around me fades into a dull hum.

I lie quietly in the numbness, a place of absence and purgatory, where only the simplest bases of my senses exist. My thoughts wander aimlessly, each one falling into the other like nonsensical waves—maladaptive daydreaming with no sense of beginning or end. Control over my nerve endings lapse, the weight of my limbs meld into the bed. Time holds no power over me as I float in numb bliss, the pain and anxiety thoroughly banished.

A distant conversation filters into my awareness. I groan as a wave of pain radiates through my chest reaches into my subconscious.

Another slap lands against my stomach and my eyes fling open to reveal Edward, landing his palm against my naval as he shouts. Vomit rises to the back of my throat when I realize his hard dick rests on my bare belly. A gasp leaves my mouth as I take in the tall, demon brother covered in tattoos with thick dark hair, the top half braided back from his face, standing in the doorway. *Ezra?* *If he's here, then… Lorcan. They must have found a way out.*

"What the Hell am I interrupting?" Ezra asks and side-eyes my uncovered chest.

Edward steps away from me. "Gideon. I'm in the middle of a session. You can't ju—"

"We're speeding things up," he states, cutting Edward off. "We can't wait anymore." His eyes travel over me for a moment. Gideon glowers at Edward, his nose scrunching.

Gideon? My hope of seeing Lorcan deflates like a led balloon. I forgot Ezra has an identical twin. I wiggle my fingers, wincing as a sharp sting radiates through my palm.

Edward swallows thickly. He touches his throat and twists his torso from view. "I'll continue once she has served her penance."

Gideon clears his throat. "*This* is not penance, and *you* clearly cannot wield the results we need. I'll take over."

"No," Edward says shakily. "I know her better than anyone. I can get it out of her."

A shiver travels the length of my body as the cold air circulates around my bare torso.

Gideon grits his teeth, then turns toward the stairs. "You have until tomorrow, or you're being replaced. Remember, human, if you fail, The Order will have your head for harboring her for all those years when she was a child."

Edward swallows thickly. "I won't fail."

Gideon glances at me. "I'm sending Asher to oversee this experiment." He doesn't look back when he leaves. Once the door closes, Edward bows his head, his shoulders slumping as he looks over the gore spattered torture tools on the metal tray. "Looks like we're out of time, Evie."

My fingers sink into the thin foam padding as I focus on him, hatred spilling through my expression until I'm clenching my jaw so hard I'm surprised my teeth don't shatter. I eye his cross, the very thing protecting him from my magic, and imagine strangling him with it. I can still kill him if my magic isn't involved.

He continues, unaware of my glare boring into the side of his head. "You refuse to open yourself to me and release your magic. I was going to wait to do this, but it seems The Order requires us to hurry things along."

CHAPTER THREE

Lorcan

That's it. I *will not* sit here with my cock in my hand and wait for shit to solve itself.

My shadows shimmer as they coat the surface of every tattoo on my body, their writhing movements akin to my own unstable state.

Dull tapping occupies the silence as I unconsciously jiggle the toe of my boot. Growling, I set my half-finished coffee and scone on the kitchen island. "Ezra."

My brother casually strolls into the kitchen, his eyes bright with curiosity, then sits on the velvet-plum upholstered stool closest to me. "Yes, Lorry?"

"Don't call me that," I warn through gritted teeth.

Ezra smirks. "Noted."

Godsdammit. Air spills past my lips in a sigh. I should not have said anything. The pads of my fingers glide through my hair as I shove a hand through it. "Do you know where The Order would take Evie?"

"Hmmm," Ezra contemplates, folding his arms over his wide chest and taps a tattooed finger against his lips. "If it were me, I'd bring her somewhere that has the most solid fortitudes." I open my mouth to reply, but he lifts his hand in the air. "Patience," he sing-songs. "They have a headquarters. It's not too far away from the witch's hometown."

"Ashmore."

"That's the one. Anyway, that is definitely where I would keep your girl if I were them."

I say nothing as I stomp towards the stove; the hood casting a skewed rectangular shadow in the space between the marble countertops and the island. Blackness swallows my boot and creeps up my leg as I enter the shadow. My brother lunges over the island, then grabs my wrist.

"Wait! I'm coming with you," he says, just like a needy puppy following at my fucking heels.

Closing my eyes, the glimmer from the silver chandelier shines through my lids with a burning glow. I focus on tracing my little witch's face in my mind. My lungs inflate, then depress with my slow breath.

My lids flutter open, and I shove Ezra away from me, his claws digging into my wrist. I glare at the demon blood dripping onto the ground, the thick drops pooling into a puddle.

My upper lip pulls back. "This is how a truce works?"

Ezra winks.

Fucking. Winks.

"Well, it does for demon brothers. We were born to split flesh and shed blood." He releases me, then elbows me in the ribs.

"For fuck's sake," I growl. "Fine. You can come with me, but the moment you get in my way, I'll gut you."

Ezra's eyes widen to saucers and his body trembles dramatically. "Oh no, don't hurt me, Mr. King of Demons. I promise I'll be good." His chest shakes as ruckus laughter fills the kitchen.

"Piss off, asshole," I spit as the shadows wrap around me, clinging to my torso as I walk through them.

There's something peaceful about the In-Between—the purgatory between the Human and Shadow Realm. After several minutes of navigating the shadows with Ezra, his lips mercifully remaining shut, I part the onyx void and slip from the darkness.

Squinting my eyes, I glare at the sky, the murky Shadow Realm sun nearing its highest point. A sea of asphalt stretches before me, a gargantuan structure casting an angular shadow over me as I walk closer.

Ezra's footsteps pad beside me and we halt before The Order's headquarters, an immense cross shaped shadow falling over the pair of us like a wraith. My brother's pale green eyes dart from the building to me. I shake my head and walk forward, blinking away bits of floating ash as my boots sink into the browning, brittle lawn of one of the most obnoxiously ostentatious churches I have ever laid eyes on, the rough grass scraping against the soles of my shoes.

Two impressive towers stand like formidable soldiers on either side of a central spire, piercing the gray sky, reaching higher than the central one boasting an enormous silver cross in a disgusting display of wealth. My gaze lingers on the intricate gables of the pitched slate roofs expanding from every angle of the church, excluding the grand entrance. Large wings expanding beneath them to the left and right.

Four more smaller intricately carved spires surround the base of the contrasting gray stones, hoisting the symbol of faith above everything for miles. I lift a hand to my brow, shielding my vision from the sun's cornhusk glow reflecting off stained glass windows lined with tracery.

"I haven't seen buttresses like this in eons," I mention. Tilting my chin to the vertically oriented structure, I step closer to an elegantly carved sign installed on the shitty grass. I chuckle darkly and drag my claws along the weathered wood, several deep scratches marring the words Christ's Blood Church. I'll never get over the way religions obsess over their 'lord and savior's blood.

"The irony, right?" Ezra notes.

I nod, then snort. "It's as if they choose to turn a blind eye to their history of endless warring, most notably the Spanish Inquisition."

Ezra bounces on the balls of his bright as fuck violet high-top sneaker covered feet. "Yep! So, let's go in."

I groan, irritation and displeasure sinking into my stomach. The hypocrisy of religious zealots leaves a foul taste in my mouth. Walking up the stones leading up to the main doors, we step inside beneath the pointed arches of the entrance doorway. Dank, cool air envelops us as I glance around the entryway of the church. The thick stone walls scream with torment, forced to witness years of willfully blind ignorance. Religion itself isn't what is wrong with humans; it's how some of them choose to share their beliefs that disgusts me.

I stroll past three sets of looming, elegantly carved double doors separated by a couple feet of stone wall. My fingers drag over the matching architraves, then focus on my bond with Evie. She's there, stronger than earlier at the manor. But the once strong, glowing cable connecting us feels as thin as a single strand of thread. My heart fucking soars.

Ezra pokes at my pulse pounding away in my carotid artery and I brush him off with a growl. "Your heart rate just went insane." One of Ezra's brows curls upward. "Can you sense the witch?"

"Yes, but it's very faint. I need to focus, so do me a favor and shut the fuck up. Go see if there are any offices or classrooms to search."

He mimes sewing his lips shut, then chomps the air like he's cutting the thread with his teeth.

If only that invisible thread were real.

Claws shoot from my fingertips as I march toward the closest set of double doors, nervous anxiety squeezing my brain. Faint screeching sounds as my claws scrape along the brass handle, grip it, and throw the door open.

I slip my hands into my pockets as I stroll down the aisle, ash swirling around me despite my slow gate. My shadows fan around me, darting behind statues of weeping saints and any other dark spaces a hidden entrance might reveal itself. I chuckle darkly, gliding over to a silver basin held aloft by a grand wooden pedestal. Water flicks against the bowl as I dip two fingers into the holy liquid, mark the center of my forehead, chest, and both shoulders, mocking the human sign of the cross. My demonic senses stretch out, ensuring my shadows missed nothing. I cock my head to the side and focus as a draft whistles through a crack somewhere in the pulpit's vicinity.

"Find anything?"

I pivot and face Ezra as he strolls from the shadows beneath the choir loft at the back of the church, rising halfway to the arched ceiling where the exposed beams groan with age.

"Possibly," I say. "And you?"

"A whole lotta jack shit," Ezra replies.

"You've returned awful fast. Are you certain you've checked every room, closet, bathro—"

"Yes, I'm sure," Ezra interrupts, then throws his head back dramatically and sighs. "This adventure is turning out to be rather dull, don't you think? We haven't even spotted one demon."

I shrug, then turn my back on him and say over my shoulder. "Well, if you're calling the day a loss, feel free to fuck off back to the manor. I, however, am going to explore a promising lead."

A loud, obnoxious crack sounds from his neck as Ezra's head drops to its normal position. "A lead? Why didn't you say that in the first place?" Ezra asks, his eyes gleaming. "I absolutely want to explore the creep factory. Lead on, Brother."

I step up on the dais, my eyes darting between the pulpit and the altar. Of the two locations, the altar is permanently fixed to the floor, where the pulpit is likely moved for different services and events. I flick the cloth covering it up, then crouch behind the altar.

"Sneaky fucking bastards," Ezra whispers over my shoulder.

We pause, analyzing the barely noticeable lines marking a square hatch. Stone screeches as my nails gouge into the miniscule crack beneath the floor of the hatch and peel it open. A thin layer of rock, identical to the ones forming the surrounding floor, line the top of a thick piece of oak. Ezra shoves his weight into my side, jockeying to go first into the unknown.

"Dibs!" He laughs. Ezra expels an oomph as a shadow wraps around his ankles and he collapses onto his front. "Oh, it's like *that*, is it?" he wheezes.

My shadows build into a gray opaque wall between us. Ezra's shadows spill from him and ram into the shield, trailing upward like smoke against glass. I laugh. "Yes, it's like that." The scent of mold and rot attacks my demonic sense of smell the moment the darkness beyond is revealed; dusty stone steps leading beneath the church. I drop the shadow shield and jog down into the gloom, my brother hurrying to catch up.

I stumble as Ezra shoulder checks me, then plants his hands on his hips, glancing to the left and right.

"Fuck me," he states, shaking his head. "I was right. This *is* a certified creep factory."

A chuckle slips past my lips, and Ezra spins to face me. "Holy shit. You *do* have a sense of humor."

"Don't get used to it. Go check to the left," I command.

Ezra clears his throat loudly and scratches his beard. Although he oozes nonchalance, his eyes and the simmering growl emitting from him betray the anger bubbling under his skin. "No. No more of this splitting up bullshit. I want to know the second you find something." My brother's pale green eyes flash with warning, the first inkling of percolating wrath I've seen so far today.

I snort, then stalk down the stone corridor. Candlelight housed in iron sconces cast purple highlighted shadows, dipping between femur bones stacked snuggly within the walls as I pass. On my left, I breeze past an open archway made of the same dark stone as the floors, walls, and ceiling.

"Lorcan," Ezra calls.

"Yes?" I question as I keep walking.

"We should check every room, just in case," Ezra says, then folds his arms across his wide chest, his ridiculous purple hoodie stretching taught against his muscles. He's right, but any delay, even a necessary one, feeds the anxiety bludgeoning my ribs.

My boots scrape against the stone floor as I stomp back to my brother. A screech rents the air as he pushes a rusty iron door open, the hinges complaining excessively. Curling my upper lip, an irritated growl rumbling in my chest as I maneuver past him into the mostly vacant space beyond.

Dust rises into the air with each of my breaths. I cough once as I wave away the offending substance. The bond between my little witch and I tightens the deeper I move into the room, as if every step I take is farther away from her. I spin on my heel, scanning every inch of the barren cell. Piles of moldering hay dot the ground lining the damp walls. My fingers trail across a patch of encroaching moss above a bucket of something vile I have no desire to examine further.

"Nice place. I see they spare no expense for their captives." Ezra whistles and glances at me. "Oh, look, they even sprang for the Cadillac of shit buckets. It's got a lid to sit on and everything."

I inhale deeply, my nose scrunching as I breathe in the putrid scent—mostly bodily fluids—expelled here. "I doubt this dungeon is used very often, judging by the level of decay." I jut my chin at a dismal hay pallet. "But it does further prove the lengths The Order will go to."

He nods, picking up a metal shackle hanging from chains secured to the wall. Ezra rotates the worn metal in his tattooed hands, the corners of his lips falling. My nails scratch lightly against my scalp as I run both hands through the longer strands on the top of my head. We need to move on. I prowl toward the exit. Metal curls inward and groans as I kick the iron door, a crater forming in the stone frame, on my way out for good measure. Ezra's quiet laughter follows me as I delve deeper into the gloom. Ignoring my brother's earlier suggestion, I speed past several more cells bracketed by even rows of skulls padding the walls and grip my bond with Evie as tightly as I can. There has to be some trace of my little witch. I just need to keep searching. The black spiky mace of anxious energy gnaws on my stomach, lining harder and harder as more time passes.

Ezra strides lackadaisically down the macabre tunnel beside me, commenting on anything and everything around him, his voice growing distant as I pick up my pace. "Shit, their headquarters is much larger than I thought. Although, I quite like the alternative material used to replace basic bitch stone. Such a delightful pattern of alternating skulls and humerus bones. Don't you think?" For a few, blissful moment's silence reigns, but my shoulders stiffen as it's swiftly disrupted. "Brother, you have to check this out."

I rub my temples as a headache drills into my skull. "What could you possibly need now?" Ezra points a thick tattooed finger at a huge marble slab pressed into an arched cut out of the stone wall. We've passed dozens of arcosolias along each twisting turn of the catacombs. What makes this one different from all the others?

Ezra's nostrils flare, and the dark, sinister magic of Wrath glows like obsidian embers in his eyes, their pastel green nearly obliterated. "Seriously, just fucking listen to me for once and take a godsdamn look, Lorcan," he growls. Seems like our time together is finally wearing on my dear brother too—about godsdamn time.

"What was it you said earlier? Ah, yes. 'Calm your tits,' Wrath," I coo, not giving a single fuck. I'm provoking the monster. My brother balls his hands into fists at his sides, the tattoos straining across his knuckles. I chuckle and stroll over to him. Shadows condense on my skin, sliding around the edges of the smooth marble. "The fuck?" I mutter under my breath. The shadows on the left side of the slab vanish, while their counterparts on the right, top, and bottom probe and wreath along a thin crack between marble and stone. A loose pebble skitters against my boot as I step closer, flattening a claw tipped hand against the marble edge and grunt. Scraping consumes all other sounds as I force a slender opening, no wider than the width of my shoulders from the side, to appear.

"Told you," Ezra declares, his anger swiftly evaporating.

I poke my head around the slab and glare at his smirking face. "Smug bastard. How the fuck did you know?"

"Unlike others in my present company, I take my time to explore shit. My shadows have traced every single crevice, nook, and cubicula carved or worn into this damn labyrinthine. Sooo, when something unusual came to my attention, I stopped to inspect it." He gestured to the north. "You can only see the gap when coming from that direction, and the shadow created by the slab makes it appear like any other shadow," Ezra explains proudly and grins.

My spine straightens, and something bitter and ugly prickles beneath my skin. I would not have noticed the cleverly disguised opening if my brother had not forced me to listen. No. I refuse to acknowledge those vile feelings. I slip into the gap, my chest and back just barely fitting as I move through it at an angle. "Good luck getting through that," I chuckle as I emerge at a set of steps.

Grunts and groans echo off the walls as Ezra squeezes into the gap. He makes it nearly all the way through, then huffs and throws a hand toward me. "A little help?" he asks.

I roll my eyes and uncross my arms. "Use your godsdamn shadows, idiot." He glares at me, but I smirk and tug him forward before he can free himself. Ezra trips, then rights himself.

"Not cool," he grumbles.

I laugh. "I was just doing as you asked."

"Mhm," Ezra hums, and rubs his chest. "We'll have to find another way out. That was too tight for my liking. I thought my sternum would puncture my heart. It's not like I can suck in my fucking ribs."

I groan as yet another bone lined corridor stretches before us. However, there is one difference. Doors peek through gaps in bone and stone walls at odd intervals, as if the size of the rooms behind them vary greatly.

Ezra claps a hand on my back as I pause and poke my head through an open archway made of the same stone as the floor, walls, and ceiling. My heart lurches into my throat. *Evie.* I stumble into the open chamber, my eyes drifting to the massive archaic chandelier on the vaulted ceiling. It's made with tibia bones connecting four levels of metal rings—each rimmed with skulls—by chains from the round, vaulted ceiling.

My nose wrinkles as the ghostly scent of roses tinged with blood cloyingly permeates the surrounding air.

"What is it?" Ezra asks, eyes the same shade as mine narrowing on my face. My palm slaps the nearest wall, sliding on mildew as I lean against it heavily.

"She's close. I can smell her."

The breath stalls in my lungs, and my eyes dart around the dim space. My little witch's bond tugs sharply, the slightest twinge of pain reverberating down its length. Fuck. *Where is she?* Panic crushes me beneath its icy waves, yet anger buoys me from the dark depths below. I shiver as the sound of my molars grinding reaches my ears. I struggle to regain any sense of calm, pinned beneath the two opposing emotions.

I sprint forward, my feet sliding on the dingy, unkept floor as I search the entirety of the circular wall. The bond tightens again and my head whips to the center of the room. An old, weathered table—no, a gurney of sorts—stands sentinel. I creep slowly toward it, my little witch's scent strengthening but still muted as it always is on this side of the mirror. My head tilts to the side as I assess the innocuous object as if it's a threat, then step onto the metal drain juxtaposed to the gurney. My witch's essence, her signature stamped in time and space between our realms, envelopes me.

Shock encompasses every thought and emotion as I whisper, "Little Witch." Bone clacks against stone as my knees collapse under me. "I fucking found her."

Ezra inhales sharply. For a moment, I stare at the drain, splashes of a rust-colored substance and bits of what could be human innards litter the pipe beneath the grate. What manner of fucking Hell have they put her through? A steady growl rises past my throat, transitioning into a roar of unfiltered rage. It's even worse than I thought.

They will pay for this.

The growl continues to emit from me, and I distantly recognize that my brother has joined mine. A deep, menacing hum rumbles with our combined sound of discontent, echoing off the beams holding back the stone above. I jump to my feet. My witch is so godsdamn close, yet I can't help her.

"Fuck!" I sink my claws into the tattered leather of the gurney and launch it across the room. A metal tray on wheels I hadn't noticed earlier crashes onto its side, and blood-stained surgical tools clatter to the ground.

"Oh, shit," Ezra says, the wheels of the blasted bed clipping his man bun as he barely ducks in time to avoid the projectile. "Unholy fuck," he hisses. "That was a little too close for comfort." He pats down his chest and eyes me. "Feel better?"

I stalk toward him, grabbing him by the collar of his hoodie and snap my teeth in his face. "There will be one less demon if you don't shut your mouth right the fuck now."

"Truce, remember," Ezra states, peeling my fingers away from his hoodie and gingerly plucking each one of my claws free so I don't tear the fabric. "Seriously, calm your tits. Instead of raging," he holds up his hands, "let's…" His gaze zeros in on something over my shoulder. Ezra jogs past me, then crouches and holds a long shard of mirrored glass aloft, his teeth glowing in an eerie grin. I bolt over to him and snatch the bit of mirror.

I twist around, noting the scratches and absence of dust on the stone floor where we stand. My lips twitch as I glare into the mirror, gripping the sharp edges so tightly it slices into my fingers and palm, and stare at a pair of men. I lean closer and note the upside-down crosses hanging from their breakable necks as they chat and sweep up bits of wood and broken mirror.

"Why are we always the ones left cleaning up after that bitch?" the taller of the two questions, tilting his head toward where I feel Evie's signature the strongest.

"First, you know she can hear you, right? And second, 'cause we'd rather be the ones cleaning up the destruction than the poor bastards he brings for her to slaughter." The man wielding the dustpan and gesturing wildly explains, his eyes lingering nervously on the center of the room.

The tall, destined to die slowly and painfully, man snorts. "She's too drugged up to understand you. Anyway, do you mind?" He nods at the pile of debris. "After this, we have to go attend our other duties in the North Wing of the abbey."

"Ugggh. Seriously, Edward needs to stop taking on captives."

I lower the shard, then share a look with Ezra. "To the North Wing."

CHAPTER FOUR

Lorcan

Ezra jogs toward a wooden door I must have overlooked earlier. "Let's go this way. It's got to be better than caving in my chest again."

I fling open the hatch of identical design to the one in the church and climb out. Ezra leaps onto the even, clean stone floor to my right. My brows furrow at our new surroundings. Everything gleams with cleanliness in the dozens of candles' dim lilac glow, as if we passed some sort of line of demarcation.

Ezra stares at me, his dark brows raised. "What now?" he asks, his baritone voice rumbling.

"Now, we shift. It will be much easier to sense any signatures in our demonic forms."

"Good call," he replies.

I close my eyes and will the shift to take hold. For a moment, it's as if the skin of my human-like appearance stretches too taut, like a rubber band about to snap. With a relieved sigh, I embrace the dark magic swirling around and through me. My eyes flash open and I bare my sharp mouthful of needle-like teeth. Somehow, Ezra's toothy grin is even more annoying without the human-like disguise.

"Oh c'mon, Lorcan. This could be fun if you let it. You've had fun before, right?" He winks, then his smile falls. "Actually, don't answer that. Anyway, we might as well use this as a scouting opportunity, too."

He's right, but I'll never admit it out loud. We need to plan every aspect, down to the most minuscule of details, in order to find and liberate Evie from this shithole. I move closer to the vast stone staircase looming before us, elaborate wrought iron designed like crawling ivy making up the banister. My shoulders draw up to my ears as Ezra steps too close behind me. Groaning, I spear my fingers into my hair. "You're like a godsdamn gnat, always infiltrating my personal space and begging to be smacked." He just laughs and blows on the back of my ear.

"Fucking heathen," I hiss, elbowing him in the ribs.

Evie's best friend must be one of the captives those fuckers mentioned. Ezra cranes his neck left and right like an owl. "Let's go," I urge. "Stop fucking gawking and move." Irritation coalesces around the mace of anxiety growing within me, adding a whole new level of unnecessary emotions to this cluster fuck of a day. I growl before sprinting up the vast stone staircase leading to the North Wing, taking two steps at a time.

"Jesus fuck. Slow down, jackass," Ezra shouts from somewhere behind me.

He will never understand the desperation rendering my mind to shredded pulp or the strength it had taken to leave Evie's signature in that fucking torture chamber and go hunt these so-called captives down. A muscle in my jaw ticks as I clench my teeth, silently fuming, my shadows skating along the plethora of stained-glass windows like a cape fanning out in my wake.

My brother's obnoxious footsteps tread after me as I come upon a series of double wooden doors with iron bracing.

I walk forward, sliding my hands into my pockets, my fingers brushing the carton of cigarettes and lighter held there, then draw them out. The cherry glows violet as I inhale and narrow my eyes at Ezra, then speak, the cigarette jerking slightly with each word my lips form. "I'm not giving you one."

His nose crinkles. "Uh, no. I don't smoke. Nasty fucking habit."

I smile around the death stick, careful not to let my sharp demon teeth puncture the fragile paper. "Suit yourself." I inhale deeply, letting the soothing, warm smoke curl into my lungs. Fuck, I am so glad to be a demon. It would be a shame if these things actually killed me. The cloying, delicious nicotine laced smoke burns as I hold the breath and focus on my senses. I know I won't smell anything in the Human Realm unless one of my bonded is near, but my demonic senses don't rely on the classic see, feel, touch, taste, and smell. There, around the bend of the corridor, something calls to me.

"There's one or more signatures ahead. Do you feel it?" I ask Ezra.

He tilts his head. "Yeppers. Huh, something about it calls to me more than usual."

"Yeppers? Really?" I scoff, blowing a cloud of smoke in his direction.

We round the bend, and a familiar signature immediately assaults me. She spends enough time around my little witch that I'd know her signature anywhere; the human rainbow. I huff, smoke rushing through my nostrils like a dragon preparing to incinerate an enemy. I reach to open the door on the right, Rosa's essence blinking within, then pivot sharply. The scent of Aiden's strong-ass cologne—a blend of mint, neroli, and sea water—reaches me. My shadows slide into the keyhole, slink around the tumblers, then disengage the rudimentary lock. A long creak issues as the door swings open, and I enter the left door of the set. I stride into the room and scour my surroundings. Muted colorful sunrays arrow through the lone stained-glass window and onto a pitiful bed. I kick at the sheets half puddled on the floor. Aiden's faint scent lingers on the bedding, but it pales in comparison to how Evie's scent crosses over from the Human Realm.

"Anything?" Ezra asks from the doorway, tattooed hands gripping the frame.

"Yes, and no. Aiden has slept here." I finger the comforter, then take a drag of my cigarette.

"Aiden? Oh, that college kid with the perpetually backward baseball cap on his head?"

"Yes, my valet. But I don't feel his signature here." I exit the room, impatience nipping at my heels.

My shadows grip the edges of Rosa's door and tear it from its hinges, sending it crashing into the hallway. The door ricochets off the opposite wall, a corner lodging into the cathedral gray wall. Bits of wood turned sawdust float in the air as I glare at the offending obstruction. I shrug, dust my shoulders off, and barrel into the room. If I were in the Human Realm, no doubt some human would scream their fucking heads off at the noise. My lips twitch upward. Sometimes the Shadow Realm has its perks.

Ezra shucks off his purple hoodie, tosses it over a shoulder, and plants his fists on his hips. "Well done, Brother. I bet they heard that all the way in Hell."

I ignore Ezra and channel all of my focus into inspecting the cramped space around me. My lip curls in disgust as I roam throughout the room. I drag my fingertips along the simple dark blue bedding stretched across the queen-sized bed, leaving long furrows in the thick layer of ash coating it, coarse fibers catching on my skin. Well, they're certainly not keeping her in a fucking cell. In fact, it appears as though all the entrapments of simple human comfort crowd the space. Yet, something is missing. I rub my jaw, ignoring the grainy feel of dust rubbing against my scruff.

An indent forms on one side of the bed as I round it. I tip my head to the side, curiosity winning out, then a shudder rakes over me as I walk into Rosa's imprint. Fuck me, that's unpleasant. I shake my head and hastily step away. If I am going to immerse myself in anyone's imprint, it will be Evie's. A sharp pain spreads behind my ribs. "Godsdammit," I growl and rub my sternum. I cannot decide which is worse, longing for my witch or a century of solitude.

"What is it?" Ezra questions as he glides over to me.

"Nothing,"

"Uh huh. Sure," he replies.

"Fuck off, Ez."

"Oh Fuckity-fuck. You called me Ez. It's just like old times."

Ezra's heavy arms wrap around me and squeeze as he rocks side to side.

A growl vibrates my chest. "Get off of me."

Ezra drops his hold, then steps back and sweeps an arm across the room. Point at something, he asks, "Did you see this shit?"

But my eyes stray to a pair of hands clasped in prayer tattooed on his triceps. My glare bores into the mockery of a religious tattoo for a moment longer before I allow my gaze to follow the direction he's indicating.

"What the Hell?" The grimy wall greets my fingers as I trace around a dark rectangle on the wall opposite the queen size bed. I look over my shoulder, noticing another similar but smaller rectangle, darker than the surrounding paint, near the simple wooden desk. They removed something. Dread coils low in my stomach. You have got to be fucking kidding me. I race into the closet sized bathroom, likely added during the abbey's renovations to make it livable, and flick on the lights. "Gods fucking dammit," I seethe while staring at the blank, discolored wall above the sink.

They removed all the mirrors.

I lean forward, my hips pressing into the cool stone counter, and read the barely legible scrawl:

SILAS WAS HERE.

Shit, of course he was. I should've known he, of all my brothers, would be smart enough not to miss that little detail; plus, he would never miss an opportunity to fuck up my life further.

Ezra leans his shoulder against the doorjamb, then nods at the graffiti. "Fucking, Silas."

My lips thin as I ponder all the ways I'll extract my brother's intestines from his body. Ezra wisely steps to the side as I storm from the room, my hands clenching and unclenching into fists at my sides. I pace soundlessly on the thin, threadbare carpet. My fingertips sink into my raven locks as I grip the size sides of my head and close my eyes. Where do humans typically place mirrors? *Fucking think, Lorcan.* A muscle in my jaw flutters angrily as I grind my molars. If there's no mirror in the bathroom or on the walls... My thoughts trail off and my eyes fly open.

Her purse.

Most human women carry them, and if everything Evie said about Rosa is true, there must be a big ass purse here somewhere stuffed with nonsense. I dart about the room, rooting in the small dresser and tearing hangers from their hooks as I swiftly search the space.

"I know that look. What are you searching for?"

I follow my instincts and yank the shitty wooden chair from beneath the desk. My eyes widen slightly as I take in the bag, for it's a fucking leather backpack, not a purse, nestled between the grooves meant for legs on the unupholstered seat. Without hesitation, I snatch the thing from the chair, unzip it, then upend the contents onto the desk. Ezra meanders closer, his gaze following a tube of mascara as it clatters to the desk, then rolls off the edge and under the bed. I shake the bag again, my claws tearing into the leather as more shit clatters against the wooden surface beneath it.

"Damn," Ezra says as he leans over my shoulder.

My elbow connects with his ribs. "Would you give me some fucking space?" I rifle through the pile of unnecessary contents, smacking away Ezra's hand as he snatches something before I can inspect it. One of my claws catches against a bat patterned coin purse as I shove it out of the way, only to unearth two tampons, a black tube of lipstick, and a baggie of blueberries and granola.

Picking up the snack bag, I roll my eyes and sigh. Bats on her coin purse and treats for him? Reminders of Fluffy Fucker are everywhere I go—something I'll soon remedy once Evie and I are in the Human Realm together. I toss the bat snacks over my shoulder, then cross my arms over my chest and stare at the remaining contents. Adrenaline bubbles into my bloodstream like liquid hope as my eyes light on something Silas missed. Of course, Rosa couldn't have a simple, round compact mirror like any other human. No, she has to have something loud—a glittery, bright purple mirror in the shape of an eggplant.

I flip open the compact and glare into the Human Realm, the same room reflecting back at me. The plastic surrounding the loathsome little mirror cracks as I grip it tightly between my forefinger and thumb. I force my fingers to relax. The last fucking thing I need is to shatter the only means of communication I have.

I snap my gaze to Ezra as a skull splitting shriek of grinding metal spears from the corner. "Shit, they could've gotten the poor monster a better cage. They haven't even given him fresh water today. What the fuck." More groans of bending metal score my senses.

A snarl twists my lips. "Would you knock it the fuck off?"

Ezra continues his rant without taking a breath or acknowledging my request. "That," he spits and jabs a tattooed finger at Gomez's crumpled cage, "is a rusted piece of shit." His eyes land on mine as he turns away from the destruction he wrought and back to me. "So, they forgot one after all. Excellent." Ezra laughs and shoves a fist full of Fluffy Fucker's snacks into his mouth while waggling his brows.

"Really?" I snarl, then shoot him a warning glare.

"What? It's a little stale, but still edible."

Satan give me strength to not disembowel my brother. Anger swells within me. This is what I am fucking reduced to, aligning myself with an idiot sidekick. But none of it matters—I'll get my witch back, even if I must look like a fool to do so. Ezra squats by the desk, pokes his finger into a crack at the base of the wall, then drops to his stomach and peers through.

"I can see all the way through into the next room."

I disregard him, keeping my focus on the miniscule mirror. The oval reflection tilts, then a pair of lips fill the space, the lower lip significantly fuller than the upper, blocking my view of the reflected room. I tap a nail against the lid of the compact as I watch her lips transform from a soft pink to a neon purple with each glide of her lipstick.

This is too godsdamn perfect.

"Oh, I gotta see this. Move over," Ezra orders, smooshing his cheek into mine.

My claws dig into his shoulder as I shove him away from me. I reach into my back pocket, then secure my mask behind my head, my knuckles brushing against my curling onyx horns. It's time for Rosa to finally meet the man in the mirror in all his demonic glory. My cheek taps against the bottom of my mask as I fail to suppress a smirk.

I dissolve the barrier hiding my masked demonic face from view and growl, "Human Rainbow." A scream rents the air and Rosa's side of the mirror swirls into a vortex of swirling colors. Silence descends and my chest rises and falls as I inhale slowly in through my nose and out through my mouth while I wait for Rosa to calm the fuck down. My adrenaline surges higher the longer I stand here waiting for something to happen. It's been too long since I scared the absolute shit out of someone. Aiden's reactions, while still entertaining, have become dull and expected. Rosa, however, is fresh prey.

I narrow my eyes as light fills the reflection once more, then one large dark brown eye widens in horror.

"What the fuck?"

"Hold the mirror farther back from your face, human," I demand.

The eye narrows to a slit, then a soft thump greets me as she sets the mirror down on the desk. Darkness creeps around the edges of the mirror.

"Don't you fucking dare close this mirror."

59

"Watch me, demon." Despite the threat, she takes a step back, leaving the compact open. Rosa's footsteps thud as she paces much the same way I did earlier, the odd glimpse of her arm or chest flashing in my limited point of view as she moves.

"Evie. Have you seen her?"

The woman continues walking back and forth at the foot of the bed, gesticulating wildly as she mumbles to herself.

A dark growl rips from my throat. "Rosa."

Teeth mashing together, food reverberates through my ears, then Ezra's face is fucking touching mine once more.

"Rosa, huh? Mmm, hey, Sugar," he croons.

"Seriously? Another one? How many fucking brothers do you have, asshole?" she shouts and throws her hands out to her sides, huffing as she drops onto the foot of the bed. She glares at Ezra and I, then circles her hand in the air in front of her face. "Can you both change all of that?"

For once, I'm grateful for Ezra's company.

I laugh sharply. "Aww, is our demonic presence too scary for you?"

A smile spreads across her face, but it appears more like a grimace. "Oh, I'm sorry. It's not like every day there is a demon in my mirror! No, two fucking demons. Jesus, fuck. You made me smear my lipstick," she seethes and rubs at a spot on the side of her mouth with a jewel blue knitted sleeve.

Ezra watches her intently. "Aww, don't be mad, Sweetness."

I grin. "Too bad, too. That shade of blinding purple paired perfectly with your petrified expression. Really set the tone of the scene for the jump scare."

"Lorcan," Ezra growls, as if he's a damn lifeguard saving me from pissing off Evie's best friend, or rather, saving her from me. Rosa scoots back and draws her knees into her chest, the fight leaving her. Shit. He's right and I fucking hate it. If my witch saw me treating her best friend this way…

My eyes dart to Ezra, widening as I decipher the rare display of seriousness on his face. "Fucking Hell, fine," I snap, then transform my features into their less terrifying counterparts.

Rosa's manicured eyebrow arches but no words move past her lips. It's then that I see it—sorrow and pain shimmers in her dark chocolate eyes. Although I hate to admit it, she, too, is affected by Evie's capture. Hell, she's a damn captive herself. Anxiety flows through her faintly pinched features, the barely there crow's feet bracketing her eyes deeper than the last time I saw her. But there's something else too, lingering just below the surface of her show of bravado.

My silence speaks for me as I tap my forefinger on my biceps. "What do you want, demon?"

I roll my shoulders back, then stiffen. My eye twitches as the persistent bat shrieks scrape down my eardrums and I wonder why Gomez has waited until now to make himself known. "Do something to shut him up. I cannot think over his nonsense."

Two fierce streaks of crimson color her cheeks. "He's trapped here just like Aiden and I. What do you expect?"

Ezra side-eyes me, nonverbally conveying his concurrence with her. "Give him some snackies. There's some in your enormous purse."

"How? Nevermind." Rosa flops onto her back, the mattress jostling beneath her.

"I need you to answer all of my questions. If you do, you might have a hope of getting out of there alive."

She covers her face with both hands. "Fine, go ahead," she snaps, her acquiescence muffled by her palms.

"Have they let you out of the room?"

"No."

"What about food? Any idea when your mealtimes are?"

"No, but Aiden," she jerks a thumb over her head to the wall separating their rooms, "swears he can hear a clock chiming the hour, every hour on the hour. He might have a better idea."

"Perfect." I clear my throat. I really don't wish to think about my little witch suffering while there is absolutely fucking nothing I can do to rectify it, but I need to know. "Are they abusing you or Aiden in any way like they are, Evie?"

"That's none of your fucking business." She huffs, sits up, then crosses her arms over her chest defensively.

"It is my business when you might very well be integral to freeing her. You must disclose any injury or handicap," I command threateningly, the deeper, gravelly tone of my demonic form breaking through.

Her features soften, and my eyes narrow. "Oh shit, you really *do* care about her."

"Fucking crazy, right?" Ezra interjects, but we both ignore him.

I roll my eyes. "Obviously. Would I be speaking to you if I didn't?"

Rosa snaps, "You're obnoxiously arrogant."

The corner of my lip twitches upward as I glance from the mirror in my hand to Ezra, and the beginnings of a plan form in my mind.

"Pass the compact to Aiden through that crack behind the desk when they return him. I have an idea."

CHAPTER FIVE

Evie

I keep my eyes clamped shut as a conversation filters into my consciousness, remaining as still as possible on the bed. Icy drafts climb over my bare arms and legs, and I suppress a shiver.

How long have I been out? One day? Two? It doesn't matter. I'm still too exhausted to open my eyes. It's better to pretend to be asleep, anyway. The moment my father becomes aware I'm conscious, his darkness comes back with a vengeance. My very presence seems to evoke a wrath in him that cannot be easily pacified.

I recognize the first voice belonging to Samuel, the evilest of all the brothers. Unlike Lorcan, whose darkness is mixed with a tidal wave of emotion, there is a notable lack of humanity behind Samuel's words. Then there's his stare with those dead, shark eyes.

A shiver ripples down my spine when I hear him shout, "The bitch is taking too long!" Then adds, "We need her magic, now! She's the last of the Fallenmoore bloodline. Without her, the world will end."

More lies. This bullshit the demons, well, Samuel in particular, has fed The Order about saving the world using my magic is so unbelievable it's almost funny. I can't believe The Order is so gullible. I've tried telling Edward the truth, that the brothers aren't angels at all, but embodiments of the deadly sins that only want my magic so they can kill Lorcan. In a way, I'm glad he didn't believe me. Otherwise, he'd have no good reason to keep me alive.

I've heard enough of their hushed talks during their watches when my father's taking breaks between torture sessions.

They want me to use my powers to decimate Lorcan and obliterate his soul. I didn't even know demons could die, but apparently, they can, and they need a living, powerful witch for that. But I won't be their key to getting him out of the Shadow Realm just to destroy him.

My heart skips a beat at the thought of Lorcan not existing anymore. Despite everything that's happened, I don't want him dead. Then there's Gomez and Rosa. I feel my little bat through our familial bond. He's okay but trapped. I know he hates being in a cage. At least he's in the same room as Rosa. Well, I assume that's the case with the feelings Gomey has sent through our bond.

65

Edward sighs, dragging me from my thoughts. His voice is strained and quaky in parts when he replies, "I'm so close. Please, if I can just get more time."

My lips twist when I hear him *beg* a demon for more time to torture me. This supposed man of God has fallen so far that he's in the depths of Hell and doesn't even know it. Religion is nothing but a smokescreen he uses as a justification for his dark actions.

Growing up with him as my parent made me realize at an early age that the religious teachings themselves are not the problem, especially when some people who believe, like my dead brother did. Caden saw the bible—a book written by men in a time far different from ours—not as an instruction manual, but for what it was, an allegory. It's the messages behind the stories that are important. Caden liked to see the best in people. He showed me that those people can exist who didn't use rules and passages like my parents did to get their way.

He tried to see the good in me, too, until my magic decimated him. Caden taught me many things, but his final lesson was that evil people often win, and that the only way to beat them is to be worse. So. Much. Worse.

Fortunately, there isn't anything I won't do to destroy my father. Until then, I bide my time and pay my so-called penance. I'll take anything he throws my way and commit every torturous, desperate feeling to memory so when I get out of here, I can sharpen that pain into vengeance.

Anger guides my thoughts as I hear footsteps stop beside the bed I'm strapped to. Samuel's voice comes out smooth, like venom. "I will break her as you have failed to."

I keep my eyes shut, but every muscle in my body tenses. Years of self-medicating and repression have buried my magic so deeply that now it comes out all wrong. Edward has tried but failed to make me release it fully through torture and murder.

I've worn that victory as a badge of honor ever since I arrived here. But as I feel Samuel's icy fingers against my temples, my magic shifts in my core like a viper coiling in preparation for an attack.

A scream tears from my dry throat, the dehydrated, shriveled membranes lining it tearing in places, as I wrestle the leather restraints pinning me in place. My eyes fling open and the last thing I see before I'm plunged into darkness is the flat gray of Samuel's eyes above me.

Inky depths pull me deeper to doors hidden in the shadows of my mind, places that my subconscious shoved the vilest memories to protect me. Pins and needles cover my entire body when I'm forced into a memory that washes over me like a tidal wave, drowning me in bitterness and rejection.

Mildew and mold hang heavy in my lungs as I'm transported to my family home, the one before Edward, Antoinette, and Caden, when I was the youngest witch of the most infamous coven in the world.

The walls of the corridors, wallpaper peeled in thick strips, pulse with the dark magic. Echoed calls from my family reach into mind as the floorboards groan underfoot, protesting my return. My bare feet smudge chalk demon circles drawn onto grimy floorboards. I glance up at a charred painting of my family, and the little girl standing with her father's hands on her shoulders. A girl who dared to believe in her own light before it was smothered by shadows.

Faded incantations scratched into the chipped, black painted walls surround the fire-damaged portrait of me and my family. An altar, scarred with gouges, scratches, and stains stands intact under it as a grim reminder of the countless rituals marred by so much Hell magic that it's impenetrable to destruction.

Words seep into me like daggers as I recall things said by my biological parents. They unfold as if I'm watching a montage of memories through my five-year-old eyes.

I wanted to be like the other kids on our street with normal families. Echoes of their laughs haunt me when I remember running with them through fields, playing make believe, and eating the food they snuck from their houses for me.

But my innocent intentions were quickly warped into something deadly.

My heart skips a beat, and I fall to my knees, clutching at my chest and gasping for air. Their little faces float back into my mind's eye. Two girls and a boy.

We were friends.

I had friends.

Until that one night, when I'd brought them to my house. Sneaking them through the window of my room so no one would see. I was desperate to show them my collection of porcelain dolls. Well, the ones my brother hadn't yet beheaded.

I'd hidden in the closet, holding the handles so my family couldn't get in. I watched through the gaps after my now angry parents discovered my friends in my room. Their faces were so warped with hatred I thought they were going to kill me for it, so I'd hidden like a fucking coward.

I thought they'd kick them out, so I watched when my parents pulled my friends from my room, their nails sinking into their arms.

Their screams rang through the house that night until I was met with silence. Those kid's bodies were never found. Missing posters hung from street posts for years until they faded along with the memory of them.

Nausea swirls in my stomach. How had I forgotten that they'd killed them? Perhaps, I never really did. Their deaths are echoed in every death since.

So many had died because of me. I had snuck my friends in. I should have known better. My family despised outsiders, keeping them from the dark secrets we held in our home.

After that, I had been so desperate to be rid of them all that telling the church about my family was far easier than it should have been, so when The Order came and killed everyone and set that fire, I was relieved.

My older brothers cried as they were lost in the flames, and I didn't try to save them. I could have helped them. I should have, but I was transfixed watching the massacre unfold.

My magic liked it.

I liked it.

I told myself it didn't matter how I felt as I succumbed to the smoke and waited to die. Except I didn't. Edward saved me. I must have looked so innocent, this poor, abused child who was alone and had lost everyone she loved. Who would have believed that I had lit the metaphorical match?

I suppose that's the catch all of evil. That's why the good fall. Evil often appears to be anything but.

My eyes fling open to Samuel, sweat beading his forehead. "See, witch. It's always been you."

My worst fear coils around me, unforgiving and permanent. I am the catalyst of my own demise. I've justified every death at my hands. None of it was an accident. My magic was me and if it killed someone, it's because *I* wanted it to happen.

Every restless and anxious thought bursts out of me in a flurry of shadows, plunging the room into darkness. The last thing I see before my shadows consume us is an unnerving, maniacal grin building on the normally steady lips of Samuel. It's the first time I've seen any light in his eyes. I grit my teeth. The fucking psychopath is getting off on this.

Darkness leaks from my pores, my nose, my ears, my mouth, each one climbing out of me with vigor until I'm cocooned with darkness. I hear a distant scream, probably Edward trying to escape. Didn't he know what would happen when I finally embraced my magic?

With each breath, I draw in the decay-laced, mildewy air. It fuels the pulses of energy surging through me. Better than any high. Any orgasm. This is pure bliss, a release of raw energy.

The shadows were never my magic's enemy. They cloaked me from evil people. Even if I didn't know their intentions at the time, my magic did.

Every person who I killed deserved it. I didn't know why at the time, but my magic could sense their intentions. Except for

Caden. He was simply in the wrong place at the wrong time, triggering something that had been suppressed by his dad—an accident in the truest of senses.

Edward is responsible for that. If he hadn't tortured and oppressed me, it would have never happened. I had no control at the time, and I've spent too long punishing myself when I should have been seeking retribution against the one man who ruined us all.

Now he wants to destroy what good is left in my life: Gomez, Rosa, even Lorcan, who enrages every part of me. But I need him, crave him even, and I'm so mad at him for it. He was always the mirror reflecting the worst parts back to me through rose-tinted glass.

The darkness settles, replaced by a vibration of red-hot magic pulsing from me like heatwaves. My death magic. Samuel's face appears from the shadowy clouds, exhilarated, while Edward cowers in the corner, holding onto his protection pendant for dear life.

My palms open to the ceiling and shadows dance at my fingertips, curling into spirals, ready to do my bidding.

The restraints at my wrists and ankles sizzle to ash, leaving scorch marks against my skin, but my shadows lick my wounds with a healing meant only for me.

This power is mine, I am it, and with every breath I feel the power of my ancestors slipping into me like a tapestry woven with threads of good and evil. Hell, maybe even the fates, forcing me to confront the buried parts of myself.

I slide my legs off the mattress, twisting my body until I'm facing Samuel. Edward's pointless prayers whisper into my ears as he begs for the god he abandoned long ago to protect him.

"Now, Witch, it's time for you to—" Samuel chokes on the rest of his command as my shadows shoot like vipers into his throat.

He grasps at his neck, attempting to sedate the shadows, but I'm stronger than him. Unexpected, certainly, by the look of pure fucking shock on his expression.

I smile, blood trickling down my lips from where I must have bitten my tongue while embracing my powers. Samuel falls to his knees. I tsk and grip his chin between my index finger and thumb. "You're next, but first." I turn to Edward, tilting my head as I watch his feeble attempt at escape.

My grin grows until my cheeks twinge as I allow him to reach the door. He thinks he's so close to freedom, his fear so palpable I can taste it. But my magic reaches the lock before he can get a grasp on the handle.

"No!" he screeches when he can't get it open, hammering his fists against the wooden frame. "Please, God, no."

"Your God can't save you here," I say sweetly, a charge of hope vibrating in my voice that fills him with dread. The color leeches from his cheeks when he turns to face me, and my shadows coil around his neck, wrists, and torso, dragging him back to me.

I'm going to enjoy this.

I grab the same scalpel Edward had forced me to squeeze, then stand over him, his limbs tied by my shadows, forcing him to face the ground. I kneel at his side, shove the blade into his palm, then whispers. "Now squeeze."

"Fuck you!" he splutters, tears bubbling from his bloodshot eyes.

"You'd fucking like that, wouldn't you?" I grab a fistful of his hair, lifting his head up. "Squeeze the blade or I'll use it to cut your throat."

He's trembling, and a faint smell of urine permeates the air surround us. The coward has wet himself.

"Please, don't do this," he begs, but his words only feed my rage until I'm blind with it.

"Now!" I shout, pulling his hair tighter until he lets out a scream. "Serve your fucking penance, you coward."

He shakes his head again. *Fuck.*

My shadows, like ribbons of darkness, tighten around him. I flick my fingers and my magic forces him onto his back.

I lean over him. I won't kill him yet. No. I plan on enjoying this torture. I'll make him see what a despicable cunt he really is.

His eyes shift a little, and I realize he's glaring at my chest. He looks up quickly, but it's too late.

"Oh, this is what you want," I say with a laughter that doesn't sound like my own. "You want me to fuck you, *Dad?* It's what you've always wanted, right? Like my magic, you suppressed it."

His nostrils flare. "I would never fuck a whore of Satan!"

My fists ball and my shadows constrict. "No?" I ask, my eye twitching. He really has justified everything, including his revolting lust. "Then why did you touch me when I was just a kid?" I scream until my throat hurts.

"It was penance."

"It was rape!" I yell, spit flying from my mouth onto his face.

"Don't pretend you didn't want it. That you weren't trying to seduce me. I only did what I had to do, to punish you."

My heart hammers so loudly I can't hear myself think. I grab the scalpel from his shaking fingers, then climb on top of him. "If the last thing I do in this world is to take you out of it, then it will all have been worth it."

Shock widens his stare when I unzip his pants, one click of the zipper at a time. "What are you doing?"

I smile. "What you always wanted. Touching your dick." I grab him through his urine-soaked boxers, and squeeze until he's writhing against me. His screams are a lullaby to the pain and hurt buried in my mind.

I squeeze tighter, digging my nails into his dick until he's screams are dry, raspy, and desperate. Bringing the scalpel lower, I free the shriveled-up appendage from his underwear.

"No, please, God, no."

My head gradually tilts to the side and my lips curl back from my blood-stained teeth. "It's for the greater good. Isn't that what you always say, *Father*?"

He almost breaks free of my shadows, but I hold him down with every ounce of my power.

I shove the blade under his foreskin, fury guiding every flicker of movement as I carve through him. Blood spurts everywhere, splattering my flushed cheeks and neck.

Slice.

Cut.

Carving away parts of his manhood is so exhilarating that I forget everything else—Samuel, Lorcan, even Rosa.

All that matters is that I show him the same pain he showed me.

Ringing resonates in my ears, but I ignore it, instead focusing on the scalpel slicing deeply into the fleshy tissue, the elasticity of the skin fighting against my makeshift weapon. I increase pressure on the blade, then blow out a breath as his foreskin rips free.

"Try to get an erection now, you perverted fuck!"

CHAPTER SIX

Lorcan

"Bro Demon!" Aiden shouts exuberantly. My jaw clenches so tightly I worry the vein throbbing along it will burst and splatter Ezra's face with gore. Aiden continues, despite my morose demeanor. "It's been sooo long since you've hung out in my head or through any kind of mirror. Don't get me wrong, it's actually been a nice break."

"So, *this* is Aiden," Ezra comments with a lifted brown, then adds. "Your valet?"

I side-eye my brother, trapping him in my glare. "That foolish observation does not warrant a response."

"You could've just said, 'yes,'" Aiden chimes. "Shit, really leaning into that evil overload persona. Glad to see your time in the Shadow Realm hasn't ruined your sunny disposition."

My brows quirk upwards. "I'm surprised you even know the word disposition."

A psychotic grin sweeps over my brother's face as he shakes me by the shoulders. "Oh, I like him."

I growl as Ezra's claws stab into my shoulders and wrinkle my nose as he winks at Aiden. "Enough, we have things to discuss, and you two fucking morons keep steering the conversation to nonsense."

Ezra snaps his teeth close to my face. "Make me."

I spin, my teeth sharpening as a triumphant smile takes over my face, and send my tattooed fist into his godsdamn throat. Ezra gags and coughs, his lips moving, but no sound escapes. "What was that, Wrath? Can't speak with your crushed larynx?" I taunt and smack his bearded cheek twice.

Rare delight warms like a sun in my chest as I bind him with shadows and deposit him in the corner by the window. "Stay," I command.

I chuckle as Ezra growls and bucks beneath his restraints. Serves him fucking right after he trussed me up with his shadows the other day.

My heart stalls. Oh, shit. I've neglected my only link with the Human Realm because of this asshat. My eyelid twitches—the reality of losing this one advantage to tedious sibling rivalry all too realistic.

I hurry back to the mirror and exhale slowly when I see it's not shattered. Aiden's wide eyes stare at me through the glass, his jaw slack. "Wha-?"

I grip the nape of my neck, then interrupt what I'm sure is about to be useless dribble. "You are going to help me free my little witch."

"Okay, sure," he says and nodding enthusiastically like a ridiculous bobble head toy. "But me too, right? Like I am going to go free, 'cause I can't get her out without being free myself."

I groan and rub my temples. *Satan, give me patience.* "Obviously. I don't give a shit what happens to you either way. All I want is to get Evie out of there."

"Fine, whatever," Aiden says, puffing out his cheeks. "If you don't care, then why should I bother helping you when I can just help myself?"

Fabric rustles as Ezra struggles and fails to free himself from the shadow restraints. The corner of my mouth twitches but I ignore him.

"Listen, *Valet.* Must I remind you of all the ways I can draw endless agony out of your body in Hell?"

He gulps, the edge of his servant's mark rippling with the movement. "Uh. No, definitely cool. Don't need another reminder. Still have nightmares from the last time."

"You need to be nicer to the kid," Ezra interjects behind me, his voice broken and raspy as if he swallowed shards of glass.

I glare into the tiny mirror, perturbed by the constant back and forth, then slap a shadow gag over his big fucking mouth. That should work for now, before he works up the energy to fight my shadows properly.

Aiden's eyes dance between mine as he pouts. "He's right, you know. I don't think you've ever been nice to me."

"Will you fucking focus? Or I'll devise a plan so that only Rosa escapes with Evie and your left here to rot."

Aiden frowns, which rapidly transforms into an impish smile. "But really, would it kill you to be, just, you know, more pleasant on occasion?"

"For fuck's sake. Will you stop badgering me if I agree to attempt it?"

"Yeppers," Aiden replies brightly, popping the P.

I don't even look at Ezra to know that he's smiling. Fucking 'Yeppers?'

A soft click sounds as he sets down the compact mirror on his nightstand, flops on his bed, then turns on his side facing me. "So, what do you wanna know, Bro Demon?"

I growl low in my chest but force it away. *The fucking things I subject myself to for my witch.* "Rosa mentioned that you can hear the abbey's bell chiming on the hour. Is that correct?" I ask, my tone brooking no argument. Reaching into my pocket, I pluck out another cigarette, rolling it between my fingers. "Anything else you might've forgot to mention?"

Aiden adjusts his ball cap and scrunches up his nose. "Nope. I don't think so," he admits, but the light in his eyes swiftly dies, like a fire doused with water. And yet, there is something intriguing beneath the surface. Interesting. "Oh, right! One of your brothers has been stalking me, following me around and shit anytime I'm out of this room."

"They've let you out? Why?"

Aiden shrugs. "The plumbing in my shower is bad and another brother of yours constantly complains 'about my stench,'" he says, making air quotes. "But yeah, anyway. He's been stalking me, and I mean in like real life, not in the mirror or anything." He pauses, then his lips turn down. "Somehow, it's even creepier. But at least he doesn't pop-up on me like a demented jack-in-the-box though. So, I win there I guess."

I push the hair off my forehead. "Interesting. Do you know his name?"

"Nope, he's mostly quiet. Always lurking around dark corners, smoking, and brooding," Aiden explains.

Fuck, that could be any of my brothers. "What does he look like?" I ask.

Aiden's eyes light up and he bobs and weaves his head as if trying to view something over my shoulder. "Actually, just like that bro demon," he says, squinting into the mirror and pointing at Ezra. "Wait! He actually is your bro. So trippy."

I twist my torso to the side, both my brows arching high into my hairline. How the Hell did I not feel him escape? Curiosity and anger blend into a potent cocktail within me. I glare through slitted eyes at Ezra as he leans on the windowsill and cleans under his claws with the blade he started carrying ever since I stabbed him.

My brother smirks and winks at me, then focuses on the tiny image of Aiden in the mirror. "Did he have an awesome bun like his and look sexy as fuck?"

Aiden grins at Ezra. "Oh, yeah. He looks just like you, it's crazy." He pauses, eyebrows pinching together. "Wait… are you guys like twins or something? That's so fucking cool."

"Isn't it though?" Ezra agrees. "Seriously, Lorry, I fucking love this kid. But yes, that demon is Gideon, my twin."

My eyes roll so far into my head the tendons and ligaments ache with strain. "Fucking fools. Your part of the plan is simple, Aiden," I state, folding my arms over my chest, and rolling my shoulders back. "Be prepared to leave tonight, just after the six o'clock bells."

"Shit, really? What do I do?" he asks much too excitedly for my taste.

"Just be fucking ready," I order. "Rosa will come collect you, then I'll take it from there."

Aiden looks off to the side, his brows furrowing and his upper lip pooching under his nose. "How?" he asks slowly, extending the 'O'.

"You get your wish, Aiden. I'll be inside your head again, pulling the strings," I say, my tone a dark promise.

"I knew I shouldn't have said anything," Aiden murmurs with a sigh.

"Pass the mirror back to Rosa," I order.

Ezra pushes me out of the frame once he sees her brown eyes, and grins. "Hey, Sugar, so here's what we're going to do. You're going to make Asher super horny."

Rosa recoils, her nostrils flaring. "You want me to what?"

"Fine. Seduce and distract him then," Ezra repeats, then winks. "Or distract, then seduce. The order doesn't really matter."

"Fucking demons," she says under her breath as she smooths her brown to ombre pink hair back into a high ponytail. Rosa shakes her head, pink locks swinging like a metronome. "There has to be another way."

"There isn't. And we both know you will do this, if not for your sake, then for Evie's," I counter.

"Ugh. Okay, fine, you're right." Rosa crosses her arms, inadvertently pushing her tits up and deepening her cleavage. "I mean, I know all the ways to bring a man to his knees, but a demon? Not so much."

Ezra whistles. "Damn, Sweetness, that confidence in seduction is sexy as Hell. Don't worry, I got you covered. The Order is fuckity-fucked, but they aren't military. The abbey is not as secure as they think it is, especially because we know our brother's weaknesses." Ezra pins me with his stare like he wants me to jump in on the conversation.

I wave him off, then glide to the window. Hues of gray and blue light trickle across my hands as I take out my packs of cigs and light a cigarette. I inhale at a glacial pace, relishing each burning molecule as I take it into my lungs. *Fuck, that's good.* The tension in my shoulders eases with the familiar habit. "Go ahead," I state, then watch two streams of smoke ripple and distort in a pane of thick blue glass as I exhale through my nose. "You've been around him more recently anyway."

Ezra shrugs, then clears his throat. "Okay, beautiful. I can already tell, even realms apart, that you weren't lying about knowing your way around seduction. It oozes from your every pore like a sensual perfume," he praises gruffly and inhales, his nostrils flaring. "Fuck, how I wish I could smell that sexy—"

Purple embers shower the windowsill as I stab my cigarette out on the stone, the weak paper collapsing into a small, flattened circle. "I swear to fuck, Ezra. Stay on topic." I narrow my gaze on the human rainbow as she hides a giggle behind her hand, point a claw tipped forefinger at Rosa. "You too."

She salutes. "Yes, boss!"

Ezra bites his lip and groans. "Don't worry, Sugar. When I get out of the Shadow Realm, we will play."

Something twinkles in her irises as she rolls her eyes, then straightens her spine. "So, Asher. The distraction?"

"Right," Ezra replies. "Thankfully, Asher is the simplest minded of our brothers. He craves everything in excess and will latch onto any opportunity to shirk his duties to fuck around."

I snort. "That's putting it lightly." Perching on the edge of the Shadow Realm version of her bed, I smooth my hair back as I monitor them.

"Well, Asher sounds lovely," Rosa states, her voice dripping with sarcasm.

Ezra laughs. "He's actually a ton of fun, but that's not the point."

I roll my shoulders back, then stand and stride over to them, glancing at Gomez's cage in the corner as I walk. I grimace when Gomez squeaks. Seeing him caged up like this reminds me of my time in captivity.

"This is taking too godsdamn long," I interrupt. "Look, Human Rainbow, we don't have time for pleasantries. Aiden confirmed that when the church bell strikes six, Asher will come and deliver dinner to you both tonight."

Rosa smooshes her purple lips to the side. "That sounds, correct. The sky darkens around that time as well."

"Even better," Ezra states.

"You will work your charm," I add. "I don't give a shit what you do, but you must make Asher believe you intend to fuck him or suck his cock at some point in the future."

Rosa laughs. "Easy."

Ezra's laughter booms, blending with hers. "Once he's so aroused he can hardly see straight, he'll be in a hurry to slink back to his room to watch porn and play with his cock."

"Precisely. While he hands you your meal and drools over you, quickly slip something from that backpack you call a purse into the door jamb so the door remains unlocked."

Rosa's brow rises over penetrating dark brown eyes. "Even demons watch porn? It's really as simple as that?"

"Yes," I state.

"Hell, yes," Ezra announces boisterously at the same time.

Rosa's hands land on her curvaceous hips. "Okay, then. Well, I don't need your instructions. I'll do what feels right at the time, once I gauge him."

I slide my hands into my pockets. "Fine. Just don't fuck it up. After you get free, unlock Gomez's cage and grab him, unlock Aiden's room, and I'll direct you through my servant bond with him to Evie. My brothers will never expect an escape attempt in the early evening. And when you get Evie, meet us back at my manor."

"Thanks for mansplaining," Rosa replies. "As if I wouldn't grab Gomey and let Aiden out."

Ezra growls and bounces on the balls of his feet. "You ready, Sugar?"

"As much as I can be."

My thoughts turn to Evie, a thrill shooting through my blood knowing I'll see her soon. *We're coming for you, Little Witch.* I try to send the vow to Evie through our bond, but yet again there's no reply. They must have her unconscious or drugged.

Godsdamn, I can't believe that stunt actually worked.

I watch the Human Realm through the compact mirror as Rosa sets it down to reflecting the most advantageous angle of the room.

Asher drags his tongue over his lips as he runs a hand over the erection forcing his navy-blue joggers to extrude.

"You know, our faces are squished into a mirror that's shaped like a fucking eggplant," Ezra whispers, his bearded face shoving against mine.

"Shut the fuck up," I growl. "There's no time for your idiotic antics."

Poor, Baby Brother. Seduction is a powerful tool, whether it's used in your favor or not. My eyes widen as Rosa bends at the waist, grabbing the weighty, ceramic lid to the toilet that she planted by the door jamb earlier. She lifts it over her head and bashes Asher's head over and over. A laugh rushes from me as dark blue blood and chunks of brain matter splatter in every direction.

"Although I'm loathe to admit, she's an intelligent woman. She at least knows that one strike won't keep a prince of Hell down. Even Asher."

Ezra hums in agreement. "Mhm."

Rosa's eyes ping frantically around the room, her hands shaking so hard she can barely grasp the handle of Fluffy Fucker's cage when she lets him out, then steals from the room.

"Hey, Sugar," Ezra calls. "Don't forget about us."

Rosa curses, snatches the mirror, then exits her makeshift prison. The reflection of the mirror turns into a phantasmagoria of colors as she jostles it around.

I hiss, "What the fuck are you doing?"

"Tucking my compact in my cleavage. I need to use both hands," she states, her words broken with nerves.

Ezra grins too widely. "I'm honored, Sweetness."

She snorts. "Enjoy it. It's the first and last time you'll find yourself there."

A sliver of crescent shaped bare skin crowds two sides of the compact as she hastily unlocks Aiden's door. The door flies open before she has a chance to turn the knob, and Aiden grins on the other side.

Handing Ezra the mirror, I plunge through the bond into Aiden's mind. Strangely, a sense of mild fondness swarms me as my consciousness weaves into his.

"Bro Demon!" Aiden shouts.

Rosa's dainty, manicured hand rises, then slaps over his mouth.

A fierce growl rolls from my chest. *For fuck's sake.* I clench my jaw and stab my fingers through my hair. *The goal is to not get caught. Stealth is important,* I snap in his mind.

"Sorry, sorry. I just got so excited," Aiden replies sheepishly.

Listen closely. I'll relay instructions to lead you and Rosa to Evie, then continue to aid your route through the catacombs once you have her. You must *walk as quickly and* quietly *as you can, but don't run.* I pause, making sure Aiden is absorbing the information. *I sense my brothers in the East wing. Thank fuck. Luckily, it's on the opposite end of the abbey, so as long as you are tactful, they won't be alerted to your movements.*

I don't bother explaining this to Rosa, as she's intelligent enough to grasp the nature of the situation.

As Ezra raises the mirror in my peripheral, my vision splits, one part of me looking through Aiden's eyes, and the other monitoring my brother as he brings the mirror so close to his face only his beard surrounded lips are in the frame.

"Be careful, Sweetness," he purrs. "Follow Aiden. Lorcan is telling him where to go."

"Okay," she squeaks as a tremble fans from her hands to her extremities. "Also, stop calling me that, you big brute."

Aiden rubs his hands together, his excessive energy zipping along the bond and raising the hair on my arms. *Fucking move. We don't have much time,* I order. *Turn left at the end of this hall.*

"What now?" he whispers. I roll my eyes.

Continue straight, I reply.

I strain my ears for any detrimental sounds, but the only things I detect are Aiden's obnoxious tromping steps, and both their panting breaths. Even Fluffy Fucker knows to remain silent as he flies with the humans. The duo quickly reaches the grand staircase and moves down them swiftly.

Stay quiet, I remind him.

"You got it, bro-demon-boss-man," Aiden says in an attempt to whisper, but it's still loud. This kid doesn't know the concept of an inside voice.

"This is a good view, but it would be a better one if you turn this thing around so I could watch those gorgeous tits of yours bounce instead," Ezra propositions.

"Ugh, you're a fucking pig," Rosa whispers in response.

Ezra chuckles as my view through Aiden tilts, then distorts wildly as he trips on the bottom step. *Fuck me, I knew the escape was going too smoothly.*

"Shiiiiiiiiiit," Aiden cries as he tumbles, then catches himself from face planting. I blow out a relieved breath through my nostrils.

I need a fucking cigarette.

Rosa whispers, "Get up, Aiden!"

Aiden swivels his head to Rosa. "Right, but apart from that fall, this is going amazing. We're the best team ever, right? Team Great Hair! You know, because we both have great hair," Aiden whisper shouts to Rosa and offers her his fist bump.

Her eyes widen and her manicured brows rise nearly to her hairline in the clearest depiction of '*what the fuck is wrong with you*' I have ever witnessed. Honestly, it's impressive.

Don't celebrate yet, I warn. *Move the rug directly in front of you. Underneath is a trapdoor.*

"What do you think you're doing?" a voice booms. Aiden's whips his head around as a member of The Order grabs his shoulders.

"Fuck," I curse.

My head tilts to the side in befuddlement as Aiden cocks back his arm and punches the man directly between his legs. The Order acolyte crumples to a heap on the floor, and Aiden celebrates, swaying his hips in a dance of victory.

"Dude," Aiden crows. "Did you see that!? I got him in his pregnancy tools! I'm just like John McClain!"

Ezra laughs, his whole body shaking with mirth as Rosa draws her leg back, then kicks The Order member in the groin a second time. "Shit, she's vicious. *I like it,*" he adds with a whisper.

I cringe as Rosa shushes Aiden and Ezra aggressively. I hate that godsdamn sound. "C'mon, we're almost there. Evie needs us," Rosa encourages, elbowing Aiden out of the way and flings open the trapdoor. Admiration trickles into me as she marches down the steps like she owns the place. Aiden hurries behind her, pressing his back to one wall, then the opposite in a lopsided zig-zag pattern as he continues to pretend he's the fictional cop who saved Christmas.

Fucking focus and keep up with her, I order Aiden.

"Right. Go team, go," he whispers, trailing Rosa closely.

My skin tightens in awareness. Something's wrong.

Aiden, stop Rosa, I command.

He manages to encircle her wrist, effectively halting her forward momentum. Her palm scrapes the wood as it slides from the partially open door to the secret chamber. A dripping sound sets my nerves on high alert, it's familiarity at once a thrill and terror. My primal senses jolt awake and search for the perceived threat.

"Pfft. It can't be that bad," Aiden proclaims, no doubt still high from his earlier actions and the adrenaline soaring through his veins. He swipes the compact mirror from Rosa and moves past her to swing the door wide.

I freeze, unable to dissect the scene unfolding in the torture chamber in my brain's discombobulated state. I take the mirror from Ezra and am immersed in a myriad of Evie's scent, the unnerving absence of sound, lashing shadows, and blood.

So. Much. Blood.

Aiden gasps, "What the shit did we just walk into?"

CHAPTER SEVEN

Evie

In retrospect, I shouldn't have cut off his dick. It was a quicker death than he deserved.

My shadows shudder against my bones as I stand over Edward's body, staring at my father's blanched face and wide, unblinking eyes. Tears fall thick and fast as years of pent-up anger swell through me.

I thought killing him would satiate the rage pulsing through me, but it only adds to it. This isn't enough. He took advantage of me when I was just a fucking child!

I had intended to keep him alive and force him to see the ugliness he'd done. I wanted retribution! I need him to know he was a bad person. That was the best way to destroy him. He thought himself a *righteous man*, justifying all his actions. I was going to reveal his true nature.

I had a plan; one I had meticulously gone over in my mind since I'd been trapped in here. I had accounted for every detail, except for my bloodlust.

"Burn in Hell!" I spit through gritted teeth.

I vaguely register Samuel behind me, spluttering and coughing as my shadows dissipate from inside his throat. A mortal would have died by now, but he's a demon and my choking him out was an equivalent of a pathetic slap on the wrist.

Despite wanting nothing more than to tear apart Edward's corpse and scream until my voice runs dry, Samuel—the twisted fuck—demands my attention.

"You're more powerful than I knew."

I turn to face him. Samuel's pupils dilate, lips trembling and glistening with splatters of dark blood. He wipes his lips on the sleeve of his maroon button-up shirt and smirks. Glancing at the door, he laughs.

I hadn't noticed them until then, standing in the doorway.

"Evie…" Rosa's voice penetrates the silence.

Gods no. She can't be here. Not now.

I stare at Rosa and Aiden, with a scalpel in one hand and Edward's severed dick in the other.

How long have they been there? How much did they see?

Rosa's eyes widen as she scans the blood-drenched scene. "Evie. Is that his…?"

I drop the flaccid organ into the pool of blood at my feet. There is so much blood, running like rivers of crimson through the cracks in the stone ground. It's too bad he bled out so quickly.

Seeing Rosa makes this ten times worse. Not because of what I did, but because of how I did it… and how much I enjoyed it. Now she sees what Lorcan saw in me from the moment he laid eyes on me—a killer.

Having my darkness reflected in the horrified expression of my closest friend makes me wince.

Gomez flaps his wings behind them, landing on Rosa's shoulder. His beady eyes scan the room and I command him not to come any further through our bond.

Seeing him breaks my heart, but I can't afford to show vulnerability now. Not with a sadistic monster watching me.

Speaking of…

Samuel's psychotic laughter echoes through the room. The fucker really has come alive in all this murder.

"Leave," I splutter to Rosa, knowing Samuel will only use her to get to me. "Now!"

Samuel tilts his head toward Aiden and Rosa and my entire body tenses. He laughs maniacally, then spits blood on the ground. "Don't run, or I'll direct my brothers to murder you all," Samuel orders, glaring at Rosa, then adds, pointing at me, "And I'll kill your favorite psychopath."

My gaze drifts to Rosa, Aiden, and Gomez before landing on the compact mirror Aiden is directing toward me. A pair of pastel-green eyes, half a straight nose and those thick lips come into view.

My heart stutters.

"Evie." Lorcan's voice comes out desperate and tortured, and I almost feel bad. Then I remember he tricked me. Used me. It was the worst of all the things he had done. I relished the stalking and chasing. But not telling me he was in love with one of my ancestors, and planning to trap me in the Shadow Realm so I could take his place, was the worst sting of it all. He pretended to have feelings for me, and I feel so fucking duped.

I blink, my lashes briefly clinging to the blood smeared under my eye, and shake my head, scattering those thoughts. Now is not the time to let emotions get the better of me.

"What an interesting turn of events," Samuel says with a hunger in his eyes that turns my stomach. "Why don't you bring that mirror here. Yes, you, with the dumbass look on your face."

"Aiden!" I yell and he flinches. "Smash the mirror. Now!" I wasn't sure if I needed Lorcan gone so Samuel couldn't reach him, or because I wasn't ready to face him. Either way, he needed to be gone.

"Oh, uh," Aiden says, stumbling, then whispers to the mirror, "Sorry bro."

Lorcan's voice come's through the mirror, as clear as if he was standing with us. "Don't you fucking da—"

Aiden drops the mirror on the ground, purple and green plastic exploding outward as the casing cracks, then smashes his heel into the glass. I hear it shatter, but Samuel doesn't make a move to stop him.

"No matter," Samuel says silkily, pacing around me in a circle, his hands behind his back. "There are plenty of mirrors in the world. What I need is for you to unlock the portal."

I shake my head. "It's destroyed."

He brings his face too close to mine, teeth bared. "Then make a new one. You have the power to do it. Or I'll kill your friends in front of you." He glances at the doorway, shadows snaking from him like serpents, and before I can blink, they've reached Rosa and Aiden, slipping into their orifices.

They freeze, only their eyes moving, as if they've been rendered statues. Fortunately, Gomez has disappeared amongst the commotion. I only hope he's hiding.

Raising my hands, magic pulses into a deadly hum under my fingertips. "Let them go."

"Evangeline said you would be powerful, but she never said it would be this much." His nostrils flare as he glances at the floor with disgust, as if he can see my dead aunt from here.

"You met my aunt?"

"I know her now," he says with mock surprise and fiery eyes. "She's waiting for you, you know."

"She's dead," I reply. "Unless she isn't?"

"Evangeline and I are doing this for your benefit too. Lorcan must be destroyed."

"So, where is my great aunt?"

"Hell," he says with an unnerving smile. "Where you will be soon if you don't build that portal."

"I'm more powerful than you."

His expression shifts into that of a predator. "Not by much, and you can't kill me." He side-eyes Rosa and my stomach drops.

"Let. Them. Go," I order with a guttural growl.

Shadows writhe with every pulse of my heart, sliding away from me in glittering, black swirls.

He laughs, eyes alight, and I realize he wants this. He loves it. We are one of the same, except he's right. I have more to lose, therefore something worth fighting for.

Samuel spits demon blood on the floor, hands in his pockets as he saunters closer. "Rebuild the portal. Now."

"No."

He scoffs. "You're fighting for someone who doesn't even care about you."

I know he's talking about Lorcan. I want to believe he's wrong, but at the same time, I know he's probably right. "This isn't about Lorcan."

His brows furrow and he tilts his head, eyes penetrating as if he's reaching into the depths of my soul, searching for the truth. It's invasive and I suddenly feel as if I'm naked. "If that's true," he replies slowly, "then help me and I'll let you and your friends go."

I swallow thickly. "So you can kill me after?"

"You have my word. I will not harm you."

I scoff, recalling everything Lorcan had said to me—every trick, when he made me believe he was falling for me. When he made me feel things for him. "In my experience, the word of a demon means nothing."

"I am not my brother," he spits, as if the unspoken comparison is so disgusting. "I keep my word."

I glance sideways at Rosa and Aiden. Her eyes are wide, pupils flitting around, revealing the panic she can't show with the rest of her body.

"Fine, I'll do it, just let them go," I relent, but he's not so easily fooled.

"Build the portal first."

"With what mirror, genius?" I ask and his eye twitches as if he's not used to being unprepared. I'm glad I can get under his skin, if only a little.

"I'll have one of my brothers bring one." When he pulls out his cellphone from his pocket, I take the opportunity while he's distracted to flick a shadow around his wrist, twisting until I hear bones crack.

The phone clashes onto the ground, and the ropes of onyx magic fade slightly. My eyes widen when I spot Rosa's fingers wiggle as she tries to move. Aiden's lips part slightly.

Samuel's growl reverberates through the room. I lash another shadow at him, and he whips it away with his magic.

I raise my fingers in the air, pulsing shockwaves of onyx darkness at him. The shadows shift and take shape, shrouding him in darkness. The deadly hum of my death magic vibrates, and the ground splits with a deafening crack.

"Enough!" Samuel's eyes darken to coal, and he shifts into his demonic form.

Unlike Lorcan, who while terrifying, looked beastly and monstrous in a regular demonic way, Samuel appeared *Satanic*.

His body swells, clothes tearing as he grows three times in size. His skin peels from his body, like a snake shedding its hide, and rows upon rows of razor-sharp teeth elongate from his gums.

Fuck this.

Rosa and Aiden fall backward as Samuel concentrates his magic on shifting. His lower body disappears as a long, pointed black tail replaces it. He drags claws across stone, the smell of sulfur thick in the air.

I race to the door, grab Rosa and Aiden by their hands before they can speak, then slip into the In-Between.

My heart pounds so hard, I worry it'll break free from my ribcage and kill me before I can get them out.

Aiden yelps when he's dragged into the shadows with me and Rosa. She clings to my arm, gasping for air as we shadow walk. We land in a shadowy corner of a room, and I slide us into another shadow, using my magic to navigate the rooms.

Samuel's roar shakes the foundations of the old building. A squeak sounds ahead as Gomez flies into view, landing on my shoulder.

Tears flood my vision. "Gomey." He nestles into my hair, and I press my fingers against his soft, warm little body. "Cling to me, baby. Don't let go."

His claws sink into my hair, and I run with the others.

"I'm going to vomit," Aiden exclaims as I shadow walk them around a corner.

Rosa's grip tightens on my arms. "Oh my god."

The cold air hits as we land outside, under the shade of a willow tree. My head buzzes as I try to stand straight, but my power wanes. Moving all three of them is draining me, but I have to keep going, even if my legs almost buckle.

"The manor," Rosa splutters. "We need to go there."

"Lorcan's?" I ask as we spiral into another shadow across the street, moving through the In-Between.

"Yes," she says breathily. "You're going to have to trust me."

My heart palpitates when we shadow walk through a stretch of darkness hidden under a tall statue and arrive onto the grounds of Lorcan's manor. I briefly close my eyes, blocking out the snow-drenched, gothic building.

Gomez squeaks in my ear, using my hair as curtains to the frosty world. "It's okay baby," I whisper and stroke his fur. It's so comforting to hold him close that I can't stand the thought of being away from him again. His tiny claws scratch my neck, but I don't mind. I know he's longing for closeness, grasping at my skin to feel it. We'd been parted before when I was in the Shadow Realm, but this time was different. He could feel the torture through our familiar bond, even when I tried to block it out. I'm hurting, and his clinging to me is his way of trying to take it away. "I'm okay," I promise, but he doesn't relax. "We're okay."

It's strange being back here in my world. I spent so much time in the Shadow Realm version of this place, where the saturation was turned down, ash floated, suspended in the air, and strings of loneliness echoed in every hall.

I wonder if Lorcan came back here after Aiden smashed the mirror.

Speaking of Aiden, he hunches over, his hands on his knees, and retches. "Let's stick to normal transport in the future."

I get it. My calves are killing me, and my stomach is a flurry of nausea. Going in and out of the In-Between, moving between shadows, is not for the faint-hearted. Gomez seems okay, though he remained tucked into my hair for most of the journey.

My breath catches when I look up. Pointed arches stretch into the sky, each one covered with powdered white. I can't even see the warped expressions of the stone gargoyles under the frosted ice.

Beyond the grounds, an ocean of snow-dusted fir trees stretches out behind the gray-bricked building, and I'm transported to the time when Lorcan had chased me through those trees, showing the true extent of his demonic side.

I stroke Gomez on my shoulder, wrapping the jacket Rosa hands me around my body. The hospital gown isn't covering a lot at this point.

Aiden wipes his mouth on the sleeve of his purple t-shirt, Darkwood College: Home of the Bats emblazoned on the front in black, then looks at the iron bars jutting downward over the entrance. "Maybe we beat them here."

"How do you know?" I ask, my eyes widening. Was this the plan all along, for Rosa and Aiden to meet the brothers here? Aiden was holding a mirror, so he was obviously communicating with Lorcan. The thought of seeing him again makes me sicker than any shadow walking could.

"Dunno," Aiden says with a shrug. "We said we'd meet them here after we got you."

I glance sideways at Rosa. "Why?"

"So you can build the portal. We need their help, Evie. Let's get inside and I'll fill you in, but first… here." Rosa reaches into her bag and pulls out a lighter and pack of cigarettes, handing me one. She's taking all of this far better than Aiden. Perhaps it's because she's a witch too. Even if she doesn't know it. Rosa, fuck, all of us need to take advantage of every strength we possess and hone it.

The first inhale of nicotine rushes straight to my head. I close my eyes, my lips curving as I relish the feeling. I have missed smoking.

Rosa returns the lighter to her purse. "Swiped them from Asher," she explains. "Thought you might want one when we rescued you. Although, it turns out you didn't need rescuing."

"Neither did you."

Aiden places a hand over his heart, looking far too pleased with himself. "Nor did I."

Rosa looks at him with incredulity but doesn't rebuke him.

I swallow. "Rosa?"

"Hm?" she hums.

"Before we go in there… I need to tell you something. Look, there is no easy way to say this," I inhale, then sprint through the rest of the words, "but… you're a witch."

I brace for her reaction, but it doesn't come. However, Aiden's hands fly to his cheeks so fast he slaps himself. "Rosa is a witch too!? That's…" He gapes, then closes his mouth. "Fantubular! Wait… Hey, how come everyone has cool powers and shit but me?"

Rosa and I glance at him, ignoring his word choice, or Aidenism as I like to call them, then I shrug and turn my attention back to Rosa.

"Are you okay?"

A gorgeous smile warms her softening expression. "Definitely." She laughs and arches her brows while planting one hand on her hip and speaks with the other. "You already told me. Multiple times actually and, before you tell me, I already know it's a different kind of magic to what your coven practice."

"The fuck? When?"

She shrugs. "Remember when you told me *you* were a witch? You also mentioned my witchy-ness, many times, when you were drinking while on benzos. And before you ask, I never said anything because I've been waiting to start practicing my magic until you harnessed your own," Rosa pauses and bumps she shoulder into me, "like I fucking knew you would. But then everything went to Hell in edible panties, and... you know the rest." She pulls me into an embrace. "Also, if I haven't said it yet, I'm so damn proud of you for getting clean, Evie."

"Thank you." Moisture wells along my lower lashes and I allow one solitary tear to fall while my best friend holds me. When I blink the rest away, we resume walking to the manor.

"Always, girl," Rosa proclaims, then her gaze heats the side of my face. "He deserved it, Evie."

I blink twice. "Who?"

"Edward."

I swallow hard against the lump forming in my throat. She always knows what's playing on my mind. *Always.*

"I know, and I don't regret it," I admit.

Aiden's eyes expand. "You and Lorcan really are meant for each other," he says and walks alongside us to the door. "*Mr. and Mrs. Psychopath,*" he adds under his breath. Aiden forces a teasing smile, but I can't be sure if it's because he's afraid of me or if he's actually joking. Except, he can't erase the horror in his bright blue eyes.

Rosa comes to my defense before I can form the words. "You should be glad she killed him. Edward was an abusive piece of shit who tortured Evie for years when she was just a *child*. He kidnapped us and would have killed us if given the chance. He used his religion as an excuse to live out his sadistic fantasies."

Aiden's light brows knit together, his lips curving into a frown. "I'm sorry, but…" He pauses, wincing at the memory. "Did you really have to cut off his cock though?"

I suck in a final drag of my cigarette, and it goes to my head. The sizzle burns my fingertips, and I throw it into the snow. "Yes. He'd also touch me as a kid, then punish me for his arousal." My teeth clench so tight I'm surprised they don't shatter. "He did it again at The Order headquarters. He was sick and twisted and I get that what I did looked severe. Perhaps in a perfect world I should have handed him over to the authorities, but people like him get away with everything. Not to mention he was murdering innocent people when I was trapped there, just to try and get me to unlock my magic."

Aiden nods, then slides his hand over the back of his neck. "Yikes. What a dick."

Rosa links her arm with mine when we reach the doors and Gomez snuggles me tighter. The warmth of his body against my neck is like a miniature blanket against the cold.

I stare at the serpentine, metal knocker on the arched wooden doors, reminding me of when I'd first come here with Lorcan. It was easier then. Although my life had been turned upside down, I somehow felt safe next to him, because even though he was a demon, he was *my demon*. What's the saying? *Better the devil you know.*

I guess I have no choice but to go inside, but even from here I can feel his presence. He's in there, waiting behind the mirrors for us to enter, and I've never felt more nervous.

CHAPTER EIGHT

Evie

I breathe in the scent of burned cigars, coffee, and polished wood as we walk into the empty, cold foyer. My eyes travel the room, over the grand staircase, marble flooring, gold-framed portraits, and the damask papered covered walls.

I never thought I'd be back here. My stomach clenches. The closer I get to seeing Lorcan, the bigger my desire to run out the door becomes.

We arrive at the living room and Rosa throws me a gray and purple sherpa blanket patterned with skull moths. I hug her jacket tighter around me as Aiden pours himself, Rosa, and me a drink, but I don't touch mine. I'm more nauseous than ever now that the adrenaline has worn off.

Fortunately, Gomez has fallen asleep on my shoulder. The poor thing is exhausted, his tiny snores a soundtrack in my right ear.

Aiden sits across from Rosa and me on the long, clawfoot sofa and says, "Okay, so before you guys do your magic stuff, what's the plan?"

My head throbs from all the new information over the past six hours. "I guess we need to find a solution to get away from The Order. I'm not going to kill Lorcan if that's what you're worried about."

Even if he deserves it, I finish in my thoughts.

Rosa's tone drops an octave. "You'll only be giving Samuel what he wants. We need Lorcan. Ezra too. The Order won't stop until they've found us. I overheard Asher talking with Samuel once," she says, then adds with a roll of her eyes, "They're either idiots or they planned on killing me, because they let a few things slip while in the room with me."

Aiden nods. "They said a lot in front of me." We both look at him and he shrugs. "No one ever sees me as a threat, so people often say things they shouldn't with me in the room. The only one who was cautious around me was Gideon." Aiden's brows furrow and it could be a trick of light, but I swear a flush creeps over his cheeks. "Anyway, yeah, I just acted as if I wasn't paying attention whenever Samuel came and spoke to Lazarus in particular. That was the only one he was like, honest with."

I squeeze the edge of the couch cushions as I lean forward. "Well, people have a habit of underestimating me too. It's their loss." He shoots me half a smile and for the first time, I feel some sort of bond between us.

Rosa places her drink on the table and leans forward too. "So, what did Samuel say to Lazarus?"

Aiden pulls his sleeves down over his hands, and I notice they're all frayed. I know the signs of anxiety when I see them. He's nervous and I can't blame him. I don't even know how he got dragged into all of this, other than what Lorcan briefly mentioned about Aiden being indebted to him. Yet, he doesn't seem loyal to him. Not really.

Aiden rushes his words out, barely stopping for breaths between sentences. "Well, okay, so he said there's some chick in Hell. Your great aunt."

"Evangeline," I confirm.

"Right, well, I'm pretty sure Samuel's in love with her. I've not been in love myself or anything, but when he talked about her it was always with like, such high regard. You know? Samuel didn't seem like the kinda dude who was scared of anything," he continues. "Except he did look afraid sometimes when he thought you weren't going to crack, because he didn't want to disappoint her. That's all he kept saying again and again, that Evangeline needs him to succeed and wouldn't let anything get in the way. Yeah, so he blames Lorcan for your great aunt being in Hell and says he manipulated her, and he wouldn't rest until Lorcan's dead." He pauses to inhale sharply, then continues, "So, your great aunt needs Lorcan dead so she and Samuel can take over Hell, because Lorcan is next in line for the throne after Lucifer retires." He pauses and shakes his head in disbelief. "I wasn't sure if I heard it right either, but yeah, he said the actual *devil* is going to retire. I don't know if they meant that as in they're going to kill him, I mean can you kill the devil?"

Rosa lets out a heavy sigh. "You're getting off track."

"Yeah, right," he says shaking his head. "So, Samuel kept making all kinds of promises to Lazarus of what he'll do once he's in charge, but like, he wouldn't tell the other demon bros that he was going to do that. If he was talking to Asher or one of the others, he just said that Lucifer was behind the command to kill Lorcan, and he told members of The Order something else entirely, saying they were angels, not demons or something." He scoffs and leans back in his chair, then kicks his feet up on the priceless coffee table. "It's a lie. From what I heard, Evangeline's with Lucifer but is secretly seeing Samuel on the side and they're planning a muttony."

Rosa nods. "Do you mean a mutiny?"

"Yeah, like they're planning on taking over behind the devil's back."

I sit back against the plush cushions and take a deep breath. *Well, fuck.*

Rosa puffs out her cheeks and releases a tense breath. "I knew about Lucifer ordering them to kill Lorcan, but I didn't know the rest." She rubs her temples and closes her eyes. "We need to get Lorcan and Ezra out of the Shadow Realm to protect us against The Order and Samuel. We can't do this alone."

Aiden hisses a breath between his teeth and slaps a hand over his neck. "Fuck, stupid servant's mark. Yeah, Lorcan's pissed. He says he's going to tear Samuel apart." He grabs his drink and downs it in one. "Okay! I hear you loud and clear," he mumbles in response to something we can't hear. Or someone. Lorcan must be communicating with him through his mind.

My muscles tense. Lorcan! I forgot all about mirrors in the chaos. He's probably watching us now and listening to everything we say. The thought sends pins and needles over my bare legs. The feeling is quickly replaced with a rush of rage. Of course, Lorcan's pissed, the woman he was in love with wants him dead.

A shiver skitters down my spine, and I shudder. "I'm assuming he needs my help to get him out first." The bite in my tongue isn't lost on Rosa, whose brown eyes widen twice their size.

Aiden looks behind me and I recall the layout of the room from when I was in the Shadow Realm. There's a large oval mirror behind me on the wall. "Yeah, but he says to make sure you rest first." Aiden adds with a mumble, "I *never* get such *sweet* treatment."

A lump forms in my throat and I'm at a loss for words. That's the first time he's communicated with me since I was in the Shadow Realm, even if it's through someone else, and all he cares about is that I'm rested so I am strong enough to rebuild that fucking portal.

"What if I don't want to rebuild it?" I question. "It's not my problem if his ex-girlfriend wants him dead."

Rosa springs to her feet and walks to me. She places her hands on my shoulders and kneels to my height. "Samuel is never going to stop hunting you. You're the only one who can open the portal. Wouldn't you rather do it on your terms?"

Anxiety threads her dark eyes. She's scared, even if she won't admit it. Out of the two of us, she was always good at keeping a cool head in crisis situations, partly because of her job, but seeing her on the edge of panic like this hardens something inside of me.

"Lorcan says…" Aiden begins to recite, but Rosa shushes him.

She returns her focus to me. "Do it for us." She slips a finger to my hair, then strokes Gomez's sleeping head. "I love you, Evie, but I don't want to spend the rest of my life on the run from these monsters, and neither do you. We deserve peace."

I run my fingers over my clavicle and sigh. "I'll do it for you and Gomez."

"For all of us. We're a family." She side-eyes Aiden. "For him too. He's an innocent in all of this, trust me. We talked a lot through the wall when we were trapped there."

A semblance of control seeps back into my mind. I can feel Lorcan's eyes on me. He could have spoken at any point but instead chose to talk through Aiden. He must be anxious around me too. Good. "I suppose I can make it a condition he free Aiden."

"Fuck, yes," Aiden pleads from behind us. "Thanks, Evie!"

Rosa smiles softly. "Come on, let's find you some clothes. There must be something you can wear somewhere in this massive manor."

Aiden bites his lip. "There is. Lorcan made me bring a bunch of your clothes here when you were trapped in there with him, for when you got out."

"Okay," I say and stand, careful with my movements so not to wake my little bat. He's exhausted and has been through so much. "I don't need rest either, I can do this now."

It's the truth, even though I'm depleted. My fingers tremble, and I sigh. There is no chance I can sleep anytime soon. Especially as my brain spins jittery thoughts over itself and my powers, now finally under control, that beg to be used.

I pull Gomez from my shoulder. He reaches out in his sleep to feel me, and I press a reassuring hand against his furry back. "Take him to a bedroom," I whisper. "I need to do something. I'll be right up."

She gathers him in her arms, swaddling him in her jacket like a baby. He remains asleep, calmed by her energy. Then again, Rosa has always been like a second mom to him.

Rosa glances behind me at the mirror. "Good luck. Remember, you always have me."

I force a smile, even though my chest is aching. "I know."

I hold my breath when I spin to face the mirror because I can feel him standing there, waiting to speak, wanting me to look at him. I don't want to see him. His betrayal cuts so deeply that I can't even begin to think about it without wanting to explode.

I hear his voice, but it's so sad it can't possibly belong to him. "*Evie.*"

My name. Not *Little Witch* or *Killer*. Just Evie.

I lift my lashes and face him. Pastel green eyes pin me from behind his black mask and I'm frozen.

Rosa and Aiden's footsteps fade as they leave the room, no doubt so I can be alone with Lorcan. I can't see Ezra anywhere in

111

the Shadow Realm version of the living room, so I assume Lorcan ordered him away too.

It's just us, alone, with just a sheet of glass and an entire realm between us.

"Your eyes," he says, voice breaking in parts. "You look—"

"Broken?"

He sighs. "Miserable."

My chest tightens. "I *was* tortured."

His eyes close, appearing as if the thought actually *pains* him. The audacity. He's trying to pull me back in with fake worry, so I help him defeat his brothers, but I won't be manipulated.

"I'm sorry, Evie."

"Stop calling me that."

His pupils dilate. "Okay, *Little Witch*. Whatever you need."

"Stop acting like you care!" I snap, my fingers flexing at my sides as I try to hold back all the venom dripping from my thoughts to my tongue. I don't want to give him the satisfaction to know that the reason I'm sad has nothing to do with me being tortured. I'm angry over that, but Lorcan's betrayal just fucking hurts.

Lorcan looks around to ensure we're alone, then lowers his mask. It's either to show me I can trust him, or to trick me into believing he cares so I lower my defenses. "I do care."

"You're a liar."

"Yes, but not about what you think."

"You were going to lock me in the Shadow Realm," I state. "You were going to use me to get out and have me take your place."

"I changed my mind," he said simply.

I scoff a laugh. "You don't even deny it."

"No," he admits, but quickly adds, "but I did change my mind. That night, in the library. Maybe even before then." He pauses briefly, as if he's catching his breath. He's a good actor, I'll give him that. Although, he's a demon so what can I expect? He continues in that heartbreak, bullshit tone, "I'm not good at this and maybe it took me a minute to realize what I was feeling was more than lust—"

"Oh Hell no. Don't go there." I shake my head and squeeze my eyes shut. I just killed a man. This shouldn't bother me at all. We didn't even have anything real. *It was just sex, something primal, and dark. It was nothing deep.*

His expression crumples. He actually has the *audacity* to look hurt. "You don't really believe that, do you?"

Damn. My thoughts were too loud. I'd pushed them through our blood bond. "I don't want to talk to you."

His tone is so soft it hurts. "Please."

One word, that's all it takes, and I freeze to the spot.

He continues. "You think I was in love with Evangeline?"

"Weren't you?" I ask, trying to keep the desperation from my tone, but my body betrays me, and my face flushes with heat. He tilts his head, and I notice the subtle shift and the corner of his lip curves.

"No," he replies, and my breath hitches. I want to believe him, but I can't. Otherwise, I deserve whatever happens to me after this. He lets out a prolonged sigh. "She'd shrouded my memories in smoke, and I only remembered everything recently. Everything I thought I felt was artificial. She loved me but I never reciprocated her feelings, and she hates me for it. It's why she wants me dead

113

and she's using Samuel to get to me. She must have figured out how I feel about you."

I shake my head. "I don't believe you."

"You should," he states, his voice now deep and gravelly like before. "I showed you my true name. I'm making myself vulnerable to you."

My gaze traces his true name inked under his eye, and I'm transported back to the night he first showed me it. The music, his singing, flood into my mind, replaying the moment he pulled me closer, when my heart first beat for him. That moment in the library I was certain I'd felt it—that song captured the essence of who we were together. What we were. Separately, we were monsters, but together, well, as Rosa would say, sometimes two wrongs make a right.

The memory crashes with the lie he'd fed me.

He was in love with my great aunt and his heart had already been captivated by a Fallenmoore Witch. It just wasn't me.

I swallow thickly, suppressing the urge to clutch the fabric at my chest. "Those grimoire entries didn't make it seem like she was a puppet. She thought she was manipulating *you*."

"*She* loved me, not the other way around," he growls, and I look at him properly, deep into those green eyes that still haunt my daymares. "Ezra helped me remember everything. I was her savior, Evie, at least in her eyes. In mine, I was just trying to escape my family and found an extremely powerful witch that I could manipulate into helping me. She was alone, an outcast in her family, and I befriended her. That is all." His breaths are uneven and all over the place. He runs a hand through his disheveled, raven locks, drawing my attention to his big, tattooed hands.

I give him an incredulous stare. "So, you're trying to tell me it was friendship?"

"No," Lorcan states. "I was pretending to be her friend. Like I said, she was very powerful."

"Ah, there's the true manipulative bastard behind the mask of niceties."

"I'm glad you haven't lost your fierceness." He flashes me a boyish smile that makes him look more angel than demon. "Look, Samuel has wanted to get rid of me for centuries, and Ezra and Lazarus locked me in a fucking cage. All of it was under my father's orders, or at least so I thought until now. Samuel has been behind everything. He always was a jealous little cunt. So, I asked Eva to help me make a prison to trap my siblings."

Hearing him call her by a nickname makes it all the more real. "The Shadow Realm," I state.

"Yes. She created it, masterfully, by manipulating purgatory into this." He looks around him. "I've never met a witch so powerful, until you."

"Those grimoire pages made it seem like she created it to trap you. That she was manipulating you!" I shout, holding onto the threads of my sanity, because he can't be telling the truth.

If he is, then I have to confront something far worse than heartbreak and betrayal, admitting that I feel something for a demon who can't ever love me back. My brows furrow when I recall the words he once whispered. *'Demons cannot love.'*

Then, maybe he didn't love her. If that's true, even if he didn't have a relationship, then he doesn't care for me either and this is all a game.

"She wrote those pages after she trapped me. Eva knew only her blood, or her descendants, could free me. By writing that grimoire, which is the very key to unlocking a portal, she knew she could poison whoever read it against me; and I hate to admit it, but it's worked." He presses a palm against the glass, then curls his fingers into a fist. "She was *insane*. I never led her on, not like that anyway. When I told her I didn't love her in return, I found love spells and potions around her house, even demon circles. She did everything she could to tether me to her, even chaining me up and altering my memories. This went on for *years*. But I still left, even after she forced my heart. That's when she locked me in the Shadow Realm with her family's help. It killed her to do it. Did you know that? She died only a few months after."

I feel the blood rush from my face. "Who's to say I won't die then, by opening the portal for you?"

"You're more powerful than she ever was. The Fallenmoore Coven has been cultivating black magic for decades, and it grows stronger with each generation. When she died, her powers were distributed amongst her living relatives, but it was tainted with her special brand of insanity, which is why when any of them since tried to suppress her magic, they went insane. But now, with the rest of your family dead, it's all yours. You hold the power of an entire coven inside of you. That's why The Order kept you alive. You're the only one who can do this."

"So, you'll risk my life?"

He shakes his head. "Just because I care doesn't mean I'm going to let fear of losing you blind me to your abilities. I know you can do this. I saw a glimpse of that when you broke the blood bond on the original portal. If I thought there was any chance you could die, I wouldn't let you do this."

Such bullshit, but I'm not doing this for him anyway. Rosa was right in what she told me. If I don't get these demons out, we'll be on the run for good. I can't protect her and Gomez forever from The Order and the demon brothers. Perhaps I might be able to take Samuel down, but all of them? I risk dying before I can finish them off. But with Lorcan and Ezra, we stand a chance.

Lorcan's intrusive gaze lingers on me, as if he's trying to read my thoughts, but based on the wrinkles forming between his brows, he can't.

"But do you believe me, about Eva?" he asks, breaking the long silence, as if my believing him is the only thing that matters.

I don't want to admit it to him, but I do believe him, only because of one painful truth—Lorcan cannot love, which means he's using me just like he was using her. I can't let any feelings I had blind me like my great aunt did. I've already put Rosa and Gomez in danger from engaging with Lorcan in the first place.

"I'll rebuild the portal," I say in way of answer, then add, "only if you promise to kill Samuel when you find him so he can't come after us, and free Aiden from his servitude."

After a heavy sigh, he nods, and I jut my chin. It's time to free my demon from his prison of one hundred years.

CHAPTER NINE

Evie

I was never afraid of dying.

I recall the counselor I'd been forced to speak to when I was thirteen asking me about it. Edward and Antionette had voiced concern over my morbid curiosity after I befriended the funeral home director's son and was caught sneaking into the morgue. It wasn't my first time going there at night when everyone was asleep, it was just the first time I'd gotten caught.

I only wanted to look at the bodies, to see what they may look like after they were dead, and yes, on occasion I would lie on an empty table and pretend I was a corpse just like them.

The counselor suggested it was trauma that led me there. I'd been around so much death that I was naturally curious about it. In truth, it was because I was desensitizing myself for the inevitable. I knew my life wouldn't be a long one. Whether I was to die young at my own hand from finally giving into the depression, or because my magic took me out, it was going to happen. Of that I was certain.

So, now when I am faced with the very real possibility of my demise, why am I suddenly afraid?

"You're going to be okay," Rosa says from the bedroom door as if she can sense my thoughts. "We don't have to do it today if you want to rest..." She tugs her bottom lip between her teeth and looks me up then down. "Maybe it's best if we wait."

"No, I'm ready. We can't wait too long. I ju..." I trail off and zone in on a spatter of blood over my hand. Edward's blood.

Rosa is at my side before I realize I was dissociating. Her cold fingertips land over the blood splatter. "Hey, look at me." My lashes flick up and I meet her warm, widening gaze. "We *can* wait. I promise The Order isn't coming here tonight. This is the last place they'd think we'd come back to, precisely because it's the most obvious choice. Aiden's idea to come here was surprisingly brilliant."

I blink thrice. "This was Aiden's idea?"

She nods and squeezes my hand. "We are safe for the time being. Besides, we have escaped them once. We can do it again. I'll even keep watch of the grounds, hmm? We all need a small respite."

"But Lorcan—"

"Has waited a century. What's another day?"

"Rosa." My words tumble over each other as I spew all the suppressed feelings I've been keeping inside. "I know this sounds insane, but now that I've killed Edward, I don't know what to do. I thought I'd feel better... but my anxiety is worse than ever."

She tilts her head, her brows lowering slightly as her gaze narrows. "Just because he's dead, doesn't mean the deep wounds he left behind are. You can't kill a memory, but you can heal your reaction to it, with time." She pauses for a moment then sighs gently, pulling me an inch closer when she adds, "Look, the adrenaline is wearing off from earlier. You're exhausted, your body has been put through so much. It's not surprising that you're anxious. What you need is a shower, clean clothes, and a good night of sleep."

"We don't have time—"

She cuts me off before I can argue that I don't need to rest. I doubt I could even sleep if I tried. "I need to rest too. We're all tired and can use one calm evening."

"Now though? We're fighting just to survive."

"Especially now. We will be okay for one night. Now, go and shower and I'll tell Aiden to nap so he can take watch while we rest later."

"But—"

"Shower," she orders and leaves the room. "I'll bring Gomez."

By the time midnight falls, we're all showered, and Gomez is wrapped in a warm, fuzzy towel. I've successfully managed to remove every mirror from my bedroom with Rosa's help. We agreed we need the privacy.

I pull open the dresser drawers and find stacks of neatly folded clothes. Aiden was right. Lorcan really had ordered my clothes to be brought here from when I was in the Shadow Realm. Which means he really did change his mind and wasn't planning on me taking his place there.

None of this makes any sense. I mull over every word Lorcan said with a fine-toothed comb, desperate to find the truth between the lines, yet each time I end up more confused than before.

I grab my loose, purple knit cardigan, a black strap top, and pair of ripped, faded blue jeans out of the drawers and place them over the back of the chair, ready for the morning.

"I'm not tired," I admit, which is miraculous considering how little sleep I've had over the past week.

"It's the anxiety. Just close your eyes and rest, you don't need to worry about falling asleep right now," Rosa replies and pulls on one of my dark purple nightgowns. She tugs on the snug fabric around her chest. "Thanks for this. I mean, it's a little creepy that he had them brought here, but I suppose we should be grateful for his stalker attitude right now."

"Yeah, I suppose." I pull on my black nightdress, then rub my temples. "I'm still so… angry at him."

She nods, then stretches out over the king-sized bed in the middle of the room. Her pink, pointed nails graze over the carvings on the mahogany headboard, and I watch, desperate for anything mundane that might slow my racing thoughts.

She places Gomez, now nice and dry, in between two fluffy pillows. He squeaks and turns to cuddle the pillow closer to him. "Oh, my baby." I lie next to him, with Rosa on the other side, and go to open my mouth to say something but the words turn into a yawn. My fingers absentmindedly meet Gomey's fur, stroking his body over and over until my headache subsides and I can hear him snoring.

Rosa turns off the dim lamp, plunging us into a darkness only eased by the moonlight seeping through the crack in the drapes. "Aiden is keeping watch," she whispers. "He'll sleep in the morning, so don't worry, there's someone here looking out for us."

A smile curves my lips. It's just so nice to feel clean sheets under my legs again, to hold a freshly washed blanket to my chest, and to feel Gomez and Rosa close, knowing we're all safe for now.

Soon enough, they're both asleep and I am alone. Except, I'm not really. As I teeter on the edge of sleep, I can feel Lorcan's presence all around me. Even without the mirrors, he's close, and a small part of me wonders if he's sleeping in this same bed in the Shadow Realm.

For a brief second, I swear I can smell his intoxicating cologne lingering on the pillow and my stomach dips.

I close my eyes as the stark reality hits me. Tomorrow, Lorcan will be free for the first time in a century and I have no fucking idea how he's going to react once he's without being bound to the Shadows Realm. I wonder if he even knows how he'll feel without the shackles tethering him to my bloodline.

I hadn't planned to wake up so ready to free my stalker from the Shadow Realm, but the moment my eyes opened, it was all I could think about. I must protect Rosa and Gomez, and Aiden too. He's an innocent in all of this.

I stand in the living room, my Aunt Evangeline's grimoire tucked between my arm and ribs, and stare at the arched windows and the snowy expanse beyond the heavy, purple drapes. A faint musk of aged furniture mixed with the lilies hangs in the air, masked only by the scent of fresh soap wafting from Gomez who clings to my shoulder.

Rosa looks at Aiden and arches a manicured brow. "You don't want to take this time to sleep?"

"I wanna see this," he states.

My brows furrow as I eye him. His eyes are bloodshot with pronounced dark circle rings under them. I understand the tiredness, as he had kept watch all night, but the pale tint to his skin and the way his eyes dart to the doors and windows every minute or so, as if he's looking for someone, tells me everything. He's afraid and doesn't want to be alone.

Perhaps the realities of The Order and the demon brothers has sunk in more now than when we first arrived. He seemed okay yesterday.

"Are you feeling okay?" I ask before I get to work.

His eyes dart to the door again. "Yeah. Sorry."

He definitely isn't okay, but then none of us really are, so I don't press him.

Rosa holds my free hand as we walk to the large mirror. Lorcan appears in it, his face all sharp angles and somber expressions. Perhaps he doubted my showing up this morning.

Ezra walks into the frame behind Lorcan, bouncing on the heels of his high-tops as he flashes me a grin. "If it isn't my second favorite witch." He winks and shoots Rosa a glance and she turns her head to look the other way.

"If it isn't my least favorite demon," I spit, which isn't entirely true, but only next to Samuel. Ezra fucking chased me in the Shadow Realm while in his demonic form, choked me out in a dream, and tried to kill me. Now he talks as if we're old friends.

Lorcan's lips curve into a smirk and Ezra just grimaces. I'm just glad that smile is wiped off his face, even if it does mean I gave Lorcan a reason to smile.

Rosa lets go of my hand and takes ahold of the grimoire, opening it to the bookmarked page. I've already memorized the incantation a hundred times, but her speaking it with me helps. She's a witch too, just one with earth magic that is classed a light magic and is the opposite of mine. Having her near calms my magic.

I close my eyes, focusing on the darkness, and allow my magic to surface as easily as my next breath. The tendrils of energy move within me, pulsing through my core and bringing with it a sense of power that pulls me higher, better than any drug.

I've spent so many years suppressing my magic out of fear of killing someone else I love that I hesitate for a moment. In some ways, it's similar to anxiety, so I remind myself that I control it and not the other way around. I can do this. I won't let myself sink into the shadows ever again but instead wield them to my will.

I place my palm outwards as the chill of the shadows seep into my hands with an icy caress. Then, all at once, my magic tears from my body like black ribbons, forming intricate patterns as my shadows creates a spiderweb over the long, ornate mirror hanging on the wall.

The deadly hum of death magic glitters like stars, lining the darkness of my shadows. They cover the obsidian frame, blanketing the mirror until the contours of Lorcan's determined expression disappear entirely. Seeing him is the last thing I want and the sooner we get this over with, the better.

The force of my ancestors' powers whooshes through me with an icy gust. I plant my legs apart and suck in a gasp of air, steadying myself. I clamp my eyes shut even tighter, gritting my teeth as I start the incantation along with Rosa, but my power only heightens with each word.

A tremor starts in my fingers, then convulses up my arms and to my chest.

I focus on my breathing and repeat the memorized words. "*In sanguine creato, terrae ac ventorum rima inter nostrates mundos aperite.*"

My heart hammers desperately against its cage of bones, every beat a shockwave of pain as my ancestors' magic works against me. My fingers curl into fists and I open my eyes.

Shadows cloud us like a thick fog, and the shadowy ribbons on the mirror has turned into a tarry substance that hangs over the glass like a sticky black web.

Rosa and I whisper in unison, "*Perde sanguinis nexum cum virtute quae per me currit. Solve cavea, sint liberi.*"

The tarry-looking substance melds with the glass, and the glass cracks into two. A tremor rumbles through the walls, and I wince when Gomez's claws scratch into my skin as he scrambles to hide in my hair.

I hold steady, but fatigue runs through me with fervor. My breaths slow and my legs feel as if they've turned into jelly.

When I glance up, I notice the tarry shadow attached to the mirror all the way to the center of my chest. Pulses are pulled from me through the bridge between the portal and me, stealing every last reserve of energy.

Rosa's hand lands on mine as I hear her drop the book. Her fingers curl around my wrist as my legs buckle. The tarry, sticky thread remains attached to me, shooting icy stabs of pain through my chest until each breath becomes so agonizing, as if I am breathing in shards of glass.

Rosa's magic blooms into me, as if she's the lifeforce keeping me alive as the portal depletes me.

"We need to stop!" I hear her yell.

"Don't," I croak, knowing what will happen if we stop midway. "I'll die if you stop it."

Stars fill my vision and my jaws slacks as shadows escape through my mouth like vipers of darkness. I choke on them, just as Samuel had, and I try to scream but nothing comes out.

Crimson veins over the glass and I realize it's not just energy that the sticky thread of magic linking me to the mirror is taking from me, but also my blood.

Just before I feel like I'm about to take my last breath, the pain and tremors ease as quickly as they had come.

Rosa's panicked cries reach me through the ringing in my ears. My vision clears and I raise my hand to my throat as the shadows curl back into me like ink into a pen.

"I'm okay," I promise, but struggle to stand. I glance up, staring at the newly made portal. The mirror is shiny and new, the glass rippling as if it's water and someone has thrown a rock into it.

A hand appears, then an arm. Lorcan slowly steps through, and my heart skips a beat. Rosa sighs in relief, Gomez flies over toward Aiden who jumps up from his chair.

I press my fingers into my temples and clamp my eyes shut. Fuck, I'm so dizzy. The room spins around me, and I grip the edge of the doorway as I stumble into the next room.

As soon as I am alone in the adjoining room, I grasp the window ledge, gasping. I stare out of the window at the bleak, snowy wonderland beyond the glass, when I hear footsteps shuffle behind me. My vision steadies and I take an extra few seconds to keep my eyes closed and enjoy the silence before turning to face him.

His brows knit together when he scans my face, the skin of his nose creasing between them. I'm certain I can withhold from him, to leave here once we've worked together to destroy his brothers, then never think about him again.

"I knew you could do it, My Little Witch," he praises and my chest heaves.

I swallow thickly. "You're free now. You don't need to keep up the game of pretend."

"Pretend?" A fiery determination crosses his pastel green eyes.

I take a step toward the doors leading to another room, when he races over to me. His hands cup my cheeks before I can push him away.

His smell, all warm and heavy, spiced with a crisp note. That cologne mixed with his skin is like damn pheromones.

"Get off me." I push him back, but he doesn't budge. He takes my fists hammering against his chest as if it's nothing, and instead of shoving me away, he holds me tighter, as if I might fall apart at any moment.

His breath is hot against my ear when he speaks into my hair. "I'm proud of you."

My heart cartwheels. "For breaking you out of the portal?"

"No. For standing up to your father and surviving when he tried to break you."

"Don't," I plead. I'm stronger when he's not holding me. I can think straight. Hell, I can destroy entire buildings if I want to. Except my magic is sedated under his touch.

He lifts one hand, his touch dragging over my clavicle. I clench my thighs and close my eyes. Just one damned touch can do this. How?

No. I won't be pulled back under his command.

"I said, get the fuck off me," I shout with the last of my resolve. "Your games won't work on me."

"Work on you?" He lowers his arms, letting me go.

"Just stop it. You're free now and you have what you want, there is no need to manipulate me like you did Evangaline. All I want to know," I say as I back away from him, "is will you still work with us to kill Samuel and keep us safe from The Order?"

He arches a dark brow. "That is all you want from me?"

"Yes," I lie.

We stand six feet apart, unblinking as we wait for the other to fold first, except I won't be caught in another game.

I turn and walk into the living room with Rosa, Aiden, Ezra, and Gomez. Ezra points at me and says, "That was fucking awesome!"

Aiden nods in agreement, but Rosa's eyes aren't on me. Lorcan is behind me, again.

Don't follow me. I push the thought into his mind and walk out of the room.

CHAPTER TEN

Lorcan

I'm free. It's all I've obsessed over for the better part of a century. Yet now the time has come, all I feel is fucking pain. I mangled my heart for Evie until it bled emotions, but she threw it back in my face.

She said it herself. All she wants from me is to kill Samuel and to keep her and her friend safe from The Order, as if that wasn't already a given and I wouldn't have burned down the world to keep her safe.

The world is bright, as if it's the first time I'm seeing color. In truth, I forgot just how vibrant the Human Realm is. My eyes adjust after a century of seeing everything with saturation lowered and follow Evie through the manor.

Either she really doesn't give a fuck about me, or she still doesn't believe me. But this time I'm not going to wait around to find out.

I dissolve into the nearest shadow, tracking her scent through the house, and silently slip out one several feet behind her.

The scent of vanilla dipped rose perfume ghosts the air in Evie's wake. My heart backflips as I inhale languidly through my nose. That fucking scent. I rub the nape of my neck as each inhale nearly sends me to my knees.

 Scent is one of the strongest triggers of all creature's olfactory senses, evoking a slew of memories from our time in the Shadow Realm. Yet, here in the Human Realm everything is stronger: scents, colors, *feelings*.

I have missed her essence drifting through the manor, saturating everything it touches with an incorporeal caress—marking me in the process.

She winds her way around the right side of the grand staircase and into the kitchen. I step into a shadow under a wall sconce as my little witch's head turns wearily over her shoulder, then quickens her pace through the exterior door near the counter.

My mouth waters as I track the sway of her hips, ass flexing with every step she takes. I ache to mark up her soft flesh with bitemarks.

Evie follows the cobble stone path to the small graveyard in a clearing near the manor, half frozen puddles splashing beneath her feet. Generations of human families and their servants are buried in this hallowed ground. I wonder what the priest who blessed this land would think of a demon holding the deed. I suppress my snort and shake my head. Said *blessing* might work on lesser castes of demons but never any of the royal bloodline.

My heart skips a beat when I see her pause by the wrought iron gate. Running her hands through her hair, she passes her fingers over the nape of her neck, drawing my eyes to her. She really does have the most elegant neck.

The gate creaks open as Evie walks through it, wandering from headstone to headstone, her fingers skating across their pitted surfaces.

She halts in front of a weathered headstone, the engraved name and dates sanded away by time's merciless touch. Her fists clench at her sides, shadows swirling along the exposed back of her hands where her rich purple cardigan doesn't cover.

I lurched forward slightly as her death magic sizzles to the surface, her steps falter. It's as if it desires to tunnel through her back and violently draw me to her.

She spins to face me, her cheeks flushing red. "I told you not to follow me."

"You talk of me playing games," I state incredulously. "You ran off. Why?"

"Why are you pretending to care?"

My jaw clenches as I walk closer. "Do you want me to care?"

That is the only question that matters, but she withholds her response, her silence like a newfound fucking torture.

"Tell me," I state, my heart hardening with each apathetic look she shoots my way. "If you were just caught up in the Shadow

Realm, when time was suspended and we were alone, then I'll understand."

"Would you?" she asks with an arched brow, and sways her hips, knowing what that does to me. "I have a hard time believing you'd understand and leave me alone. You just want to fuck me. To use me."

Gods I do.

She's absolutely right.

I think about all the ways I'd use her mouth and I'm fucking hard. Something animalistic takes over my emotions, shrouding them until all I can think about is pushing her up against the headstone. I dart my tongue between parted lips, sensing her arousal from here. Her thighs clench together, coaxing a growl from my chest. "Don't you want me to use you?"

I walk closer and push my chest against her back. I slide my hand up her sternum to her neck. My eyes briefly close as a gasp shutters through her. My other hand caresses the shell of her chilled ear as I tuck a loose lock of hair behind it.

"So that *is* all you want?" she whispers.

I growl sensually, the carnality of it rumbling between us. *No, it's not,* I confess while stroking the threads connecting the most essential parts of ourselves.

A sigh slips past her lips, then her throat bobs against my palm as she swallows. "You lie. Demons cannot love. So, what is it you want from me?"

What am I supposed to say to that? It's true. Demons are not supposed to be able to love, so what do I feel? Infatuation? Or something else entirely?

All I know is it feels like I'm wearing my fucking heart on the outside of my chest.

I smooth a hand over her gorgeous, silky hair, and bring my lips to her temple and whisper, "All I know is right now, I just want to be close to you." I squeeze against the sides of her throat gently, then trace my finger to her clavicle.

I draw my tongue down the side of her tense neck, flicking the tip over her carotid artery in time with her pulse. I loosen my hold and turn her to face me.

I hate, no, I despise how vulnerable she makes me feel. The weak and desperate emotions I vowed to never resurrect from my centuries in that Hell cage.

Her inner voice filters into my mind. *Don't pretend to care. Just tell me the truth, all you want is to fuck.*

She looks at me as if that's what *she* needs to hear. As if my emotions are too much for her. I want to hold back, to show her this means more to me than she realizes, but before I can try, she slides her hand down my pants, wrapping her fingers around the bulge of my cock.

Fuck!

I collar her flushed throat and use my hold to drag her lips to mine in an impassioned kiss. I release a guttural moan as her tongue twirls against mine. She sucks my tongue into her mouth, the sensual assault spurring a desperate craving to claw my insides with fervid need.

So much fucking need.

My hips buck as my cock swells painfully and pulsates, copious amounts of pre-cum leaking down my veiny shaft. I tip my head back and suck in a breath. Cool misty rain dewing on my overheated face. My chin tips down and my gaze connects with Evie's lust drunk orbs, then skates down her rosy cheeks to her sexy swollen lips. I bite my lip hard, relishing the sting on the fresh cuts and feather my thumb over her lower lip, collecting the fine dewy drops of rain, then push it onto her waiting tongue.

I groan, "Evie, fuck." Backing her into the nearest headstone, I kick her legs apart and grind between her thighs. Evie hisses as the cold rock penetrates her thin jeans and I smile against her mouth. My tattooed hands cup her ass, lifting her onto the headstone.

I rest my forehead against hers. "Fucking Hell, Baby Girl. Do you know how badly I've missed being buried in your pretty cunt?" Our lips battle savagely for a moment, then I draw back and stare into her lust drunk chocolate eyes.

"Call me Little Witch," Evie commands, spearing a hand into my hair and brushing her peaked nipples against my chest.

My heart swells with warm, fuzzy feelings and a shooting pain sears through my chest, as if my body is trying to push the feelings out as if they're poison.

Her other hand squeezes my biceps as an emotion I cannot comprehend floats between us like a heavy fog. Streaks of lust illuminate the building tension like lightning.

"Fine," I say breathlessly. "Little Witch."

She grabs my hand and directs it past the waistband of her pants, her hand gliding on top of mine. I inhale sharply, no further coaxing necessary, as two of my fingers slide into her needy little pussy. I swirl them against her walls, remove them, and swiftly suck the digits into my mouth. Her pupils widen and darkness sweeps through her irises, pure primal need and magic merging into one. My shadows tear through her jeans just as hers deftly unbutton and shove mine to the ground.

"Evie," I pant, "your cunt tastes fucking delicious. Now let's see how good it feels." My cock leaks copious amounts of pre-cum as I line it up with her entrance and thrust. Our joint gasps fill the frozen air as my cock slams into her cunt, her slick squelching between us. Evie's fingers dig into my ass cheeks.

Pain ripples through my scalp as her shadows pull on my hair. I growl, rolling my hips into her with inhuman speed. Her head falls back as I continue thrusting and suck her nipple into my mouth. Her core clenches against me signaling her impending release.

"Uhghng," I moan. "I hate you for being so damn perfect." My lips connect with her neck as I attack it with kisses and bites.

"Oh, fuck," she moans. "I'm so close. Lorcan, don't stop."

My balls slap heavily against her damp skin as I rut into her. I throw my head back and my hipbones smack into the headstone, the bite of pain spurring me on. "Hold onto me," I command, and Evie's legs wrap around my waist, her feet crossing above my ass. "Don't let go." My palms connect with the cold stone, claws digging in as I use the headstone for leverage. I angle my hips until I find her G-spot and relentlessly grind against it.

My witch mumbles and moans incoherently against my neck as I drive into her pussy harder and faster, my pending orgasm just out of reach.

"Gods!" she screams.

"That's right, come for me." Three more mind bending thrusts, then her orgasm drenches my cock.

I moan as my pleasure builds to unstable heights. "Ahhgh…MmUhgnhgn…Fuuuuck." My orgasm swirls into existence like a sudden tornado. Roaring, I paint the fucking walls of her pussy with my cum.

Evie hugs my neck. "I love how you fill me up."

"Shit," I groan as another unexpected wave of pleasure milks several more jets of cum into her.

I watch with pride as the liquid of our combined releases leaks around my cock and drips onto my balls, then nestle my face into her neck and bury my face in her soft hair.

I lean to the side and yank up my jeans while holding Evie steady on the gravestone. My shadows smooth down her back, then cloaks around us to shield her from the winter elements.

"Did you just put a shadow cloak on me?" she asks.

"It's freezing out here." I raise a sardonic brow. "Plus, it's more of a shadow blanket."

A bubble of silence builds between us and is swiftly popped as we both belly-laugh.

The sound of her laughter, especially after everything she's gone through, breathes something warm and fuzzy to life behind my ribs, but its quickly quelled as she automatically rejects the emotion. I feel it in our bond, as if she needs the lack of feeling between us.

Evie's happiness fades as quickly as it came, the sparkle in her eyes dimming. She needs to be taken care of. Even if she rejects my heart and wants to believe I want nothing but to fuck her. I'll take care of her until she realizes I'm not going anywhere.

Her legs almost buckle, and I pull her upright.

"I'm fine," she says, blinking several times, but I can see how much creating the portal took out of her.

She rests her head against my shoulder as I scoop her into my arms, wrap her tighter in my blanket of shadows, then trudge back to the manor.

CHAPTER ELEVEN

Evie

The security and warmth from Lorcan's body quickly fades as reality rudely encroaches on my post orgasm high. He sweeps me into a bathroom I have yet to make use of—the jade color scheme blurring at the edges of my vision.

Panic claws at my throat, and my heart flees to the back of my ribs, clutching onto the bones with its atriums and veins. I squeeze my eyes shut as memories slash across my mind's eye, the cruel hands of someone carrying my freshly tortured body, sheer agony radiating every bone, muscle, and nerve. My lungs inflate a quaking breath and Lorcan's scent dissolves the daymare.

I open my eyes and fix my gaze on his neck, working to unlock my joints and unknot my muscles one fiber at a time.

My demon cuddles me to his chest as I crawl back to the present, banishing all painful thoughts into my subconscious. His throat tattoo faintly vibrates as I trace the lines of the two facing skulls with my index finger, as if coming alive under my touch. I relax further into his arms as magic goes to work at his behest, preparing us a bath. But too soon my muscles tighten once more.

Lorcan doesn't do *nice*.

If I knew this side of him existed, I might have fled to the graveyard sooner... like when we had endless alone time in Shadow Realm. Well, except for Ezra.

Still, I am unused to him being so gentle with me. "Put me down," I choke out too loudly, my words seeming to reverberate off the walls. I squirm in his arms, but he only holds me tighter.

"Shit. What's wrong, Little Witch?" Lorcan questions softly. The muscles in my legs tighten as the icy black honeycomb tiles meet the souls of my feet.

The automatic response of 'nothing' curls on my tongue but I swallow it.

Lorcan sets me onto the vanity. I sigh, hanging plants tangle in my hair and tickle the side of my face. His nostrils flare as he slams his palms against the mirror beside my head. "Don't you fucking dare say 'fine' or 'nothing', Evie." A shadow curls around my throat, it's pressure oddly comforting. "We both know those words only temporarily hide such pretty lies."

He slides a finger over the tattoo on my chest and whispers into my ear. "You can keep fighting against me, but I'm not going anywhere." Lorcan presses his thumb against the ink on my breast and gnashes his teeth close to my earlobe. "You are *mine.*"

My eyes narrow on his lengthening, sharp teeth. Our breathing mingles as he leans into me, our chests flush. I grit my teeth, ignoring my hardened nipples sliding against his bare chest. A deep growl rumbles behind his ribs, my sensitive skin soaking in the vibrations.

The momentary anxiety retreats as quickly as it came, but it's too fun to play with my demon. The corner of my lip twitches upward. "Perhaps."

Lorcan's eyes squeeze shut for the length of a heartbeat, then he throttles me with his gaze. He holds my stare with unwavering, determined focus, and emits a growl so low and deep it raises the fine hair all over my body.

Fuck—that sound.

"Must you be so combative, woman? I just want to take care of you. When will you accept that?" he utters so close against my lips, kissing me with every word. His continuous growling lining his words with a thrilling and seductive, yet deadly purr.

My lips part. "You're serious."

"Of course, I'm godsdamn serious. I don't waste my fucking time spewing words without meaning. Enough of this, My Witch."

Lorcan grabs me around the waist, then deposits me in the half-filled claw foot tub. The water stings my cold, rain dampened skin, and I hiss as lift the lower half of my body to hover over the water. A palm presses against my sternum and my arms shake, then I fall back into the water with a splash.

Lorcan looms over me, his claws scraping against the smooth, rolled edge of the tub. "You *will* be a good girl and let me bathe you. Your skin is like fucking ice," he commands, fury sharpening the skin along his cheekbones and jaw, then rises and reaches blindly for a green jeweled tone bottle sitting on a convenient shelf to the left of the vanity. His tattooed knuckles tighten around the delicate-looking glass. "Don't fight me on this. You. Will. Not. Win," he pontificates, as if I have no choice in the matter.

I remind myself all I wanted to do was get under his skin a little, then willingly concede… for now. "I know." Surprisingly, he's making it nearly impossible to deny it otherwise.

His anger sharpened features smooth out and his always present smirk slides into place.

"Good girl."

My stomach swoops.

Bubbles froth to the surface as Lorcan pours a healthy dollop of the liquid under the running silver faucet. I gasp as I catch the reflection of something dark, yet housing a soft yellow glow, moves behind us in the long, shining neck of the spout. My neck twinges as I whip my head to the side and twist my torso, but I can't see past the muscular tattooed bulk of his body.

His fingers caress my cheek, then folds them into an easy grip on my chin as he looks down at me with a smirk. "Be easy, Baby. It's just my shadows lighting some candles," he says, then rests his jean clad ass on the edge of the tub.

I blow out a breath. How long will it take for my nerves to stop buzzing in my veins this time? Trauma is not new to me, and for years, the only person I had to rely on was myself. But now… I have Lorcan.

My emotions knot into a ball even a cat would struggle to unravel.

Fuck. *Focus on the present, Evie.*

I roll my shoulders back and force myself to lean against the tub. My eyes trace the v-lines dipping into the top of his unbuttoned pants, the subtle shifts of his movements flexing the slabs of muscle. Lust blooms in my core.

Lorcan's shadows fetch another bottle, this one a gorgeous, jeweled azure, then he deposits a puddle of citrus and sage scented liquid into his palm and lathers it onto my roots.

"I can smell your arousal," Lorcan mentions causally.

I moan as his thumbs and strong fingers massage my scalp and I relax into his touch as his strong, nimble fingers clean my hair. "I'm positive that's true."

He laughs. "Close that bratty mouth and let me pamper you. Well, for now. I'll need it spread nice and wide when I fuck your throat later."

My moan dances among the bubbles floating on the water, and I release a satisfied sigh as he continues to wash my hair. "Promises, promises."

Lorcan hums, "Mmm. That's it. Relax your muscles and allow the heat to soak into your bones." His fingers pause their soothing ministrations, almost hesitantly, then resumes. "You've been through so fucking much… I won't ask you about it now. But at some point, we need to have a discussion," He coils a tendril of my wet hair around his index finger, "but not until you're ready, Little Witch."

My gaze fixates on the large flakes of heavy snow falling behind the two expansive arched windows making up a nook for the tub, their tracery thick between the panes of clear glass. I rest my neck on the rolled towel and close my eyes, exhaustion and emotional overload zapping my energy.

There is something about watching it snow while cuddled up in the warmth indoors that makes my heart throb with contentment.

I look away and play with the bubbles tickling the upper curves of my breasts and let the conversation drop completely.

My demon skillfully rinses the shampoo and croons, "Rest, I've got you." Then works conditioner into my hair.

His warmth teases my senses awake, surrounding me in a cocoon of safety. Lorcan swirls his index finger slowly in the hollow of my throat, lightly stroking whirls and other unknown patterns onto my delicate skin.

"What time is it?" I ask him groggily and blink my bleary eyes. The bedroom looms around us, one shadow indistinguishable from another. I note the absence of moonlight, only the glittering, inky cloud-free sky meeting my tired stare through the ornate window.

"Almost three. Plenty of time for more sleep…" Lorcan splays his fingers on my lower back. "Or anything else you might want to indulge in."

Figures. Fucking insomnia. I usually wake around this time each night. In fact, it was close to three when he scolded me for drinking coffee back in my apartment. Longing for the place that was my home, the only thing close to a safe haven I had at the time, sweeps through me. Memories of Gomez and I living our lives pre demons curve my lips in a small smile. "Nearly the witching hour," I say through a yawn. "Did you get any sleep?"

"I have better things to do than waste the night reliving nightmares," Lorcan grumbles. With his words, I realize my sleep was inexplicably dreamless, despite the recent torture and all the bullshit from my past haunting my waking hours. I wriggle my body backward into his, my ass rubbing against his groin in the process. Lorcan growls softly in my ear as his cock twitches between my naked cheeks.

"What could possibly be better than sleep?" I ask.

Lorcan inhales but holds the breath in his lungs as if he needs the time to formulate a response. "I was watching your chest rise and fall," he says through an exhale. "Counting each heartbeat. It soothes a part of me I thought died centuries ago," he grumbles as if put out by the feeling.

I sigh contentedly, the languid exhale kissing his skin where my head rests on his biceps, then skate my fingertips over the goosebumps rising on his skin. My demon hums and guides my hair—the heavy mass silken from his expert washing and moisturizing hours earlier—away from my neck to the fluffy cloud-like pillow behind us.

Lorcan growls lightly and grinds against my ass while parting my thighs with his knee. His precum covered tip glides against my

145

me, pleasure sparking everywhere it touches, then notches himself at the entrance of my wet pussy. "I missed this," Lorcan says hoarsely into my neck, and peels his hand from my hip to skate his palm down my belly. I gasp, my core warming pleasantly as he cups my sex possessively and my clit throbs under the heel of his large hand.

This demon is overwhelming at the best of times, but the sweet and sexy way he's acting now? Catastrophically devastating.

Lorcan leans over my torso, his chest pressing onto my side, then hovers his lips over mine. "The tortuous days you were... gone," he says brokenly, the rich bass of his voice cracking in places. "I dreamt of nothing but fucking murdering them all, then making you come all over my cock while you're draped over their corpses." He kisses me softly, the action in direct contrast to his violent rage filled words.

Lorcan swallows thickly, pulling back and our eyes lock, the same searing lust setting my skin ablaze reflecting in his hungry stare. Tension filled angst simmers between us like the frothing waves of an ocean during a hurricane before we reach for each other with greedy hands.

Taking.

Claiming.

Consuming.

I reach backward and grip the nape of his neck as we kiss, forcing the weight of his sculpted, tattooed upper body onto my awkwardly twisted torso. I don't give a shit if my spine snaps from the position.

I need him.

All of him.

Our bond sings with intensity as his tongue duels with mine. Lorcan sucks on my tongue, and I moan into his mouth. His teeth sharpen, nicking my lips, the taste of iron fueling my desperate desire. Lorcan rocks his hips against my ass, his thick cock gliding through the mess he created at the apex of my thighs.

I startle as he parts his fingers around the head of his swollen erection. Groaning, he rubs his cock between the V of his tattooed fingers and cups my pussy. Arousal slips between his fingers as his hand glides easily over my clit, pleasuring us both at once.

A whimper slips from me, but no words are spoken between us.

We don't need them.

Our bodies speak louder and more coherently than our tangled thoughts ever could. In fact, the presence of his noticeably absent shadows makes this all feel vastly more intimate. It's just us, who we really are when stripped down to our souls, skin against skin. I arch my back, urging Lorcan to sink inside me. He chuckles and traps my throat in his free hand, growling long and deep as he thrusts into my aching, needy pussy.

Time blurs by, its meaning nonexistent as we rock against each other, my hips meeting his every thrust. Delirium clouds all rational thought as I moan and whimper, the pressure within me building to mind boggling levels. Lorcan moans and his fingers flex tightly around the column of my throat. I don't know how long we lose ourselves in each other's arms, but eventually, his hard, deep thrusts penetrate me with ravenous intensity.

He nips my earlobe, then groans. "Are you going to come for me, Baby Girl."

"Yesss," I moan, teetering on the edge of orgasm. I jerk as he pinches my clit between his thumb and forefinger firmly. He strokes the skin around it in an upward motion, massaging the epicenter of nerves. My breath stalls in my lungs as I crash violently into my climax—pure rapture. I bite into his tense shoulder as my toes go numb, riding the brutal ecstasy filled waves.

"Good fucking girl," he praises, the words rolling from his tongue in a half growl, half moan. I slide my hand between my legs and wrap my fingers around the base of his shaft. He jerks against me and grunts out a gasp as I tighten my fist, the silky skin of his hard cock sliding erotically within the circle of my fingers and into my body. "Ughng, fuck me that feels so damn good," he groans, then wraps his arms and legs around me and shudders. "Evie," Lorcan moans with a voice like it's been sifted through gravel. "Evie. Evie. Evie." His cock swells, then gloriously hot cum splashes inside my pussy.

I shiver as another small wave of bliss zips through me. "I love when you come inside me," I say, my words slurring with exhaustion. I stroke my fist down his still hard cock a few more times, milking him until his cum spills around our cuddled sexes.

Lorcan's mouth tips upward wolfishly, then his head lowers and caresses my lips in a kiss. "Good," Lorcan says passionately, "because I will never stop."

CHAPTER TWELVE

Lorcan

Is it more appropriate to burn the manor down, therefore smoking out my *houseguests*, or violently evict them with shadows?

"Fuck," I curse and stab my fingers into my hair as I pace in front of the pool table. This was the only room I'm positive the others have yet to explore. No doubt if Aiden and Ezra knew, my hideout would be no more.

Perhaps Evie had the right idea with the graveyard; dead humans don't speak—well, most of the time.

A memory of a young female ghost singing and swinging on a playground crosses my mind's eye.

Evie's presence consumes every breath and pours down my throat.

The Human Realm finally awaits, no phantom strings yanking me back to the Shadow Realm.

I'm fucking *free*.

My heart rate slows and a true smile eases onto my face. Yet, the only place I want to be is wherever my little witch is.

I exhale with a barely detectible growl, and rub a hand over my face, enjoying the momentary reprieve from my mask.

Baby Girl, I call down our bond. A minute passes in silence and my throat clogs with anxiety. Shit. Mayb—

Yes, My Demon?

Oh, thank fuck. *Come to me.* I feel more than hear her sweet, mental laughter.

Desperate?

Yes, I growl and send the memory of her face slackened with bliss as I fucked her in the graveyard.

That's cheating, she gasps in my mind.

I'm a demon. It's a rite of passage. Evie's lust builds, strumming our bond and hardening my cock. I groan. *Come. Here.*

Well, since you asked so nicely, she replies, then smooths her end of the bond shut.

My lips quirk to one side as her soft, unhurried footsteps sound moments later.

Depraved thoughts skitter across my mind as she walks into the room, closing the door behind her. Her long, unbound hair swaying against the small of her back with the movement. Evie presses her back against the door and bites her lip.

I growl darkly. "That lip... What have I said about biting it?"

Evie's mouth parts and her teeth release the plump flesh. She glances up at me as I grip the edge of the pool table, and my breath catches.

Her smile falters as she scans my face seriously. "Why am I here, Lorcan?" she asks, rounding the game table and halting at my side.

I straighten my spine, then cross my arms over my chest, forcing my hands to obey and not pull her to me. "Nothing. I've changed my mind. You can go back to whatever you were doing," I state casually and shrug.

Evie's eyebrows pitch inward, and her eyes darken. "No," she says simply.

"No?"

"No. I'm not going to leave when you have that look in your eye."

I scoff. "I do not have a look."

"You do. It's the same look you get when you tell me to run."

"Fuck," I moan and tip my head back. "Baby Girl, I don't have enough restraint for this."

"Why did you call for me?"

I exhale and grip the nape of my neck with both hands. My gaze lowers and pins Evie with a heated glare. "Because I... godsdamnit..." I exhale through my nostrils.

Words, Lorcan.

My hands flex at my sides. "Fucking, Hellfire. I missed you, Little Witch. Okay?" Evie's jaw drops and her lips form a perfect O, then her teeth snap together and her lips pinch inward, her brown eyes sparkling with... Is that mirth? Oh, for fuck's sake.

I need to move this conversation onto familiar ground. "And I want you...I *always* want you," I growl and take a step toward her, shadows swirling on my arms and covering the ground by our feet. "No, I fucking *need* you. The craving to be buried inside you, drawing out your pleasure haunts my every fucking breath. I can't stay away from you. I. Won't."

"I never asked you to, Lor," Evie says. "There has to be a happy medium." Pausing, she inhales sharply. "Despite my better intentions, I crave you too. But I never know if I want to suck your cock or slap you for all the shit you've put me through."

I raise a brow and will a shadow to grasp her chin. "I don't know what you expect me to do with that statement. There is no middle ground for me. If I touch you, I'll fuck you."

Evie laughs darkly. "I thought you had more control than that."

A growl crawls out of my throat as I step up to her, push my chest against her, and force her neck to tilt backward. "And I thought you had better sense than to goad me," I snarl, my hands shaking, the need to grip her throat and claim her all over again pounding through my entire body. My shadows swell and pulse around us in time with the muscle in my chest.

My witch laughs. "You need me," she states. "Now, shut the fuck up and kiss me, Demon."

I raise a hand, hover it near her cheek, then lower my lips until they skim hers as I speak, and Primal lust sharpens my words. "Is that a challenge?"

"Absolutely."

I groan. "Fuck." My shadows explode in a tsunami of darkness, erasing the space between us. I loop Evie's long, gorgeous hair around my hand and plunder her mouth with my tongue. Dark musings plague my mind as Evie and I stumble and crash blindly into the wall. I moan as her tongue teases my tastebuds. Damn. Her mouth is fucking sinful. My hips buck against her involuntarily.

I need to be inside her.

Throbbing desire spreads throughout my balls the more I imagine thrusting my cock into her dripping cunt. Evie moans as my erection rubs against her pussy, the only barrier between us my fitted gray joggers and her thin leggings. My witch's hand curls around the back of my neck as she pulls her lips from mine with a gasp.

For a moment we just stare at each other, our panting breaths mingling between us, then I roll my hips slowly, grinding salaciously against her. The heat of her seeps through the fabric barrier tauntingly. Pressure builds in my balls, and I hum as I cup the back of her head, spearing my fingers through her silky strands.

"The things I want to do to you, Little Witch." I brush my nose against hers, tilt her head back, then wage war on her mouth once more.

My shadows condense, swirling into the tattoos on my body, but don't calm. They vibrate with unspent lust and magic. Evie moans and my cock twitches against her, pre-cum soaking into the fabric of my pants. "Godsdammit," I breathe, absolutely consumed by lust; the urge to spread her out on the green felt and feast on her vulnerable body nearly overwhelming.

My tongue bumps along the ridges on the roof of her mouth, then I cup a full breast in my hand, squeezing and kneading it through her shirt. "Remind me to fuck these tits again soon." The muscles in my neck tighten as my demonic senses pick up a loathsome sound in the hallway.

No. Nothing will stop me from drawing as much pleasure as I can from her.

I throw all of myself into our kiss, gripping our bond and stroking a claw down its length with every caress of my lips, while willing the tenacious annoyance away from our location.

I continue kissing Evie as I cup her ass, stride to the pool table, lower her onto the Kelly green felt, then follow her down. My forearms slide against the soft fabric as I crawl up her body and spread her thighs with my knees. Evie moans beneath me, the scent of her arousal-soaked pussy clouding my thoughts. Cringe worthy wing beats cleave through the haze of desire, stroking my body and mind with flame coated fingers. I should've known better than to wish for her familiar to leave us be.

Fucking foolish.

Evie squirms, pool balls clacking as she tries to get up, but I trap her to the table with my hips. My exposed neck zings with slight pain as Gomez's fangs puncture the skin. "Godsdamn bat," I hiss. Disentangling my fingers from Evie's hair, I blindly swat away

Fluffy Fucker. He screeches, his wings displacing the air as he flies away from us.

He's gotten even worse with his constant interruptions. I thought his behavior was intolerable before, but now he's a horrible nuisance that will never disappear.

Evie smiles against my lips as I exhale sharply through my nose, then twists her face away from mine, our cheeks pressing together as we seek out the annoying fucker.

Gomez hovers about two feet away, his beady little eyes narrowed with distrust. They flick to Evie, and I swear to fuck the bat smiles, two tiny fangs peeking past his lips. Evie laughs, then curls her arms around my sides.

I glare hellfire at the cute little shit and my shadows rise around him threateningly. Squeezing Evie's cheeks with a tattooed hand, I twist her face back to mine, then move to claim her lips. The soft pads of my little witch's fingers press against my puckered lips.

"We can't make out in front of him," Evie whispers.

I growl, then climb off the pool table and cross my arms. My growl rumbles throughout the room as Evie sets her clothes to rights, swivels her ass on the felt, and jumps to the hardwood floor. "What the fuck does he want?"

Her head tilts to the side as if listening or rather, sorting through the bat's emotions, then glances from me to her familiar. Her shoulders fall. "He doesn't trust you."

My nostrils flare, then I spear Gomez with a poisonous glare. "I have done nothing but care for our witch." I jab a finger into the air between us and the bat flinches.

Shit.

It's not like I would actually harm the creature.

Wait… What the fuck am I thinking?

My fingers curl into tight fists. "Every time you interrupt us is less enchanting than the last," I growl. "It. Will. Cease."

Gomez chirps, then flies to Evie's shoulder and snuggles against her. Her fingers sink into his fluffy fur and for a moment something ugly pierces my brain.

Those fingers should be wrapped around my cock right now, not giving him godsdamn belly scratches.

My eyelid twitches again and my growl increases in volume as a realization stuns me.

I'm jealous of a fucking bat.

I exhale sharply, stabbing a hand through my hair.

Absolutely ridiculous.

"I don't think blueberries will solve this one," Evie jokes, the corners of her kiss swollen lips twitching.

I glare at her, then rub the skin of my eyelid, attempting to stop the skin from fluttering inconveniently. "Very cute, Witch, but I'm serious." A headache throbs into existence over my left eye.

"What if you got him a present? Gomey loves them," Evie ponders and scrunches her lips to the side.

"A present… for a bat."

"I honestly think it could work. Rosa is always getting him little treats and gifts, and he loves her," Evie elaborates. Her fingers scoop Gomez up under his wings, cuddling him to her chest in a hug. I scoff, striding to the opposite side of the pool table. It's better to have distance between us before I snap his fragile fucking neck.

"Gomey, can you go find Rosa? I'm sure she can find you a yummy treat to nibble on," she coos, then kisses him on the nose. Gomez chirps once, glares at me, then flies through the doorway.

"I think you both are jealous of each other," Evie says, her eyes twinkling with humor.

I growl defensively. "I am not jealous of your fucking bat."

"So, you say, but the twitching of your eyelid and permanent snarl face in his presence shows otherwise," she aptly points out.

I lower the lip I didn't realize curled away from my teeth. "Shit," I mutter.

Aiden shouts excitedly in the hall, "Hey, you two love birds!"

"For fuck's sake," I growl under my breath. I twist my head slowly, then stare at the side of her smiling face with darkening, narrow eyes as I slip my mask from my back pocket and slide it over my face. She flicks a glance in my direction and her body jerks, a boisterous snort turned into a laugh breaking past her control.

"Hi, Aiden," Evie replies, and waves. Aiden bounds into the room, his laughter joining hers, then adjusts his peach ball cap, his blond hair curling around the edges.

Slipping his hands into his pockets, he bobs his head and looks around the room. "Sooo, what are you guys up to? I'm so bored."

"I have an idea," Evie says, a smirk playing across her lips. Oh, Hell no. "Aiden, why don't you go with Lorcan to town? He wants to pick out a present for Gomez."

"Absolutely not," I hiss, but my denial falls to the wayside as Aiden's joy circumvents my attempts.

"Hell yes!" he screams, then holds up his hand as if waiting for someone to slap it. He lets it hang there for a moment, then drops it, a brilliant, shiny smile taking over more than half his face. "Bro bonding time," he continues," I've wanted to hang out with you forever, Bro Demon. You're not so bad when all of your time isn't spent threatening to torture me in Hell." Aiden's blue eyes flick from Evie's watery, mirth filled ones to mine. "You know, to peel my skin off or feed me to the wild dogs in the pits. Remember?"

Fucking traitor, I send down the bond to Evie.

Relax, I promise I'll make it up to you later, Evie responds in kind and saunters over to me, her hips swaying sensually. Her pointer and middle finger walk up my sternum, then jab into my pec. *Don't be such a grumpy asshole. Take him with you. I'm sure he will be much better at picking out a present than you would alone.*

"As a matter of fact," Evie says, speaking aloud, "you should ask Ezra to come along too." My jaw drops as my witch winks, then glides from the room.

I growl into her mind, *You'll pay for this, Witch.*

She replies huskily, *Looking forward to it, Demon.*

Her voice filters into my consciousness and wraps around my cock as if it's her tongue, then a shiver skates over my skin.

I've created a fucking monster.

Evie's laughter floats down the bond before I disengage our minds and focus on the present.

CHAPTER THIRTEEN

Lorcan

"Fuck, no." My skin screams to be itched under the thick layer of concealer Evie slathered over my true name. According to her, a mask would be too out of place in the Human Realm this time of year. I bring my lit cigarette up to my mouth and stare at the mom-and-pop store with disdain. Although I donned one of Ezra's plain black hoodies, the hood large enough to hide most of my face, uncomfortable doesn't begin to cover it—I feel utterly naked without my mask. "Martha Doyle's Doilies and Gifts," I read aloud, then cross my arms over my chest.

"C'mon, Lorcan. It's not so bad. I bet there're loads of awesome stuff in there," Aiden encourages as he leans against the front window and peeks inside, his breath fogging the glass.

"Yeah, demon the fuck up," Ezra agrees.

"Oh look, they have embroidery!" Aiden crows.

"And?" I drawl.

"And my mom owned a sewing store when I was a kid. She taught me some cool things, like how to use her embroidery machine," Aiden explains with a shrug.

I gape at him. "I think that's the most coherent sentence I've ever heard you speak, Aiden," I admit.

Aiden grins at me, "Evie was right, we're totally bonding and shit."

Ezra snorts, then marches over to the entrance and shoves the door open, the welcome bell clanging so hard the bronze brackets holding it in place loosen from the wall. Aiden and I stare as it dangles by a lone screw. I smirk and watch from the shadows beneath my hood as Aiden cringes and lays a hand on Ezra's thick shoulder. "Dude, you gotta be careful with human stuff. It's not made for big demon bros like you," Aiden whispers poorly, then turns a toothy grin on the elderly woman behind the store counter as I cross over the threshold.

"Beg your pardon? You'll have to speak up, I'm afraid my hearing is not what it used to be."

"Sorry, Ma'am. We're just so excited to look around your store!" Aiden shouts. I reach my fingers to my left ear, then pull them away and inspect them. Huh, no blood. I'm positive he ruptured my ear drum.

She laughs quietly and lowers her hand from over her heart. "That's quite okay, dear. I remember how it was to be young and full of energy."

"Oh, you do?" Ezra asks as he leans his hip against the worn but serviceable stained pinewood counter, the top polished to a shine despite the many scratches from customers.

The elderly woman turns to Ezra. "Aren't you a handsome one."

I roll my eyes. Sure, he's attractive, but my incisors are sharper than his. My eyes squeeze shut as I struggle to acclimate to my nauseatingly bright surroundings. Dammit, these fucking florescent lights are scouring my retinas. I don't recall the Human Realm being this full of color, especially compared to the Shadow Realm; I feel like I'm viewing everything in godsdamn technicolor. I tug my hood farther forward and use Ezra's bulk to edge farther into the store. Aiden meanders down an isle packed with a combination of creepy-as-fuck porcelain dolls and... monogrammed toilet paper? I blink a few times, the perplexing isle options remain unchanged.

Something tugs on the lower half of my pant leg and my muscles lock up. *What the fuck was that?* I whirl around, then my eyes drop to a tiny, blonde human girl. She teeters on her chubby little legs, then presses a spittle covered face to my calf and babbles nonsense into the fabric. Shit. I'm so fucking distracted I didn't think to count the heartbeats in the store.

"Angelia? Angelia!" A woman with the same color hair as the toddler crashes into my chest. "Oh!"

I glare down at her from beneath my hood, gesture to the child, then speak, a growl vibrating my words. "Is this *yours?*"

"Oh. Um. Y-yes, that's my d-daughter," she stutters and lifts the drooling, shit scented monstrosity from the ground, but grubby little hands clench my pants in a death grip.

"No! No, no, no!" the girl wails.

I recoil and swallow a hiss, wrenching my leg away. The toe of my boot clips a fold out display of glittery cherry red and lime green cards, then stumble away down another isle. *Godsdammit.* My molars grind as I retreat as far as I can from the humans. What the fuck was I thinking. I'll never forgive Evie for this. Samuel should be informed, all it takes is a sticky human child to thoroughly discombobulate me. Fuck. Me. I inhale sharply, then force my pulse to slow as I exhale through my lips at a molasses pace.

My eyes blink several times, then my vision finally clears as I take in the newest isle of terror I've found myself in. It's been quite some time since I have explored the Human Realm, but we're doilies ever a thing? Well, enough of a *statement piece* that they require an entire fucking store dedicated to them? I scoff and shake my aching head.

I will *never* understand humans.

My boots scuffle along the thin, speckled brown carpet as I near a shelf packed with little figurines of deceptively innocent looking angels. "That's not even fucking close to what they look like," I say under my breath, then reach out and pinch one between my fingers. A fine fissure streaks across its previously smooth, unblemished face, and one of the wings crumbles to dust. Shit, too much pressure. "Oh well, it looks better now anyway." I place the now beautifully disfigured angel back on the shelf with distaste. If humans only knew what those dickbags are really like. Pretentious assholes.

The deep drone of Ezra smooth talking the store owner floats by as I turn down yet another isle at an awkward angle and proceed to crab walk to the other end. Frustration and anxiety stir into a clumpy cocktail within my stomach, like a protein shake left in the sun. There is so much shit packed into this fucking building that moving through it is near impossible. My shoulder knocks into a stack of doilies placed near some display of delicate looking glassware. "Oh, for fuck's sake," I utter, then send multiple shadows to catch the falling items and discreetly put them back in place. I straighten my spine and glance around. Shit, I forgot I'm in the Human Realm. Shadow magic would definitely draw unwanted attention. I grip the edges of the hood and bend at the waist, my blood rushing too fast through my veins.

Where's Aiden? I'm over this bullshit. I'll have him pick a random object and call it a gift. Gomez is a godsdamn bat, it's not like he can hate it. Although perhaps I should have just gotten him some damn trail mix at that shitty gas station down the road. The hoodie pulls tight against my skull as I grip the nape of my neck. I'm overthinking this. I know I am. But even though I'm aware of that fact, there's no helping it. I can't stop a loud growl from tearing free.

The things I do for my witch. This is fucking torture.

A gasp sounds from the checkout counter. "Oh my, what was that?"

"Hm? Oh, that rumbling sound? I think it was just some hooligan teenager speeding by," Ezra replies smoothly.

You're welcome, Ezra pushes down our bond.

I'm not going to thank you.

You should. The next thing we know there will be a witch hunt or some shit on our hands. Oh! Maybe they'll think you're a werewolf and pelt you with wolfsbane.

I blow out a breath and clench my eyes shut.

A bit overwhelmed, are we? Ezra prods with smothered laughter in his voice, but I don't miss the genuine concern underlining his question.

Do you blame me? I've been in the Human Realm for less than a handful of days. It's not like I've had the time to fucking adjust, I shove the thought at him, then close my end of the bond. I move to the front and spy Aiden dithering away by a glass display counter, his baseball hat curiously absent. My head tilts to the side as he places his palms on his knees and crouches low. He's so absorbed with admiring the many embroidered bags, hats, and bath towels, I decide to make the best of it. I can't have him becoming complacent just because I'm no longer trapped behind mirrors. A sadistic smile unfurls across the lower half of my face, perhaps Evie will think better of forcing me to socialize.

I sneak up close to Aiden, then casually reach behind my back and snatch a small plushie from the overflowing basket, toying with it absently between my fingers. *What are you doing?* I growl into his mind.

"Shit," Aiden yelps and jumps to his feet, cracking his head on a dangling metal basket full of painted rocks of all things. "Fuck. Ow." He faces me and glowers while rubbing the top of his head, the circle depressed into his dirty-blonde hair from the band of his hat shifting slightly with the movement. "Why do you always have to do that!? It's like you enjoy startling me or some shit."

I laugh darkly and lift a shoulder. "I couldn't pass up the opportunity."

"Plus, you've got your hood up, raising the creep factor to the max because I can barely see your damn face."

"You didn't answer my question," I remind him.

Aiden stills, then his eyes glaze as if he's searching his mind for the answer to said question, then they refocus on me. My gaze flicks to the pulse hammering away in his neck. "Oh, right," he says, the corners of his lips curling into a small smile. "I'm waiting for my hat. It's getting embroidered. I'm so stoked bro."

Ezra's eyes bounce from me to Aiden, following our conversation with one ear while listening to the old woman with the other. My brother's eyes dart to my hands, and my attention returns to the soft plushie in my fist. I hold the thing a loft and a crooked eyed chicken stares back at me from a fuzzy feathered face. Ezra mumbles to the woman, then pats the counter once and walks a few steps to Aiden and me.

"That's what you've come up with, Brother? A fucking chicken?"

"Have you got any better ideas?"

"Naturally," he scoffs and his familiar pale green eyes glitter. Ezra laughs, crowding me into an end cap of overly floral candles to my right. He winces as my fist makes contact with his shoulder but continues interloping on my personal space and reaches around me, shoving a dark purple plushie into my chest with a shadow. "You want this one instead."

Aiden's eyes ping pong between us like he's watching a high stakes tennis match.

"Guys," Aiden whispers loudly. "Put the shadows away. Humans, remember." Ezra and I glance at him, then separate. Shit. I inhale deeply and tame the growl building behind my ribs.

"For once, Aiden is right," I acknowledge.

Aiden's jaw drops open comically and his eyes bulge. "I…I…wha?" he stammers.

Ezra twists toward me, then raises his tattooed hand in front of his mouth and speaks at regular volume. "Utoh, I think you broke him."

My eyes narrow on Aiden, then every single muscle in my body tightens rapidly as he tips forward and traps me in a bear hug. "I knew you liked me," he cries in my ear.

I release a dark growl. "Aiden. Get. Off. Me."

"Oh, shit. Sorry. Like, for real dude," he blurts while aggressively smoothing his hand down my hoodie like he intends to rid it of wrinkles.

I reanimate as an elderly male struggles to get Aiden's attention. "Sir? Your hat is done."

My legs twitch to life as I spin on my heel, then chuck the fucking bat shaped plushie at Ezra over my shoulder. "Pay for that. I'll be outside." The dilapidated bell tinkles weakly as I stalk out the door and seek some place to wait.

I sprawl onto a red bench across the street, the paint peeling in large chunks, then reach into my pocket and draw out a lighter and pack of cigarettes. Fire winks to life within my cupped palms, a rich orange glow highlighting my fingers. I take a long drag, spread my legs, and lean my elbows on my thighs. Exhaled smoke rises from my lips as wind curls into my hood and threatens to uncover my head. "Fuck," I curse and tug it as far forward as far as it will go, my claws extending slightly and puncturing the fabric. *They better hurry the fuck up.*

As if the thought summoned them, Aiden and Ezra leisurely cross the street and stop in front of me. I glare at them beneath my hood. "Let's go." I stand, leading them down an ally and into a shadow formed by the clumped dumpsters and into the In-Between.

The scent of roses curls into my lungs as I depart a long shadow juxtaposed to a framed painting of the manor's graveyard. "Evie," I call.

"Any luck?" She leans against the back of the couch.

"Perhaps," I reply, then hold a brown paper bag out to her.

Evie laughs and folds her arms over her chest. "Oh no, you're going to give it to him."

"No," I growl.

"Yes," she growls back mockingly.

"Frustrating fucking woman," I retort. "I don't want to bicker with you right now, just give the damn thing to your familiar."

"Nope," Evie says, then backs away with her hands raised, palms out.

"Godsdammit," I curse. "You deserve a punishment for your earlier meddling. You don't want to make it worse, do you?"

Someone clears their throat, and my eyes slowly slide to the group before the fireplace. Rosa, Gomez, Aiden, and Ezra now lounging in the seated area. Rosa lifts her brows and speaks authoritatively. "Well, what are you waiting for? Give our sweet little night puppy his gift."

I bite my tongue and swallow my creative vitriolic response before I lash out at Evie's best friend. Dropping my shoulders, I force my fingers to uncurl. My shadow dives into the wrinkled bag midair, absconds with the plushie, and drops it onto Rosa's lap next to Gomez.

"Satisfied?" I stab my hands into my pockets, so I don't murder the lot of them. Fabric rustles as my legs walk toward Evie before I make the conscious decision to do so. I loop my arms around her waist from behind and rest my chin on the top of her head, her soft brow hair tickling my stubble.

"Good boy," Evie praises.

An unexpected bolt of lust heats my skin.

I force any arousal producing thoughts away and glare at my witch. "I'm so fucking furious with you," I rumble, then shackle her wrist with my thumb and forefinger, intent on dragging her from the room. My breathing halts as something twinges the demonic senses in the back of my mind like an early alarm system. Out of the corner of my eye, through the wisps of my witch's hair, I glimpse a pair of pastel green eyes frames by black lashes peeking through the window.

CHAPTER FOURTEEN

Lorcan

Ezra and I whip our heads to the right and lurch toward the window on the back wall. Two tandem shadows give chase, but mine is faster.

Glass splinters, a web of fine cracks spreading from the point of impact, as I spear a shadow through the window and around Gideon's wrist. Ezra's shadow joins mine and secures both his wrists at Gideons lower back. A crack sounds under my heal as my boot connects with his ribs, then wrap another shadow around his throat. Gideon's shadows lash out but it's too late. He grunts and curses as Ezra and I drag him through the jagged maw of glass between lines of tracery. Blue demon blood splatters the dark velvet drapes.

"Hey Lor, want to redecorate?"

"Not. Fucking. Following." I pant as Gideon wrestles with our shadows.

Ezra nods to the drapes. "New pattern, I call it Blood Motif at Sunset." He grins and his pale green eyes twinkle, the madness behind them trickling through, then sighs. "So pretty."

The air punches from my lungs as I barely miss grabbing Gideon and his booted foot lands against my stomach. I watch temporarily stunned as my brother, the King of War, spins from my path mid-air, then connects his fist with Ezra's face in three quick jabs. Unfortunately for Gideon, Ezra has his unhinged side in his favor. He leans into the blows, allowing his face to become the canvas of a grotesque abstract painting. Ezra laughs like a maniac. I gasp in a breath, before jumping on top of Ezra and Gideon. At this point, I don't give a fuck which one my elbow comes in contact with. They're both assholes.

Shadows cloud around us thickly. Although I can no longer see which body is Gideon's, I tear into flesh with my serrated teeth while stabbing my claws into anything but myself. I will more shadows to join the fight as someone yanks on my hair. Pain radiates from my jaw to my temple as something cracks the bone.

I lash out blindly, no longer able to discern whose shadows belong to whom. Gideon is a fierce fighter, no doubt a result of endless battles in Hell honing his skills, but I'm sure he never anticipated Ezra and I capable of working as a team.

I tense as agony radiates from multiple wounds, every inch of my skin absorbing inhuman blows from every angle. Shit. My eyes close as I block everything out and search my mind for my brotherly bond with Ezra. I find it, then rocket down its length and spear into his mind. As I roar, someone's body jerks in the fucked up doggy pile.

This fight will continue unless we do something about it.

And how do you think we should do that? Ezra replies.

Ez, fucking focus. Shake off the blood lust and tell me when I find you. I search through the tangle of limbs and other body parts until my fingers find a face in the impenetrable darkness within the shadows, then hammer my fist into the nose.

Jesus fuck, Ezra grows into my mind. *Yep, you found me. Great job.*

My laughter swells into his mind. *Now that's established, use your shadows to bind his legs together and I'll use mine to capture his arms and torso. We keep piling on layers of shadow ropes until he can't move.*

Agreed, he growls.

My claws sink into Ezra's face, and he hisses. *What? It would be a shame to lose you in the melee.* With my free hand, my shadows and I work together to locate Gideon. A tendril of shadow finds Gideon's neck and squeezes until pleasing rasping breaths issue close by. Some of the other's shadows clear and I catch a glimpse of Ezra curling into himself as Gideon knees him in the balls, heedless of his twin choking him. Ezra laughs, then jabs his thumbs into Gideon's eye sockets while his and my shadows dip and weave around our errant brother. A grunt rushes out of me as Gideon writhes, testing the strength of my onyx ropes, then stills abruptly. The remaining shadows dissipate, and I aim a glare at Gideon.

Ezra pants, then shakes out his arms and bounces on the balls of his feet. "That was over too soon. Wanna go again?" he asks me, the five perfect lacerations on his face from my claws quickly healing as he speaks.

I shake my head, then stand.

"Look at us, working together and shit." Ezra's arms raise, then spread. "Celebratory hug?"

My palm skims the back of his head with a crack.

"That was uncalled for," Ezra says with mock outrage, rubbing his skull. "Asshole."

I clap him on the shoulder, then immediately go to my witch. Evie smirks as I cup her cheek with a bloody hand. "Now, where were we?"

Evie laughs, a brilliant smile blooming brightly across her face and *finally* meeting her eyes. There's my girl. "That was actually entertaining," Evie says. My heart gallops as a rare, true grin spreads across my face, mirroring her own. If pummeling my brothers makes her this happy, I'll gladly do it as often as she pleases.

"Damn, Gid. You've got yourself into quite the fuckity-fuck of a situation," Ezra says to his twin.

My hand slowly lifts from Evie's face, blood smearing down her cheek, then intertwines with one of her hands, my thumb stroking the lush purple rose magically tattooed on the back of it. I angle myself toward Ezra, my brows tilting down. "But more than that," I pause, raise our clasped hands and kiss the back of hers, then unravel our fingers, "it was suspiciously sloppy." My boots thump against the floor as I stalk back to Gideon with a measured gate. "How does the King of War get caught?"

Gideon's face remains impassive. "Maybe that was my intention," he conveys flatly, like he murdered the emotion in his words before they could form. Damn, I forgot how ragged Gideon's voice is, shouting orders to his troops daily for centuries rendering his vocal cords permanently damaged.

Suspicion thickens heavily in the air with Gideon's statement. Then from one blink to the next, quicker that even my demon eyes can track, Gideon tears through his shadow binds and rolls into the shadow behind the couch. My heart takes flight and lodges into my throat as the King of War exits a shadow cast by one of the high back chairs angled toward the couch like bookends— directly in front of Rosa. Fuck. Her shrill scream grates on my eardrums as Gideon grabs Rosa and captures her against his front.

Gideon chuckles. "Did you really think me, of all people, would make a novice mistake like allowing you fools to detect me?"

Out of my peripheral, Ezra's body shakes violently in direct contrast to the smooth cadence of his twin's words, seeming to almost blur in and out of focus. I glanced at him, then tense.

He's about to go full beast mode.

Gideon winks at Ezra as he presses his sharp claws over Rosa's heart, then Ezra simply disappears. I track the slight distortion in the air marking his movements. Although, Ezra's King of

Monsters powers allow him to seamlessly cloak himself like a chameleon. Those abilities, combined with his demonic speed, are essentially akin to teleportation to the untrained eye.

Gideon roars as Ezra reappears behind him and rips the arm crossing over Rosa's chest clean from the shoulder joint. Ezra lets out a bestial growl and tosses the offending appendage. Aiden's head as he screams as it flies over his head and curls into a ball on the other end of the couch. Gideon levels his eyes on Aiden and tilts his head to the side, all his attention zeroing in on him like his shoulder isn't spirting blood all over the living room. Gideon's eyes blink once slowly, then he spins, drops to the ground, and kicks out all in one move, catching Ezra hard in the kneecaps with the momentum of his descent.

This is getting out of fucking hand. I shake out of the trance their fight compels and cross to Evie. I wrap my arms around her waist and drag her farther away from my dueling brothers.

"Wait!" she shouts, then reaches for Rosa's hand and pulls her along with us.

Ezra's body swiftly swells as he wills his King of Monsters powers to rise and blend with his demonic form.

Evie inhales sharply while my eyes widen when a palpable tension brackets the silence, the chiaroscuro of my brother's ominous shadow spilling across half the room. Blue horns rise from just within his hairline, curving up and back in an arc akin to a giant sable antelope's as he continues to grow at least a foot taller. Flames rise higher in the hearth, sparks crackling loudly as if in celebration of the bloodshed, casting an eerie tangerine glow on the twins' profile. Soft looking, black fur sprouts from the back of his hands and wrists, while navy-blue spots appear on the pelt, their pattern an organized chaos of magnificence. The fur spreads up his arms, over his shoulders, and onto his chest, slowly decreasing in length and volume as it grows into barely visible fine hairs along his abdomen. He bounces his weight from foot to foot and cranes his neck to the side as if to alleviate the strain from shifting.

While Gideon operates on strategies and carefully choreographed plans, Ezra relies on his unhinged nature and the numerous monster forms he houses in his arsenal.

"Are you finished?" Gideon growls.

"Not even fucking close," Ezra snaps through serrated teeth and unsheathes the dagger strapped to his thigh. The weapon gleams in the firelight as Ezra angles the demonic blade along his forearm.

"Did I touch a nerve, Monster?" Gideon says, then bares his teeth in an aggressive display of emotion his twin easily provokes.

Shit. I reach for Ezra's mind only to come face-to-face with an impenetrable shield—a solid barrier of uncut black diamond. My brothers are the only beings able to block me out like this, Lucifer teaching all of us simple mind shielding as adolescents, but I sense madness swirling like a whirlpool behind the barrier. I slam a mental fist against it. *Ezra, let me in.* Ah, fuck. I brace myself as a furry, clawed, yet still skeletal hand spears over the wall, then flicks me out of his mind, while continually circling his twin.

Gideon chuckles darkly, nodding at Gomez who is hiding his face against Evie's chest and my palm, his new plushy tucked securely under his wing. "I'm surprised you haven't adopted the bat

175

into your pack of rabid Hell monsters yet." Gideon's lips twitch downward. "Those mutts were always the most important things in your life. Weren't they, Brother?"

I growl as my demonic powers creep from the depths of my magic. I might not like Fluffy Fucker, but no one threatens him but me. The air shimmers over Ezra like a second skin, then dissolves into nothingness as he uses Gideon's lapse of concentration and cocky overconfidence to his advantage. I angle my head and track him through our brotherly bond. Ezra darts from one side of Gideon to the other in an irregular pattern as Gideon slowly turns in a tight circle.

"Don't hide, Monster. We used to have so much fun together," Gideon growls, then slashes the air with his claws. Ezra appears an inch away from his twin, towering over him. Ezra grunts but shoves forward as Gideon's claws stab into his chest, however, he doesn't seem to feel the pain.

My arms tighten around Evie and Gomez squeaks in protest as I watch my brothers, waiting for an opportunity to jump between them if necessary. The twins have always fought, but we always knew they never intended for death to end their games. *This* fight, however, is swiftly shifting to murderous territory.

Ezra shoves his body further onto Gideon's claws, arcs his elbow to the side, then slashes the demonic blade across Gideon's throat. Navy blue blood pearls on Gideon's skin in a thin line, then the tattoo of crossed swords inked onto his neck splits wide, a deluge of the thick liquid pouring onto his chest. Firelight flashes on the dripping dagger as Ezra flips the blade and grasps it upright in his palm, plunging it into Gideon's gut. I wince as Gideon crumples to the floor before the hearth with a groan.

Fuck. It'll take Gideon days to completely heal from those wounds.

He flashes a gruesome smile at Ezra, blood coating his gums and bubbling between his sharp demonic teeth as he coughs. "I've taught you well, Ez." Pride threads through words before his eyes roll into the back of his head as he passes out.

My brows arch as Aiden's head pops up from the circle of his arms like a turtle peeking from the shelter within its shell. "Shiiit. That was fucking terrifying," he says, then gulps. "Is it over?"

I disregard his question and eye Ezra seriously, fine hairs raising all over my body. He looms over our unconscious brother, his chest rising and falling rapidly like bellows, one hand white knuckling the drenched demonic blade, the other clenching and unclenching into a fist, his claws repeatedly stabbing through his palm to the back of his hand. A dark puddle of blood blossoms underneath Gideon, viscous drops of the substance steadily feeding the pool from Ezra's healing chest.

I open my mouth to speak, but Rosa steps away from Evie. "Ezra," she calls softly. His pointed, softly furred ear twitches in response but he maintains his pose. "Ezra, I *really* am okay."

"Human Rainbow," I warn as she takes a step forward but jerks to a stop as Evie clamps onto her wrist with a shadow.

"Don't go near him. It's dangerous," Evie implores, then swallows thickly. "We don't know if he's in his right mind yet."

Rosa smiles gently at Evie, her eyes conveying a world of unspoken communication with her best friend. Her brown eyes flicker to me, then narrow as one of her brows lifts.

"Just let her go. She can make her own mistakes," I say to Evie.

A shadow tears from Evie's hands before I can process what's happening and coils around my throat, my shadows stretching to their breaking point as she pulls me away. Fury whips down our bond as she states, "He's *your* brother, you help him."

I brush a kiss to Evie's hair as she easily snaps my shadow binds, then I draw back. My eyes fly to her chest as Fluffy Fucker strokes his furry cheek against my hand.

My heart backflips, then my brows bunch together before the corners of my lips fall.

What.

The.

Fuck.

I yank my hand away, stepping to Evie's side and secure her with my shadows. I use another shoot of shadow to encourage Evie's to lift from Rosa's wrist, her magic squirming in my grasp before it dissipates. "If Human Rainbow wants to try first, I'm not going to stop her. Ezra is more of an asshole than usual when coming down from blood lust and his shift. Plus, I'm fairly confident Ezra flipped the fuck out because Gideon threatened her."

Rosa takes Evie in, her eyes softening. Nodding at me, she shakes out her trembling hands as she marches over to Ezra. She holds out a trembling hand palm up to my brother as she delicately steps over Gideon and places her spike heeled ankle boots into the pool of blood. "You got him. It's okay," Rosa assures quietly.

Ezra's head slowly twists to the woman boldly standing before him and turns his unblinking black predatory stare on her. Rosa glides forward and places her hand on the center of his chest, seemingly no longer afraid of the monstrous demon she met in the compact mirror.

The room exhales as Ezra shifts from his unhinged state to his regular humanoid form, shrinking inches and collapsing his mass. He shakes his head aggressively, his sweat dampened hair lashing in all directions, then clears his throat. "Well, now that we've got him down. What do we do with him?"

And just like that, Ezra's back to normal. Well, Ezra's version of normal. I draw shadows over to Gideon and around his unconscious form. "These won't last for long as you witnessed earlier," I mention and run a hand through my tangled hair.

Evie steps several feet away from me, the death glare in her eyes promising retribution. "What if I spelled something to secure him with? They'll be stronger than the temporary shadows, at least. Although, judging by the power he displayed, they likely won't hold for more than a couple of days."

I sigh heavily. When will Evie understand that I don't give a shit about anyone else but her? If her friend wants to throw herself at an enraged demon, that's her choice. "That should work," I grumble.

Rosa pats Ezra on the arm. "I've got just the thing." She grins, then shines her amused expression on Evie. "I'll be right back."

I pace behind the couch, stopping at invisible markers like its muscle memory. A cold sweat dots my brow. That's because it *is* muscle memory. I paced the exact length of my cage, its dimensions carved into my brain matter itself. *Fuck,* I utter internally and Evie's attention flashes to me. Panic coalesces sharply in my gut, twisting my intestines in on themselves painfully as if Ezra stabbed me instead of Gideon. *Did I accidentally send that thought down the bond?*

Yes, you did, Evie replies softly. *Are you okay?*

Later. I inhale for three seconds and exhale for four, begging my mind to recenter itself on the present. *We'll talk later,* I concede, then block my end of the bond, cutting off communication. Rosa jogs into the room, her tits nearly bouncing out of her shirt. Ezra moans audibly, eyes dilating as he tracks her.

Rosa winks at Ezra as he prowls toward her. She ignores my brother pressing against her back as she removes the strap of her leather backpack—I refuse to designate it as a godsdamn purse—from her shoulder and drops it onto the mahogany end table. The blue, purple, and gray stained-glass lamp shade shudders as its new burden jostles its base. My eyes narrow on the pair of them. Ezra inhales noisily at Rosa's neck and her eyelids flitter briefly, then her stare hardens as if she's slipping on a mask—a dominant one. Interesting. Rosa dips manicured fingers into her bag of tricks and removes a pair of baby pink...

Fluffy.

Fucking.

Handcuffs.

"You've got to be fucking with me," I say, rubbing my temple, then stabbing a hand into my pocket in search of my cigarettes and lighter.

Rosa rolls her eyes and cocks her hip to the side, dangling the handcuffs from her fingertips. "I don't give a shit if you like them or not, Lorcan. My good leather pair is at home," Rosa claims, raising her chin. "A good sex therapist always has a pair handy for demonstration."

Aiden laughs boisterously and finally uncurls his body from the floor.

Ezra crowds into her further and drapes his arms over her shoulders while rooting through her bag with curious tattooed fingers. I snort and shake my head as Rosa smacks the back of his hand. "Naughty demon."

"Ouch," Ezra says playfully, his voice husky. "Do you have any more of those bat snackies? They were fucking delicious."

I shake my head and move over to Gideon. "I'll take him up to one of the spare bedrooms," I announce, then throw my brother over my shoulder and stalk from the room.

CHAPTER FIFTEEN

Evie

I finish my fourth coffee of the evening and glance at the clock. Midnight. Yet, again, I haven't followed by body's cues to go to bed at a normal time.

I hold my breath for a few seconds when Lorcan sits on the chair next to me at the kitchen table along with Ezra, Rosa, and Aiden.

In the Shadow Realm, everything was muted including our chemistry, and even then it was off the charts. Now it's like I've been transported to a whole other level of desire.

His curious voice booms into my mind unexpectedly and I almost drop my coffee mug.

What are you thinking about, Little Witch?

I exhale slowly then respond, *Just thinking about your sins. Lust in particular.*

Oh, do tell.

The corner of my mouth lifts and I watch Lorcan in my peripheral vision, his gaze burning into me. I track his fingers as he glides them to the inside of my thigh, tracing them up and up until… my quads clench as he flicks a finger against the jean fabric between my legs.

I've missed the way you taste.

"There are other people in this kitchen, you know," Ezra says, eyebrows raised.

Heat floods my cheeks. Fuck! Normally I wouldn't mind an audience, but these are people I know. At least Rosa and Aiden are. Thank the devils that Gomez is sleeping on the couch. He's been scarred enough by shit like this.

"Right." I clear my throat and have to push Lorcan's hand away when he doesn't move it, because it's not like he gives a fuck who sees.

Lorcan's claws protrude from his fingers, digging into the jeans over his knees. A low growl rumbles in his chest as he grumbles into my mind, *Later*, sounding more promise than request.

"It's okay. I get it," Ezra exclaims sultrily as he watches Rosa gliding her tongue over the few remaining sprinkles clinging to the whipped cream on the rim of her mug.

Lorcan makes a face and Rosa shoots him a look I can only equivalate to murderous. I'd like to believe she's not charmed by Ezra, but when she leans forward, the sudden arch to her back and wiggle of her hips tells me otherwise. She fucking enjoying his attentions.

Damn. If he fucking hurts her.

"So," Rosa says, pulling me back to the present. "We're all here for your idea. What's up."

I cast a glance at the grimoire that I've been reading ever since an unconscious Gideon was thrown into one of the spare rooms. My magic pulses in my fingertips, ready to be used. The desire to let it out on the rest of The Order is the equivalent to a damned orgasm. Gods I just want to rid the earth of them, but killing one of the demons is going to be harder than I first thought.

I clear my throat and announce, "It will likely kill me to destroy Samuel, something The Order likely knew when they tortured me."

Lorcan's claws extend again, but out of anger this time as I watch them slice through the fabric of his pants. "You won't. I'll fucking kill him myself."

I shake my head. "That's sweet, except you're not a powerful witch and you can't kill your own kind."

Ezra smirks as Lorcan's cheeks flush with pink. "Yeah, Lor. That's *sweet*, but she doesn't need your help. Let your girlfriend take care of the big bad men while you sit looking pretty."

Girlfriend. I watch Lorcan carefully for his reaction, but that doesn't seem to be the part that's pissing him off.

I shoot Ezra my best psycho gaze and intone, "I'll take care of *you* in a minute."

Lorcan pushes his elbows against the table, muscles flexing under his rolled-up sleeves. "I can kill Samuel. I don't need to be a witch to do that. I kill demons all the time."

Ezra nods as he stands, scraping his chair backward. "Lor's right. I can too."

Rosa grabs his arm and pulls him back to his chair. "She said you can't kill your own. I assume Evie's done her damn research," she says, then adds with a roll of her eyes. "Fragile. Fucking. Egos."

Aiden snort laughs then quickly slaps his hand over the servant's mark on his neck. "Ouch, bro. It's Rosa that said it, not me."

"Gods, I'm going to need more coffee." I look at the empty cup, then slide it across the polished wood. "Look, I've been thinking."

"Me too," Aiden adds unexpectedly.

Lorcan laughs. "That's dangerous."

I suppress a smirk for Aiden's benefit and mask my laugh as a cough. "I've been thinking that we need to go to Hell."

Ezra blinks twice, exhaling a tense breath. "Sorry, my brain just seized up for a second. Because *you* did not just suggest we go to Hell."

Aiden puffs out his cheeks and leans back in his chair. "Yeah, dude, I'm out. Like, I am not going to the place that made these two." He points at Lorcan then Ezra. "Plus, there are demons there and I've experienced my fair share of those."

Ezra chuckles. "There are much worse creatures in Hell than demons, Kiddo."

Aiden and Lorcan exchange a glare, but we don't have time to unpack whatever history is there. I clear my throat and announce, "The Order will be on their way. If Gideon is here, then surely the rest of your brothers know. We can't take on all of them including The Order, or maybe we can but…"

Half of us will end up dead. I finish the last part in my head. I continue, "Even if we can kill them, they'll just go to Hell and be able to come back. We need to obliterate their souls or whatever is needed to actually wipe them out of our existence." Ezra winces and I remember that I am talking about his family, and even if he hates them, bonds like that don't break easily. So I add, "Or just Samuel at least."

Ezra and Lorcan both nod.

"Samuel needs to go," Lorcan says. "But what will going to Hell do? You don't want to go there, Evie. It's not a good place."

I roll my eyes. "Well, I didn't think it would be a vacation."

Rosa laughs along with Aiden and Ezra while Lorcan, unbeknown to them, speaks into my mind.

You need to be dead to go to Hell, Baby Girl. I'm not going to see you dead before your time.

My stomach does a cartwheel at his words. I mentally kick myself for swooning over a nickname when we have much more important things to discuss.

I saw that in the grimoire, except there is another way. We go through one of the gateways to Hell.

His response comes all too quickly. *Absolutely not. It's still a risk and there are far more demons there than there ever were in the Shadow Realm. Their favorite pastime is tearing human souls apart. The answer is no.*

I glance sideways at him. *I wasn't asking for permission. You let me open the portal even though it was risk… or was that just because it benefitted you?*

I knew you would be okay. I've seen how powerful you are.

I nod. *Then you can trust me on this. You're not my damned keeper and I'm going. It's the only way to get us out of this mess.*

Rosa clears her throat and we both turn our heads to look at her. "You know, we can't hear whatever you two are saying to each other. I know about your blood bond through the portal or whatever." She waggles a finger between us.

"Technically, it's because of the Fallenmoore blood spells tying my family line to Lorcan," I say, but Lorcan quickly rebukes it in my mind.

It's not that. It's a mating thing. I can imprint on a witch's mind, if I… feel a certain way.

My eyes widen and Ezra grins as if he knows exactly what it is.

The question burns in my mind. *What way?*

In a bat-plushie buying, hair washing kind of way.

I'm dying to dissect exactly what that means, but Ezra interrupts us. "So, Hell? Why?"

"Right." I tap my fingers on the table in a rhythmic motion. "We need to talk to Lucifer. Err, your father."

Aiden's eyebrows shoot halfway up his forehead. "The *Devil*? You mean you want to go to Hell to see the *Devil*?"

"Where else would she go to see him?" Rosa asks, earning a smirk from Ezra. "For real, though. Is this really our best plan? What if we're wrong about it all and he's in on it?"

Lorcan shakes his head. "He's not. I thought so too, but Samuel and Evangaline are pulling the strings."

Ezra nods, his leg bouncing under the table. "I never heard an order come from Dad himself. They don't allow us to go see him. I agree with Evie. We should go. Dad has the power to banish or destroy anything."

I can feel Lorcan's eye roll without looking at him. "Such a daddy's boy." He sighs. "Well, I suppose, Evangeline won't stop until I'm destroyed. I guess we need to go to the bitch herself."

My stomach knots. I hadn't thought about that part too deeply. Instead, remaining willfully delusional about never having to meet the woman who manipulated Lorcan, and was the most powerful witch in the world before me.

Rosa arches a brow. "Can we die while we're in Hell?"

Ezra shrugs nonchalantly. "No, because you need to die before you go. Do they teach humans nothing?"

She slaps him on a toned forearm, right on the face of a crying stone angel tattooed there, and he feigns pains. "I mean is there any other way to go there? I'm not killing myself."

Lorcan's grin widens. "I can do the killing if needed."

"He's joking!" I say before it escalates. At least I hope he is. "We can go through one of the gateways to Hell."

Aiden slowly stands. "Gateway? Where?"

"Hellam, Pennsylvania."

"Aptly named," Rosa jokes, although I notice a bead of sweat collecting on her forehead, and Ezra snickers.

Aiden hisses a breath between his teeth and professes, "You all have fun with that. I'm going to head off to Mexico or some Caribbean Island."

"With what money?" Ezra questions.

Aiden shoves his hands into his sweatpants pockets. "Uh, I don't know. I guess since you're all dying, I'll just sell this place."

Lorcan's chair screeches back as his tattooed knuckles land on the table. "You fucking try it. You sold your soul to me first, Valet, or have you forgotten. Just because we are allies doesn't mean your servitude is over."

Aiden's mouth forms a perfect 'o'. "Evie said—"

"I agreed to let you go, but there was no contract. I am not required to do anything."

I place a hand on Lorcan's arm, pulling him back to sitting. I forget sometimes how angry he can get with all that power contained behind those untamed eyes. "You did promise, but…" I add before he can lose it again, "perhaps we can add another layer to the deal. That you remove it on the condition Aiden goes to Hell with us." I look at Aiden and sigh. "I wish we could cut you free, but the truth is you're in danger on your own. They'll never stop hunting you because they know you were with us at The Order."

Aiden pauses for several seconds, then throws his hands in the air. "I'm not swimming through any lava pits and God help you all, if there are any clowns there, I'm out."

Ezra rolls his lips in and Lorcan snickers.

"There are, aren't there?" Aiden asks, and I shake my head, as if I'm the authority on it. "Look, I'll make sure there's a contract this time. So you can be free."

Rosa shrugs and points at Lorcan. "It has to be better than spending a lifetime attached to him."

"She's right," Ezra says to Aiden. "I've had Lor at my side for centuries and it's a fate worse than dying in a lava river."

Aiden's face blanches. "Lava river? You're kidding, right?"

Rosa grabs my hands from across the table, ignoring Aiden's freak out. "It's a good plan."

"I wish you didn't have to come. That I could keep you and Gomez safe."

"You are." Her smile widens, although I detect a flicker of fear in her brown eyes. "Besides, it's not like we have any other choice. We're not safe here anymore."

I close my eyes, clenching my fingers as she releases my hands. I hate that I dragged her into this. I only hope Ezra's little crush means he'll actually focus on protecting Rosa in Hell. Although, going by the type of person he is, it doesn't seem likely.

CHAPTER SIXTEEN

Evie

Lorcan's hands land on my hips as he comes up behind me.

I lean further out the open window and take long inhale of the cigarette, the cherry glowing red. I hold the smoke in my mouth before inhaling when Lorcan spins me around and brings his lips to mine, parting them with his tongue.

He sucks the smoke from my mouth and into his, pulling away to exhale the white puff. "Everyone's asleep."

I close my eyes, my back against the window, the cold air prickling over my exposed neck. "Are they?" I take another drag of the cigarette, enjoying the buzz of the nicotine in my brain and trying to ignore the throbbing between my legs. I inhale the last drag before throwing it out the window, then turn to face him.

His thoughts flow like a faucet in my mind.

Now that we're alone, why don't you tell me more about those thoughts you were having earlier?

My gaze travels downwards, to the bulge straining under his gray sweatpants.

I lick my lips, fever sweeping through my body as my demon straddles me against the windowsill, the wood digging into my lower back.

I couldn't, possibly. Those thoughts are sinful, I tease, dragging my teeth over my bottom lip, enjoying the way I can so easily pull his attention to any part of me.

His growl reverberates behind his teeth as he brings his mouth to my neck. *Tell me what you want,* he commands.

I press a hand on his chest, pushing him backward smiling when I notice the thrum of his heartbeat race under my splayed fingers. *Not this time.* I press my other finger to his lips as they part. *This time, you're going to tell me what you want.*

His eyes widen, surprise shining in those pastel green irises, but hunger quickly consumes his gaze. Maintaining eye-contact, I pull down his gray sweatpants. His eyes stay focused on me as he thrusts his cock into my awaiting hands, letting out an incoherent sound when I squeeze. "The last time I did this, I cut a man's cock off."

The line between what I should want, and the moral ambiguity of my desire, blurs. I need to feel powerful. Fuck, I *do* feel powerful. After years of being afraid, I am finally in control.

I stare deep into his eyes, unblinking, as I grasp his engorged cockhead, smearing the thick bubble of pre-cum leaking from the slit with my thumb.

Tell me, I command.

I want you to be mine, he groans as his shadows unfurl from the small gap between my hips and his questing hands. Ropes of darkness make quick work of my pants, shredding them into ribbons around my feet. *To be yours.*

Then beg me.

My words come all too quickly, but I know I've done something right as he engorges in my hand, his head throbbing. My dripping pussy clenches the air as I take in his every breath, breathing in the scent of his arousal mixed with nutmeg and smoke.

I don't beg, Witch. He pushes his cock between my legs, and I grab the base, rubbing his head against my clit. His other hand slips down to my ass, and palms the cheek, squeezing hard until I gasp. When he releases my sensitive skin, the pain radiating through my buttocks only adds to the pleasure building in my pussy.

His other hand tangles in my hair as he grabs a fistful and forces me closer to meet his lips. His tongue flicks against my sensitive skin.

He rocks against me harder, grinding his cock against my labia and a guttural groan sounds in my throat. *Look how well you stretch for me.*

Oh, Gods. No. Fuck. I want him to submit to me, to feel him explode when *I* desire. Just like when he controlled when I could come.

I clamp my legs around his throbbing length, before dropping to my knees. *Beg for more. Show me you will submit to me.*

I don't submit to anyone. Not even you.

His gaze flicks to mine as I moisten my lips with the tip of his cock, smearing the pre-cum gathered there. My lips close over his swollen head, and he makes a desperate, needy sound I've never heard issue from him before. *You taste so good.*

His fingers grip the sides of my head, holding me still as he stares down at my lips stretching around him. My shadows inject inky magic into his wrists until he releases me. We turn slightly until his back is over the open window, his legs pushing back against the windowsill.

Hold still, I command, my shadows slinking around his throat and pinning him in place. *Or the next thing you'll feel is pain.*

His cock transforms as I dab my teeth into the skin. The ridges of his length pulsate in the 'O' of my mouth, stretching my lips further.

Lorcan moans. *Uhghn. That's not the threat you think it is, Little Witch. You know I like pain.*

He tilts his head back, the muscles in his throat working beneath my shadows as I explore the ridges with my tongue.

Look at me as I take control, I command.

My shadows tremble as his own attempt to strangle mine so he can fuck my face harder, but my death magic hums in warning, infusing every shadow with searing heat.

Fuck me, Little Killer. Careful with those shadows.

I guide my tongue down his shaft in slow circles, alternating between soft sucks and long licks until he's growling.

My magic traps his hips as he attempts to buck them. *Fuck, you're so big.* I take him deeper into my mouth, savoring every long inch until his cock hits the back of my throat, and I can't breathe. *I love it when you make me gag.*

Unholy-fucking-shit, Evie. Arousal floods my pussy as my demon growls so forcefully it vibrates all the way down to his cock and punctuates each of his words with a small thrust. *Let. Me. Fuck. You.*

I hum around him. *Not yet.*

My clit throbs, swelling and aching for friction. Why is this so hot? I hollow my cheeks and the answering thought trickles into being. Because I'm dominating him from my *fucking* knees. *This* is power.

His legs quiver, body shuddering as I take him as deep as I can until I'm gagging, his cock hardening further in my throat.

My lips tingle as I taste his pre-cum. So fucking good, like my personal nectar.

Even his inside voice is broken. *Your mouth feels fucking incredible.*

His exhale comes in short, stuttering bursts, hips arching in response as I pull back just as his erection twitches against my tongue with signs of his impending release.

Let me fuck you, Evie.

I bite my lip, the arousal dripping between my legs as his charcoal stare lands on my pout. *Beg for it.*

Lorcan snarls. *I told you, Witch; I don't beg.*

Fine. Then, you won't get to touch me.

My shadows tighten, like a full-body straight jacket until he's unable to move. A lick of satisfaction curves up the corners of my lips as his muscles strain and twitch against my shadows. My smile grows brighter, an orgasm is buildings just from watching him desperately trying to fuck the air. Pre-cum drips into bubbles and I swipe the drop before it can fall, then rub it all over my lips.

My stare fixates on him as he remains restrained to the wall and windowsill, his ass flexing. I stand slowly, bringing my lips to his and say through our bond, *See how good you taste.*

His lips meet mine with fervor, his short beard rough against my chin as we inhale each other. I gasp as his cock jabs between my bare thighs, and I back away enough so that only his dripping head can reach my clit.

"Dammit, let me touch you." He wrestles against a shadow, and it takes all of my energy for it not to snap against his strength.

My mouth parts as I fist his length and rub slow circles over my clit with the head of his cock. *And you call me a needy little slut?* I project a sultry moan down our bond, fueling it with my untamed desire. *How does it feel? Being forced to submit.*

His words take a few moments to form, before flittering into my brain. *I'm going to fucking ruin your cunt for this.*

Gods, I hope so.

What did I tell you before? I'm your god, Evie.

I bite my lip. *Then show me.*

My shadows tremble when I tear off my sweater, revealing my breasts and peaked nipples against the cold. His eyes close for a brief moment, his head hanging as he shakes the windowpanes with a primal growl.

"Fuuuuuccckkk!"

My heart rate skyrockets when he snaps one of my shadows as if it was my damned neck, but my others take over, and the blazing heat of my death magic seeps into them, burning his skin. Lorcan snarls, his abdominals flexing as his craving, no, his *need* for me sprints down our bond.

I glide back down his body, dragging my teeth over the skin. His cock twitches and I trace the outline of his ridges with feather light kisses until he's dripping all over my breasts. *Good, show me your pleasure, Lor.*

A flash of desire floods my clit as Lorcan moans gutturally. "Hellfire! Fuck! Evie."

He tries to lift his hips, but my shadows form a rope around him, keeping him in place. My demon roars, his elongated teeth winking in the moonlight as his jaw slackens and beads of sweat trickles between his pecs.

I slip my thumb across his taint, the gland throbbing under my touch, then circle the index and forefinger of my other hand around the top of his scrotum and pull hard enough that I feel the line between pleasure and pain blurring in slick, tightening skin. My lips graze his head, which pulses another mouthwatering drop of pre-cum. "Ungnhhhgh. Fuck, Little Witch!" My shadows stretch as he slams his cock between my lips, but I pull back, panting, just as his erection jerks hard.

"Aghhhh, godsdammit!" he yells, the sound hoarse and growly. Shit, I've tipped him over the edge, I worry, then blow out a breath as only a thick stream of pre-cum leaks all over his shaft. I drag my fingers to my clit, then push a finger inside my aching pussy until I hit my G-spot. "That was so fucking hot."

I bring my lips to his length and rock against my fingers, allowing the vibration of my moans to graze his sensitive skin. *Watch me pleasure myself to you.*

My other hand slides to my nipple. Holy... fuck. I pant, wishing my fingers were his teeth. I hear his sharp inhale and then...

Do. Not. Stop.

His voice pierces my skull, and I stop moving, rising to meet his eyes. My shadows prickle heat over his skin and sweat drips from his forehead. *I love seeing you disheveled like this. It's so fucking hot.*

Lorcan pants. "Let me taste you." I guide my finger to his lips. My demon sucks the digit into his mouth and swirls his tongue over my skin, eliciting a pleasure-soaked moan from my throat.

I spread my legs and drift my hands back down my stomach to my aching pussy. I slide my fingertips along my swollen vulva, slowly tracing circles around my clitoris until a fever consumes me, my orgasm drawing tighter like an invisible coil in my core, ready to snap at any moment—

Please, Evie.

I whimper, the need to come cresting unbearably behind my clit. "Oh, fuck." I crash to my knees as my legs give out and swallow down his cock, my throat muscles quivering around him. Drool leaks from the corners of my lips as I deep throat him and fuck my fingers feverishly into my pussy, unbearable pressure building as I taste his arousal.

I close my eyes and force my body to inhale. It's all too much. I'm so fucking close.

My inner walls spasm around my fingers as I come, ecstasy throwing stars across my closed eyelids.

My shadows dissolve just as my orgasm quells, and I pull back as another climax threatens to swallow my senses. But it's too late. Lorcan's free. He pulls me upright with trembling hands, claws tearing into my skin with his fervent movements.

I moan as I take in his gritted teeth. His black eyes dart to mine and a primal growl rips from his throat, the sound akin to a feral animal more than a demon. He roughly turns me away from him, throws me onto the windowsill, and presses a palm flat against my spine, driving my hipbones into the wood. My screams echo into the night as my arms and torso dangle out the open window and I stare down all three stories to the snow-covered ground. Fissures of pain thread through my back muscles as I struggle to hold myself up in this awkward position. If he drops me, I'll die. My throat closes and my arousal slips down my thighs on the heels of the thought.

His voice stings my mind. *You have no fucking idea what you do to me, making me beg like that.* The cold air wraps me like a blanket as pleasure-edged pain shoots through my ass cheek. He spanks me again and again until I'm red and raw. His racing heartbeats thrum in my ears as he devastates my pussy. *You swallow me so perfectly, My Witch.*

He places a hand under my lower stomach, lifting and angling me as he stretches me unlike every before. Pain washes with pleasure and he slams into me, forcing my breasts to bounce over the edge of the window. The icy gusts are welcome because I feel like I might die from the heat of us.

Tell me your mine, that every part of you belongs to me. His command comes out desperate, or dare I say, vulnerable. *Tell me.*

My heart flutters, my mind caught between unescapable lust and something else. *I'm yours, Lorcan. I always have been.*

He grasps my hair, those strands being all that remain between me and certain death. As if he can sense it, his shadows curls around my throat, the pressure increasing on my jugular.

The snow-powdered world fuzzes and falls to stars in my vision as he emits a deep roar, slapping his thighs against my ass cheeks and ropes of hot cum fill me until they're pouring out.

A scream tears from my throat, entangling with his as I fall into a deeper, longer orgasm the second time, my toes curling against the air.

CHAPTER SEVENTEEN

Lorcan

My eyes light with pleasure that morning as Evie walks out from a shadow cast by a long bookcase to my left. I'm so godsdamn proud of her for learning to shadow walk on her own.

"Nice of you to join us," I say, smoke curling around my masked face. I inhale another drag of my cigarette, leaning my back against the mahogany rolling ladder and keep my attention riveted to the arched ceiling. My eyes trace the painted black and purple swirls, enjoying the painted scenes of dark, depraved events in the Human Realm. Those were the best of times.

I turn to face her, holding out a cigarette in my palm like it's a peace offering. Her lips twitch as if she struggles to hold back a smile while I think back to last night.

I muffle a groan as she wraps her lips around the filter and waits for me to light it. Her lips part slightly as I observe her closely. I don't miss the subtle shift of her legs, her black jean clad thighs rubbing together. I step into her space, slipping my fingers into my pocket to snag my lighter. With a stroke of my thumb, the gas within wooshes upward and ignites into an orange flame.

I hold it suspended in the air between us for a moment, enjoying the scent of her sweet arousal permeating the air as I exhale slowly through my nose, then ignite the end of her cigarette and kiss her temple. She inhales deeply, and I watch the flame catching, transforming into a tantalizing glowing ember.

I skim my hand across her lower back as I move past her into the stacks, then tuck my hands into my pockets and stroll toward the plush seating area.

"About time, Brother," Ezra teases as he sits next to Gideon on the black leather couch he moved in here from the living room. I watch Ezra drool over Rosa as she walks to the fireplace and places her hand on her hip

Ezra grins, casually ignoring Gideon's heavy silence on the other cushion, before flicking his gaze behind me.

I turn my attention to Gideon. "Now, what to do with you?"

Gideon's serious expression sharpens as his gaze drifts from Aiden's to mine at a glacial pace. While I'm curious to know what the fuck that's about, I have no time to dissect it now.

"Obviously, we cannot leave you here," I add when he doesn't answer.

Ezra brings his index finger to his scrunched lips and taps them a few times. "I'd say we kill him, but I'm a selfish fuck and won't risk something happening to me because of our twin bond."

Gideon's eyes track to Ezra, cold fury mounting in his pale green depths.

Ezra scooches farther away from Gideon dramatically. "Woah. Calm down, War. I was just dicking with you."

Gideon returns his attention to Aiden and remains silent.

Evie points to Gideon's bound wrists. "What if I bind myself to him? He wouldn't be able to flee, and I can keep track of him at all times."

I bite back a laugh as Gideon's claws lengthen and cut into his hands as he clenches his fists, knuckles whitening. The fuzzy pink padding shifts and the cuffs dig into Gideon's straining wrists.

"Absolutely not," Rosa and I say together.

I arch a brow at Evie's friend, and she mimics my movement.

Rosa hisses vehemently. "Evie, you cannot bind yourself to another demon!"

Evie's lips curl around her cigarette, the corners tipping up, and my cock twitches. Damn. I miss those lips. They would look better wrapped around my cock instead. "I said bind, not bond," Evie responds. "I'll tether myself to the handcuffs, which Gideon is already bound to, not to the man himself."

203

Gideon's eyes widen the slightest bit, then he quickly masks his expression. That rare display of emotion tells me everything I need to know. My witch managed to surprise the King of War. I smirk and shake my head.

My clever girl, I say into her mind and her cheeks flush pink.

"Sounds perfect to me," Ezra agrees, his words ending in a groan as he stretches his arms over his head.

"Agreed," Rosa says croakily. I narrow my eyes on Rosa as she stares at the exposed skin where my brother's t-shirt rides up, then licks her lips before quickly looking away.

"And how do you know a spell to accomplish that?" I snap, instantly regretting the bite to my words as the determined expression flees from her bright eyes.

My intentions tighten painfully.

I never intend to cut her like that, but the anger often controls my tongue.

"In your library," she answers.

"I see," I state flatly and fold my arms across my chest.

I look around and realize everyone in this room has their eyes on someone, whether it's an intention to kill them or fuck them.

I soften my gaze and stroke her tattooed arm with a shadow, the dark smokey magic twisting into shapes to match her rose and skull tattoos.

She glances at me, then quickly walks away. Yep. My words, or tone, hurt her. She walks over to Rosa. Her best friend wraps an arm around her shoulders, then plucks the finished cigarette from Evie's fingers and tosses it into the fireplace.

Evie continues, her eyes focused on me. "When I discovered the grimoires months ago, I noticed another dark book of magic, but I forgot about until now since I was so desperate to find the grimoires."

"Show me, Little Witch." I trail my gaze after Evie's departing form. She quickly returns moments later with a plain leather-bound book, crisscross stitching binding the book and forming the spine.

Evie cracks open the book and places it on the coffee table, flicking through the pages quickly until she finds one marked with a scrap of paper. "Here."

Rosa peers over her shoulder. "What can I do to help?"

"Not much, actually," Evie replies. "I only need cinnamon, a dried basil leaf, and blood."

"Okay, I'll go see if I can find them in the kitchen."

Evie glances at Rosa and a smile unfurls across her face. "Thank you," she calls as Rosa leaves the room.

Every muscle in my body tenses as I linger on the last ingredient. "Whose blood?"

"Mine and Gideon's," Evie replies without looking at me.

Gideon's nostrils flare when he finally speaks, hushing the room into silence. "So, my choices are imprisonment or allowing you to leash me further like your little pet demon?"

"Fuck me, he does speak," I say. "But yes, those are your choices."

Gideon's face remains passive, but his eyes frost and I swear I catch a glimpse of chilly lilac flames rising in his irises. The middle finger on his right hand taps an even beat on his thigh.

I chuckle darkly, then nod curtly at his hand. "You must be really bothered by all of this. I see you've not learned to control that little tell yet. You've been struggling to master it since what, adolescence?"

Ezra nods. "At least that long. In fact," Ezra says and glances at me, "I think it's gotten worse."

Gideon inhales and exhales at a pace that is far too measured to be natural, holding his silence.

"Well? What'll it be, Gid?" I ask.

He stares at me stonily. "I decline your offer."

"It wasn't a request," I spit. "Oh, how could I have forgotten. You do have another choice. Allow my witch to bind you, or we lock you in the Shadow Realm for eternity."

The muscles in his jaw feathers. "You'd imprison me in the Shadow Realm after the hell you suffered there?"

"Absolutely."

He growls. "Why?"

"Because I'll do everything in my fucking power to keep Evie safe. If that requires me to banish my entire family to that damn realm, I'll do so without a second thought," I state. "Besides, why do you think I had Evangeline create the Shadow Realm?"

Gideon blinks and a curious expression flits across his face before I can analyze it. "I see." He sits forward and rests his bound wrists on his thighs.

Ezra claps his hands together, turning the topic back on our preparations. "So, who is carrying the humans? It's not like they can shadow walk on their own."

"No shit, asshole." I pause, then sigh. "Any suggestions? "

"I call dibs on Rosa," Ezra quickly demands, dragging the attention back to him as usual.

"Why?" Evie asks before Rosa can come back and hear this. She's probably wondering if her friend is in danger, which she likely is if Ezra desires her.

Ezra lifts his heavy shoulders in a shrug. "What? She smells nice." He looks around the room, stopping briefly on all our unimpressed faces. "Annnyway, Gid can go by himself. You and Aiden should go together, and Evie can bring herself," Ezra suggests.

"No."

Ezra and I swing our faces to Gideon.

"No," he repeats firmly, then stands. Ice glitters across his knuckles.

"Care to explain?" I ask, my patience wearing thin.

"I will only go on to two conditions," Gideon expresses.

Ezra snorts. "Which are?"

"One, I take Aiden through the In-Between."

Rejecting his request is too easy. "Shit, I completely forgot," I drawl. "I don't cater to the whims of my younger brothers."

"Anymore," Ezra scoffs.

An image of the cage slices across my mind's eye and my throat constricts. I shake my head, scattering the thoughts and twist to the doorway as Rosa crosses the threshold into the library. "I got the cinnamon and basil," Rosa announces. "I brought a bowl too."

"Perfect." Evie accepts the supplies and places them on the top of the bar beneath the concealed stereo system along with the spellbook. A beat of awkward silence reigns before I return my focus to Gideon with a raised brow.

"Two, you allow me to retrieve and carry my sword," Gideon continues, dismissing Ezra and my opinions entirely.

Rosa snorts and rolls her eyes. "Yes, because that sounds like a great idea. Let's arm the enemy demon with a sword while we take him on a grand adventure."

Ezra cloaks himself, reappearing behind Rosa, then whispers close to her ear., "Fuck. I wanna lick your mind, Sugar."

Rosa shivers, gasps, and recoils. "What the hell does that even mean?"

"Wouldn't you like to find out," Ezra teases then trips over his own feet as Gideon yanks him backward by his elbow.

"I may be your captive, Wrath, but I won't stand by and allow you to continually pester the woman. She obviously abhors your attentions."

Ezra jerks his arm away from Gideon. "Fuck off. That's none of your business."

Rosa turns a brilliant smile on the twins. "Thank you, Gideon," she says, her words sickly sweet.

I laugh. Ezra's upper lip pulls back from his teeth and his skin ripples like it's begging to shift into something horrific.

When Rosa turns, her attentions shifting onto Gomez, Ezra twists and whispers, "Watch it. Twin or not, I'll fucking gut you Gideon."

Gideon snorts. "You could try."

Ezra squares his chest. "I already beat you once, remember? Or did you forget as you bled out in the living room?"

Gideon's stare hardens. "You won because I allowed you to win. How have you not put two and two together when I literally told the lot of you that I *wanted* you to catch me?"

Ezra crosses his arms over his chest and nods, then lowers his gaze to the ground. "Yeah, you know what? Excuse the shit out of me. You *did* mention that. But I don't recall you explaining the reason behind it."

Gideon's lips twitch like he's holding back a smug smile but says nothing. A growl emanates from Ezra and I sidestep closer to Evie. I cannot stand the two of them together.

"For fuck's sake, enough," I command, intoning every word with my growl. I walk forward and shove them both in their chests. "If you two cannot at least tolerate one another, stay away from each other. Have you learned nothing in the centuries you've been alive?"

Gideon swallows, then walks to the other side of the room, his middle finger tapping against the side of his leg. Gideon is a master at disguising his emotions behind a serious, yet bored and indifferent expression. He's skilled, but I'm better. I spent countless hours analyzing my brothers' faces, marking their ticks and micro expressions in my long-term memory. These small, seemingly innocuous habits betrayed them, informing me exactly when they intended to strike, or when I would have the opportunity to do the same to them. Gideon's gaze is cold and hard, but the barely visible narrowing at the inner corners or his eyes tells me Ezra's comment about killing him broke something deep within him. Ezra always said idiotic, sometimes cruel shit, but he's never gone as far as this before.

Perhaps the looming threat of The Order and my brothers coil the tension within him to his breaking point, like a needle continuously pricking his awareness and fight or flight instincts. The same worries plague my thoughts as well, but I'll never speak the words aloud. Unfortunately, something within me urges to soothe their tension and anxiety, as if an instinct as the eldest sibling grows like a weed. I fucking hate them all. I don't need any of them. All I need is Evie. She's my family now.

"Fine. If it means that damn much to you, you can shadow walk Aiden to Hellam and keep the sword on your person. But, if anything happens to him, or anyone else in this group, I hold you directly responsible," I growl.

"You really do like me," Aiden whispers towards me, the awe in his voice audible to the group.

I cringe but don't acknowledge his comment. He's right. The fucker has somehow grown on me like a godsdamn mouth sore. The skin so raw and inflamed that one cannot help but chew on the spot, spreading the infection.

"Noted," Gideon acknowledges.

"Gideon, your wrists?" Evie asks and Gideon complies without complaint. Interesting. Evie accepts a tiny silver key from Rosa, then utilizes it to unlock and remove the fuzzy pink handcuffs. "Lorcan, break the chain off both cuffs."

"Gladly," I purr, then snap the thin link of chain where it's connected at the two ends and bring my darkening gaze to meet Evie's. She sinks her teeth into her lower lip, then shakes her head as if she wishes to clear it and faces the bar once more. Although the handcuffs broke easily between my hands, Gideon, despite his immeasurable power from his royal demon blood, could not remove them with the secure binding spell counteracting them.

"All of you back up. Give my witch room to work," I order, pushing a wall of shadows against Ezra, Rosa, and Aiden's shins, then nod at Evie. Her chest rises as she inhales deeply, her pulse fluttering rapidly at her neck and in my ears. My arm lifts toward Evie, the desire to curl around her back while she works chipping away at me. I snatch my hand back, clenching it into a fist.

"Shit, I forgot a knife," Evie says and looks over at me.

"Not a problem, Baby Girl," I purr, but it quickly transitions into a growl as Gideon's claws lengthen as he holds his hand over the bowl.

"My claw will work just fine," Gideon suggests, then slashes into his outstretched palm. Denim blue blood wells along the deep cut, gushing down his skin and into the bowl as Gideon offers Evie his bloodied claw. Fuck no.

A shadow snatches my brother's proffered hand, twisting it sharply until a crack fills the silence. "No one makes my little witch bleed but me," I growl darkly, the words almost obscured by my threatening rumble.

"Jesus fuck, Lor!" Ezra exclaims. "Ease up."

I watch Gideon through narrow slits and bare my teeth as he hisses and clenches his teeth. "It's okay, Ez," Gideon reassures through gritted teeth, then smirks. Searing heat bites into my shadows, a muted lavender glow spreading beneath them.

"What the fuck," I growl and recall my shadows as agony peaks where my shadows touch Gideon's Hell fire.

"Keep your shadows to yourself," Gideon growls, his expression quickly shifting into a feral visage.

"As long as you stay the fuck away from my witch."

Gideon's intense expression clears and his blank, serious one ripples into place like water smoothing over a river rock. "Are you two done?" Evie asks.

"Yes," we both reply and a headache blossoms to life over my left eye. I step up to Evie's back, then reach around her and gently take her hand in mine. I extend the claw on my other index finger.

"Is this okay?" The back of Evie's head rubs against my pecs as she nods. My shoulders tense as I quickly and efficiently cut into her palm, just deep enough to extract the blood she needs for the spell. Retracting my claw, I slide my it up her torso, across the length of her sternum, and halt with my fingers around the column of her throat. Evie's arousal sweetens the air as I use the hold on her neck to draw her back into an embrace, then whisper, "Good fucking girl." A shudder works its way from her toes to the crown of her head as I draw my arms to my sides and back away.

Evie swallows thickly, then squeezes her bleeding hand over the bowl. I watch each drop intently as it drips in a thick stream to join Gideon's. Her brows tip inward with concentration, then she glances at the page with the ritual instructions. My thumb tingles with the need to smooth out the little V forming between her brows. Damn, she's cute. Gideon plucks the cuffs from the table, purple flames igniting the pink fuzz in a cloud of noxious smoke.

My shadows rise around my brother, poised to strike if he's so much as breathes negatively in my witch's direction.

Gideon chuckles, rolling his shoulders back and focuses on the cuffs. Frost crawls along the metal of each, and for a moment nothing happens. Metal shrieks and grinds as each handcuff splits in half along the circumference. The severed metal bits thump to the table and a smile tips the corners of Gideon's lips as he holds them out for Evie.

"Um. Thank you."

"Don't thank me. I simply wished to remove that hideous pink fuzz," Gideon explains and gestures for Evie to continue.

Evie blinks rapidly a few times before narrowing her eyes on the blood. Her husky voice floats over my skin as she chants the words of the spell under her breath, shadows spilling from her chest. Taking the modified handcuff bands, she dips them into the bowl of thick dark purple blood. Evie continues to chant as she sprinkles the herb mixture onto the waiting bracelets that drip steadily over the bowl with her shadows. Thick white smoke rises from the surface of the bracelets and clouds around them. My witch's shadows split, one carrying a metal band to Evie and the other to Gideon. He holds up his wrist without comment, letting her shadow glide the band over his tattooed, scarred hand and secure it to his wrist. The band shrinks, fitting to his wrist snuggly.

A thin shadow glides around the circumference of the metal, then rushes to Evie's, repeating the process. Evie lowers her wrist, rolls back her shoulders, and straightens her spine. "It's done," she exhales.

"Thank fuck. That was intense," Ezra says.

"I know, bro," Aiden agrees, and walks over to Ezra, knocking his elbow into his. "Cool as Hell to watch, but I've never been into the spooky stuff."

"Ironic, considering you sold your soul to a demon," I interject.

"Don't worry, Aiden," Ezra says, then flops his arm around his shoulder. "We're besties now, remember? I'll keep you safe." An oomph rushes past Ezra's lips as Gideon's palm connects with his sternum.

Ezra stumbles back a step, his arm falling from Aiden. "What the fuck was that for?" he growls.

"Don't. Touch. Him." He enunciates each word crisply.

"Fuck off, Gid," Ezra huffs, moves to crouch by Rosa. "Hop on."

"Excuse me?" Rosa asks skeptically.

"Climb on my back, Sugar. I know you're eager to explore the shadows with me," Ezra says and bounces his eyebrows.

A sigh pushes past Rosa's lips, then her arms and legs coil around my brother. "Let's go."

Ezra laughs as Rosa squeals and tunnels her fingers into his hair to keep her seat as Ezra bounds into the shadow juxtaposed to the fireplace.

"Rosa!" Evie calls.

"I'm not gonna drop her, Evie," Ezra replies with laughter in his voice from the entrance of the In-Between.

I raise my brow, then clear my throat. "Evie and Fluffy Fucker are with me," I remind Gideon. "Follow your bond with Ezra."

Gideon ignores me and stalks into a shadow near the door without another word. I tilt my head to the side. *Is he attempting to run?* I ask Evie through our bond.

Her lips purse and her brown eyes glass over as if all her concentration has turned inward. *No. He's still somewhere on the property.* Evie pauses, then tucks her hair behind her ear. *Actually, he'll come back through that same shadow in a couple seconds.* Gideon returns precisely two seconds later, just as Evie predicted.

Impressive. At least we know the ritual worked.

I raise my brow, then clear my throat. "Evie and Fluffy Fucker are with me," I remind Gideon. "Follow your bond with Ezra."

Gideon settles his great sword's sheath strap over his chest, strides purposely toward Aiden, and pulls the top half of his blue-black hair into twin war braids. My brow quirks as my brother plucks Aiden from the ground and secures him against his chest in a bridal carry. Aiden yelps and covers his mouth with a hand, a deep rosy flush creeping up his throat to his cheeks and ears. Gideon adjusts Aiden's fucking hat, then disappears into the In-Between.

CHAPTER EIGHTEEN

Evie

My eyes fluttered close as we enter the In-Between and the noisy world falls into silence. The experience is akin to taking a benzo. Gomez's wings close around my forearm as I hold him to my chest, and a sense of calm washes over us both.

Perhaps it's knowing what's coming but being here is like standing in the eye of storm. I peel back my eyelids to reveal shadows dancing in illusory spirals around us, the mist and fog clouding everything in this aimless plane.

Lorcan struts to my side, his hands shoved deep in his pockets. I hear a pop when he rolls his shoulders, pressing a thumb against the muscle in his neck. We both needed this quiet, it seems.

His voice comes between a whisper and his normal, deep tone. "This plan of yours is good."

My eyes widen as his approval gleams through our bond. Speaking of... "You said the bond we have is more of an imprint. You never told me that before."

"I did and it is." His hand squeezes my shoulder as I step forward. "Let's take our time getting there."

"The others are at least four shadows ahead of us," I say as Gomez climbs up my chest and onto my shoulder.

Lorcan shrugs. "I know. I want to talk."

My brows raise. "The King of Demons wants to just *talk*?"

The corner of his lip tilts. My eyes track his large, tattooed hand as he runs it through his disheveled, raven locks. "I'm just as surprised as you, Baby Girl."

My stomach dips on hearing my nickname. While I love Little Witch, this one is far more intimate and makes my heart flutter. With the absence of arousal, I realize my feelings are stronger than I knew. "The bond," I say as we amble slowly through the In-Between. "You were saying that it's an imprint."

He wets his thick lips with his tongue. "I'd only ever heard of it in Hell," he admits, his eyes flitting everywhere but on me. "How when a demon feels certain things for a human—or witch—it's possible for a bond to form, like a mating bond."

I exhale shakily, and Gomez purrs in my ear as if he can sense the swell of my heart. "So you feel certain things?"

The muscles in his arms tense, straining the sleeves of his shirt. "Yes."

"Except, you cannot love," I add, wishing I didn't sound, or *feel*, all doe-eyed and desperate.

"Supposedly I can't." He lifts a hand to his chest, placing it over his heart. He doesn't elaborate but instead shifts the topic to one that halts me in my tracks.

"What happened at The Order, when you were tortured?" He turns to face me, and tucks a lock of hair behind my ear, gently brushing Gomez's fur as he does. "We never properly discussed it, but your magic is more powerful than ever now."

"You saw what happened." I lower my stare to our shoes. "In that compact mirror."

His thumb tucks under my chin, with a gentle nudge, he lifts my gaze back to meet his. "All I saw was a result of what he did and I'm proud of you for it. You know I don't care about murder."

"I do," I admit, my eye twitching as memories flood back from before our time in the Shadow Realm. "I mean, not about Edward, because I know I did the world a favor. But I can't help but think about all the people that have died because of me. Like, some had it coming but others didn't." I pause, recalling the neighborhoods kids that died because I had let them into our home. But I'm not ready to talk about that, so I mention another that I haven't properly addressed. "Like Jay," I bite out. "He was an asshole, but most people are and that doesn't mean he deserved to die, not over me. I was using him."

"Let go of that guilt," Lorcan orders, and runs a thumb down my cheek. I lean into his touch as he whispers. "It's not yours to carry."

"Wait, are you saying *you* feel *guilty*?" I ask, blinking twice.

He grimaces. "No, I don't." Reaching up, he drags his thumb over my bottom lip. "Don't do that."

"What?"

"Expecting me to be human just because I happen to care about you. I don't give a damn who dies, as long as it's not you."

"That's…"

What is it? Disappointing? *Romantic?*

My heart balloons when I look at my demon. At least he isn't pretending to be anything other than what he is.

Gomez wings flap unexpectedly, sending a whoosh of air into my ear and Lorcan laughs.

"Calm down, Fluffy Fucker," Lorcan states and Gomez hisses in response. "You're a part of my witch."

I pat Gomez on the back. "That's about as close as he'll come to admitting he cares about you too."

Lorcan tsks under his breath. "Don't think I didn't notice you shift the conversation away from the torture. What is really bothering you and don't pretend it's about your old fuckboy." Our bond ripples as his intrusive gaze bores into mine, plunging into the depths of my dark soul.

We continue to amble at a snail's pace, shifting from one shadow to another, moving through a monochrome kaleidoscope. "Edward, my father, he, well, I can't remember everything but when I came around, his… cock was on my stomach. It's not the first time it happened." The rest of my words evade me as a rage simmers through me, piping hot and ready to explode. My father might be dead, but I want nothing more than to kill him all over again. "Do you think he's in Hell?"

His fingers ball into fists. "I fucking hope so!"

"It's not just him either," I choke out. "Samuel showed me who I really am. I killed people because I wanted to. I used to think I was born evil, but he made me remember things in my childhood that I'd forgotten."

"Evie." He grabs my shoulders, feet planted apart, grounding me. "*I'm* evil. You are *not* close to that. Look… " He huffs and glances up with a growl. "God gives humans all these insane fucking emotions then expects you all to do no bad with them. Give me a fucking break. It's why he cast my father out. Lucifer questioned shit and you can't do that there." His pupils swallow his irises, his nostrils flaring as he stares at me. "My brothers are complete dicks, but my uncles are worse."

Uncles?

At times I forget how biblical all of this is. Lorcan is the son of Lucifer, a literal fallen angel and his uncles are freaking angels in what, Heaven?

Wait, so then his grandfather is God?

I press my fingers into my temples and puff out a breath as my lens widens and the bigger picture sinks in. I can't wait to discuss this with Rosa because it'd sound insane to anyone else who isn't in this situation with us.

"Are you okay, Little Witch?" Lorcan asks and I nod slowly.

"Yeah, it's all just really sinking in. So," I add as curiosity takes over the pain in my chest, "who is your mother? In the abstract I guess I know you have one, but it's sounds so strange to say"

He chuckles. "Her name was Lilith."

"As in Lilith from the bible?"

Of course it is. Who else could it be.

"Mmhmm," he says and whistles a breath as if all of this isn't mind-blowing. Which, to him it isn't, I suppose. "I didn't know her well. My father destroyed her eons ago when she tried eating us."

My jaw slacks. "She tried to what?"

"Eat us," he says with a shrug. "I guess she wasn't particularly maternal."

I suppress a laugh, but he sends a comforting tug down our bond, telling me it really doesn't bother him.

A tree passes through our next step into a shadow. Pain radiates in my forehead as Gomez pulls on my hair, clinging to me for dear life. I pat him on the side. "Your father has really had bad luck with women."

Lorcan stops, pauses, brows furrowed, then laughs that boyish laugh I rarely get to see. "Yeah, he hasn't. It's why it'll be hard to convince him about Evangeline's motives. I'll need to find a way to show him."

"I hadn't thought about that."

He ushers us along. "I haven't stopped thinking about it, but we need to focus on getting to Hell first. We should be arriving soon."

I shake my head, scattering my thoughts. "Are you nervous to return to Hell?"

I notice the subtle shift to his breath and the crease forming over his left brow. "No."

Tenderly, I speak through our bond, *It's okay if you are. I am.*

I think about Edward and how he's probably in Hell along with other people I've killed and realize I'm not the only one with metaphorical demons I need to face while there.

Just stay close to me? he asks in a moment of vulnerability.

By the time we arrive at the dense wooded area, my brain feels like a sponge that's been wrung dry. I glance up as the sky darkens from a deep indigo into an inky black, and silvers dots pinprick the rich night sky.

The group comes into view. Rosa taps her fingers against her hip, shaking her head when she sees us walk up the dirt road between the trees. "Take your time? It's not like we're on a schedule or anything."

Ezra side-eyes Rosa then smirks. "They were probably fucking again. At least this time we didn't have to listen to it."

My eyes bulge. *They heard us last night.*

Good. Now they all know you're mine, Lorcan responds, and I realize I unwittingly pushed my thoughts into our bond.

They're your brothers, I admonish. *You don't need to prove anything.*

It wasn't too long ago that Ezra had his hands around your throat in the Shadow Realm, he reminds me and my cheeks flush with heat.

My arousal was not my fault. I despised him at the time, but you know, I like being strangled a little and…

Lorcan's fingers flex at his side. *Don't make me mark you again, Little Witch.*

My neck flushes this time, and a bloom of desire veins through my chest all the way down to between my legs.

Ezra tsks and Aiden sighs from behind them, with Gideon standing a few feet away. "We're not doing this again," he says, wagging a finger at us both. "We can't hear you when you talk through your bond, so all we see is some broody and pouty looks with longing glances between long bouts of silence. It's crazy awkward."

"Say that again," Lorcan threatens.

Rosa hisses a breath between her teeth. "Why don't we just get going. Before *some* of us overreact."

She glances at Lorcan who's giving Ezra a murderous look and I quickly realize they're now talking through their demon brother bond. And you know what? Ezra was right, it's awkward. "Yes," I agree. "Let's go."

"Agreed. Let's stop playing with each other." Gideon's words cut through us like a blade. His words holds more gravitas than all of ours combined.

Ezra huffs and crosses his arm in mock sadness. "But why must we stop, Gid, when you're so much fun to be around?"

Gideon rolls his eyes and holds up a flashlight for Aiden. Rosa plucks out her phone and uses it to illuminate out surroundings.

Ezra bounces on his heels, his hands shoved in his jean pockets. "Alrighty then, lead the way, Witch." He nods his head in my direction, and I look around, trying to familiarize myself with the map I'd studied at the house.

"The first gate should be right off the road up here. It's visible any time of day."

"What and the others aren't?" asks Aiden. "Why are there even gates to Hell here of all places?"

The group look at me, although I am certain the demon brothers know the true reason. "The legend says there was an asylum that burned down here with the patients inside who tried to run," I explain to Aiden and Rosa, after having read through the human's urban legends on the gateways, versus the history as written by witches. "The locals believed the gates were built to stop those patients from escaping, and another legend tells of a doctor who built them to keep trespassers out, but neither story is true."

Aiden glances into the darkness between the tree line and shudders. "Great, your version is going to be so much creepier, isn't it?"

Lorcan grins from ear to ear as Aiden backs away, closer to the edge of the dirt road strewn with vines and leaves. "It's so much more terrifying. If you knew what was truly in this woods, you wouldn't be moving so close to the tree line."

Ezra, cloaked with shadows, appears behind Aiden and yells "Boo," into his ear, sending Aiden wailing with his hands in the air.

I slap my hand over my mouth, snort-laughing behind my palm while Ezra and Rosa's hands are on their knees as they belly laugh. The only one not impressed by Ezra's stunt is Gideon, who swiftly strides next to Aiden, taking a protective stance that Aiden seems to lean into.

Do I detect something there? Gideon bridal carrying him was one thing, but now it seems Aiden reciprocates. Well, fuck. It seems we all might end up with a demon brother, although I am determined to keep Rosa from Ezra. Mostly because I don't quite trust his intentions and she deserves so much better that a demon who can't feel love.

Aiden places his hand over his heaving chest and groans. "Fuck the pair of you."

"I'm good," Lorcan replies.

Ezra chuckles and says, "Me too, although I'm sure Gid will take you up on that offer."

Aiden's cheeks turn tomato red. "That's not what I meant," he says but checks to see Gideon's response, who has gone so still he could almost pass as a statue.

Lorcan pulls his pack of cigarettes out and pushes one between my lips. His zippo lighter flickers blue as he flicks the lint a few times until it flames orange. I inhale deeply, closing my eyes as I bring the smoke to my mouth, hold it there for a couple of seconds before dragging it deep into my lungs.

Mmm.

My shoulders relax and I look at the group, Rosa in particular, who's tapping her nail over her bottom lip. "Are you going to tell us what happened? Don't tell me I have to hear it from him?" She points at Lorcan.

"No," I reply, exhaling a puff of smoke. "The so-called asylum runes here is actually an old mill. But the violent energy many feel here is real. What most don't know is that just a little past the ruins of the old mill is the birthplace of my great aunt Evangaline, before she moved to my hometown. This is the original place where the Fallenmoore Coven originated and it's also where they practiced a lot of dark magic. She's the reason these gateways exist."

Lorcan scrunches his lips. "Unfortunately, she's right. Evangeline wanted a link to the human world so she could come back after her death and *visit*."

Aiden pulls on the strings of his hoodie. "That's not that bad. You made it sound like something really creepy happened here."

"It did," I bite out. "My ancestors loved practicing sacrificial magic, meaning a lot of men, like yourself, were strung up in these woods and slaughtered."

His eyes widen twice their size, the moonlight making the blue in them even more potent. "You scare me sometimes."

I smirk. "Good."

Rosa rolls her eyes. "She's not as frightening as she thinks she is." Her hand disappears into her bag, surfacing with a fistful of granola and feeds it to Gomez who grabs it in his tiny claws, from on top my shoulder. "We should go before the ghosts of all those men start haunting us."

The group moves in tandem, and Aiden whispers to Rosa, "Do you *have* to say that?"

Lorcan presses his lips into a tight line and speaks into my mind, *He's really not going to do well once we're in Hell.*

CHAPTER NINETEEN

Evie

Remnants of dark rituals litter the open spaces. Half-burned black and purple candles, salt wrappers, and scorched rope lay captured under a scrawl of vines, as if the woods claimed the items for itself.

We must be close.

I place a hand on Gomez's back, keeping him in place on my shoulder as he naps. At least he's warm against the side of my neck.

Rosa's voice sounds from ahead, her phone light, along with Aiden's, guiding us through the woods. "Does anyone else feel like we're being followed?"

I glance behind me as a rustle of leaves sweeps the twig-strewn ground. A shiver skittles down my spine when I turn my head and spot a ghostly figure flicker in and out of the darkness, entrenched by shadows. "Yes. We must be close."

She cocks a hip, then continues walking ahead. "Try saying that again without smiling."

Lorcan's voice penetrates my mind. *Scared, Little Witch?*

A little, I admit and keep walking.

Thought so. A growl reverberates in his chest, earning him a glance from Ezra. *I can smell your arousal from here.*

Jealous? I tease, and he yanks his fist into his hair.

The only thing you should fear in these woods is me.

I drag my tongue over my lips, my chest heaving. *Perhaps you've lost your touch.*

Wait until we're in Hell. He bites out as he matches my pace. *I'll remind you how terrifying I can be.*

My thighs clench as we walk, warmth pooling in the pit of my stomach. I hope he fucking does. Lorcan lets me play out my darker fantasies in a safe-ish way. While it's unpredictable with him, it's totally different from when I was being tortured at The Order.

His fingers flex at his side as if he's contemplating the last time we were in the woods together, and I'm reminded what he used those hands for.

Rosa huffs, snapping me out of my thoughts, her voice tinkering as she whispers to Ezra, "They're doing it again."

"Why focus on them?" Ezra asks. "I am far more entertaining."

I can hear Rosa's eye roll from here and suppress a smirk.

"Is that it?" Aiden whispers, as if we might awaken the spirits haunting these narrow trees. "It's a rusted old thing."

Ezra strides to the brown-orange metal gate, half buried behind tall grass, the bars strangled with ivy. "Oh, this is it. Feels like home."

Aiden grimaces. "So, if we go through that…"

"You won't be dragged to Hell. Yet," Gideon says before Lorcan or Ezra gets the chance to scare Aiden. "We need to go through all seven first."

Aiden shudders. "Dragged?"

Ezra nods. "How else did you think we'd get there?"

"I don't know," he says, shining his phone's flashlight around. "I thought there'd be a portal or something."

"It makes sense," I chime in. "A portal would be the most likely scenario for someone not well-versed in this. We used one to get to the Shadow Realm."

Lorcan walks ahead of me, his focus on Aiden, twigs snapping under his heavy boots as he reaches him. "Yes, but this is Hell and there are few ways in. None of them are portals."

"Mhmm," Ezra says, his foot bouncing against the ground. "The ground opens up and swallows you whole. Or so I've heard."

"Heard?" Rosa and I question in tandem.

Ezra lifts his arms in an elaborate shrug. "What? I've never been to Hell via a gateway before."

Rosa lifts her brows in mock horror. "How do you normally get there?"

Lorcan walks through the gate first, then looks back at us, answering in place of Ezra. "We walk through dimensions, but that's not an option this time, else we would land directly into Lucifer's Court, and they'd know we were coming. We need the element of surprise. Besides…" His intense gaze finds me. "This is the only way mortals can get there. Well, this or dying."

"Lucifer's Court?" I repeat, imagining a weird underground hell castle upon a moat of lava.

Ezra nods and follows Lorcan through the gate. "Yeah. It's a big castle filled with spirits and demons and balls. It takes up most of Hell."

"Balls?" I grimace, unable to even imagine the balls that would be held in Hell.

"Oh yeah," Ezra replies.

Lorcan's statements shoots through our bond. *They're horrifying. You will love it, Little Witch.*

The light dwindles from Aiden's phone, and he bashes it against the side of his hand. "Batteries dead."

Rosa's phone flashlight fades, too, along with Gideon's flashlight, plunging us into darkness only remedied by a silver of the moon. "Mine too."

The atmosphere shifts. An icy chill shrouds us, the scent of sulfur permeating the usual smell of decayed leaves and damp earth. Within the tree line, a translucent woman flickers, ambling through thickets of leaves, as if she's searching for something.

Beyond her, a second woman leans over a makeshift pentagram of twigs, muttering spells. None of them seem to notice us.

"Oh my fuck," Rosa exclaims when she spots them.

"They're just ghosts," I say with a flick of my hand. "They'll draw from our energy, but they're not sentient like spirits."

Aiden's eyes are twice as wide. "Sentient? Like they don't have feelings?" His shoulders droop. "Great! Psychopath ghosts are even worse."

Lorcan sighs. "That's sentiment, you idiot. She means the ghosts are not aware. They're just imprints of time left on this earth."

"Oh." Aiden falls silent and Gideon shoots Lorcan a glare filled with promise and threat.

Gomez stirs from his sleep as I walk through the first gateway, his claws digging into my shoulder. "It's okay Gomey."

His noses twitches as he curls his head around to get a better look at me, his round eyes somehow appearing bigger than normal. Once satisfied that everything is okay, he nuzzles back into my neck.

Once we're all through the rusted, iron gate, Gideon takes the lead with Aiden in tow. If my research is correct, the second gateway should reveal itself to us soon.

"Fuck," Ezra whispers, slowing his pace to match mine, and by default, Lorcan's. "We're going to have to go through the trials."

Lorcan blows out a long exhale. "I forgot about those. But I'm sure we'll get through them quickly."

I flick my gaze to Lorcan, admiring how the blue-ish hue to his hair is even more prominent under the moonlight.

"*You* will," Rosa points out. "Because you, Ezra, and Gideon are princes of Hell. What about us mortals?"

Ezra takes the opportunity to lean closer. "Awe, Sugar, I'll take care of you."

She leans in the opposite direction. "As much as it pains me to admit it, I may need you too."

Silence envelops us as we delve deeper into the woods, the spray of pale moonlight casting shadows from the branches onto the well-beaten dirt path.

We tread carefully over the mossy mattress below. I grab Lorcan's biceps when my feet slide over a slick rock. Gomez's claws dig into my shoulder as we weave our way through the labyrinth of twisted trunks, then past a circle of stones.

Heat sizzles in my fingertips, warming them against the icy gusts. My death magic hums the closer we venture, my skin prickling with electricity. "We're close," I exclaim.

Every log, twig and blade of grass is etched with the magic of my coven, of my family. It calls to me, the whistles of the wind echoing their chants.

The trees narrow, along with the path through them, and we venture off the beaten track.

"Agh!" Rosa jumps back a foot as a snake slithers across our path, its obsidian scales shimmering under the moonlight.

I watch the creature disappear into the underbrush. "It's more scared of you, than you are of it," I say as she hugs her arms around her, slowly backing away into the tree line where I'm certain more of them are.

She shakes her head. "I highly doubt that."

Ezra pats her on the back. "It's not venomous, sweetness."

"Is that supposed to make me feel better?" she asks.

Aiden rushes to Rosa's side. "I'm with Rosa. I hate snakes. I can't believe I'm saying this," he adds, rubbing his palms up and down his arms, "but how long until we reach the final gateway?"

Lorcan's dark chuckle sounds in my mind, his words searing through our bond. *Does he think Hell is going to be any better?*

Give him a break. I bite back. *We're all tired. He doesn't need you adding to his misery.*

Why not? Lorcan flashes me a white, wide grin in the darkness. *The crueler I am to him, the less he'll think about the real dangers surrounding him.*

My brows flick up in surprise. *So you're doing him a kindness? You?*

I catch the angle of his smirk before he turns his head to look ahead. *Sure. I mean, I'd do it regardless. I do enjoy being the source of his terror.*

How bad are these trials going to be? I ask as I watch Gideon place a good three feet between him and Ezra, who falls back to walk with Rosa and Aiden.

They're intended to test new souls who are sent to the underworld. Except, we're arriving in our mortal forms. Well, you are, he explains, then continues in a somber tone through our bond. *Humans are usually dead when they arrive—with just their souls. The spirits are ferried across the river by Asher before entering the trials from the beginning. Evangeline's gateways to hell will likely drop us in the middle of some trial, so it's likely we won't have to go through as many. I doubt she'd want to wade through hundreds just to make her way to the Human Realm.*

A soft patter of rain drizzles onto my face and hair. I cover Gomez with my dark strands like a curtain, pulling my hood over my head, searching for pockets of warmth.

You think she visits the Human Realm?

I notice him shrug in my peripheral vision. *Maybe. I doubt she can sneak away from my dad for long enough.*

I pause, peering into the darkness as the abandoned mill comes into focus, its decrepit walls cloaked in the shadows of the trees, windows dark and hollow with vines choking the ancient stones forming what's left of the building.

My magic vibrates the closer we get, and I spot another iron gate, this time less weathered and taller.

"Thank fuck," Ezra says, sighing. "I'm ruining my shoes."

Lorcan rolls his eyes. "We're going to be dragged through the earth, fuckwit."

Ezra leans closer to Aiden and Rosa and snickers. "He's extra grumpy tonight."

Ignore him, I command, unwilling to listen any more of their bickering. Partly because I have a headache, but also because their sibling rivalry and quips remind me of my relationship with Caden—of when I had a brother.

Gideon storms through the gate first, his sword glinting from the moonlight, still strapped to his back. His long, braided hair catches against dangling vines hanging from a low branch, that brush his shoulders like the fingers of the grim reaper.

Ezra goes next, followed by Aiden, then Rosa, who accidentally runs her fingers through a web stretching between two trees. She screeches, making Aiden and Ezra jump, her entire body rolling with a shudder.

"I'm done," she exclaims breathlessly. "I need light." Her eyes focus on Ezra as she places her hand on her hip. "Can't you do something? You are a demon."

Ezra snort-laughs. "I'm not a damned flashlight, Sugar. Just stay close. We'll be there soon."

My heart skips a beat when I reach the gate, creaking against a gust of air. The magnetic pull of the mill draws me closer, beckoning me to wander inside and join the lost souls of my ancestors.

My magic pulses as the violent energy of the Fallenmoore witches and their sacrifices bubbles around us. Except no one seems to notice except for me. Their ghostly desires knot with mine, and I'm suddenly nauseous and dizzy.

I whip my head around to look at the spirits watching me from the mill with charcoal eyes and smoky forms, like slow-moving tornadoes growing closer. They want me to go to them. They can sense my magic.

Lorcan's voice is sharp and pointed when it arrows into our bond. *Tell them to fuck off.*

I flick my gaze to him, noticing how his black hair shadowing his eyes has curled against his forehead from the rain.

Dark lashes frame his intense, pastel-green eyes when he says aloud, "You're alive. That means you are so much more powerful than them. That includes Evangeline or any of the demons or spirits in Hell."

"Except for you," I reply, focusing on him until the spirit's translucent, glowing figures fade from my peripheral view.

His boyish smile makes my heart leap. "I'm the exception. I was born a demon, not made into one."

I blink twice, the moment holding us together with an invisible tether, until he locks his fingers with mine and pulls me toward the gate.

The second I'm through the gate, the nausea dissipates.

The third, fourth, fifth, and sixth gates are unremarkable, and the ghosts and spirits don't bother us again, as the wrought iron entrances emerge in the darkness along the long, winding path through the dense woods.

But the seventh gate is unlike anything else.

I hold my breath when we see it, shimmering in dark purple and obsidian as it appears out of thin air between two twisted trees, the bark on the trunk resembling skeletal beings trapped in time.

The spires on the top arrow through the canopy above.

It's far too quiet and still. There's not a breath of wind or a hoot from an owl. It's as if we've stumbled into hallowed ground, except it's anything but that.

Aiden whistles out a breath. "I'm not going first."

Rosa steps back. "Yeah, me neither."

Lorcan and Gideon stomp toward the long, twisted bars, and I flex my fingers at my side.

"Gomey, hold on tight to me, okay?" My little fruit bat nestles closer, his body trembling against my neck. "You can stay here. Until I get back."

He flaps his wings, his fangs grazing my skin in warning.

I whisper. "Okay, but Hell is dangerous."

His claws grip into my skin in a way that tells me he's not leaving my side, and my stomach dips, knowing I must protect him at all costs.

His wings tangle in my hair, knotting into a mess which is going to be impossible to brush out, but I don't care, not now when we're about to be dragged through the mud and into Hell.

My voice comes out a hair above a whisper. "Let's get this over and done with."

Rosa looks at me, her brown eyes glossy, and nods. We both know she's seeing this through to the end too. Poor Aiden looks as if he's going to pass out.

Lorcan and Ezra smile while Gideon looks completely unbothered, as if this is a regular Tuesday.

I grab Rosa and Aiden's hands, and we walk through the gate together—slowly at first, then into a run before we lose our nerve.

Then everything changes.

I struggle to hold on to them as the ground quakes and splits with a roar. Vines and phantom fingers snakes from the clammy mud that gurgles as if it's alive and intends to devour us, gripping my ankles.

Aiden's scream tears from his throat, as he's pulled waist deep, his fingers clawing at the ground.

Adrenaline floods my veins, and the more I struggle, the faster I sink.

A low rumble resonates through the Earth as smoke spirals from the gate in illusory waves, and I watch Lorcan and Ezra smiling as they're dragged to Hell, their arms crossed upwards, palms flat against their chests.

"Stay calm," I shout as we're dragged deeper. "No matter what happens, we must stick together."

The sticky, wet mud clings tighter, enveloping us from a soft embrace to something far more sinister. The vines and fingers tug harder until I can't breathe. I'm holding onto Gomez with every ounce of strength I have, but he's torn from me the moment he hits the soil.

The soil is in my nose now, my mouth gasping for one more lungful of air before I'm pulled underneath, mud muffling my call to Gomez.

Then I'm falling through a void, grasping at the black air for something tangible to hold on to. The landscape transforms around me into fog and smoke and darkness. My descent slows, and I'm spiraling through shadow creatures twisting in the corner of my eye, just out of sight. Demons lurk on the fringes of the darkness, their occasional red eyes flashing as the air is mercilessly pulled from my lungs.

"Fuck!" I scream as my body slams onto cool, stone slabs. Slowly, I look around, taking in the fog and what appears to be an eerie graveyard.

Every sound is an echo in the void.

"Rosa?" I croak. "Gomey? Lorcan?"

Lorcan?

Our bond is broken, at least temporarily, and I look around. I'm completely alone.

CHAPTER TWENTY

Lorcan

Evie's gone. They're all fucking gone.

I land on the cold, stone ground, coughing black, gritty Hell dirt from my lungs, every violent expulsion of air sanding rough, course particles along my esophagus. My watering eyes lift to what first appears to be a cemetery, with its curling black patina speckled wrought iron archway. I peer around both sides, then scan the expanse of something akin to Human Realm ivy twisting through the metal, visually tracing the two words formed in a slight upward bend at the peak of the arch. Intricate metal flowers sit on either end of the words like bookends. Magnolia Medows. I snort, then a few more coughs wrack my body as I expel the rest of the dirt stubbornly clinging to the membranes of my lungs. I squint into the thick, creeping mist and the hairs raise on the back of my neck. There are no headstones or crypts—just foreboding statues as far as I can see.

Fuck.

"Evie!" I yell, my voice suffocated in the gray ether.

Adrenaline surges through my veins as I race to find her, fingers clenching into fists. If anyone's hurt her, I'll fucking kill them.

The faintly glowing fog wraps around me like a cloud, the chilling caress of its tendrils sending shivers down my spine as it slows me. Echoes of my footsteps break the unnerving silence as I run through the labyrinth of stone walkways. I swear to fuck I've seen that same gargoyle multiple times. Foreboding prickles my skin like miniature icepicks. I'm going in circles.

This must be Samuel's doing. He was always going on about creating trials for the unfortunate souls who ended up here to go traverse. Dad only went along with it because Samuel added that the human souls would learn something as they went through each trial, essentially making them better people. My lip curls. I know better. These trials are torture under a guise—Samuel never does anything unless it inflicts suffering. If this is a trial, then Evie's stuck in one too.

I ball my t-shirt at my chest, clutching tighter as anxiety shreds what's left of my waning sanity. She's already so fractured from what that sick fuck Edward did to her. There is no possibility that she leaves the trials unscathed—none of us will.

I've never felt anything like this. I thought I'd experienced every side of fear until now, but caring this deeply, it's like wearing my heart on the outside of my chest—vulnerable, bloody, and raw, exposed to the elements. I run a hand through my hair and spin in a pointless circle. My shoulder clips a statue and I freeze. I swear the stone just twitched. No. That's not possible, it's just Samuel fucking with me in the cruelest way he knows—extended, creeping psychological torture.

My claws shoot out of my fingertips. Godsdammnit. I have to get the hell out of here so I can save her. So, what's the fucking trial? I'm going in circles surrounded by creepy ass statues.

I stare at the tall and twisted stone statues, slick with moss and decay, searching for clues. In the distance the fog lights up as if something moves, hidden amongst it. The trials are linked to some kind of lesson. Perhaps after each of us? Lust, Wrath, Envy... but they'd be torture. Emotions were the simplest and easiest way to fuck humans up, so what were the darkest ones? Depression, loneliness, grief...

As I draw closer to the statues lining the bisecting gray stone paths, their expressions shift and the sorrow etched into their faces distorts into something more sinister—more *alive*. My heart stalls, then gallops at an untenable pace. Unblinking eyes seem to follow my every move. The statues watch me with feral hunger, as if they're waiting for me to falter.

Loneliness seeps into my thoughts, a heavy weight pressing down on my chest, utterly suffocating and unyielding. I call out for

Evie again but only a whisper from the mist responds. No one is here to hear me. Fuck.

I'm truly alone, separated from the rest. Even the illusory wisps of barely illuminated fog resemble the bars from the cage I was trapped in for decades.

A statue moves in my peripheral vision. I glance over my shoulder, half-expecting to find someone—or something—trailing behind me. But the graveyard is empty, save for the looming statues that seem to shift just beyond the edge of my vision.

The air thickens so rapidly I choke, and I can almost hear the statues gasping, their stone mouths warping. I lean closer, just making out the trapped, intelligible voices from within.

"Shit, you're alive," I whisper, my voice too loud in this oppressive silence. I straighten my spine. They're fucking real. I lift a finger, then poke the tip against the solid, stone chest. The statue's feminine lips twist and I leap back. "Godsdammit!" I shout. "Fucking creepy, Sam." I really hope the asshole can hear me. I stare into the stony, pained expression of the woman and cross my arms. "What did you do to end up trapped here?" I glance around at the pathways, clogged by fog, when I realize the statues are people who never made it out of the trial and succumbed to the sin it embodies.

That means… Evie. Gomez. Rosa. Aiden. Gideon. Fuck. They're all at risk of becoming statues. Vivid scenes of my witch and her bat encased in stone carousel in my mind. I shake my head, trying to remove the thought, but it only stabs deeper like icy claws into my brain matter, distorting my reality into a grotesque caricature of itself.

A whisper climbs through the branches of dead trees that post like soldiers between statues on the sides of the path, reminding me I will *always be alone.* It's in my nature. A muscle under my eye twitches. I am a demon, immortal, and Evie is human. One day, she'll die like all the others, and I won't have anyone.

Shapes twist and morph in the mist. I spot a statue's arm, and for a fleeting moment, I swear it twitched.

I stumble backward, dread pooling in my stomach. I have to find her before the statues take my witch and turn her into one of them.

The fog coils tighter. Shadows flit just beyond my sight, darting away whenever I turn to see what the fuck is moving.

The statues' faces blur together, their muffled voices growing louder, a chorus that haunts my every step.

I turn down a narrow path and catch sight of a shorter statue—a woman draped in tattered robes, her face twisted into a mournful expression. My eyes widen and I barre my teeth. I. Can't. Look. Away. Her stone eyes latch onto mine, luring me deeper into her sorrow—a feeling so palpable, my heart launches into my throat. No, fuck this. I tear my gaze from hers.

My heart races, a frantic rhythm that matches the pounding of my thoughts. I feel myself sinking deeper, desperate to suddenly lie on the ground and give up. It would be so easy to drift into the icy loneliness pulsing from the statues, its frosty claws a relief of sorts. The voices grow louder, reaffirming what I already intimately know—I deserve to be alone. I sink to my knees, and stare at my fingers as they curl inward and slowly turn to stone, but a sudden burst of clarity jolts me upright.

What the fuck am I thinking?

Alone.

Loneliness.

This is the godsdamn Trial of Loneliness.

The statue moves in my peripheral. I sense more of them, their presence lurking in the fog, inching closer every time I look away.

I know how to get out, but as soon as the thought flits my mind—an acceptance that I may be alone again someday, but I'm not right now and everyone deserves to be loved, even demons—the veils fade away into tatters and the fog dissipates. I spot Rosa first, running from a statue that chases her toward a collection of dead trees. Aiden wanders beyond her, none of them able to see each other, crying into his palms as he tries to not look at the statues.

Then I see Ezra, smirking right at me. "Found your way out then, Brother. Took you long enough."

"Where's Evie?" I growl.

He shoves his hands in his pockets and glances over his shoulder. "She's back there, but you can't help her. They can't see you and if you touch them, it'll just feel like the fog is suffocating them."

I take off in the direction he indicates, my heart racing when I hear the squeaks of Gomez flying over Evie. The bat shoots me a scowl, and I sigh in relief. "I've never been happier to see you, Fluffy Fucker."

He does not appear to share my sentiment.

"Where is she?" I ask and he flaps his wings down a path. I sprint after him, then my steps falter. This trial is destroying her. I walk closer to her crouched form, and swallow back a curse as my witch cries so softly it could break hearts. A statue of a cloaked man looms over her and focuses all of its nefarious energy Evie.

"Baby Girl," I whisper, but she doesn't shift. Instead, a statue moves behind her, gnarly stone fingers reaching toward her. "No!" I grab the statue's hand, but I'm thrown back by what feels like hundreds of volts of electricity. Suddenly, their eyes are on me and the awareness in them surges ice through my veins as I lay twitching in the dead grass. It's taken me less than a heartbeat to recover, but they seized their opportunity with voracious malice. They're not demons or helpless souls, but the worst of the worst— murderers, rapists, serial killers, devoid of any humanity, hungry to pull anything good and living into themselves.

Ezra finds me and cups a hand on my shoulder. "I have to hand it to Samuel. He did a good job."

Shrugging him away, I turn to face my witch, fists clenched as the statues grow closer. "Run, Evie. Stand up. Anything. Do not give up!"

"We're not strong here," Ezra proclaims. "This place zaps your energy, so you can't help anyone else when you wake up and can see through the veil. It's smart."

"Yeah, it's so fucking stupendous," I snap sarcastically. "Are you going to help, asshole?"

"Help what? She needs to figure it out like we did."

I growl. "You don't *understand*! She can't take this."

"Ye who has little faith. Give her a chance. I'm going to check on Rosa."

I arch my brow. "Oh. So, you *do* care about someone other than yourself. Consider me shocked."

He shakes his head. "I don't, I just can't stand here and watch all of this." He waves his hand over the area of Evie slowly breaking as she cries into her palms. "It's too damn depressing."

With that, he races away and my stomach knots. I kneel in front of her. Even though she can't see me, I touch her arm anyway, and she flinches, sensing the chill from what she thinks is fog. "I'm here, My Witch. You can do this. Please, Evie, come back to me. You're not alone. You never will be."

She lifts her eyes, but looks past me at something I can't see, her beautiful browns devoid of any hope.

Whistling greets my ears as Ezra strolls through the fog and walks toward me. He ignores my glare as he pats my back heavily. "She wouldn't want you to torture yourself like this, Lor. Come wait with Rosa and me until it's over. You can't do anything. It's fucking tearing you apart."

My fists ball at my sides and a growl rumbles in my chest as I turn away from Evie. I'll go with him, for now, but only because the temptation to hold and comfort her is too great, it will only worsen her pain.

I can't watch her suffer like this without trying to soothe her.

CHAPTER TWENTY-ONE

Evie

A sharp slice of ice digs into my shoulder and I shrink away. It's then that a detached certainty crawls over me as I crouch near the closest statue's stone feet.

These statues want me to fail.

I squeeze my eyes shut and try to reach Lorcan through our bond again. *Lorcan? Can you hear me?* My stomach hollows as only silence deigns to reply.

I don't want to be alone here. I need to find the others before it's too late.

The air shivers against my skin as five statues circle me, bending at the waist and reaching for me. Pain lances through my chest, sobs tearing from my throat. Something tickles the back of my mind, like an awareness that isn't mine. This is reality and yet, it's not.

My heart shrivels as whispers so low I can only just make out the words rise around me as I stare into three cold stone faces.

Alone.

Alone.

Alone.

You are alone forevermore.

The whispered voices hook into my mind and send pulse after pulse of anguished sorrow filtering into my thoughts and mutating them until I no longer know the difference.

Memory after memory pelts unwantedly into my mind's eye like spattered paint. In the first, I'm watching myself playing dolls by myself after my only three friends vanished without saying goodbye.

The scene unfolds into the next. Flames engulf my visions, my family. Burning. Dead. Because of me.

If it wasn't for my brothers dying in that fire, their souls at least savable still then, I'd be glad for the fire that got rid of my family. The rest of them were nothing but a stain on this earth.

The scene swiftly shifts into a spiral of smoke as the fire dissipates, and I stare at myself. The sole survivor among blackened corpses.

The last memory comes with a migraine. The scene, our bedroom, white pillows, and my brother, Caden, my adopted sibling, and the only family that loved me, exploding into thousands of gory pieces.

All alone. As it should be.

I dry my damned tears with my sleeve, tired of crying, then lift my head and stare into every one of the statue's twisted faces.

The reel of memories assaults me once more, but something is different, like a dimmer switch in my mind crawls toward an understanding I can't quite grasp.

But I know this—I can't let the statues touch me.

With the revelation, time seems to stop. No, the statues still come for me, but their movements are so slow it seems like they aren't.

Icy pain sears through my toes and creeps up my legs. I claw at my pant leg, but my jeans are reluctant to glide against my skin. An expanse of rough gray appears as I finally tear the stitches off the hem.

My eyes widen and vomit burns the back of my throat. I reach out with shaking fingers, but instead of skin greeting my fingertips, it's solid stone.

"No! I will not become like you!" My chest inflates as I gasp. The realization in my mind sparks, and awareness floods my stagnant thoughts with light.

This is a fucking trial! I need to get out of here.

My stomach swoops when I think the words.

My hair flings around me as I dart my head around. There must be a way out of this cage of stone bodies.

I'm okay with being alone. I have people who love me and they're waiting for me. The pain quickly disappears from my foot, and I'm free.

I risk a glance over my shoulder and immediately regret it. The five statues turn, stone dust peppering the air as their joints grind against themselves, then step forward as one.

Nope.

My tongue throbs as I bite it, swallow my scream, and sprint away. Gods, I really don't want to move deeper into the thick fog, but there are no other options.

How am I ever going to find my way out?

Whirls of fog whip toward me as wing beats join the melody of my panicked flight.

"Oh, thank Gods. Gomez!"

My night puppy flies into view, then glares over my head and hisses.

I catch a glimpse of something gray moving quickly toward me in my peripheral, then shriek as a stone hand reaches toward my hair as it ripples behind me like a sail.

Shit, shit, shit!

I veer sharply to the left, Gomez keeping pace at my side. "Can you show me the way out?"

He chirps, then takes off, his wings slicing through the thinning fog.

My feet pound against the ground as I pick up speed and follow Gomey's encouraging cries, dashing down stone paths and dodging more stone hands. The oppressing fog clears just as my face connects with something solid and warm.

"Evie! You fucking did it." Lorcan's nutmeg and ash scent rushes into my nose, where it's pressed against his chest.

All the tension in my body melts away. "Oh, thank gods." I peel open my eyes as a hand rubs my back, then smile at my best friend.

"You're okay," Rosa whispers, tears welling along her lashes.

Ezra clears his throat. "I vote we get the fuck out of here before those statues change their minds about leaving us alone."

Lorcan's chest rumbles against my ear. "Absofuckinglutely." Rosa's hand falls away, then Lorcan's warm knuckle nudges under my chin.

I blink and the last of my tears drip down my cheeks as I take in his soft expression. "That was…"

"I know," he reassures me, then feathers a kiss across my lips and smiles against them. "I need to speak to my brothers for a minute, but I'll be right back."

I watch him go, each step of his determined stride taking him farther away from me. My attention swings to Aiden as he meanders over to me.

"Is it just me, Bromina, or was that harder on us than them?" Aiden asks me as he curls his thumbs around his belt loops and strolls beside me.

I offer Aiden a slight smile as he blows out a breath, his cheeks puffing with air. "Bromina?" I ask him and hope he hears the sincere sympathy in my voice.

"Oh, you know like bro but for a chick. It's your nickname," he laughs but it decidedly lacks mirth. "I'm not very creative."

I've been called worse things. I shrug. "I like it."

Silence descends as I monitor the backs of Lorcan, Rosa, Ezra, and Gideon as they walk far enough ahead of us for the illusion of privacy. "Do you want to talk about," I jut my chin over my shoulder toward Magnolia Medows, "all of that?"

Aiden hesitates, then his shoulders lift and fall heavily. "Do you think it would help?"

My lips purse as I think. Could it really cause any more harm? "Yes. No. Maybe?"

He laughs, and this time a smile accompanies the action. "Maybe it would help, but can you go first?"

"Um, I guess." My mind spins incoherently, like the aftereffects of a spinning ride at an amusement park. Where to even start? "I've been on my own for over a decade, ever since I ran from my past." I paused, hesitation curdling my will to divulge, but I pushed past it.

"Right. The Order and that dick Edward," Aiden clarifies.

I nodded. "Yes. They've been hunting me since I was a teen and ran out on Edward." My lips pursed and Aiden shivered. "Long story short, that trial… I honestly thought I'd never make it out. It would have been so easy to give in to the misery as those statues loomed over me, to let loneliness envelop me like a cold, bitter embrace." I cleared my throat. "Um, what was it like for you?"

"It was like I was reliving the worst years of my life."

"Even worse than bargaining your soul to a demon?" I ask with forced levity.

Aiden fiddles with the brim of his peach ballcap, repositing it as if it's a nervous tick. "Unfortunately. From Kindergarten through high school, I had no friends, and I mean *none*." He scratches the side of his neck, then lowers his voice to a hair above a whisper. "It's not something I've really said aloud, but I like men."

I nod and offer an assuring smile. He continues.

"I knew I was gay for as long as I can remember. It wasn't ever a question, just a vital part of me. You know? But the town where I grew up was, uhh… Well, they didn't believe it was possible for anyone to be born queer." He sighs and his gaze drops to his sneakers, his voice quiets as he continues to speak. "My parents were freaking amazing, still are to be honest, but their love couldn't make all the other bullshit disappear. Although, I really wish it could've. Anyway, I was so fucking lonely it hurt. It sucked, dude. That's why I stopped telling people I'm gay. I can't deal with that shit anymore.

"I'm sorry people can be so fucking narrow minded," I say, "but you're safe with us. It's no ones godsdamned business who someone is attracted to. It's ridiculous people even try to manage other's feelings on that. Since when did we decide that being straight was the norm anyway?"

His dimples deepen when he smiles and my stomach sinks. Fuck, I hate that anyone made him feel that way.

"Yeah, anyway, whatever the fuck that cemetery on steroids was, it drug all that loneliness to the surface and amplified it. Those zombie statues reminded me of all the shitty times I spent alone. Like that I ate lunch in the corner of the dark music room so no one would harass me or how I had no one to play with a recess…" Aiden trailed off.

"Did it help?" I ask, offering him a sad smile.

He inhales, then raises his head, a small smile curving his lips upward.

"Evie? I need to speak with you." I glance over as Lorcan weaves through his brothers and stalks toward us.

I fight to control the anxiety ricocheting jarringly around in my guts, like a bouncy ball with sharp spikes. If this was my reaction to the first trial, how would I survive the rest? I rub over my heart as it flutters nervously. Lorcan cups my face, his tattooed hands so large his index fingers sit where my jaw hinges and his pinkies press lightly under the sides of my jaw. My lungs expand as his ashy nutmeg and sage scent lights me up from the inside out. It's as if his very essence demands my body to relax, like I'm a marionet and he controls my strings. A blush steals across my cheeks as the intensity of his full, unwavering focus wraps around my mind and body like a soft silky cloak. I raise my chin and open my mouth to speak, but Lorcan shakes his head gently. He steps closer until our bodies touch from chest to thighs, then lowers his forehead to mine.

Why does his mere presence soothe me? The dominant yet gentle press of his hands demand I submit to his overbearing control without speaking a word. I don't need him to put me back together. I've been doing that myself over and over again since I ran after I killed my brother. I inhale a stuttering breath. But part of me begs to admit, if only to myself, that maybe I truly *do* want him to take care of me.

Slight trembles course down Lorcan's fingers and through his forearms where they brush against the sides of my breasts.

"Are you okay, Baby Girl?" he asks quietly, his voice rough and gravelly.

I honestly don't know how to answer that question. A million emotions knot behind my breastbone; it's impossible to pull apart the threads and inspect each individual feeling. "I'm fine. I passed and now we can all move on, that's all that matters."

"I don't give a shit about them," Lorcan growls softly, lifting his face away and narrows his cold green eyes on mine but never relinquishes the hold he has on my face. "Surely, you're aware of that by now. You are and will always be my first and only priority, Evie." The knot in his throat bobs as he swallows, then he closes his eyes as if the words he wants to express pain him in some way.

My brows furrow, then my lips flatten into a straight line. "But I really am fine. I've been through worse than this. I can't fall apart now, after one damn trial, and expect to magically complete the rest." I tug on our bond seeking entrance to his mind, but he has it walled off on his end. Frustrating but not entirely unusual. "Let me in," I whisper.

"No. I need to say this aloud. I know you're not fine, but I'll let it go for now. Don't think I didn't notice that you nearly gave up back there. I almost lost you forever to a fate far worse than death. So, please, let me speak."

"Did you just say please?" I blurt.

Lorcan chuckles deeply and the corner of his lips twitch as if he's suppressing a smile. "Yes, but don't get used to it. As you know, it's not a word I use loosely."

I roll my lips together, then nod seriously. "Okay, go on."

"I've been meaning to give you something." He pauses and gestures to the cemetery, gritting his teeth. "I almost missed the chance and I'll be fucking damned if I continue to put it off any further."

I narrow my gaze on a folded piece of paper as he slips it from his front pocket and tucks it into mine. The hand still cupping my cheek glides down the side of my neck, collaring my throat. I gasp as he lightly squeezes and my heart backflips.

Damn I love this demon's touch. I wish I didn't but there is no denying it any longer, he saw to that in the Shadow Realm. "Don't open it until after we complete the trials."

I quirk a brow curiosity roaming through my veins. "You insist I must have, whatever this is," I say, smoothing a hand over my pocket. "And now you want me to wait?"

"I can't explain it now, that's why it's written down." Lorcan blows out a frustrated breath and the blue-black tasseled hair tickling his forehead lifts briefly. "Swear it, Evie."

My gaze narrows on him as I peer up through my lashes. "Why?" I inquire further.

Lorcan growls, long and deep, then closes his eyes briefly. They flash open and inky darkness replaces their normally gorgeous pastel green. "For once in your life, just fucking do as I say." It comes out as a plea, but his continuous growl underscores the sentiment with a command. I skate my fingers along the edge of his mask. Shit, he really means it. I rise to my tiptoes, brush my nose against his, then plant a kiss on his lips before dropping back to my heels.

"I won't read it until after the trials."

A dark eyebrow arches as if silently asking, *And?*

I roll my eyes and sigh. "I swear it."

"Good girl," he rumbles, pressing his palm to my lower back and guiding me forward, punctuating our conversation.

CHAPTER TWENTY-TWO

Lorcan

With the first trial complete, a low hum of determination settles over the seven of us, including Gomez.

I move closer to Evie as she takes in the hellscape surrounding us. She tips her head back and her lips scrunch together, begging me to smooth a kiss over them. "What are you thinking, Baby Girl?" I ask aloud, rather than reaching through our bond.

"How do you tell if it's day or night? Nothing around us has changed to indicate a time shift."

What a smart witch. "Correct. There aren't any markers for several reasons," I expound and follow the direction of her gaze. Varying monochromatic shades of a cloud-like substance drift lazily far above us. I rub my temples; it's a poor mimicry of the Human Realm sky. "Time is simply irrelevant. For better or worse, it does not exist in Hell. Not to mention there is no sun, moon, or stars to speak of because Hell exists in a realm of its own." My scalp prickles, and I can sense how intensely the others are listening to our conversation. Although my brothers are already aware of the ins and outs of Hell, just as any child is taught about where they live, they're still a couple of fucking nosey busybodies.

Aiden chimes in. "So, a realm is different?"

"Mhm, because realms are like pockets within the same plane." I return my gaze to the road ahead and ignore the ever-present desire to feed my obsession and stare at my witch. "For example, Hell is one of many realms on the same plane as the Human Realm, but the Earth exists within its own solar system."

"Blergh, why does it have to be so confusing?" Aiden complains and Gideon hums in agreement.

"That's just how it is and always has been. There are immeasurable amounts of realms on any given plane," I elaborate, gesticulating with my hands. "Hell and the Shadow Realm are just two that exist simultaneously."

"Like a stack of pancakes," Rosa suggests and laughs. A shiver rolls over my shoulders as Evie's laughter joins Rosa's. Fuck, I love that sound.

Evie runs her hands up and down her biceps, then shudders dramatically. "Please don't remind me of The Ugly Pancake right now. I can practically smell the bacon grease."

"Uh, Bro Demon, your girl makes a good point. This doesn't look like the Hell you threatened me with," Aiden huffs as he walks to squeeze past my other side, his shoulder brushing mine. I straighten my spine and wrangle my irritation. This road was not meant for three people to walk side by side. Aiden's sneakers scuffle against the edge of the cobbled black moonstone road as he struggles not to knock me into Evie on my right. "Where are the other demons, and you know, pitchforks and shit?"

I eye the fog by his shins, his movements flaring their glow brighter, then slide my hands into my pockets. If he only knew. "Oh, you noticed, did you?"

Aiden's eyes widen. "Um, yeah. Were you screwing with me this whole time!?"

"No, everything I mentioned is still a possibility," I say, the corner of my lips tilting into a smirk. "But have some patience. We'll get to that in a moment."

The hairs on the back of my neck prickle as Gideon growls low where he strides behind me, but I shrug it off.

Ezra slows his pace but remains at the head of the group with Rosa. "First, you have to understand how the trials work, then we can explain the lay of the land. Let's put it this way, God and his own *powerful angels*," Ezra intones, making air quotes with his fingers, "judge the fuck out of souls when they get to Heaven."

"Meanwhile, in Hell, the souls judge themselves. Personally, I think self-judgment is by far the crueler option of the two," I elaborate. "What we're going through now, every soul goes through; however, they don't know what's happening to them. They aren't clued in on the fact that they're in the trials or what they will face. The catch twenty-two of it all is if a soul cannot complete a challenge, they remain trapped within it for eternity—suffering the same fate over and over like a death loop."

"Fuckity-fuckery at its finest," Ezra concurs.

"How many trials are there?" Rosa asks over her shoulder as she walks next to Ezra.

"Seven," I reply.

"Five," Ezra speaks over me.

I growl and smack the back of Ezra's head. "To be clear, there are between five and seven trials. However, as Evangeline's gate dropped us in a later trial, we have two trials left, three at most. The intention is to keep the souls uncertain if they will ever end." Realization sweeps over me and my shadows swirl into a frenzy, trapped within me. "Actually, the souls would never have that information to begin with. Godsdamn sadist."

"You forgot to mention the worst aspect," Gideon drawls. "The average soul goes through these trials completely alone. Pure and simple—its psychological warfare." He pauses, his eyes drifting to the countless switchbacks carved into a sheer cliff face rising over a cluster of trees in the distance. "Can you imagine if there was a way to utilize the principles of the trials on the battlefield?" He clicks his tongue. "Unadulterated carnage without a drop of blood spilled."

"And what happens if a soul passes all the challenges?" Evie questions, then cocks a brow.

"They gain entrance to Lucifer's Court," I explain. "Don't give me that look. It's actually really spectacular. Pleasant even."

"Pleasant?" Rosa says, heavy skepticism lacing the question.

I sigh and run a hand through my hair. "Humans have a completely warped view of Hell. Yes, there are parts of it that are torture, fire, and brimstone, but the vast majority is occupied by Lucifer's Court."

With that profound thought, the group falls silent; the fog illuminating our footsteps. The cracked and weathered cobbled black moonstone path winds through a scattering of trees and extends into the distance, shrouded by the same thick fog as when we arrived. So far, the trials are shaping up to be more intricate than I expected. I know Samuel is a sick fuck, that's not new knowledge, but a taste of worry sits at the back of my throat, bitter and acidic.

Lush bushes dot the edge of the path as we continue our stroll. Their dark black, shiny leaves and plump pink berries dusted in shimmering gold, tempting passersby to have a taste.

"Berries!" Aiden shouts. I turn an ear toward him as the sound of something like shuffling feet blinks into existence.

"Aiden," Gideon calls sharply.

Curious, I glance over my shoulder, arching a brow as I take in the scene unfolding at our backs.

Gideon's fingers dig into Aiden's forearm, jerking the appendage backward just as Aiden's fingertips graze a plump neon pink berry. "Eat nothing unless my brothers or I say it is safe. There are edible foods in Hell, but the vast majority are poisonous, especially to humans."

Aiden closes his eyes briefly and his throat bobs as he swallows audibly. "Shit. I-I didn't know." Gideon's lips flatten into a thin line as he nods, then drops Aiden's arm.

Evie's shoulder brushes mine as she turns to face Aiden and Gideon. "You alright, Aiden? I don't blame you for wanting to taste one. Those berries look delicious."

"Yeah, just a little freaked out. It's like, is there anything in Hell that isn't trying to kill us?"

"No," my brothers and I state unanimously.

Evie laughs, rolls her beautiful browns, and walks on. Her hands fly to her belly as a distinct grumble voices her stomach's need for sustenance. I chuckle and wrap a tendril of my witch's hair around a finger. "Hungry?" Evie glances at me and I wink.

"Starving."

I hold her heated stare, then dip my gaze to her lips and back up. Her eyes dart away, her hair slipping from my hold as she increases her pace. "I actually don't know when the last time I ate was."

"Evie, what have we agreed to? You cannot continue to skip meals. It's not healthy, girl," Rosa says as she faces Evie and walks backward next to Ezra.

Evie's head lowers. "I know, I know."

Her shoulders tense as my growl crawls up her back. Why does she continue to abuse her body? "For once, I agree with Human Rainbow. You need to take better care of what's *mine*."

"I could eat," Aiden says, seemingly oblivious to the rising tension. "It feels like we've been walking forever. Is it dinner time yet?"

Thank fuck I don't require food or drink to survive. I roll my eyes internally. Humans and their weak countenances. I can consume whatever I'd like, thanks to my superior demon biology. I sigh and my eyelid twitches. I never thought I'd crave the solitude of the Shadow Realm, but here we are. "We have no way of knowing. Hell lacks fluid time, remember?"

"Oh, right."

I tilt my head. *Do you hear that?* I ask Ezra mentally.

Sounds like rushing water?

A river, Gideon insists, breaking into our mental conversation with ease. *Also, I advise against ingesting any of their blood. The trials are swirling our minds and weakening our defenses, just waiting for us to slip up.*

Ezra laughs. *Struggling with a craving, Brother?*

Gideon sighs, frustration tinging the exhale. *Just a word of caution. Don't come bitching to me when you inevitably fuck up while on a blood high.*

He has a point, I supply.

Ezra huffs. *Fine. But something about the growing sound of rushing water reminds me of how blood moves through veins.*

Don't be surprised if Samuel worked a craving for human blood into the creation of the trials, Gideon reiterates.

I growl mentally. *Conniving bastard.* The humans jump as Gideon and Ezra's answering growls rumble into being.

What is the point of communicating through our bonds if you two imbeciles react outwardly? Is that a twin defect?

Excuse us if we haven't had as much time fucking around with bonds. Are you positive your link to your witch is closed, and she's not privy to everything we're discussing?

Shit. I've gotten so used to leaving our bond open since my return to the Human Realm. I scan my mind and find the mental pathway leading to my little witch, but my shield stands strong, smooth, constant vibrations filtering through that always accompany the connection. Evie speaks to Rosa, their murmuring voices like white noise as I focus on the internal conversation with my brothers.

Gideon, are you positive? You don't know anything else about the trials, I ask him. *Anything that might be of use.*

Silence greets me, but his presence lingers on the edge of my mind.

I wasn't part of the trial's development. Father made sure of that when Samuel pitched a fit when he suggested our brother include all of us. One trial for each brother.

I scoffed. *So naturally, Dad agreed to leave it all for his precious Samuel.*

Actually, Ezra rumbles, *Lazarus was also involved, but only in the vaguest sense. He might've had a hand in one trial, but not all of them.*

Fucking figures.

Be that as it as it may, hopefully the worst trials are behind us and we got dropped in toward the end, Gideon says. *What lies ahead is not safe for any of us, especially the weaker creatures in our care.*

Don't underestimate them, I retort. *I have a bond with Evie and Aiden. They're stronger than you think.*

Ezra shrugs. *Don't forget about Rosa. While none of us have a bond with her, I have a feeling she's not to be trifled with. And then there's Gomez, of course. Fierce little bat. Do you remember when he clawed out that Order lady's eye to save Evie?*

This smart mouth asshat. *You mean to save her from your imbecilic ass? No, I definitely don't recall that.*

As if he senses our silent conversation, the flapping breaks through my concentration and Gomez flies off Evie's shoulder, then lands on Ezra's.

Have you always been jealous of Gomez? Gideon hums, implication heavy in his raspy, deep voice.

Excuse me?

Ezra guffaws. *Of course, he's jealous that little Gomey likes me. We both find those bat treats to be delicious. And don't pretend like you hate him. Evie and Rosa told me you enjoy feeding him blueberries.*

I growl, then snap. "It was one fucking time." My witch cocks her head in my direction, her eyebrows arching. Ezra and Gideon snicker loudly.

"I'm fine," I mutter, then stroke my knuckles down her cheek and drape my arm over her shoulders.

You both are incorrect, Gideon retorts. *Gomez is likely drawn to Ezra because of his affinity with monster kind. He is a monster, after all, in his own right.*

I'm not sure if that was a compliment or a dig, Ezra ponders.

Take it as you wish, Wrath, Gideon states, then his presence vanishes from my mind.

Ezra throws up his hands and nearly dislodges Gomez's perch on his shoulder. "What the fuck is that supposed to mean?"

267

"Don't you dare hurt my precious little night puppy, Ezra," Rosa hisses and snatches the bat from him, tucking him against her shoulder and neck like a godsdamned infant. Evie giggles, then strides forward and scratches a nail under Gomez's chin.

"I hate that fucking bat," I grumble.

Evie glances back at me, a smirk pulling at the corner of her lips. "No, you don't. You just wish you did." As Evie speaks to me, Gomez's beady black eyes swivel from Evie to me, the biggest non-verbal 'fuck you' I've ever received in his gaze.

Something gnaws on my nerves, begging for attention. My skin feels too tight, as if my demon form presses too closely under the surface. It's as though I'm craving something intensely, but I have no idea what.

In the distance, the trickling sound grows.

"What trial do you think is next?" Ezra ponders aloud.

I stare at the back of my witch's head, her shiny, chestnut hair swaying side to side with her steps. It's been too fucking long since I've been inside her. The longer I stare, the filthier my thoughts become. Image after image spill across my mind's eye like rapidly flipping pages of a debauched book. Evie is on her hands and knees, her pretty pink cunt glistening as my hands dig into her hips. Squirming on my lap, or how I hold her face to the mattress. My claws pricking her skin as I grip her hips and pound into her from behind. Shit. I can practically taste her slick arousal, scenting the air as it drips down my shaft.

I blink twice, my eyes drifting away from the back of Evie's skull and the temptations it provokes, then adjust myself, tucking my throbbing cock into my waistband. *Fuck. Don't think about her wet, pretty pussy and how good it tastes.* I clear my throat, pretending as if I didn't lose all sense of self in a delicious montage of my witch. "It could be anything. The options are literally limitless."

"Wrath," Gideon suggests.

Ezra snorts. "Really?"

"It would be a glaring opposite of the Trial of Loneliness we just completed," I agree. "Throw us directly from one emotional upheaval to another."

A wave of sound detonates as the path curves around a thick copes of trees like they were a sound barrier.

"Woah," Aiden says, his voice full of awe.

Evie's hand flies to her clavicle. "That's not at all what I expected."

My lips curl and the muscle behind my ribs swells as I watch a myriad of emotions flit across her face. Gorgeous. I swallow, thickly my tongue sticking to the roof of my mouth as if the trickling river stokes my thirst—but not for water. For her.

The cobbled black moonstone beneath our feet traverses down a short slope of short swaying gray grass, ending at a bridge about a quarter mile downriver.

On the other side of the black wooden bridge, the cobblestone path trails into a clearing.

"Damn that's beautiful," Ezra says as he takes a step forward.

He's right, it's beautiful, but something about it seems off. What business does a three-story Victorian house have in Hell? The house commands the meadow before it and looms over anyone who dared pass over its threshold. I folded my arms over my chest, as I analyze as much of the exterior architecture as I can from my position, but I hardly absorb any of the details.

"It's the windows," Gideon states, then glances over at me from three feet away, his stance mirroring mine.

"What?"

He juts his chin at the cathedral gray and charcoal house. "I feel it too, the unseen threat… that something lay behind those walls."

I nod. "Yes. Exactly."

"I can't shake the feeling that it's watching us, a sentry hiding in plain sight." Gideon shivers, then raises his chin, the picture of composure once more. "We need to set aside whatever has us bristling for now. The witches and Aiden need food and rest." Without another word, Gideon returns to Aiden's side.

I scan the gothic monstrosity once more, my growing arousal temporarily forgotten as my attention snags on those two circular windows positioned side by side, too intricate, and more out of place than the dwelling itself. My eyes narrow on the miniature pitched roofs extending outward from the main slate roof over both windows. The hair along my forearms rise. Tracery bursts from a much smaller circle like the spokes of a bicycle wheel. Within each wedge created by two spokes, another thinner one bisects the slim wedge two-thirds from the top.

I continue my inspection as I stalk to the center of the bridge. Mirrored arches break from the thin central line of tracery and connect to the outer border. The smallest circle yet rests on an inverted V above all the other details and completes each individual section. I count the wedges, then deem it a waste of time once the total reaches over twenty. An icy chill runs down my scalp as my stare catches on the center circle present in both windows, painted black like an inky void.

Ezra bounds across the bridge whistling, freezing at the halfway point. He turns to face us as if just realizing no one followed his lead. "What are you assholes waiting for?"

"Right behind you!" Aiden says and jogs over to Ezra.

Gideon growls. "Pay attention and whatever you do, don't fall in."

Rosa walks forward slowly, then halts at the two posts supporting this end of the bridge and eyes my brother warily. "Why?"

"It's teeming with water wraiths!" Ezra shouts, cutting directly through the translucent, blue-gray tinged shoulder height vegetation staking a claim where a lawn in the Human Realm normally resides. "Oh, and I'd run to the front porch. Many Hellish beasties love to hunt their prey in the tall grasses." He bounces his eyebrows, then dark laughter filters to us as he sprints to the front door beneath a covered porch, Aiden, Gideon, and Rosa hot on his heels.

CHAPTER TWENTY-THREE

Lorcan

I glide my knuckles down Evie's forearm to link our fingers as we climb the gently curving staircase and onto the covered porch. My witch reaches for the doorknob, but the door swings inward before she can make contact.

"Did that door just opened by itself?" Evie asks cautiously.

"Yes."

She gasps, turning her face up to me, grinning from ear to ear. "Maybe it's haunted."

A smirk curves up my cheek. "My creepy, Little Witch." A pulse of need rolls through me. Fuck, my lust only grows stronger. Perhaps we could... No. She needs food and rest. I hinge at the waist and lift my witch with an arm under her thighs and upper back, then step over the threshold into the house.

Evie yelps and smacks my chest. "I can walk on my own, you know."

I shrug, set her down on her feet in the foyer, and reclaim her hand. "I'm aware."

A beautiful, rosy blush stains Evie's cheeks. "So, why did you pick me up?"

I growl, then nip the shell of her ear. "Because I wanted to. Plus, I've watched humans use that move and it *always* ends in fucking."

She laughs, then touches a hand to her stomach as it growls. "Like you need any *human moves*."

We stroll down the long hall straight from the foyer to a hardwood door propped open at the end, following the scent of freshly cooked pizza.

Aiden jumps up from his seat and rushes over to us as Evie moves to take retrieve Gomez from Rosa. I struggle to take my eyes off my witch and focus on Aiden.

"So, yeah, Bro Demon. There was even a hot pizza in the oven. This house is, like magic or something!"

I rub the nape of my neck. "You all are consuming food from some magical source, without a thought that it might be tampered with?"

Aiden laughs. "Well, yeah, we're so, so, *sooo*, hungry. What's that saying? You don't look a gift whore in the mouth?"

"It's gift horse, Aiden."

"Oh yeah, that's it. Anyway, this whole kitchen is stuffed with food! Like, seriously, the whole thing: the pantry, the cabinets, the fridge…"

I tune him out as my eyes dart over to my witch.

She lifts her nose and sniffs lightly, then fucking moans. "Is that coffee?"

"Hell yes, girl," Rosa replies, lifting her mug heaped with whipped cream.

The sense of wrongness treads on my senses. I have to figure out what's causing this damn unsettled feeling. I slip a hand into my pocket to extract my lighter, and turn it end over end between my fingers as Evie undresses me with her eyes, sultry, desire drenched heat licking over my body.

I smirk, then wink. "Eat, Little Witch. I'm going to look around." My boots hardly make a sound as I tread over the hardwood floor. Placing one hand on the swinging door, I pause. "Have fun with your heathen misfits."

There's a breath of silence before Ezra's booming laughter shatters it. He laughs so hard, hacking coughs shake his body as he chokes on whatever food he shoved down his gullet. "Ah, fuckity-fuck! I love it, Brother."

I run a tattooed hand through my hair, careful to avoid my mask, then walk over to the counter and cross my arms. "I don't see how that statement is humorous."

The others burst into laughter, joining Ezra and startling the bat.

Gomez beats his wings, flying toward the counter I'm leaning against, and hangs by the intricately shaped metal handle of the upper cabinet. I glare over at the bat, and he glares back, but neither of us move. My gaze narrows, then I roll my eyes and look away. As long as Fluffy Fucker leaves me be, I'll allow his proximity. Although, I have no fucking idea why he'd seek my company of all the people present.

A hum of excitement vibrates our bond as Evie notices where her familiar flew off to.

I shake my head. *Leave it alone, Little Witch.*

She bites her lip and a delighted squeee skips into our bond. *I can't help it. This is the first time you've actually gotten along.*

I pin her with a glare, but my witch just grins.

The group's laughter quiets down when Aiden clears his throat and gestures with a beer bottle in his hand, looking just like the drunk frat boy I made a bargain with. A moment of nostalgia waves through me… selling his godsdamn soul for a red mustang.

What the fuck is wrong with me? I do *not* think fondly about my soul bargains.

"You know, Bro Demon is right, we're definitely heathen misfits," Aiden says, then smooshes his lips to the side. "Well, you all are, but I'm a good boy." His eyes widen, then he covers his face with his hands.

Gideon visibly stiffens in the seat across from Aiden's.

Evie laughs. "It's okay, Aiden. We understand what you mean. Go on."

Aiden lowers his hands, chugs the rest of his beer, and a sheepish smile unfurls across his face. "Yeah, so, uh, first of all, we have two witches, three demons, an amazing frat boy." He pauses and arcs his thumbs toward himself. "Oh, and our favorite fuzzy buddy over there," he expounds, nodding at Gomez next to me. "But one of those witches does some dark shit, and the other is a sexy therapist. No, a sex therapist. Well, she's really hot too." A rolling growl rumbles from Ezra's throat, but Aiden ignores it, probably not realizing the warning was meant for him. "I don't even want to analyze what's wrong with you two." Aiden wags a finger between Ezra and I, then turns glazed blue eyes in Gideon's direction. "But I haven't figured you out yet," he mumbles and looks away.

Ezra claps his hands and the humans jolt in their seats. "We are the heathen misfits, here to crush the fuckity-fuckery that is the trials."

An annoyed growl issues from my throat. "Why do you have to make everything into a godsdamn thing?"

"Because that's what fun people do, Lorry." Ezra winks with exaggerated slowness. "So, obviously, you wouldn't understand."

"Yep," Aiden agrees and swigs his beer.

I trail my gaze to Evie and dig my claws into the underside of the counter as the primal urge to take her sears through my veins.

My witch quirks a brow. *What?*

I caress a claw down our bond and Evie shivers. *I don't know how you put up with these fuckers.*

She licks her lips. *Maybe I have a high tolerance for bullshit because I worked in customer service.*

The pad of my thumb leisurely glides over my bottom lip as she undresses me with her eyes, a sultry, desire drenched heat licking around my balls. Time to use this to my advantage. I cross my legs at the ankle. *I can think of* much *more pleasant ways to pass the hours.* My cock thickens behind my fly. *Eat something so I can tuck you into bed, My Witch.*

Evie reaches for a slice of sausage and green pepper pizza from the center of the table. *Are you going to carry me over the bedroom threshold too?* she quips.

An external conversation floats to my ears at a distance as Evie and I devour one another with our stare. Fuck. How does she make the simple act of eating look sexy?

Someone sighs. "They're doing it again."

A bark of laughter rumbles. "Just ignore them. They'll stop eventually."

Gideon's low, bass tone cuts through the expression of mirth, cracking like a frozen whip. "I don't see why it should bother any of you. They're just silently communicating, which some of us appreciate."

Evie finishes chewing her last bite of food and dabs her lips with a napkin.

I step from the counter and send praise down the bond. *Good girl.* A sweet flush blossoms across her chest and neck. *Mmmm. I fucking love how much you blush when I use words of affirmation.*

I've never hidden my praise kink.

My witch pushes back her seat, then meets me by the door. "We're going to bed. Gomey, are you coming up with us?" I glare at the bat over her head. But he's too distracted eating a banana to notice. Evie shrugs. "See you guys in the morning... er when we wake up."

Ezra snorts, leaning back in his chair and rests his hands behind his head. "I doubt there will be much sleeping. You forget, I know allll about your sexcapades."

I raise my middle finger over my shoulder, then push through the swinging door, hugging Evie to my side with a hand around her waist.

Evie laughs as the smack of skin against skin and Rosa's whispered hissing arrows through the gap of the swinging door. "When Lorcan attacks your ass for comments like that, remember that you fucking deserve it."

We wind our way through the house and up the creaking stairs to the second level. I nudge open the first bedroom door we come across, slipping my arms under Evie. She smiles and plucks the mask from my face, dropping it to the floor. Her giggle-scream shivers over my skin as I toss her body onto the bed and follow her down.

I don't bother taking in our surroundings. All that matters is that there's a bed and I have my witch in my arms. My lips crush against hers passionately as I glide a hand over her sternum to her throat, then spear my tongue into her mouth, her moans encircling it. Absently, I note the soft snick of the door closing on its own as I grind my erection between her thighs.

I pant against her lips. "Fucking Hell. I want you."

She bites my tongue, then sucks it into her godsdamn mouth. *So, take me,* she replies in my mind.

278

My teeth nip across her jaw and onto her neck. I grind against her harder, friction digging claws of desire into my bones. *Ughnm… No. I can't. You need to sleep.*

Please? she begs.

Pre-cum smears against my boxer briefs as I growl against her throat. I fight past the surge of lust drunk fog and pull away onto my forearms and press a soft kiss against Evie's lips as a delicate pout shapes them. "I'm doing this for you, Baby Girl. Trust me, I'd love nothing more than to wreck this pretty cunt, but we might've been in this trial for days already and you haven't rested once." I brush the tip of my nose against hers and growl, "I promise we'll play later."

Evie's brown eyes sparkle as she stares up at me. "You really have changed, My Demon." I narrow my eyes at her and she laughs. "It's a good thing."

"I've been trying to tell you that since you freed me, My Witch. Now, sit up and I'll get you something to wear." Evie does as I've asked, crossing her arms to remove her black long sleeve shirt.

I retract my claws and rifle through the drawers in the cathedral gray dresser, a sea of soft, silky fabric greeting my fingers. A smile creeps across my face as I hold up an elegant, azure silk sleep short and tank top set. It'll do, at least until I rip it off her later.

Evie's brows rise. "Wait, you actually want me to put clothes on?"

I chuckle and narrow my eyes on her. "For the purposes of actual sleep? Fuck, yes. You need some kind of barrier, no matter how flimsy it is, or I'll fuck you into a cum covered puddle."

"Um, yes, please."

The corner of my lips curve. "Lift your hips." A tantalizing tendril of her arousal stokes my cock as I strip the jeans and panties from her body, then remove all my clothing.

Evie's hungry gaze settles on my rigid cock. "But if you're going to sleep naked, what will protect you from me?"

I close my eyes and breathe through a primal growl. *Keep it together, Lorcan. Now is not the time to be blinded by pussy. But she smells mouthwatering. Fuck. No.* My eyes blink open, then I pull back the covers and lie flat on my back. "Come here."

My heart throbs as my witch curls into my side and rests her head on the junction of my chest and shoulder. I inhale slowly, exhaling a long, luxurious sigh and relax each of my muscles one by one.

"Goodnight, Lor," Evie murmurs through a yawn.

"Goodnight, Little Witch."

I press a kiss to the top of her hair, then close my eyes, a soothing warmth blooming behind my ribs.

My eyes blink open, then I push a hand through my hair. Fuck. I forgot how disorienting it is not having day or night, not to mention the weather. I allowed the subtle nuances of the Shadow and Human Realm to force me into complacency.

Scratch.

Scratch.

Scratch.

My shoulder's tense. Oh, good. I was wondering how quickly the bat would come pester us. I skim a knuckle down Evie's sleeping face, then slide quietly from the bed. My fingers lightly brush the wooden floor as I snatch my mask, slip into a pair of sweats I discovered earlier, then crack open the door. Gomez clings to the top of the frame and squeaks in my face.

A grimace contorts my features. "Quiet, Fluffy Fucker. Our witch is sleeping. Come with me." I gently poke him in the fluffy belly, then duck under him. Gomez's head swivels to mine, then he drops into the air. "For fuck's sake," I hiss as he flies past me, clipping my cheek with his wing.

If this little shit wasn't her familiar…

"If you listen, I'll supply you with those damn berries you love so much."

The bat chirps quietly, then lands on *my fucking shoulder.* I force measured breaths into my lungs, then stalk across the hall to the only other unoccupied bedroom and place him on the bed. "I don't know what room Human Rainbow is in or I'd send you to her." Mind made up, I gather extra blankets from the wooden trunk at the foot of the bed and arrange them into a nest. Gomez watches me with what I fucking swear is a batty version of a smirk. "There. Happy?"

He just stares at me further with those beady, black eyes. This little asshole. "I'll be right back." I trudge down the stairs and into the kitchen, not bothering to light any candles. An ominous weight presses on my shoulders, but I ignore it.

Fucking house.

Fucking bat.

I cross my arms and glower around the cooking space. Something prompts me to scan the counter again, then I spot them—a carton overflowing with ripe blueberries. I could ponder how exactly they appeared just as I thought about them, but at the moment, I don't fucking care. Actually, while I'm here, I might as well get food for Evie too.

I grab a wooden tray from the table, then heap it with the blueberries, chocolate truffles, strawberries, and a container of orange and cranberry scones from the cupboard. My footsteps thud quietly as I jog back up the stairs and into the room with Gomez.

I drop the container of blueberries next to him, a couple berries spilling onto the bedding, then stride to my room as Fluffy Fucker purrs and snuggles deeper into the nest of blankets.

Evie's deep, even breaths soothe my agitation as I close the door and set the tray of food on the dresser. My cock hardens painfully the longer I stare at her sleeping form. I slip a hand past my waistband and stroke myself, swirling my thumb through the pre-cum. Lust consumes my every thought, and I thrust into my fist without the conscious thought to do so. I pad over to Evie's side of the bed on near silent feet, kicking off my sweats and resume pleasuring myself.

Has she slept enough?

I want to bury myself in her needy cunt so fucking badly.

As if the thought summoned it, I choke on a moan as an orgasm rips through me. My fingers grasp the side of the headboard, and I jerk my cock feverishly as cum spurts all over the blanket, Evie's rose and skull tattooed arm, shoulder, and neck, plus the side of her face. I bite my tongue hard enough to draw blood as pleasure threatens to send me to my knees. *Fuuuuuuuuck.*

My witch moans. "Holy shit that's hot."

My gaze darts to Evie's as she smirks, gathering my cum from her cheek, and sucking it off her finger.

I pant as I crawl over her and roll onto my back, taking her with me. My fingers wrap around her throat, dragging her face down to me and lick the rest of my orgasm from her face.

Evie rolls her hips against mine. "Ahhg… Oh, gods."

I growl against her lips and cut through her sleep shorts with a claw on either side. "Ride me, Little Witch."

Hours, minutes, perhaps days, pass by in a haze of orgasms, sweat slicked skin, and moans.

Evie moans as I slowly thrust my cock into her cunt and slip a third finger into her ass. "Fuck, Lorcan! That feels so good. Please fuck my ass, you've been prepping me for hours."

A chuckle vibrates my throat as I grab a toy and lube from the nightstand drawer. "Not yet, edging you is half the fun."

"For you maybe."

I slather the metal anal plug with lube, then circle her puckered hole with the tip and growl, "Fucking brat. I want to play

283

with you first, but I promise I'll destroy this ass soon," I pause, inhaling our combined arousal perfuming the air, "but only if you're a good girl and wear this plug until I say otherwise."

Evie tenses but quickly melts into the bed. "What if I have to use the bathroom?" she asks breathlessly.

I slowly dip the plug into her, working it farther into her ass. "Take out the toy, clean it, then reinsert it with some lube when you're finished."

She groans. "It sounds like you plan on me wearing it for days."

My lips caress her ass cheek in a kiss. "Would that be so bad? Imagine how desperate you'll be for my cock. So full, the plug rubbing inside you every time you move."

"Evie sighs as I seat the metal toy fully inside her. "I suppose that doesn't sound too torturous." Her back muscles flex as she whips her head around. "But we should probably go see what the others are doing, right?"

I pull out of her and watch our cum mingle between her thighs. A dark chuckle issues from my throat. "I suppose. Either way, I'll never get my fill of you."

She rolls over and presses her face into a pillow. My palm cracks against her ass cheek.

"Get up, Witch. I'm sure your bat misses you."

"Shit! Gomey," Evie says as she jumps out of bed.

"He's fine. I made him a little nest and gave him some blueberries." I drag a shirt over my head, face Evie, and laugh as she gapes at me, her jaw practically on the godsdamn floor. My knuckle nudges her chin until she closes her mouth on her own. "He's quite easy to manipulate now that I know what he likes."

"I'll say it again; you *really* have changed. I like seeing this side of you, Lor."

My lips curl up at the corners as I grin, then toss a pair of black leggings and an oversized gray sweater at her. "Get dressed and maybe you'll see more."

Evie and I reach the bottom of the stairs, then move into the living room. But Ezra and Rosa don't look up from their seats by the window as they hold each other's stare. Rosa swirls her drink in a tall glass, then sucks on the straw. Ezra's pupils dilate rapidly as a wide, unhinged smile creeps into his expression.

Evie clears her throat. "Um."

I sigh. "I'm not getting anywhere near," swirling my fingers in Ezra and Rosa's direction, "that."

My fingers close around my cigarettes and lighter as I remove them from my pocket, light one, place it between Evie's lips, then kiss her temple and peruse the room. The hair on the back of my neck prickles as my eyes land on a cabinet tucked into the back corner of the living room. That same eerie presence I've felt since our arrival renews with vigor the closer I get.

My boots halt in front of the black walnut cabinet and I trace my eyes over the filigree design arching over two doors with polished handles that beg to be opened. I tilt my head to the side as Gideon's scent surrounds me.

I nudge my chin toward the curious piece of furniture. "Do you feel that?"

"Yes, it exudes power, but it's difficult to tell if it's," he pauses, "friendly or not."

I snort-laugh. "Since when is anything in Hell fucking friendly, Gid?"

My brother glances at me and the corners of his lips curve upward slightly. I would've missed it if I were not aware of his every micro expression. The eldest sibling part of me warms about the fact that I can make him smile when he's seen so much war and death. Generally, these things aren't a burden for demons, but something about Gideon has always been different. I believe he feels things more intensely than the average demon, let alone one of Lucifer's sons.

Gideon chuckles, his deep bass voice rumbling like an engine.

My smirk falls. "But why doesn't Ezra seem to be affected by this unknown presence as we are?

In my peripheral, Gideon's middle finger taps his outer thigh. "I believe it's because Ezra hasn't faced the same level of suffering that you and I have."

"Perhaps."

My brother's gaze drifts to the doorway as Aiden walks over. "What's up? Why are you guys staring at this thing?" Aiden hums, stepping in front of us and flings the doors open so hard they crash into its sides. His squeal of delight lacerates my brain as he pulls armfuls of nonsense from the cabinet, his smile nearly shattering his face with its brilliance. "Dudes, do you know what this means!? The house wants us to play beer pong!"

Rosa laughs, then shrugs. "Why not? But first, I want to try it."

"Me too," Evie agrees.

Everyone steps back as Rosa takes her place at the head of the group, then opens the cabinets.

I massage my temples. "For fuck's sake, woman."

Evie elbows me in the ribs as Rosa struts by carrying the most massive, bright pink dildo I have ever fucking laid eyes on.

A growl issues from Ezra's throat. "Godsdamn, Sweetness."

Evie's lips smooth over my stubbled cheek. "My turn."

I wrap my arms around her as she waits for the two doors to close before she walks forward and opens them once more. "Don't worry, I've got the booze," my witch says as she turns around, arms laden with beer and spirits. Part of me uncoils as I realize she could have easily wished for benzos instead.

Aiden, Rosa, and Ezra cheer. Then I help Gideon shove the furniture against the walls as the others move the table from the kitchen into the living room.

I relax onto the couch and run a hand through my hair, surveying the group. Like me, Gideon has no interest in playing the foolish game, but he hasn't removed his stare from Aiden since the moment he entered the room.

Aiden waves around the foam finger, *TEAM Heathen Misfits* printed in bold letters, that he received from the magic cabinet as he splits them into teams: Evie and Rosa on one side, Ezra and himself on the other. I chuckle quietly. I can't deny it's rather amusing, and endearing seeing Aiden completely in his element. He's blending into our group extremely well.

My gaze narrows on Evie's best friend as she tosses the small white ball.

It seems as if a fog of lust floats over the entire group. Everyone exudes some level of fuck me vibes, even if they're not obvious about it. Well, my witch definitely isn't subtle, but I'm not complaining. I'll never tire of those sultry looks she casts in my direction as she arches her back and tosses her ping-pong ball across the table.

I hold her heated stare and growl down the bond. *If you keep looking at me like that, I'll shove my cock into your cunt right here and fucking now in front of everyone.*

Evie responds, but I don't hear her as something tingles in the back of my mind. My eyes scan the room, and I count the bodies present, but there's two missing. "Has anyone seen Gideon and Aiden?"

As if the question summons it, an ear bleeding scream rattles the windows.

I sprint out the door and race through the candid grass to the riverbank within seconds, Gideon's growling warrior cry piercing my ear drums and his body trembling with the ferocity of his rage. His sword glows as he unsheathes it from across his back, slices it through the air and into a water wraith half curled over Aiden's struggling body. However, because of the ever-changing shape and consistency of water wraiths, it's difficult to tell where he injured it.

More water wraiths creep to the surface as their brethren's noxious green blood leaks into the water. Aiden screams and claws at the bank. Gideon's biceps bulge against his rolled sleeves as he roughly clamps a hand around sopping wet Aiden's forearm and drags him onto the bank, stabbing another wraith directly in its skull-like face as it appears out of its drifting body. The skull shatters into hundreds of pieces and drifts down to the bottom of the river.

I lift Aiden's arm over my shoulder and help him onto the gray grass near Ezra and Rosa. My eyes track Evie as she steps past Ezra and Rosa and walks over to me. "Make a cut on my hand, please."

"Evie?"

"It's time I release Gideon from the binding. He's more than proved himself."

I pause and glance at Ezra. He nods, gesturing toward Gideon like he's a fucking game show host. I extend my thumb, cut it shallowly into her palm, then press a hand to the small of her back as we go to my brother. Gideon crouches at the water's edge and cleans his sword with the bottom of his shirt, but stands as we approach, holding out his wrist.

"Thank you for saving him," Evie says and smears her blood over his cuff, then hers.

CHAPTER TWENTY-FOUR

Lorcan

My shoulder taps the doorframe of the porch on the second floor as I lean against it and trace Evie's curves with a searing gaze.

I inhale my next breath sharply as undeniable, primal lust squeezes my veins, forcing nearly all the blood in my body sprinting toward my cock faster than the white water tickling my ears further down the river. I want her. I always do, but this insatiable drive to devour my witch right here and fucking now is on a level I've never experienced.

A groan slips past my lips as a lash of Hell fire coils around my balls and tugs.

She turns toward me and caresses our bond. *What's wrong?*

I fucking need you, Baby Girl. I prowl toward her as she steps back and presses her ass against the wooden railing. I peel off my mask and chuck it on the wooden rocking chair, then collar her with my shadows and lower my lips to hers.

She bites her lip. *Now?*

Now.

The pulse in her neck hammers beneath my shadows, each beat sending an electric current across my skin. I skim her hot cheek with the bridge of my nose, inhaling as I continue to the shell of her ear and whisper. "I need to be inside you."

My witch arches into me as I sweep my lips against hers, pushing my tongue into her mouth. Evie gasps and I delve deeper, thrusting in and out of her mouth like it's her cunt. Sweet vanilla rose scented arousal curls around us, thickening the more our mouths dance. I uncoil the shadow from her throat, then leisurely trickle it into her shirt. Evie moans as my shadow splits and attacks her tits with primal intent, rolling her nipples into tight, hard buds. My fingers glide over her hips and grasp her ass, lifting her, and grunting as she crosses her ankles at my lower back, grinding against my swollen cock.

The wooden planks reverberate with our combined weight as I drop to my knees and pant against her mouth. "Take off your jeans."

My witch scrambles off my lap, stands, then drags her pants down her mouth-watering legs before stepping free of the puddle of fabric. I grunt as a searing wave of desire hardens my cock further. "Fuck, you're gorgeous. Come here."

Evie shrieks as I dive forward, and her feet flow out from beneath her before she can comply with my request. My fingers cradle the nape of her neck and the small of her back as she falls, turning us so my back hits first.

Evie lets out an oomph, then laughs. "Impatient, are we?"

I stretch out on the porch beneath my witch, grip her hips, and lift her to kneel over my face. "Godsdamn, Evie." I lift my head and smother my face with her drenched panties. The fabric clings to my mouth and nose as I draw in a torturous breath of her musk. My cock thickens to the point of pain as I consume her essence and she groans. Evie turns to look over her shoulder as the clink of my belt buckle sounds, followed by the zipper.

"Lorcan, what--?"

"Eyes on me," I demand, nipping her swollen pussy through her panties. Evie's heart rate speeds as I sneak a claw under both sides of her panties, slice through the thin lace, then yank them off her and ball them in my fist. "Such a dirty little whore, soaking your panties instead of my face." I bring the fabric to my nose and chuckle deeply as her eyes widen, a blush stealing across her cheeks. "Now be a good girl and ride my fucking face. Let me taste that needy cunt."

Evie moans and lowers herself, her glistening pussy barely touching my lips.

No.

I need more.

I grip her ass with my claws and her blood scents the air, driving my need higher. My stubble covered face rubs against her soaked cunt, a growl vibrating against her sensitive pink flesh. "I said sit on my fucking face. Not. Hover."

Finally, she sighs and allows her full weight to rest against my mouth. I swipe my tongue through her slit. Arousal blazes within me, stealing my breath. I continue pleasuring my witch with my tongue as I reach down, tug my cock free of my pants, and wrap her wet panties around my shaft. I groan against her pussy. "Ugmphm. You taste so fucking good."

A breeze rushes past, igniting the low hanging fog's illumination as it lingers around us.

I shuttle my fist up and down my aching shaft as pleasure tightens my lower abs. I tug on our bond and absorb just how good I make her feel, then speak into her mind. *What a messy cunt. So damn needy you're practically drowning me.*

"Lorcan," Evie cries, grinding her pussy lips down and chasing her pleasure. I stab my tongue as far as I can into her pussy, then curl it backward, her sweet slick pooling on my tongue. My cock jerks, the friction of her panties a mind-numbing combination of pleasure and pain. I smile against her vulva as a brilliant idea forms. I will my tongue to shift into its demonic counterpart, elongating and splitting in two. My witch trembles against me as I sweep my tongue against her inner walls, moaning as the taste of her desire sweetens. My arousal only worsens the more of her I taste, pre-cum leaking continuously into her lace panties as I fuck into them. Shit. I'm so close.

That's it, Baby Girl. Fuck my face so hard I'll never be free of your mouthwatering taste and scent. The rhythm of her thrusting hips falter, then speeds up as I growl, the sound traveling down my demonic tongue as it vibrates within her.

"Holy fucking shit," she pants. "Oh Gods, I'm close." I dig my fingers into the outside of her thighs and press her further into my mouth, gliding my stubbled chin against her silky, slick skin. Evie whimpers as I retract my tongue, then gasps as I massage her tits with my shadows and smooth my demonic tongue from the base of her slit to clit. I cuddle her bundle of nerves between the two halves of my tongue and growl, swallowing as a fresh wave of arousal floods my mouth. *Mmm, do you like that?*

"Y-yes!" she screams. "Mmm... Ughng... Why does that feel so good? What are you doing to me?"

Look down and see for yourself.

Moaning, Evie sucks in a breath as she draws back slightly, taking in the scene beneath her. "Is your... tongue split?"

I laugh, then suck her clit between my lips. *It is.*

"Oh Gods, yes. Please. More." The ground vibrates as her palms meet the wood just above my head.

What a needy fucking slut. I pinch her clit between my teeth and suck hard, my climax cresting as her sounds of pleasure rise in pitch and volume. *Make this pretty pussy come all over my face.*

"F-fuck, I'm coming!" Evie screams my name over and over as ecstasy claims her, washing through our bond and taking me with her.

I grunt and groan as my cock throbs painfully and my sinful pleasure tightens around my balls. My head falls back against the porch and mind-numbing bliss consumes me as I orgasm. I moan, words of praise falling from my lips. "Ahh… Ughngh… Baby Girl… Fuck!" I gather her panties around the head of my cock as cum shoots into the fabric and drips onto my stomach, the lace over-saturated with my release.

Evie climbs off me, then curls into my side. We stay there, soaking in comfortable silence for several minutes. I rub circles onto her back as we catch our breath.

Evie leans up onto her elbow. "What now?"

"Now, I find you some food. Don't think I have forgotten how neglectful you've been of your body."

"So, we need to talk about the trials again. I know you're the embodiment of lust, but I think what we're all experiencing surpasses even what you're capable of."

My throat tightens and something within me crumbles. No response came to mind, so I let my silence answer for me. The absence of sound rings with warning, begging her to shut that pretty mouth of hers, the post coitus glow plummeting. It's complete folly to argue the same point over and over. I pinch my eyes shut briefly and ignore the chasm opening behind my ribs.

My madness stirs, breaking the surface of my mind like shattered glass. "I suppose this is when you use the trials as an excuse to pull back from me again."

"What? No! I'm serious, Lorcan. No one is acting like themselves. For fuck's sake, I swear I caught Rosa and Ezra watching each other masturbate!"

I pinch her cheeks roughly between my forefinger and thumb, then jerk her face toward me, the claw on my thumb digging in a little too hard. I lean forward and lick up the trail of blood trailing its way to her jaw. Fuck, that's good. "I told you I'd show you I can still terrify you."

"I don't know what you're talking about, Lorcan. Listen to me. This is just the trial of desire pulling your strings! Snap the hell out of it!"

I growl sharply, then fold my arms over my naked chest. "No, it's not. It's honestly fucking pathetic that you think you'll escape me again. I can see it in your eyes. You want to run. Try it. I dare you, Witch. I'll collar your pretty neck so fucking fast it'll snap." I hiss in a breath. "Better yet, I'll drag you around on a leash like my personal pet whore. Always by my side where you belong."

She storms toward me, then pokes me in the chest. "You're going to have so much groveling to do once you realize I'm right."

Evie's back bows backward as I lean over her, pressing my chest against hers. "You keep speaking, but I'm too busy imagining shoving my cock down your throat to shut you the fuck up."

"You're being intentionally cruel."

I tap a clawed finger against my lips. "Perhaps." My cock jerks against her belly as I catch her throat in a palm and squeeze. "But you wouldn't want me if I was nice."

Evie shivers, then takes a backward step toward the bedroom door. The heel of her back foot lifted, ready to pivot her at a moment's notice. No, dammit. I squeeze my eyes shut, trembles cascading to every limb as I fight to maintain my sanity. She will never forgive me if I allow my madness to spew vile words at her whenever it pleases me.

My eyes flash open and she gasps. "Your eyes." Her torso tilts toward me as she stares, mouth forming a perfect O. What a good little distracted prey she is. "They're split down the middle of each iris, one half green, one half black. I've never seen anything like it."

Her breathless comment washes over me like ice water, numbing my shock and chipping away most of my madness induced anger. I don't even recall what she said to send me into a rage. I melded my madness with my self-aware mind. I've tried countless times over the centuries but failed. Every. Time.

I will not let this opportunity go to waste.

I tunnel a hand into her hair, then drag her head back sharply. "If it gets to be too much—"

"It won't."

I growl and shake her with the hold I have on her hair. "I need to know you're okay. Communicate through the bond if you're unable to speak. Green for good and yellow for if you're getting close to your breaking point. If it's too much or you don't feel safe, shout red down the bond and everything stops. Do you understand me, Baby Girl?" My question rushes from me, husky and deep, my lust clear in every syllable.

Evie nods. "I need your words, Witch."

"Yes, I understand, Demon."

"Run, Evie. Before I do something that cannot be undone."

"Now?"

I will my demonic self forward, my skin zapping as the shift quickly takes hold. My voice growls out of me in its full, demonic timbre. "Go. Before I do something that cannot be undone. You have two minutes until I hunt you."

CHAPTER TWENTY-FIVE

Evie

Like a two-minute head to start will give me any sort of advantage over the King-of-motherfucking-Demons.

My breaths puff in and out of my lungs as I run from the room, not even stopping to grab clothes, and slide on the hardwood floors, relying on my instincts to lead me.

I run, although it's an entirely moot point. I *want* him to catch me and reorganize my organs with his cock.

All thoughts of getting him to realize this is a trial scatter as I scamper down the staircase with quick feet and careen into the corner of the banister. My adrenals flood my system, sending want, excitement, and light fear into a dizzying cocktail of emotions.

I fly past the living room and the front door swings open on its own. "Thank you!" I pant to the house and continue running as fast as I can over the covered porch and down the steps.

Fuck. Which way?

My pounding footsteps hesitate before the field of whispering, translucent grass, the faintest blue tinge reflected in the glowing fog at their bases. Do I go through the field and risk contact with whatever monster lives there? Or do I take the long route and hope I can skirt the edge of the candid grass to the riverbank? I bounce on the balls of my feet, legs tingling with the urge to move.

Lorcan's deep, gravelly voice drifts over the yard and my entire body jolts. My feet decide for me, and I disappear into the meadow, soil squishing between my toes. The grasses sway higher than my head with an unseen wind, their movements thankfully making it impossible to see through the vegetation as they cross and bend over one another like an ever-changing net.

I relish playing the prey, especially as every fine hair on my body stands erect while I subconsciously decipher the lyrics he sings across the meadow, of Every Breath You Take. He could not have picked a more apt song.

Grasses glide along my bare breasts like wandering fingers as I run.

His singing cuts out and my shoulders sag, but the muscles tighten as it immediately resumes…in my head—somehow that's worse. Way fucking worse in the creepiest, best way possible.

I freeze in the center of the meadow, legs barely holding me up upright as they quake with anticipation, then slap a hand over my mouth. Too loud breaths warm the side of my palm with every exhale as Lorcan's gravelly baritone voice glides into the chorus, the volume swelling and filling the chambers of my mind to capacity.

My heart launches into my throat, somehow still melting with lust and beating out of control at the same time. This feels too damn real, the intensity straining my weak mortal heart.

Would he stop if I screamed red? I'm not ready for this to end.

My muscles stiffen as I slowly revolve, expecting the worse. An exhale stutters from my lungs. Nothing. I rise to my tiptoes and search my surroundings in vain. He's gone.

A moan threatens to spill past my lips as I rub my legs together, arousal slicking my inner thighs, unconsciously seeking the friction I crave more with each passing second.

Do I want the game to stop? Yes. Fuck, no? Dammit. Gods, my thoughts are crawling over themselves.

Oxygen ices over in my lungs as a hot breath caresses the back of my neck.

Don't look, don't look, don't look.

Don't. Look.

I look and nearly stumble over my feet as I peek over my shoulder and see a nightmarish version of Lorcan less than ten feet away. My pussy clenches on air as my stalker closes the distance between us with the measured pace of a born serial killer; the candid grass releasing blood-curdling screams as his clawed toes rip their roots from the ground with every step.

A scream ravages my throat and my core throbs sharply as I behold his fully shifted form, my eyes raking over every inch of his terrifyingly gorgeous body.

The air trembles with unleashed power around his nude body, dark cobalt fur dotted with large black spots covering nearly all of his skin. I choke on a half gasp, half moan as my eyes lock onto something that looks like a tail curling over his hip and circling his arousal inducing, engorged, dark blue-ish gray, ridged demon cock.

My thoughts trip over themselves—Yep-that-is-a-motherfucking-tail.

Pre-cum leaks onto his soft looking tail as he uses it to pleasure himself with long, leisurely strokes, a growly groan pouring from his chest. *Like what you see, Baby Girl?* His laughter vibrates the air and throughout my mind, layering over itself as I stand paralyzed, absolutely mesmerized and at his mercy.

Mercy?

I know there will be no *mercy* for me, and that's fine because I don't fucking want any.

I want this lethal predator to unleash himself on me. I stumble backward a step as the thought resonates.

I want this.

Him.

All of him.

I just want him in any and every way possible, demon form or not.

His growls deepen to a carnal, sinful pitch that makes me wet every time. "That's right, Evie. You. Are. Mine."

My enlightening perusal ends as my gaze reaches his face, his serrated teeth filled mouth stretching wider than I've ever seen, like the gaping maw of a wolf. Oh, gods, *yes*. I don't know or particularly care why I'm so attracted to this more unhinged version of my demon. But I am, I definitely am.

Words rush past my lips before I can reclaim them. "Are those fucking horns?"

Yes, he replies. *And if you're good, I'll let you hold on to them as I tear you in half with my demon cock.*

This is the King of Demons. The person demons and humans alike fear. And I've pissed him off. Just fucking perfect.

An inappropriate, choked giggle explodes from me, then my hand twitches, freeing me from his thrall. I spin and trip over my feet as I sprint as fast as my legs will carry me until I stumble out the high grasses and fall to my hands and knees on the sandy riverbank, the metal butt plug jostling further into my ass.

On shaky legs, I scramble to my feet and fight for breath with each pump of my legs, my blood pressure steadily climbing to dangerous heights. Yet, heat floods my center, and desire radiates between my thighs. The longer he toys with me, the hornier I get.

The back of my neck prickles. It's too quiet. When did he stop singing?

"Eeevie." Lorcan's voice sounds far too close to my left ear. I risk a glance, but he isn't there. My bones go cold. He could be anywhere. Why is that thought so fucking hot?

Stubby dry grasses stab into the soles of my feet as I clap a hand over the stitch in my side and slow to a jog.

I cannot wait to catch my witch. I could be balls deep in her right now, but the chase is too thrilling.

What the hell?

Lorcan's gravelly voice drips lust as it comes through the bond.

Look at her trotting along like good little prey.

I trip, then face plant on the sloped bank as the truth bitch slaps me. Holy-fucking-shit. These are his thoughts. I groan as my pebbled nipples scrape on the ground. Maybe I should just lie here and wait for him to find me. My clit pulses with desire. No, I love that he's chasing me. Wait, did he say look at her? Oh, Gods, he's watching me right now.

His crazed inner monologue slips through our bond. *Fuck, I want to lick that bead of sweat right off her neck. Her fear smells... So. Damn. Good.*

A whimper escapes my lips. I sit back on my heels and swivel my head. "L-Lorcan?"

It's far too soon to end our fun. She needs to run.

My legs collapse under me as I struggle to stand, my vision swirling as my pulse thrums like a hummingbird's wings. Shit, he's going to catch me. The pit of my stomach falls. I dig my nails into the sandy dirt and crawl forward as speedily as I can.

Godsdamn, she's crawling. His laughter cleaves the air. *My poor, Evie, she's exhausted. But her cunt is soaked, begging for me to fuck it. I need to be inside her. Right fucking now. I can't take this much longer.*

I scream as pain radiates across my left ass cheek.

Ugnghn. Look at that ass jiggle. My teeth ache to bite it. Mark her all over. Mine.

Lorcan moaning inside my mind is too much. I want him. This is more arousal than I've felt in my entire life. Sweat trickles down the groove of my naked back as I keep crawling away.

It's cute that she thinks she can get away.

Another stinging slap bites against my other cheek and Lorcan groans from behind my ear. My breaths stutter from my lungs as my forearms collapse and claws pierce the skin of my hips as my ass is jerked into the air and a hot, thick tongue stabs into my pussy. *Lorcan!*

He drives me higher and higher with his lips and split tongue. *Is this want you want?*

Yes! More, please, I beg. My hips rock, chasing the pleasure he's coaxing from me, his fur tickling my inner thighs. My power sizzles within me, but there's nowhere for it to go. *More. More. More.*

A whimper slips from me as the pressure in my ass vanishes, Lorcan tugging the metal plug from my body.

He surges upward and three of his fingers spear into me, spreading my pussy wide. He thrusts them deeply, gyrating his hips into the back of my thighs in time with his fingers. Lorcan's fingers curl, stroking my G-spot. *I need you inside me. Fuck me, Lorcan.* Oh, Gods. His moans are like ambrosia. More slick pools in my pussy as his pre-cum smears over my ass and completely opens the bond on his side, his conscious thoughts licking along mine.

I need to fuck her. His pleasure and mine swirl together into one carnal, insatiable desire. *Look how well she takes my fucking fingers. It's not enough. I want her cunt wrapped around my cock.*

Mmm. I'll come without her if she keeps moaning and begging like that. Godsdamn, she's throbbing around my fingers. She can't come unless it's around my cock. I'm so damn hard for her.

I think I'm going to die. It's so good. Too good. The hellscape dissolves. I know nothing but bliss. Our power connects and swirls through our bond, blending with my pleasure. I'm so fucking close.

Please, I moan.

My scalp screams as he shoves a hand into my hair, his claws lightly scraping. I gasp as he coils my hair around his fist and yanks my head back. Pressure blooms within my clit. I want to come. A ragged, pleasure-soaked groan swims into my mind as he finally sinks his cock into me, his pace feverish.

Ahguhngh. So hot and wet.

My walls stretch around his erection. Those fucking ridges. I explode without warning as he thrusts into me, his bone deep desire encouraging wave after wave of ecstasy to obliterate me.

Gyrating his hips, his ridged cock swirling circle after circle of targeted pressure against my pussy walls, working me through my orgasm. My pussy clamps around him in squeezing bursts.

Lorcan roars, a moaning string of praise cutting off his own words. "Hellfire, that feels so fucking good. Ughngh! Ev-." His cock throbs so hard, his thick ridges rub against my G-spot with each pulse.

Spurt after spurt of thick, abnormally hot cum fills, then overflows my pussy as he comes, never stopping the blissful stirring movements of his hips.

His absolute euphoria soaks our bond, his pleasure soaring straight to my core as he steals another climax from me as exhaustion puddles my limbs at my sides.

I choke out a breath and speak through my pants. "Gods. I can't come anymore."

His growl rumbles over my skin as he grunts through his serrated teeth. *You. Will.* Both words punctuated with a punishing jut of his hips. Moans pour from his lips as I absorb them with mine. *You can't deny that you love how I'm terrorizing your body in my true form.*

I suck in a breath as his hand clamps over my mouth, muffling my throaty shriek of his name as something prods at my ass. *Trust me, you'll love it. And when I'm done, you'll beg for more.* The heat simmering in his lusty gaze affirms the words as truth.

Wait.

One of his hands pulls my hair, and the other covers my mouth…

Oh, no.

That can't be what I think it is.

My muffled words hardly reach my ears over the drumming of my pulse and the sound of our flesh slapping together as he ruts into me. "Lorcan? What the Hell is that?"

My demon untangles his fingers, then palms the back of my head and shoves it into the sandy dirt. He lowers the weight of his body onto my back, trapping me against him and the ground, then whispers, his sharp teeth scraping against the shell of my ear. "Shhh, Little Witch. It's just my tail."

Just.

His.

Tail.

Stars spark across my darkening vision, then my eyes roll back into my head as an unexpected orgasm rips through me just from the thought of him fucking my ass with his tail.

My body jostles and my back meets the riverbank, spasms of release still tearing me apart as his cock glides back into my pussy, our cum squelching with every penetrating thrust of his hips.

I cough as fresh, sand free air eases into my lungs. I'll be covered in bruises after this. My core pulses at the thought. Lorcan looms over me, his biceps bulging and abs flexing with every roll of his hips. *I want to see your face as I fuck another orgasm out of you.*

His hips rise as he pulls out of me slightly. My stare darts down our bodies as his dark blue, lightly furred tail swirls around his thick cock and through the cum pooling between my hipbones. It tugs out the metal butt plug, a dull thud sounding as it drops to the ground, and slides between my ass cheeks.

Damn, that's sexy. I could watch you lust for my tail every second of every day and still not get enough.

My lips part on a moan. "Oh, Gods. I don't think I've ever been more turned on in my life."

Lorcan chuckles, then thrusts his tail into my ass, the glide smooth and nearly painless from the extensive prep earlier. My back arches as he thrusts his hips in time with his tail.

"Breathe, Evie. I've got you."

I chant his name over and over as he thrusts his cock in tandem with his tail. "Lorcan, please. Fuck that feels good. I want,"

I gasp in a gulp of air and drag my nails down his back, "your t-thoughts. Give them to me one more time."

His pace falters as I beg, then resumes with fervent vigor.

My demon's teeth close over the front of my throat, the barest bite of the tips breaking my skin. Blood trickles down my clavicle and my heart seizes, but he doesn't go any deeper. Lorcan snarls low in his throat. "As you wish, Little Witch."

Shiiiit, my tail is so godsdamn sensitive. Her ass feels like hot, wet silk squeezing around me. I want to be inside her constantly. I will never get enough of my witch. Evie has no idea how long I've wanted to do this. Fucking Hell, she takes me so well. I need to come. Ughng, I can feel my tail rubbing against my cock through the thin barrier.

I enter a state of complete aphrodisia. "Yessss. Holy shit. That's so hot. Fuuuck, Lorcannn."

His tantalizing horns slice through the air, begging to be touched, as he grinds me harder into the ground.

I reach a hand toward them and graze their cold, smooth surface with the barest of touches, trembles of fatigue traveling from my forearm to my shoulder.

Lorcan grunts, then sucks in a breath and releases a moan laced shout. "Unholy Gods-of-motherfucki—I'm going to come!"

My thoughts fizzle as I transform into nothing but a vessel filled to the brim with mind numbing pleasure.

He collapses onto his forearms, locks our pelvises tightly together, and bellows a thoroughly satisfying chain of blissed out moans and groans underscored with a low, resonating growl. "Ughngh, fuck yes. Eeeevie." Lorcan presses into me harder as he comes deep in my pussy. Bursts of cum jet against my cervix, pressure rapidly growing where his fat cock seals off my entrance.

You're so beautiful when you come, Baby Girl.

My head whips side to side as my over stimulated body fights against another release. I can't survive another orgasm. He's already wrung every drop of pleasure from me. "No, no, no, no. I c-can't."

A shiver skates over my body as he presses a soft kiss on the sensitive skin behind my ear and stills.

My eyes trace the sharp edges of his face as he rises on one hand and his eyebrows bank together, his stare filled with concern. "Tell me your color, Baby Girl. Do you really mean that?"

My lips purse and it takes a few seconds for my brain to circle back to his question, but it's gone, lost in the haze of cum-drunk peace. "What?"

Lorcan laughs lightly, the pleased sound vibrating my ribs, then smirks. "I said, tell me your color. Green, yellow, or red?"

I close my eyes and consider the options as I check in with my body. I think I'm done. I've had enough for one intense scene, but if he wants to use me to come again, I won't stop him. My eyes blink open, then a smile tips my lips upward. "Yellow."

"Good girl."

A heart-stopping grin spreads across his deep blue face, his serrated teeth on full display, as he cups my cheek and smooths a claw tipped thumb over my kiss-swollen lips. "I'm so fucking proud of you for being honest, Evie."

Something within me shifts and my belly swoops. Shock mutes any reply I might have uttered. *I* did this. *I* make him comfortable enough to accept happiness, if only for a moment, all while wearing his true skin. Unabashedly showing me who he is at the core—every dark, twisted, and fucked up part of him—and I couldn't be happier he trusted me with this.

His smile falls, an emotion flicking across his face too quickly for me to catch, as power ripples over him and cloaks his demon features.

My guts twist. "Lor?"

He drops his face into my neck, tunnels a hand into my tangled mess of hair, and cradles the back of my skull in a palm. For several moments we just stay there, his stillness weighing on my chest, then he lifts his head. "You're right."

My eyes narrow. "About what?"

"That this is a fucking trial." He sits up and stabs both hands into his hair as he blows out an exasperated breath. "Specifically, the Trial of Desire. I should've realized sooner. I'm so fucking sorry I didn't believe you, Evie."

Holy. Shit. Lorcan just apologized. I burst into an uncontrollable fit of laughter.

A low growl creeps from his throat and his lips spread into a thin line. "I fail to see what's so humorous."

I glance over at him through watery eyes, my laughter bubbling behind my lips as I press them together.

"What the fuck, Evie? Stop this."

I gasp for breath and lean up on the heel of my hands. "You apologized! I can't fucking believe it."

His gaze darkens. "No, I did not."

I hurl myself into him and his arms squeeze me to his chest. "Yes, you absolutely did." My lips graze the hollow of his throat as

I press a quick kiss against his skin. I breathe him in and sigh. "You did. But I'll let it go because you gave me so many fucking orgasms I literally can't stand."

Lorcan pulled me tighter against his body. "A wise decision, as I'll never admit to uttering such horseshit." My heart backflips as he presses a kiss to the top of my head. "Let's go back to the house and try to convince the others."

CHAPTER TWENTY-SIX

Evie

Shutting out the desire for benzos, alcohol, and sex suddenly feels like the hardest thing in the world. As if there's a part of me that wishes we can all stay in this house forever, trapped in a blissful delusion.

I glance down at the bridge beneath me, my eyes tracking the shadow of a large water wraith ominously slipping under my feet—a reminder of what happened to the souls who came here and thought the same thing.

Lorcan's at my side first when I walk away from the house, his illusion already shattered, although I feel the desire pulsing through our bond like an elastic band that could snap at any moment. My ass is still aching from earlier and all I can think about is him taking me again like that, again and again until I'm so sore I can't walk.

Careful, Little Witch, Lorcan says into my mind. *You smell like you need to be fucked.*

I smirk, wanting nothing more than to tease him into chasing me again. But we can't. We have to keep going and not to mention, we're surrounded by my friends. Damnit. How can he occupy my thoughts like this so damned much?

We keep walking and I exhale shakily, pulling a loose shard of grass from my hair and bite my lip.

Aiden clears his throat from behind us, and I glance over my shoulder. Aiden and Gideon walk a few paces behind us, followed by Rosa and Ezra, who can't keep their eyes off each other.

Rosa catches my eye after ogling Ezra's muscles and I lift a brow. I mean, I get it. It's not like I haven't felt the allure of a demon brother. In fact, I still can't keep my eyes off him now.

Rosa points toward a forest of tall, brittle gray trees wearing a crown of purple leaves. "That wasn't here earlier."

"It was," Lorcan says with a grunt and shoves his hands in his pockets. "We just couldn't see it through our haze."

Rosa shakes her head, her fingers pressing against her temples. "I should have known better," she says, breathlessly as she cradles Gomez in her arms, "than to have lost myself in a blissful feeling. Especially one artificially created." Her brown gaze travels briefly

314

to Ezra, who's waiting a few paces behind us, then back to me and sighs. "Let's go. Hopefully, Lucifer's Court is just beyond those trees."

Gideon shakes his head. "It's another trial."

"Ever the pessimist," Rosa retorts, but Gideon's right. It probably is.

I glance over my shoulder. The house fades the further we walk, like an out-of-focus photograph. The heightened desire slips away the further we walk, the feeling quickly replaced with uncertainty.

I breathe in Lorcan's scent, my stomach flipping at the smell as he comes up beside me and slides his hand in mine. I guess we're holding hands now. My heart does a little stutter, to remind me I am falling, even though I shouldn't. He's a demon and while things have been fun, seductive, and even intimate, Lorcan cannot love me. Demons cannot love.

Yet, with a gentle squeeze to my fingers, I'm reminded of all the things he's said, of all the sweet touches and caresses and wonder if he can and if he does. It's just he was so thoughtful of me earlier, of my pleasure and consent. Surely, it means something.

His dark eyes find mine as he side-eyes me, his voice sultry and deep in our bond. *What are you thinking about, Little Witch?*

Heat flushes my neck and cheeks, and I look away. *Nothing.*

He clears his throat, then speaks through our bond. *You're flustered. Now I'm really intrigued.*

Don't be, I bite into his mind. *It's not about sex.*

Fuck. Why am I acting like such a bitch? I don't look at him when he tugs me closer.

His voice comes through tender, more inquisitive. *Are you thinking about us?*

I don't answer. Because why? Am I embarrassed about feeling this way? For falling for him. Oh, Hell. I really am. Every word he spews is either a fucking bruise to my heart, or the ointment that heals it.

The rest of the group walk forward onto the purple-leaf carpeted ground and into the entrance to the woods, while Lorcan pulls me to a halt, turning me to face him. Those eyes. My gods. Then his lips, so perfect that all I want to do is a spread a kiss over them.

He pushes a lock of hair from my eyes, his thumb dragging goosebumps over my cheek. "I am just as intrigued, if not more, about matters of your heart, Evie."

"I—I know you care about me, but how much do you… you know, care?" Gods, I'm fucking rambling. What the hell is wrong with me?

His smile widens and my stomach flips. "Read the letter," he says, as if sensing my question. The one I've wanted to ask since he came out of that mirror: Do you love me?

"I thought you said to wait until after the trials?" I ask.

He shakes his head. "You need to hear what I have to say now."

I peer behind him to the group, who have disappeared into the fog beyond the trees. "It's in Rosa's bag. Can you just tell me?"

He smirks. "Can you tell me first?"

My eyes narrow. Fucker. "Fine. I'll read the letter."

"Let's go find Rosa then," he quips. "Wherever the Human Rainbow has gone." His pastel-green eyes are swallowed by blackness as he peers into the trees. "Stay close."

I nod and follow him past a rickety, wooden sign unfittingly labeled Wildflower Woods. Flowers punctuate everywhere an 'O' would be in the words, the carvings crisp and defined despite the overall wear of the wood itself. A dark greenish-blue ivy crawls up the post and around the edge of the sign, and I suspect it's the only thing holding it upright.

Goosebumps prick my ankles as a dense, glowing fog creeps around my feet, swallowing the trees ahead in a ghostly wave.

"Rosa?" My voice echoes, the sound so lonely as it's lost in the eerie silence.

A twig snaps up ahead, drawing my gaze to a large, dull cobweb caught between two branches. A shudder skittles through my bones. "That must be one big ass spider."

Lorcan's eyes narrow. "What spider?"

I point at the cobweb. "None, it's just a web."

Lorcan's brows knit together, a pearl of sweat on his forehead as his focus turns to the underbrush. "Did you hear that?"

A panicked flutter sounds in the beats of his heart as he leans closer. "I swear, I heard a fucking snake. Probably Ezra."

"Maybe," I say with a shrug. "But I'm not really scared of snakes." My eyes lift to the web hanging dully under the gray sky. "Spiders, on the other hand?"

Boots hammer against the ground ahead, multiple footsteps, crunching leaves and twigs like bones.

Aiden appears in the tree line, tendrils of fog shrouding him like spectral fingers. I back up a few paces when he looks at us and screams. The blacks of Aiden's large pupils gloss with unseen horrors. Behind him, Rosa follows, thickets of brambles slashing at her arms as she looks right through me.

"What's wrong?" I shout, and Lorcan's grip tightens around my palm.

"Ghosts!" Rosa screams and runs in the opposite direction.

Lorcan pins me to the spot before I can chase her. "She's hallucinating," he spits, then takes a step toward Aiden, who falls to his knees, kicks his legs out from behind him, and scrambles backward.

"No!" Aiden's yell pierces my eardrums as he scuttles until his back presses up against a large trunk. The bark crumbles under Aiden's touch, the wood of the tree bleeding crimson rivers. "C-c-clown." Aiden points at Lorcan, tears streaming from his bloodshot eyes. "P-please, no."

Lorcan's panicked expression shifts easily into a psychotic smirk. Aiden jolts, his hand clutching his chest and crumpling the fabric of his purple shirt as Lorcan jumps close to him, hands extended with the creepiest smile I've ever seen. "Boo."

"Ahh." Aiden clamps his eyes shut, his fingers desperately skating over the bleeding tree trunk, as if it might save him.

Shaking my head, I grab Lorcan's arm and pull him back to my side. "Stop terrorizing him… and enjoying it."

Lorcan chuckles darkly. "I can only promise to stop."

"Aiden, it's okay. It's Evie."

Aiden stumbles over his words when he finally climbs to his feet, point a shaky finger at me. "You ate Evie?"

"No, I *am* Evie."

Aiden's jaw slacks. "You're not her!" Aiden's cry echoes deep into the chasm of the woods and my eyes widen.

"What the fuck?" I say, stepping backward.

"Your words are changed in his point of view," he explains and looks around.

His hand is back in mine, but his fingers are furry now, and all too warm and twitchy. My eyes drift upward, and I notice Gomez, who disappears into the branches above.

My eyelashes flick up as I watch his wings curl around his body in an attempt to get out of the thickening fog surrounding us.

A chill creeps over my body, my breath coming out in a puff of smoke as I turn to look at Lorcan and instead discover a spider the size of a human, the creature's body glistening with tiny brown hairs.

I drop the creature's leg and scream, and the spiders looks at me, taking me in with those black, soulless orbs. Clicking erupts from its mouth when it drags the top of its leg over my forearm, its sticky threads grazing my skin in a sickening, gentle caress.

Heat burns through my legs as I turn and run into the dense woods, the tall, blue grass feathering my thighs.

My feet ache as I navigate the uneven, mossy mattress below, littered with rocks. Webs stretch across the path ahead, strands of ghostly threads caught in the dappled light, and I divert into taller grass.

Fuck, fuck, fuck!

Tick, click, tick.

The spiders clicking sounds through mine and Lorcan's bond, halting me. My breaths come in ragged bursts, my lungs aching with each breath of icy air.

Lorcan! Lorcan!

Bile bites the back of my throat, and I slowly stand. A tickle glides over my shoulder. I shiver under the chill wrapping me when the tickle turns tangible, gliding down my arm.

A scream tears from my dry throat, echoing through the clearing as I notice the body gift-wrapped with web, suspended between two gnarled branches.

Threads surround me, caught between the gray, cracked bark of the trees, glistening with the promise to ensnare me if I get too close.

Suddenly, I'm the fly.

I pivot again, ducking under a web, my stomach gliding against the feathery grass. I grab a branch, the bark crumbling, turning into sticky blood oozing through the gaps in my fingers as if the trees are people, bodies even, and I realize that like the other trials, they probably are. Souls who never got out of here.

Click. Hiss.

My eyes flick upward to the source of the sounds—gigantic spiders, their spindly legs curling inward as they descend from threads of web toward me.

"No!"

My mind races, adrenaline coursing through my veins when I run again, the woods blurring around me.

Wait.

This is a hallucination.

His words from earlier come back to me with ease. That's all it is. A fucking hallucination.

It's not real. Not real.

I clamp my eyes shut.

"Not real," I yell this time as more clicking sounds through our bond. "Not real. I am not afraid."

I hold myself still, going against every primal instinct in my body. How many times have I sought things that make me afraid? I used to long for terror and I won't let damned spiders me my downfall.

A fog of silk creeps around my body, encompassing my every limb until I can't see anything but web as spindly legs make quick work of me.

My heart sticks in my throat as my powers thrum, begging for me to at least attempt an escape, but I hold still instead and allow myself to be taken my these eight-legged horrors, keeping my eyes closed.

Either I'm incredibly fucking stupid, or this works.

After a minute, the sticky silk leaves only threads of phantom feeling on my skin. I blink. Once, then twice, and look around at the still woods.

No spiders. No webs. It was a trial and from the sounds of distant screams and yells, I'm the first to break out of it.

Gomez's chirps reach me through the sporadic screams and oppressive silence. "Gomey," I exclaim as he uses his wings to climb down the trunk, his little claws gripping the bark. Every few

321

seconds, he pauses to look at me, and I notice the little purple leaves clinging to his shining, black fur.

He reaches the last branch, then swoops down and lands on my hand. I bring him to my face, nuzzling my lips and nose into my little puffball.

"Are you okay?" I whisper into his fur, and he lets out a contented squeak, playfully tugging at my hair. "Go on, jump on," I say with a tap on my shoulder. He curls up against my neck, using my hair as a curtain as we walk through the woods. "Don't worry," I say when he chirps and squeaks. "We're going to find Auntie Rosa now."

A hiss pulls my attention to the underbrush. A snake. A real one, or at least a Hell snake. The creature's brown and red body coils tightly, ready to strike should I come too close.

Gomez squeaks and I shush him. "Don't act like prey around predators," I whisper.

An icy breeze circles my body, carrying the pungent smell of decaying vegetation with the recent fragrance of rain.

A glimmer of green comes into my vision as Rosa runs through the woods without looking where she's going, her face buried in her palms.

I race to her, calling her name. She uncovers her face then claws at imaginary figments on her skin. "It's not real. Come on, you know how to see through imaginary bullshit better than anyone." I grab her by the shoulders and shake her. "You're a goddamned therapist and the strongest person I know. Pull it together."

The tough love aches my heart, but it seems to do *something*. Her blinking slows, and the golden rivers in her irises shine a little more. "Ghosts."

I shake my head. "It's all a hallucination."

She lets out a tense breath and pushes me back at arm's length. "Do you see that tree?"

She points behind me, so I whip my head around and then nod.

"And that grass, there?"

I nod again.

"That snake?" I arrow my gaze toward the direction she's pointing and watch as a brown tail slithers into the tall grass.

"Yes, I see it."

She swallows thickly, her throat bobbing. "The ghost next to you."

I look around me and shake my head. "There's nothing there."

She nods and closes her eyes briefly. When she opens them again, she pulls Gomez into her arms. "What a perfect little distraction," she whispers to our bat while tickling him behind the ears. "None of this is real," she tells Gomez as if it's some big secret. "Were you afraid too? You flew off earlier."

He squeaks sadly, and she snuggles him tighter.

"We need to find Lorcan," I say. "I ran from him earlier because I thought he was a gigantic spider."

Her eyes flash with concern. "Oh, Hell no. Maybe I should be thankful all I had was ghosts chasing me."

"Spirits," I correct, only because it's important to know the difference between them when we're literally surrounded by them here. But she waves a hand, ambling ahead and no longer listening.

Lor? I'm coming back, I whisper through our bond, but am met with a chilling silence.

CHAPTER
TWENTY-SEVEN

Lorcan

It's too quiet.

My ears ring as I note the absence of sound, other than the ones created naturally by my body moving through the wood. This section of trees looks just like any other. Aside from the mild upward slope to the ground, it's impossible to tell one section of the woods from another.

I freeze as a dark, blurred shape, creeps over the leaf strewn ground.

I have had enough of these fucking trials.

Fuck me.

I take a step back, a fallen branch snapping under my heel, and the snake launches itself at me. A snarl tears from me as I kick out my foot and extend my claws, but it doesn't veer from its path.

Fine, have it your way.

I slice my claws along its disgusting, scaled belly and breathe hard through my nose as I struggle to regulate my heartbeat.

Leaves crinkle and move as I rotate in a tight circle. No, those aren't leaves, they're snakes, hundreds of them in all shapes and colors.

No. Absolutely not. This will not be how I go down.

I growl and rush the oncoming hoard, claw tipped hands swinging like a metronome of death. Vile black blood sprays into the air, drops of it sticking to my face. This is a fucking nightmare. I curse and continue cutting my way through the snakes, leaving a trail of their mutilated corpses in my wake.

Shit, I hope the snakes haven't found my witch too. I swear to fuck, if any of them bit her, I will commit far worse atrocities than murdering Samuel. No, I'll keep him alive, drawing out his death for centuries and inventing new methods of torture.

Every.

Single.

Day.

There are no limits to my depraved creativity.

I fall back into the present and bare my teeth in a snarl as pain rips into my forearms, dark blue blood joining the gore already splattered all over me. Oxygen saws in and out of my lungs as I fight to control the panic seizing up my muscles.

Fuck. I can't afford to be distracted.

My feet run faster, Hell dirt flying out behind me with every step, and I'm still cutting down the slithering bastards blocking my way to freedom. A flood of relief washes over me as I spot clear ground beyond the line of snakes. I just have to make it, then I'll find the others.

I cut through the last of the snakes and sprint up the boulder strewn slope, slamming my back against a wall of rock. My hips hinge and I plant my hands on my knees. It's fine now. They're dead. I eviscerated them all. I slide my body sideways, keeping the rock at my back as I reassure myself.

My neck pops and I hiss as I dart a glance around the blind edge to my left. Thank fucking Satan. I exhale and drop my shoulders, darting into a shallow cave. My lips flatten into a straight line. Does this qualify as a cave? While the natural space has two sides and a roof of sorts, solid impenetrable rock fills almost all the space. This doesn't make any fucking sense. The outer edge I crept along is far longer. This *should* be a cave, but it isn't. Fuck it, no time to dwell on that thought now.

I cannot fathom why my mind and body are reacting this way. It's not as if I fear snakes… but there is something abnormal about them I cannot put a name to.

I flinch and bolt upright as something thumps to the ground not five feet in front of me. My eyes darts overhead and my blood freezes solid as wave after wave of snakes slither over the top edge of the cave's entrance.

My heart seizes and my guts twist painfully, the overwhelming panic returning worse than before. Then I whisper a stream of nonsense under my breath, madness rising within me. "No! No, no, no, no!"

The snakes form a loose semicircle, trapping me inside the shallow cave. My hands shake as I grip the sides of my head. For a moment, I'm at a loss.

What the fuck do I do?

The snakes hiss in unison, then one darts forward, snapping its fangs onto the toe of my boot. My vision blackens at the edges as a growl rips free and I jerk my foot away from my body, hoping to dislodge the scaly fucker. But it clings on. I inhale as a single rational thought scrolls across my mind's eye like writing on a wall, and I temporarily forget all the other snakes awaiting their turn.

If its fangs are stuck, kill it while it's incapacitated.

My head flicks side to side fruitlessly as I fail to discover another solution. I *really* don't want to purposely put myself in such a vulnerable position.

Godsdammit.

I must.

I fill my lungs with oxygen, then strike out with my bloody claws.

Agony spears through my unprotected neck as the snake stabs its fangs into my skin and bites down. Utterly useless words spill from my lips. "Well fuck, not stuck after all."

Venom flows into my bloodstream, branding everything in its path with an emotion I have no experience with navigating encased in Hellfire, and I stumble forward.

I grimace and suck in a deep, painful breath.

What the fuck is this feeling?

I squint into the trees and my chin quivers as a bloody, mutilated visage sways at the end of a noose. My knee cracks against stone, sweat beading across my brow, then I go utterly still.

Hanging from a noose derived from a gore splattered spinal column...

Evie's.

Dead.

Fuckboy.

I don't recall his name, but the emotion surging through me with the venom reaches a climax.

My shoulders draw up and I pin my arms to my stomach, curling in on myself. Maybe I shouldn't have killed him.

The fuck? He touched what *is mine*.

I swallow repeatedly as another face replaces the boy's, but this time it's not human, then I recoil as a demon's revolting, rotting, smashed in face appears. I have no memory of killing or torturing this demon. Its unremarkable face could be one of the thousands I tore into. Yet, my heart curls in on itself.

Fuck, fuck, fuck.

My claws scratch at the side of my face.

What is happening to me?

My hands curl inward against my chest as I rock.

It's then that I remember the rest of the problem.

A chorus of hisses rises in volume. I try to catch myself, but it's too late for that. My legs lose all feeling and crumple beneath me, a loud crack ricocheting through my brain as my skull smacks into the hard ground.

"SHIT!"

Heavy, scaly bodies slither on top of me, striking me with their fangs wherever they can reach. My clothes shred as my shadows burn within me, snake after snake, adding their weight to the knot of slippery, slithering bodies. My madness roars within my mind, but I can't acknowledge it, my awareness seeping from the blood pooling under my cheek.

Perhaps I should just give in. Lay here and let the fuckers have their way with me. An unhinged giggle cracks from my throat. "At least I'll make a good meal."

A sharp fang stabs into the back of my hand.

I suck in a deep, stuttering breath as my vision blurs and my body loses physical form.

What the Hell?

I grip the sides of the Fallenmore Coven's mirror, the rose design digging into my palms.

I rub my sternum hard enough to bruise.

I.

Can't.

Fucking.

Breathe.

Evie?

My witch laughs, her head thrown back as Rosa and a man stand with their backs to me, arms draped around each other with obvious familiarity, shoulders shaking with mirth.

I take in their location, twisting my neck to see around the edge of the frame.

I focus on Evie's face. Her lips move, but I can't make out the words.

Fuck. I need to know what she's saying.

I close my shaking hands tighter around the mirror, struggling to keep on my feet. My eyes close as I will the portal to life and step through into the Human Realm.

My feet drag with every step toward Evie. It's as if every drop of strength in my body disintegrated at once. I reach for her, but my opaque hand drops through her shoulder.

Why can't I touch her?

My lips tremble, and I inhale sharply through my nose.

"Evie!"

My witch continues chatting animatedly with Rosa and the unknown man, but I only have eyes for her.

Words crack from my throat as I try again and again to touch Evie, to get her to *feel me*. "Baby Girl, please…" A single tear spills over my lashes. "Can you hear me?"

Evie jumps off her stool, fixes her apron, then walks *through* me. My breathing gutters to shallow pants.

It's as if she's forgotten my very existence,

I blink and slap a palm against a glass surface.

No.

How am I back here?

I slam the side of my fist against the mirror, whipping my head around frantically, vague, low saturated surroundings blur around me.

The Shadow Realm? But she freed me?

Air rushes into my lungs as I gasp, slithering bodies crawling over me, but nothing's changed.

Forgotten… once more. Pressure builds on my chest, a heavy weight spreading across all my extremities, and my pulse weakens. But just as I allow my eyelids to drop, I see a pair of familiar eyes framed by dark lashes in my mind—*Evie*. She could be facing the same thing I am.

I suck in a breath and roll onto my side, dislodging several sets of fangs from my flesh. My body aches as I move, the overwhelming quantity of injuries throbbing in tandem, then burst from the pile of wriggling bodies.

I turn on my heel and pump my legs as fast as they will go down the sloped hill, trees passing by in a blur.

Sweat runs down my back as I peek over my shoulder, but no snakes followed. Thank fuck.

"Lorcan!"

My head whips back around. I could've sword I heard my witch. Something connects with my cheek, and I blink several times as the sting resonates.

Evie's husky voice registers first. "Shit, Rosa, why did you do that?"

"It's the most affective and quickest way to bring someone out of panic induced hysteria. Well, other than smelling salts or straight adrenaline." *That doesn't sound correct.*

A growl rumbles low in my chest as I rub my fingers over my smarting skin, and Rosa and Evie come into focus. "What. The. Fuck."

"Our thoughts exactly. Welcome back."

My hands drop to my sides, then I rub my temples as a headache blossoms within my skull. "Are you being deliberately confusing?"

Rosa scoffs. "Are you being deliberately obtuse?"

Evie walks between us and holds up her hands, then faces me. "This is a trial."

The breath stalls in my lungs, then I dart to my gaze to her as my heart careens into my ribs. I squeeze her against me, a trembling hand smoothing down her long, straight hair to the small of her back.

Evie encircles my torso with her arms and hugs me back.

She can feel me.

Thank fucking Lucifer.

"L-or?"

Evie's muffled voice reaches me as I step back just enough to take in her bemused expression.

I peer at her through a slitted gaze and fish a cigarette from my pocket, then pat down my pants. "Godsdammit. My lighter must've fallen out when I ran."

My witch huffs and strides over to a pile of demolished vegetation, plucks something from the remains, and hurries back to me. "Lorcan. Listen to the words coming out of my mouth. This is a trial."

I squint at her over the purple flame she holds to the end of the cigarette between my lips, inhaling as it catches. My eyes close as reality sets in.

Fuck.

She's right.

All of those human emotions were forced on me. A relaxed smirk tips my lips. I knew I didn't give a shit about killing the fuckboy. In fact, I reveled in it. "The Trial of Terrors. Did he have to make it so obvious?"

A snort-laugh peals from Rosa. "Riiiiight, obvious. Because you weren't slashing your claws at hanging vines while you growled and screamed."

My upper lip pulls back and my nostrils flare as I shoot a glare at Evie's best friend. My annoyance dissipates slightly as Evie brushes her mouth against mine and drapes her arms around my waist. "Ignore her, we need to find the others. Although, she's not wrong. It was hilarious once we figured out what was going on."

My cheeks hollow as I take another drag and the lavender cherry flares brighter. I hold the curling smoke in my mouth, grab Evie's chin, and blow the hot nicotine laced smoke between her lips. A grin smooths over my features as she moans. Satisfaction rolls over my skin as I cross my tattooed arms, free of any injury because it really was all in my fucking head. "Who do we hunt first?"

Rosa hums. "I don't think Aiden went very far. He crashed into the woods over there." She points a manicured nail to our right and I chuckle.

Evie laughs. "He could have made it a bit more of a challenge."

I pass my cigarette to Evie and shake my head as I note the clear path of destruction zig-zagging drunkenly through the woods for no more than a hundred yards, then spot the top of a peach ball-cap and half of an embroidered bat wing design sticking out behind a tree.

Rosa takes a step forward. "I'll get him. You two," she drags a finger in the air between Evie and I, "stay here."

I scoff and make to follow her, but my witch raises a hand and lays it on my chest. "Let it go. I'd rather Rosa calm him down and explain quickly, then have Aiden run off again if he sees you. You have a habit of scaring him for fun."

I laugh. "And I'm not even fucking sorry."

Several minutes go by in comfortable silence, and I massage Evie's shoulders as we wait.

Evie's muscles finally loosen under my hands, my thumbs digging into a stubborn knot.

"What the Hell did you think you were seeing earlier?" Evie blurts.

My fingers tense. "Snakes."

"Cute little danger noodles?"

I turn her to face me. "In what possible fucking way are they cute?" I sigh down my nose, glancing over her head and speak through the bond. *It wasn't about the snakes at all. Never mind. We'll get back to this later. I need to understand how you like those scaly fuckers. They could consume your bat whole, for fuck's sake.*

Aiden ambles over to us with Rosa on his heels as Evie rolls her lips and shakes with silent laughter. *I mean, not a garner snake, though.*

Aiden covers his mouth with a hand in my peripheral, then whisper shouts, "They're doing it again."

Rosa looses a long sigh. "I can see that."

Evie clears her throat and turns toward Aiden. "Glad to have you back."

"Are you sure he's not going to turn into a clown again?" Aiden asks, a barely noticeable quaver to his words, and side-eyes me.

Evie's gaze slides toward me. "I'm sure."

I chuckle into Evie's mind. *That's what he thinks. Fucking with him is too much fun. Even more so now that I know he abhors clowns. Well…*

Lorcan, Evie admonishes, then claps a hand over her mouth, her muffled laughter still seeping through.

Rosa clears her throat and plants her hands on her hips. "If you two are done with whatever it is you're doing, should we go search for Ezra and Gideon?"

Evie steps away from me, following Rosa as she speed walks up the slope. How she manages that in high-heeled boots, I have no fucking clue.

I glance at Aiden as we trek after the women.

"How are we going to find them?" Evie questions over her shoulder.

"Well, I suppose I could track them through our brotherly bond."

Rosa muffles a laugh. "Yes, I don't think they will be as easy to find as Aiden was."

"What do you mean? I had a great hiding spot," Aiden says, nodding to himself.

I sigh and flick the brim of his hat. "We could see your damn hat sticking out behind the tree."

Aiden laughs and flashes his too white smile at me. "But I'm telling you. If it wasn't for the hat, I would have been completely invisible. You dudes would never have found me." For a moment he looks so fucking proud of himself, but his grin falls. "Oh, but then, you know I guess I would still be afraid clowns were chasing me…"

My hand claps over his shoulder and he jumps, making me chuckle. Just as I open my mouth to exacerbate Aiden's sorrowful demeanor, Evie speaks in my mind. *Please, just leave him alone.*

I smooth a hand through my hair and exhale through my nose. *I'll consider it, in exchange for a sexual favor to be claimed at a later date of my choosing.*

Evie snorts and Rosa's head swivels to her, then back at me. *You can have me whenever you want, Lor.*

So, it won't be a problem accepting my bargain then.

Fine. I mean it, leave him the fuck alone. He's had a rough day.

I shake my head but refrain from yet another smartass response. She's well aware that all of us have had a *shitty day.*

"All of you keep your mouths shut. Any needless blathering will delay us, and I'd really like to get the fuck out of these woods."

Rosa scoffs but doesn't comment.

I turn inward, locate my brothers' bonds, and focus on their location. Dammit, they ran much farther than Aiden, which isn't surprising as they're demons and he's a weak human, but at least they're near each other.

The fuck? That can't be right.

I track their energies down our bonds once more. No, I was correct. It's as if they're practically on top of one another.

"Lorcan? Did you find them?"

My eyes drift to Evie. "Of course. However, be on alert. Their signatures are far too close, it's likely that they're locked in a fucking brawl again."

"Could you pick up on any landmarks?" Rosa asks, stopping to face me.

I raise my brows, even though I know she won't see the questioning expression behind my mask.

She sighs and speaks with her hands. "It stands to reason that if we all know what to look for, they will be located sooner."

"Oh! Good point," Aiden remarks, lifting a hand in the air and holding it there.

A smile blooms across Evie's face, and she arches a brow. "Well, don't leave him hanging."

"What the fuck are you talking about?"

A sonorous gasp vibrates my eardrums and my nose wrinkles.

"What? Bro, Demon, are you telling me you've never given someone a high five?" Aiden shouts, his eyes wider than dinner plates. Of course, I'm aware of the odd human behavior, but I have no intention of enacting said *high-five*. Aiden reaches toward me with his free hand, picks my hand up, then slaps it against his own, smaller, clammy hand. My nostrils flare as Evie and Rosa burst into a fit of laughter.

A growl seeps from me, low and deadly. "If I were you, I'd remove your touch from my hand immediately."

Before Aiden gets the chance to follow through with my demand, Gomez flies over and bites the back of my hand, and retreats to my witch's shoulder. I glare at the cute bastard, then close my eyes for a moment. My fingers curl at my sides and my blood boils. *You cannot kill the bat, or the human, Lorcan. Evie would never forgive you.* My eyes flash open and my neck cracks as I twist it side to side before speaking over my shoulder and stalk to the head of the group. "We are all off topic yet a-fucking-gain. Yes, Rosa, they're near a fairly large boulder, perhaps a quarter mile or less to the North."

We walk in silence as I track my brothers. I have no way of knowing how long we've searched for, but it's clearly long enough that Aiden forgets to remain silent.

"Are you sure we aren't lost?" he asks.

"Yes, I'm sure. You can't hear them?"

Aiden tilts his head. "Uh, no?"

I release a pent-up growl. "Of course not, because you're talking loud enough to wake the fucking dead."

"Hey, asshole, that certainly looks like a big ass boulder to me," Rosa interjects.

I spin toward her, following her stare with my own. Sure enough, just over a crest in the slope, part of a massive boulder rises.

Fucking.

Finally.

I jog toward it, picking up on more sounds as I eat up the distance between my brothers and me.

"Get it away from me!" Ezra screams, tears shining along his lower lashes and dripping into his beard.

Gideon roars, "It's not here for you. It's here for me! Run, Ez."

My eyes narrow as I round the side of the boulder, then I laugh. "Oh, this is just too fucking perfect." Three heartbeats register in my ears, and I glance over my shoulder at Evie, Rosa, and Aiden.

Ezra peers out at me with wide eyes, all his featured stretched with fear from beneath a cute little doggy pile of zalvie spirit monsters. So, that's what manifested the hallucinations, the zalvie's most potent power.

Ezra sits up and at least twenty of the fluffy creatures fall off him. "Lorcan, did you see where it went?"

I dart my gaze over his head and slowly widen my eyes. "Don't move. It's right behind you." The look of horror on his face will forever be etched into my memory.

Aiden whoops. "Are we messing with Ezra instead of me now?" He slaps his hands to his cheeks. "Oh no, bro, you better run. It's gonna get yoouuuu."

Evie looks toward Rosa, sighing. "Stop. Enough of this."

Aiden's brows furrow and fine wrinkles appear on his forehead. "But, Bromina, someone else was final—"

"No," Evie and Rosa say, cutting him off.

Aiden's shoulders droop as he sighs. "Okay, fine. What are those things anyway?" Gomez flies into the fray of fluffy bodies and rolls around with them on top of my brothers. "Whatever they are, Gomey sure likes them."

My attention drifts back to my brothers as Gideon crawls over Ezra, kneeing him in the gut before crouching next to the boulder. "Get over here, Wrath. It won't see us if we take cover behind the boulder."

I laugh so hard my cheeks dig into the bottom edge of my mask. "You two are fucking idiots." I reach out a hand to pet a periwinkle zalvie, but it bounces on feet too big for its body and bites my finger. I hiss and shake my hand, flinging it off me. "You fucker."

"Let me try," Aiden proposes, then removes his hat, attempts to scoop one up inside it. The cornflower blue monster hisses and narrows its cobalt eyes at Aiden. "Oh, common, little guy, I just wanna give you pets."

Rosa sucks in a breath. "Shit. Aiden, I wouldn't do that."

The zalvie parts its jaws far past what it should be capable of, then sinks its fangs into the back of Aiden's hat near the Velcro sizing strap.

"That's mine," Aiden says, then tugs his hat backward, but the little zalvie doesn't release its hold.

I roll my eyes as Evie and Rosa laugh at the absurd tug of war.

Crouching down in front of Ezra, I shake his shoulders. "This is a trial. Trust me, whatever you think is happening isn't." Ezra stops flailing and coughs as a zalvie jumps onto his face and hangs onto his beard. Three more of the little assholes cling to Gideon's warrior braids and swing along with the momentum of his head as he turns. "He's right, Ez, there's no duck."

I squint my left eye at the twins and mutter under my breath. "What fucking duck? You know what? I don't even want to know."

Gomez flies back to Evie, squeaking and rubing his fluffy cheek against hers. "I know, Gomey. Aren't they so cute?" The bat releases a soft, pleased purr, and wraps his wings around his body.

Ezra falls flat on his back as one final periwinkle zalvie bounces on his chest, the others climbing onto the boulder. I narrow my eyes on the tiny monster, then realization dawns.

Ezra grabs the fluffy creature with two hands and smothers it against his chest. "Rupe? Rupert!" Ezra and Rupert roll around on the ground, a convoluted symphony of two extremely different pitched growls emitting from their aggressive cuddle.

"What's a Rupert?" Aiden asks.

"Rupert is the name of Ezra's pet zalvie," Gideon say laconically, then stands and brushes his hands over his pants.

Ezra stands, cuddling Rupert against his bearded cheek, and eyes all of us. "No one say the word duck to me ever-a-fuckin-gain."

The group's chatter fades into a buzzing as something scratches at the back of my mind, then a flash of the cave from the zalvie's vision darts across my mind's eye. I lace my fingers with Evie's and stroll farther up the hill, confident the others will follow.

"Shit. Where the Hell are you going, Lor?" Ezra shouts.

I press a kiss to my witch's cheek, smiling against her skin before answering my fucking pest of a brother. "To test a theory."

Evie's mind brushes against mine. *I'm curious too.*

She shivers as I stroke my thumb in leisurely circles on the back of her tattooed hand. *I saw a cave in a vision. Something was off about it. It's not far. Less than one hundred yards, just over the final crest of the hill.*

The feeling of power grows as the group takes in a tall archway cut into the rock of the shallow cave. My eyes trace over the ancient demonic language carved above it. Snorting, I glance back at my brothers.

"What does it say?" Rosa asks.

Ezra shrugs. "Essentially, that going in is a risk of death, etc… Standard posturing. Nothing to be concerned about."

"Is that such a good idea, Bro Demon?" Aiden asks, his lips tugging down.

Gideon steps close to Aiden's back and quietly hums. "It's most likely only a deterrent."

Both of my brothers are right, but I'm done fucking explaining every detail of my thought process. I squeeze Evie's hand, tuck our laced hands close to my back, then stoop below the arch and saunter into the swirling darkness.

CHAPTER TWENTY-EIGHT

Lorcan

Ezra whistles a breath while rolling back onto his heels. "Home sweet Hell."

He and Gideon pass us as we stand on the uneven, stone path leading from the archway. Fog shrouds the castle walls and candles flicker from the dark, arched windows above like dying stars. Nothing has changed. Even the same spirits haunt the courtyard, except the remnants of their human forms have mostly faded.

Evie's grip on my fingers is tighter than usual, as if she's aware how stepping foot onto these grounds affects me. How my heart stutters and sweat trickles down my spine. The last time I was here, my brothers dragged me into a fucking cage. I exhale with forced slowness through my nose.

"So," Evie says with a tense breath, "this is Lucifer's Court."

Rosa adds, "It is, right?"

"It is."

Rosa and Aiden sigh in tandem, the trials now behind us, left for the next unsuspecting souls. I walk ahead, a bittersweet heartache spilling through my veins as I recall the good and bad times here.

"Did you grow up here?" Evie asks, her brows creasing, a smirk shadowing her lips as if the idea of me as a child is incomprehensible.

"Yes."

The hollow eyes of spirits follow us as we walk through the courtyard. My gaze drifts to the tallest turret, and I trace each stone step leading from the window down to the roof, now suffocated with purple vines. It feels like a lifetime since my brothers and I would play up there. Granted, much like the human game hide-and-go-seek, except our version was more like torturer-and-victim. Once, we found Asher after three days, struggling to breathe while trapped in a chest. Then we threw him down those steps.

Evie glances up at me with those soft, brown eyes. "What are you smiling about?"

"Remembering playing here with my brothers."

"Awe." She gently squeezes my hand, and I chuckle.

"You wouldn't say that if you knew what games we'd play."

Aiden rubs arms with Rosa as they cautiously step beside us now that the path to the doors has expanded for us all to fit. "I can imagine," Aiden says, gripping the back of his neck. "Are there demons here?"

"Of course there are," I state.

He swallows thickly, the bulb in his throat bobbing up and down.

Rosa rolls her eyes and tugs Aiden closer. "Ez!" she yells as Ezra stands under the gigantic, arched doors. They're using fucking nicknames now? Fucking Hell. She's going to become a permanent part of my life, isn't she?

Demons in their human forms—giving fresh energy to the saying a wolf in sheep's clothing—loiter the darkened foyer, bathed in purple candlelight and glowing fog. Once they see us, they fall back into the shadows, their eyes never leaving us. Wrapping my hand around Evie's waist, I pull her closer, making it very fucking clear that she's mine.

A low growl resonates in my chest and Evie cranes her neck to look at the demons.

Can I use my magic here? Now that the trials are over

Yes, and you absolutely should if anything tries to hurt you, but don't let on what you can do.

"Ezra!" Samuel's voice echoes around us like nails on a fucking chalkboard. "Gideon. And is that little Lorcan I see behind you?" He appears through a cloud of mist in the middle of the spiral staircase, his fingers grazing the intricately carved banister of human suffering.

Ezra hisses, "You say that, but you're the shortest out of us all."

Gideon scoffs a laugh, his sword glowing on his back as a reminder that he could easily strike Samuel down with it. In fact, he just fucking might.

Samuel's smile drops and for once I'm glad Ezra is on my side. It feels good. Like having a brother, a teammate, and I almost say thanks. *Almost.*

Samuel's flat, gray eyes trail to Evie, the corners of his thin lips curling up like a caricature of a damned villain. "You brought humans. How intriguing. I've always wanted one as a pet." He points a clawed finger at my love. "Maybe I'll take this one. She's feisty like her aunt."

I shove Evie behind me before she can say a word, wanting her out of this vermin's view. He doesn't deserve to even look at her, to breathe the same air as her. "I'd like to see you try to take her from me."

Gideon clears his throat, stepping between us as Samuel descends the last few stone steps. The demons have all but melded themselves into the wall, too afraid to make themselves seen but too intrigued to leave us. "We're here to see *your* queen," Gideon intones.

Footsteps thump behind Samuel as Lazarus appears in his finest suit without a blue-black hair out of place as usual.

Ezra laughs and smacks Gideon's arm. "And here she is."

An unexpected, hearty laugh bubbles from my stomach and into my throat. I almost choke on my next words as I watch Lazarus turn a satisfying shade of pink. It's so easy to get to him, but then, he's the embodiment of pride and has the biggest ego out of us all.

Ezra glances over his shoulder at me and winks.

The muscle in Lazarus's jaw feathers as he stares down at Ezra, murderous intent etched into every crease of his mouth. "Ever the joker, Brother. Let's see how long you'll keep that smile on your face when Father learns you helped him." He points at me.

Silas and Asher join the fold, their reddish-blonde hair reminiscent of our mother, except Silas's is neatly trimmed short on the sides and long on top, while Asher's shaggy strands fall in waves around his shoulders.

Asher leans against the dark, mahogany banister and sighs, looking bored already. Samuel likely ordered him down here the moment he learned of our return. "Father doesn't even know—hey!" Asher shouts when Silas kicks him in the shin.

If Evie wasn't here, surrounded by demons and princes, I'd be at each of their fucking throats by now. Instead, I glare at Samuel and growl, "Where is our father?"

A flicker of panic crosses his dead stare, and I know at that moment, even without Asher blurting it out, that Ezra and I were right. Lucifer doesn't know the truth.

"He's not available."

"The Hell he's not!" I shout back and Evie wraps her fingers around my wrists like manacles.

It's Lazarus who approaches us first, closing the gap between us and them. He stands before Ezra and Gideon, and several paces in front of me, without a hint of fear. "None of us have seen him in a decade."

I flick my gaze from him to Samuel. "Not even that piece of shit?"

"Father is in solitude," Lazarus explains, deadpan. "He's working on something important."

"A ritual," Samuel adds.

"Fucking bullshit." I shake my head. "Where is he?"

Ezra pushes past Lazarus, whose aquamarine eyes narrow. "We're going to him now."

"Wait!" Samuel's deep voice echoes around the cavernous foyer. "First, Evangeline wishes to speak with you."

"Fine. Let's get this over with," I spit, but Lazarus holds out a hand when I try to pull Evie along.

"No humans *or* witches." He eyes Rosa, then Aiden, and finally Evie. "They can go to the East Wing while you see her."

I tug her to my side, pulling her against my hip, my pulse racing at the thought of being separated from her, here of all places. "I'm not leaving her."

"We won't touch the witch," Lazarus says with a grimace, his nostrils flaring as if the thought of my caring about Evie is the most disgusting thing he's seen in years, despite Samuel standing right behind him.

Gideon steps back and stands between Aiden and Rosa. "You and Ezra go, Lorcan," he says with wide, green eyes. "I'll guard the East Wing."

My throat dries. "No."

Evie curls around to my front, and rests her head on my chest, her voice in our bond, soft and caressing my hard edges. *Go deal with her and find out where your father is. I'll be okay. I trust Gideon, and besides, I have my powers. After everything you've told me, it'll be best not to provoke her in my presence.*

I don't give a fuck about her, I reply and wrap my arms around Evie, placing a kiss on the top of her head. Fuck, she smells so godsdamn good. I just want to hold her like this forever.

I know. I trust you. Now go. This is your chance. Manipulate her, just like you did before. Whatever you need to do to find out where Lucifer is.

Evie unfolds herself from me and I flinch with the desire to keep her close, but she's led away with Ezra, Gideon, Rosa, Gomez, and Aiden before I can. A chill skates over my flesh, the chasm behind my ribs gaping without her. Without all of them, I suppose. A shockwave pierces through my bones like an electric current and my breath catches.

"I always hated you, Lorcan," Samuel says once they're gone and it's just me, Ezra, Samuel, Lazarus, and Asher, who's no longer paying attention. "But at least I respected you. Look at you both with those humans," he spits, sneering sneers at Ezra too. "It's pitiful."

Ezra balks, his shoulders squaring when he faces Samuel. "I can still beat you in a fight, Sammy. You know that. Go on, test my wrath."

Samuel laughs but visibly shrinks back against the banister. "All brawn and no brains. As always, nothing changes. How disappointing."

"I'm heading to my room," Asher says, completely unaware of the tense atmosphere. Or more likely, doesn't care. "See ya."

Samuel grasps at his hand, but Asher slips away before he can force him to remain. "We agreed to go together."

"There's no reason for me to be there," Asher says from halfway up the staircase, his voice always the same, flat and unbothered. Even when he saw Rosa, which was a surprise, considering she knocked his ass out. "If Lorcan tries to hurt Dad, you're all more than capable of stopping him."

I scoff. "I have zero interest in the throne and Dad fucking knows that." Without Evie to protect, I turn to face Samuel, leaning closer until he's poising backward. "Listen to me, you *cunt*. I don't know what you've done with Dad, or where you and the bitch have hidden him, but I am *not* leaving until I find him."

"Enough," barks Lazarus. "There's no need to fight. Evangeline's already waiting for you."

It takes less than a minute for the five of us to shadow walk to the small solar at the other side of the castle.

Samuel gestures his arm out to the open door when we arrive, and I halt at the threshold, reaching my shadows within first. The dark smoke of my magic curls around the corners of the solar until I'm satisfied it isn't a trap.

Ezra huffs out a breath, pushing past me to walk inside. "See, it's fine," he says, arms wide open as he stops beside the bone table that takes up most of the room. He pulls one of the eight chairs out, screeching it back until it stops at the stone hearth of the fireplace. "Come on. It's been an age since we've sat in here."

Slowly, I walk inside, hands deep in my pockets and look around. Everything is the same, from the stone walls covered in tapestries showing each of the deadly sins as humans suffering, to the small arched window with fractured stained glass, and the black cabinet displaying books bound in skin and swords that ended the grisliest of battles.

Lazarus stomps behind me, then brings the fire to life, the purple embers settling between half-charred logs. He brushes any remnants of ash from his double-breasted jacket and takes the seat next to Ezra.

I grab the seat at the head of the table before the bastard Samuel can. Ezra glances at Silas, and with a mocking smile, pats the seat next to him. "Come sit, Sil. I know you don't really want to sit next to *him.*" Ezra gestures to Samuel, who takes the chair at the bottom right of the table, leaving the chair directly opposite me empty.

After a few heavy seconds of silence, Ezra slams his hands on the bone slab of the table with a grin. "Well, this is nice. All of us together after all this time. I mean, except Gid." He points down to Samuel. "You should be glad about that. After he realized you lied to him, he wanted to run you through with his sword."

Samuel shifts in his chair. "I'm not afraid of Gideon."

Ezra laughs with his whole chest. "Oh, you should be. Truly. Even I am. Just don't tell him that."

I cut through the bullshit, my eyes fixed on Samuel. "Where's the bitch?"

His dark brows pull together and his lips crease into a deep frown. It's only when the second entrance to the private sitting room opens does he offer even a hint of a genuine smile. He must genuinely like her. I'd never have guessed it. I'm shocked he has any emotions.

The purple hue of the candlelight flickers shadows over Evangeline's square jaw and angular cheekbones when she saunters into the dimly lit room. Drips of blood fleck her ivory bone corset. She rolls her shoulders, pushing her chest out when she locks eyes with me for the first time in a century.

Those dark brown eyes, with flecks of gold, which used to soften when she looked at me, now pin me with contempt. She stops at Samuel's side, standing over him. He reaches his fingers close to hers, but she pulls back before he can touch her. Of course, they have to pretend they're not fucking. She's meant to be my dad's bride, not his.

"Lorcan." Her voice echoes, sounding throatier from when I knew her. "How good of you to stop by."

The glow of her skin waltzes between translucent and opaque. She's dead, yet somehow preserved, unlike the other spirits. She really has manipulated my dad. He's the only one with the power to do that.

"Let's save the niceties," I spit. She holds her expression steady, unlike when she was alive and trapped me in the fucking Shadow Realm. "Where's my father?"

She exhales slowly, her face unreadable as she flicks her eyes to Samuel, then slides into the seat directly opposite me, but fortunately the furthest away. "He's not taking visitors."

"I am his oldest son," I snarl. "I *know* you're keeping him from me, from all of us."

Her laugh is girlish, a tinker of insanity lacing each giggle of disbelief. With her hand pressing over her heart, she says all too sweetly, "You think I have any power over Lucifer, the almighty King of Hell?"

"We both know you do."

Silas shakes his head in my peripheral vision and leans forward. "Do you hear yourself, Lorcan?"

"She's a manipulative bitch."

"Says you?" she asks, her dark brow quirking up. It's surprising how much she looks like my Evie, albeit her features are sharper, less refined. Yet, she repulses me with every micro expression and movement.

I lean back in my chair, pleased I finally provoked a hint of anger from her. "Says *me*." I place my tattooed hands in my lap and smirk, evoking a twitch in the corner of her painted lips. "Tell me, how did you convince Samuel that you love him?"

Her brows crease, her eyes wide with worry as if I'm in the insane one. "I love all of my stepsons."

Bile bites the back of my throat. "You know exactly what I mean, you harlot."

She laughs again. I know that sound will find me in my sleep, a damned soundtrack to my fucking nightmares. "I don't know what you're insinuating, but I love your dad."

"Hmm. Enough to convince him I'm trying to steal his throne, if he even knows that story."

"Throne?" Her brows rise up her forehead. "I never, ever told him such a thing."

Samuel nods. "It's true. Eva had nothing to do with it. I told our brothers that, which is the truth."

I exhale sharply through my nose and shake my head. He said otherwise to Evie. He's protecting her and he doesn't even realize she's making him into a scapegoat.

Silas looks at Samuel. "Wait. I thought you said Evangeline knew?"

"Me too," Lazarus adds, and I smile as I watch his lie unravel.

"I thought she did," Samuel offers. "Father didn't discuss it with her."

"We fucking hunted him," Lazarus admonishes, gesturing across the table to me. "You said we were working under *her* orders."

Evangeline has the audacity to look shocked. She even throws in a small gasp for good measure. What an excellent performance. I can't wait to choke the fucking life from her. "None of that matters now," she says softly, placing her hands between them. "All that matters is finding out if this is true."

"You know it's not," I state, and she shrugs, lackadaisically resting her wrist upright against the chair rest. Her red nails drum against the splitting wood, each thrum evoking the madness deep-seated in my mind.

That's when I hear my Evie and my heart quickly settles.

Lor? Is everything okay?

I close my eyes briefly. *It's going as well as I thought it would. I'll come to you soon.*

Evangeline tilts her head, knowing flashing in her eyes, but says nothing.

Evie's voice softens the sharp edges of my madness. My own personal medicine. *Did you find your dad?*

No. They won't tell me.

After a few seconds, her reply filters through. *That's because they think you're a threat. Convince them you're not or seek him out yourself.*

I cut the bond off once I realize Evangeline's stare has warped into that of a succubus. "I know that look," she says when my attention falls back on her. "Tell me, is my namesake enjoying her chambers?"

"You mean the witch? Your niece?" I shrug, forcing as much icy intention into my expression as possible. "You think I was talking to her?"

"Why else are you so focused? I know the look. You each have it when you're using your inner voice."

A cruel smile twists my features. "I wasn't talking to her. I'm using her, just like I used you. *Remember?*"

Her eye twitches and my muscles relax. I've won. At least in aggravating her. But Evie's right. I need to convince them I'm not a threat, when all I want to do is tear her and Samuel apart, limb by limb, and watch their skin melt from their bones as they burn in Hellfire.

Ezra chimes in. "He was talking to me, if you must know." He sits back and mumbles under his breath, "Nosy bitch."

I clear the hoarseness in my throat. "He's right. Look, I don't care what's been said about me wanting the throne. About being locked in the Shadow Realm. Any of it. I want back in Hell, to be in control of my demons again." Lies. It's all fucking lies and Samuel knows it. So does Evangeline, but her eyes narrow, her lips parting an inch. She wants to believe me. Her heart rate picks up slightly, and I know exactly what I need to do. "I'm not a threat to Dad. I want my life back, that's all."

Her smile almost betrays her to the rest. "Fine. Let us talk alone then."

Ezra scoffs and looks from me to Evangeline, then back to me. "Are you fucking kidding?" he asks incredulously. "I did not go through all of that just to miss the real gossip."

Samuel grunts as Evangeline whispers something unintelligible in his ear. "Let's leave them," he says, and Ezra's pastel green eyes widen twice their size.

"Since when the fuck are you the authority? I'm staying."

Evangeline flashes her pearly whites at Ezra. "There will be no gossip. I must simply dissect whether Lorcan is a threat to your dad."

Ezra shakes his head, a laugh of disbelief bubbling past his lips. He stands up, murmuring under his breath. "Unbelievable."

Before he leaves, I hear his voice clearly in my head. *You better tell me everything. Also, if she tries anything, I'll happily help you get rid of what remains of her soul before Dad finds out.*

I shoot him a smirk, and he grins, which only annoys Samuel more. He pushes his chair out and hurries after Silas and Lazarus in what I assume is an attempt to do some damage control.

Once we're alone, Evangeline stands, her gray dress flowing around her ankles as she stirs a scattering of sparks from the fireplace. "Now, my love, why don't we drop all the bullshit?"

CHAPTER TWENTY-NINE

Lorcan

I cannot hide a glare as I exhale a tense breath. Evangeline stands in front of me, taller than Evie's short stature, but still five inches shorter than me. She smells like musk, death, and lilies—all the trappings of a funeral. "Samuel tells me you've fallen for the witch, but we both know you don't have a heart."

I don't stop her when she walks her fingers up my chest, at least until she reaches my throat. I grab her fingers and gnash my teeth. "Touch me again and you'll lose those fingers."

She laughs but recoils her hand. "Your threats don't scare me. Your father will never let anything happen to me."

"He'd never hurt his son, either."

She smiles. "You're right, but I've been whispering sweet, poisonous little lies into his ear for years. He thinks you abandoned him. That you hated him. It broke his heart." She pouts and bats her long lashes. "You should have seen him."

A growl rumbles in my chest. "Enough! I know it's impossible to reason with a fucking insane person, but—"

"Insane?" Shaking her head, she turns from me to stare out the window. "You still take no responsibility for what you did to me, do you?"

"You got your revenge. I was locked in the Shadow Realm for a godsdamn century."

Her palms lay flat on the stone windowsill as she hunches over, her spine misaligned at an odd angle. Her body quakes as she sucks in a lungful of air, and I grip the back of a chair. "You were never supposed to be locked in there in the first place!" She spins to face me, her head tilted at an almost inhuman angle before she straightens herself out. "You forced me to lock you in there after you betrayed me."

"I used you, just like you're using Samuel and my dad."

She runs her long, ringed fingers through her dark, dull strands and lifts her gaze to me mine. "Well, you know the saying. If you can't beat them, join them."

"You're fucking psychotic," I say, realizing being nice isn't going to work. Lying about my intentions won't either because of one fucked up truth—she's still in love with me. I can see it in her dilated pupils and the way she keeps floating closer to me as if she's magnetically drawn into my orbit.

"Thank you," she hisses. "Are you impressed?"

I scoff. "Do you want me to call you a good girl?"

Her brown eyes alight with gold. "You're more playful now. I thought all that time in solitude would destroy your spirit. Or was it my great niece? Did she warm the cockles of your empty heart?"

I grimace. "No."

"Good," she whispers, then glides her hand up my arm without actually touching me. "I wonder what she'll do to you when I tell her you're using her like you did me? How did you convince her, by the way?" she asks, drawing closer. "That what I wrote in the grimoire wasn't true? She must have believed you because she destroyed the portal."

I'm just so fucking glad she doesn't think I care about Evie, else my witch would be in genuine danger.

I tilt my head. The purple flames from the torches on the wall flickering in her mad stare. "You Fallenmoore witches always were so damn gullible."

She brings her face closer to mine, then spits, "I don't believe you. I know you've been protecting the witch."

"I'm not."

"Then prove it," she hisses, her fingers dancing into the ruffles of her white dress. "Kiss me."

"I'd rather tear out my tongue," I snarl, and she swallows thickly. "I don't want her, or you."

"You will never see your dad," she replies with a shake of her head as she steps out of my proximity. "He's mine and for as long as he is, I'll never let you know peace for what you did to me. You destroyed my life." Tears gloss her eyes, and I realize she doesn't recall how she treated me. No, she just remembers the bad things *I* did to her. "You pretended to be my friend. You made me love you, and then you tossed me aside like I was nothing."

I lean in and whisper, "And does Samuel or my dad know about that?"

She shakes her head. "They know we were friends, and you threatened me."

I chuckle darkly. "You've left out quite a bit."

Her smile wavers, lips quivering as she attempts to pull herself together, but she can't rid herself of the twitch in her eye. Perhaps she convinced herself that seeing me after all this time would be easier. She wipes the single tear trickling down her cheek onto the back of her hand and sniffs. "I won't let you break me again. I died because of you, because I had to lock you away after you refused to… well, you pretended to love me."

"I never did that," I snap. "I used your friendship, yes, but I never showed that I was fucking interested."

"You did."

"You invented an entire convoluted romance in your head," I yell, placing my fingers to my temples. "You were a fucking anchor around my neck, Eva. I didn't care about you then, and I sure as fuck don't care about you now."

She juts her chin. An icy coolness seeps into her expression before the mask of apathy returns. Except now she looks as evil as Samuel, with pointed, dark eyes.

A waft of spicy cinnamon and rich, buttery dough pinches the air around my nose. At first, I think someone must have lit a candle, until I hear clashing in the next room of metal trays hitting the ground.

Dad's voice filters through the door. "Bugger it, damned things."

The door opens and Lucifer walks in, a tray in one hand, a second on the floor, with cinnamon buns everywhere.

He hasn't aged a day in the last century. In fact, he looks a few years younger than I remember.

Patches of flour douse the dark curls against his forehead, and cling to his gray and black trimmed beard. His silver eyes—a hallmark of an angel, even a fallen one—meet mine. Placing the buns that didn't fall on the table, he extends his arms out in a warm gesture as he walks to me.

My eyes widen, fear piercing through my veins as he pulls me into a hug. A fucking cuddle.

"My boy," he says, patting me on the back. The scent of vanilla and cinnamon cling to the flowery apron of lilies and black dahlias, covering his white shirt and black pants. "One of my demons told me you'd returned to court. I didn't believe it, but here you are."

Evangeline forces a smile, putting several feet between me and her. "Hi, my love. I was just coming to tell you your son was here."

He waves a hand in her direction. "Get my other sons, Darling. We're going to have a ball tonight."

She sucks in a deep breath, holds it, then says with forced cloying, "Another ball?"

"Of course. It's a celebration. All my sons are back home, where they belong." He steps back to get a proper look at me, and I hold still, not sure what to say or do. "I'd worried we'd lost you to the Human Realm for good."

My brows quirk up behind my mask, my eyes flitting from him to Evangeline. Did he really believe I was in the Human Realm this entire time?

My brain fritzes, quickly catching up after struggling to process him just walking in on us. "Evangeline said you were not to be disturbed."

"That was Samuel," she adds quickly. "We know you've been so busy, working on your project."

"Cinnamon buns," he announces. "I had the perfect recipe some centuries ago but lost it somewhere in the Human Realm." He shakes his head. "No matter, no matter. My oldest son has finally returned."

He wraps me in another hug, and this time I allow it, fold into it, and close my eyes. Every crevice of my chest aches. Ever since Evie cracked it open, it's like I can't force the desire of more than lust out of it.

It's fucking painful to love. It hurts so godsdamn much that I want to tear the organ out of its bone prison.

He pulls away again, tousling my hair. "I hope you're planning on staying this time. I know I've no right to expect it," he says with an arched, dark brow, "and I know a century is nothing to us, but you could have sent a letter. I've missed you."

My throat tightens. "I've missed you too, Dad." I pause, evaluating his face. He really knows nothing. "We need to talk. I wasn't in the Human Realm the whole time."

"We will catch up tonight," he promises, and grabs a cinnamon bun. "Try this."

"Uhh." I pick up the swirl of golden brown and white pastry and sniff it first. "I'm not really into desserts."

"Please, tell me what you think of it," he says. "While it's still hot, and be *honest*."

He watches, eyes wide with anticipation, fingers spired together as I bring it to my lips.

The warm dough sinks easily between my teeth, the sugary sweetness subtle with a hint of orange extract, walnut, and vanilla. The filling is perfect as the dough breaks down between chews. "It's good."

His shoulders slump. "Good?" He nods his head. "See, I told you it's missing something," he says to Evangeline without looking at her, who rolls her eyes to the ceiling.

"I really do like it," I offer and place the rest back on the tray.

"If it was perfect, you'd have finished it," he announces. "Hungry or not. No matter, nothing will match up to my original recipe."

"Wait, is this what you've been doing?" I ask, thinking back to Samuel's comment about him being locked up, working on some ritual. "*Baking?*"

"Well, how else am I supposed to spend my time?" he asks, glancing toward the window. "The demons do all the grunt work, and your brothers handle their tasks, which, you've been slacking," he says with a waggle of his finger. "No matter. Now that you're back, I assume you'll be taking the reins back on your duties?"

"About that," I begin, "I really do need to talk to you about Samuel and—"

Waving a dismissive hand, he cuts me off. "I don't get in the middle of squabbles between my children. You can work it out at the ball tonight." He rubs his hands together. "I love a party, and I haven't seen Asher, Gideon, Ezra, Lazarus, or Silas in almost as long as I haven't seen you. They're always so busy with their duties, always somewhere on the other side of Hell or up to something in the Human Realm," he rambles, completely unaware that he's been isolated by the bitch behind him. "I know I can't force any of you to visit."

At least she has the sense to look terrified now we're back and our dad knows it.

"Now, head on down. I know you have guests. I've sent them something to wear."

"Already?"

He nods and grabs his tray. "Come now, Eva. I still need to visit the rest of my sons before the ball."

She quickly races to his arm as he walks out, cinnamon buns in hand. "Love you, Lorcan," he says before the door closes behind him. "I'm so glad you're home."

I press my hands to my forehead once I'm alone, smoothing out the deep lines forming.

Dad hasn't changed a bit, I tell Ezra. *He found me. Wants us all to go to a ball tonight.*

Ezra tone skates through my mind like a current of energy. *I just got the invitation. I'm going to go find him in a minute.*

No need. He's coming to find you soon. I pause, adding, *He knows nothing. We need to get him alone, to tell him what they did.*

He won't believe us, Lor. You know that because he won't want to believe it. He loves her and he'll have to punish Samuel, and you know how he feels about punishment.

I walk out the room and shoot back to Ezra. *Then we need to prove it to him. Evangeline was easy to get a rise out of.*

Then, that's what we'll do. There's a brief pause. *Lor, I'm glad things worked out this way. I know it's not what you wanted, but we are back together again and now we know the truth. I'm sorry, if I didn't say it already, for everything I did to you. You always were my favorite.*

I hold my breath. *What the fuck am I supposed to say to that?*

Thanks, probably. Hmmm… perhaps, something nice too. I hear Ezra's chuckle in my mind. *Go to your old room. I'll meet you there after I talk to Dad so we can plan.*

He cuts out before I can answer that I want to see Evie first, but with Evangeline's spies hanging around, that'd be a disastrous idea, anyway.

I glance down at all that remains of the cinnamon buns—a few crumbs—and wonder how a man in charge of Hell can be so upbeat.

He was always that way. Everyone expects the devil to be evil, often mistaking him for a demon, but he's not. He's an angel, and they're born from light. Out of the eight of us in our family, Lucifer is perhaps the nicest, yet most powerful of us all.

I replay the memory in my mind of him tearing apart a soul in punishment, releasing his untapped, terrifying power in a split second, then sitting down and playing fire blocks with us after as if he hadn't obliterated a soul out of existence.

I reach the entrance to my childhood bed chambers, happy to see nothing in here has been touched since then.

Except for the tuxedo on my four-post bed, along with a note. He'd only been gone for fifteen minutes, and Dad has already done this.

My son, this is for you.

You will accompany your stepmom tonight while I greet our guests and then join your love.

Love, Dad.

He knows. Of course he does. I just hope he doesn't relay anything to Evangeline. He would have had his demons report everything to him by now, about my time in Hell. He might even know about the trials if he's spoken to Ezra.

I pull the velvety fabric of the suit jacket between my fingers. The entire thing looks as if it's been plucked from the night sky. I suppose it's easy for him. Dad can manifest almost anything into reality, a gift no one else has.

I'm sure the dress he's spun for Evie is just as beautiful. Not that it matters. She'd look fucking stunning in just about anything… or nothing but her rose and skull tattoos.

Evie. Fuck. She needs to know that we must be careful around Evangeline. I don't trust the cunt not to attempt to hurt Evie if she knows, even more than she wants to now.

I reopen our bond, removing the mental barriers until I reach her. *Evie? Little Witch?*

Lor? An edge of anxiety hangs in her tone, and I suddenly feel awful for keeping her cut off that long.

Are you okay?

She hesitates than answers, *Yes, but I was worried about you.*

Don't be. Look, I found my dad, but I couldn't convince him. I need you to listen to me carefully.

CHAPTER THIRTY

Evie

Lorcan's voice comes through in an unusual, panicked flutter.

Evangeline cannot know we are together. She will destroy you and until I can convince my dad of the truth, we need to play it safe, for you, Rosa, and Aiden too. You're all at risk here.

We chose to come here, I say into his mind before he can blame himself.

Your aunt knows the bonds between demons well, he explains. *She'll know if I'm talking to you in your mind and that can only be done to a witch or human after imprinting, even partially.* He pauses briefly, then continues through the bond. *Evangeline is not a fool. I will not risk your life by risking her finding out, so we can't do that when we're together, okay? Just know, everything that is about to happen isn't real. My feelings for you will never change, but you must play along.*

I shoot a message back through our bond. *Play along with what?*

Lorcan's voice splits into my mind in an instant. *I'll explain later, Little Witch.* His voice echoes in my mind, thrumming softly as if it belongs there. *Lucifer has left a dress for you in the wardrobe for the ball later. Remember that letter I gave you? Did you read it?*

Not yet. I reply. *It's still in Rosa's bag.*

His reply comes all too quickly. *Read it and hold on to the words. I must go.*

Lorcan? What happened?

Silence greets my question, and I sigh. My stomach knots at the thought of him being in such close proximity to Evangeline. Who knows what she's fucking capable of? If she's anything like the rest of my family was, then I can only dread to think of the damage she will inflict. And from everything I've heard, she's worse.

I need to find Rosa to retrieve that letter, but first, he said there's a dress the actual devil, made for me, which is insane since I've never met the... *man? Demon?* No, *Angel.* He's a godsdamn angel. It's insane to think how much my life has changed. Sometimes I wonder if I'm trapped in some prolonged fever dream.

I climb out from the cocoon of darkness in the massive fourposter bed and push back the black, velvet curtains draping the intricately carved posts. I shudder as my bare feet hit the ancient stone and look around. Gomez has cradled himself on top of the tall, black wardrobe.

"Come here, baby," I call, the echo of my words lost to the shadows shrouding the ribbed, vault ceiling. Everything here is in black and white, as if I'm trapped in a monochromatic dream.

His wings unfurl as he yawns, his beady eyes tracking me. Standing, his nose twitching before taking flight, his wings a soft rustle as he glides down to me, disrupting the shadows cast from the flickering, purple hues of the candelabras.

"Do you want to stay here tonight?" I ask when he yawns again. His wings flap twice, which means yes. I don't know why I bother asking. If there's ever an option to stay inside and sleep, he'll take it.

I grab a handful of granola I pocketed from Rosa's bag, and hold the clumps out for him in my palm. His fur brushes against my skin as he sniffs the air, then takes a clump between his claws and nibbles on it with his tiny teeth.

My heart rate slows, watching him do something as normal as eating out of my palm, as if we could be back in our apartment on a dreary Wednesday afternoon when it was just us.

After he finishes the granola, his small, black tongue gently licking the last few crumbs, he climbs onto my other hand. Those big, black eyes widen when he looks at me with such affection that I feel guilty for not spending as much one-on-one time with him lately. I remember when I found him, trapped in a thorn bush after he escaped from a zoo or a previous owner.

As soon as I saw him, I knew we had something special, the bond opening between us in a gentle hum. Since then, he's been a part of my soul, and I can't imagine being without him. My fingers dance over his back, stroking him slowly until a small sigh escapes him, his body heaving in one huff. His body curls against my palms, small claws gripping my fingers as I cradle him like I used to. My eyelids slowly close as I pull him to my chest, the warmth of his body seeping into my chest.

For a beautiful moment, everything is calm and beautiful. All the torture and painful memories are forgotten when it's just me and my little familiar. But every moment must end, no matter how much I want to stay like this and go to sleep for a week.

"Here, baby." I slowly lower him onto the bed, prop up a pillow at his side so he won't accidentally roll off, then pull the cover over his stomach. "I'll be back soon."

He purrs against the bed, the sensation seeping through our bond, sending a tingle into my heart. "You sleep," I say, then turn to the window.

I creak the glass windows open, but it does nothing to change the temperature in the room. There's not even a breeze. The lack of weather is enough to drive a person mad.

My gaze drifts to the courtyard below as I grip the cold, stone sill. My morbid fascination forces me to lean further out to get a better look as the spirits forms swirl in a tempest of smoke and gray mist. One man, echoing his human form, moves in slow motion across the stone patio, the silence deafening as his mouth opens in a silent scream, reminding me of my dreams when I'm trapped between sleep and paralysis, where my body feels too heavy for my soul and moving even an inch is a struggle. To be in that state all that time must be Hell. I suppose here, that's the point.

Tears of smoke drip down the man's face as he trudges slowly forward, his fingers clawing at the air as if he might find some secret door in the air that can free him from this torture.

I understand the need for punishment, but as I stare out at the lost souls wandering the castle grounds, I wonder what they could have possibly done to deserve such a horrific fate—forever lost and broken.

My throat tightens as the realization washes over me—if I never met Lorcan, I would have joined those tortured spirits after my death. At least now I know I'll be spared that, but I'm still going to end up in Hell no matter what. I've murdered people and as much as I want to be good, I know that the truth is I am inherently bad.

Having compassion doesn't make me a good person. It just makes me human.

I turn to face the stone fireplace, a gaping hole of soot-stained logs upon a bed of ash and cast my death magic to heat the wood into a flicker of purple flames. The crackling instantly soothes my soul, and I turn to face the wardrobe. Surely Lucifer wouldn't have made me a dress. I mean, he's the devil, and when would he have had the time to bring it up here? We only recently arrived, and I've not left this room. Although, I guess, he's the devil and can do anything here.

I grab the gargoyle handle of the hand-carved, black wardrobe door, and pull it open. Holding my breath, I glide my fingers over the glossy, swirl carvings, then gasp.

For all that is unholy! My gaze travels the length of the gown hanging inside. I never, in my wildest daymares, thought the devil would have created me a dress, and such a beautiful one, too. It's almost too perfect to wear. *Almost.*

My fingers trace the luxurious layers of silver silk and black tulle billowing beneath the fitted velvet bodice, accented with black lace. Each thread embroidered into delicate roses shimmers like stars plucked from the night sky.

I retrieve the velvet hanger and turn to face the oval, silver-framed standing mirror. With a quick sweep of the drawers, I grab a pair of silver lace gloves and pull them up and over my elbows, then pair them with a pair of silver earrings.

It takes several minutes of careful maneuvering to undress, then pull on the corset, lacing the ribbons of the bodice and around my waist, but it's worth the effort when I finally admire myself in the mirror.

Like the rest of the court, the room behind me is shrouded in a ghostly gray, purple candlelight flickering from the candelabras coated in dripping wax, illuminating the glass beads on the voluminous skirt as I sway.

I gasp, tracing the seven diamonds on my black choker—a stone, I realize, for each brother. This ball must be to honor them all being together again. The thought of being close to Samuel again sends a murderous, icy-hot vengeance through my body. Pressing my fingers to my temples, I take a long, slow breath in. I can't react like this at the ball. Lorcan said we need to play along, and this is his world, not ours.

"You are stunning!" Rosa's voice jolts me as she appears in the doorway, a pop of color in all the darkness. "I found one in my wardrobe too."

"Lucifer made them for us," I explain and look at her. "Damn, you are… wow, Rosa. Ezra is going to lose his mind."

"Girl, I'm not dressing up for him." Her lips quirk into a crimson smile. "But he *will* lose his mind." She spins, her crimson skirt billowing outward, longer at the back, and shorter at the front, reaching the midpoint to her thighs. "Wow. The devil is quite naughty, putting me in this."

I can't help but agree. Spikes of black tulle cascade from the ends of her crimson, patterned skirt. Her cleavage is accentuated by a v-neckline and the shiny, black corset cinching her waist. Lucious, black stockings reach her knees, and tight curls flow down her shoulders.

"We should go," I say. "The devil waits for no one."

She chuckles and pulls a curling wand from her bag. "Not yet."

I'm forced onto the stool in front of the black, sprawling dresser, watching as Rosa makes quick work of my hair. When she's done, her red nails graze the circlet of black beads holding the waves of my dark hair into a half-up, half-down style.

"You are amazing. Honestly, I'd be lost without you," I admit.

She shoots me an incredulous look. "I know." Pausing as I stand, she says, "If Lorcan doesn't immediately fall to his knees when he sees you like this, leave him."

"Oh, wait!" I reach for her bag, rummaging through it until I find the letter. "I almost forgot. I need to grab the letter from Lorcan that I left in your purse."

I unroll the parchment and trace my gaze over the inky, cursive text. My jaws slacks as I back up against the stone wall to steady myself.

"What does it say?" Rosa asks as I read it twice, the words nestling so deep into the crevices of my soul that my heart aches.

My Witch,

I didn't know how to tell you this, and I know I should have told you when I first knew, so I needed you to have something tangible so you know my feelings for you.

Love, although a simplistic word, must suffice to express my uncontrollable feelings for you, Little Witch.

There is no word in existence that encompasses the depth, the all-consuming craving I have for you.

I will not say I love you beyond these written words. How can I when my soul fucking growls for you—You are my eternity.

Your Demon

I have to remind myself to breathe after finishing it. I've never had anyone love me. Especially not a demon who told me he cannot feel such deep, human emotions. Two weeks ago, I'd have been convinced he was manipulating me, but now?

"Girl, you look like you've seen a ghost," Rosa teases, then glances around. "Although that is probably the case in this castle."

I bring the parchment to my chest and close my eyes. "Lorcan, well, he…" I want to show her, but I'm not ready to part with his words, wanting nothing but to hold them as just ours. "He admitted he loves me."

Actually, his words were *you are my eternity,* which feels so much more pronounced and intimate.

"Well duh," she says as if it's obvious, when for me it's been anything but. "Do you love him?"

"I… I…"

She tilts her head up. "Don't feel pressured to say it back to him if you don't. He can swallow his pride. Honestly, it wouldn't hurt for him to get humbled a bit. Although, maybe do that after we leave Hell, you know, when he's not in control of what happens to us."

"No, I *do* love him." My stomach flutters into a thousand butterflies with broken wings.

She taps her crimson nails against her purse. "Well, if you want to be with him, then what's the problem?"

"Problem?" My eyes widen. "He's a demon. How can that work?"

"Or is that an excuse so you don't have to be vulnerable?"

I huff out a breath. "This is why I don't tell you things." I tuck the letter in the gap between the wardrobe and wall.

"If you love him, *and* only if he's good for you, then be with him," she adds cheerily, turning to the door. "You have a habit of catastrophizing. Live in the present with me. It can all be taken from us in a second."

"You've changed your tune on demons," I say as I follow her, a trail of tulle and lace flowing behind me.

"Hmm." She shrugs. "I guess Hell will do that to you."

I tsk under my breath. "Or maybe another demon has you romanticizing."

She shoots me a glare. "I don't have a crush on Ezra."

"Denial," I sing-song, making her cheeks tint with pink.

"Shh, now hold on to me," she orders, steadying herself on her black heels. A haunting melody grows louder as we descend the grandiose, silver-gilded staircase. I'm about to bring up Ezra again when we reach the bottom, but spot a man across the foyer, waving at us.

Dark curls adorn his head, and a trimmed, salt and pepper beard runs the length of his chiseled jawline. His silver eyes find mine, a gentle smile curves the wicked angular edge of his face. "Bellissima, Evangaline, Rosalia." His velvet, midnight tux fits his muscular build, the cufflinks shining the same color as his angelic eyes. "I apologize for not introducing myself sooner. I am Lucifer."

Rosa chokes on her inhale. "*You're* Lucifer."

Oh my gods. Or devils. With all the depictions of Satan floating around, I pictured him as something cartoonish with horns and tail, or at least something hellish. But just like his son, he appears human, except, unlike his children, he walks with an ethereal softness that can trick the most well-intentioned.

"In the flesh," he states with a wide-toothed, affable grin. "Ah, Evangeline, you are beautiful. I have to say, the family resemblance between yourself and your aunt is unmatched."

"It's actually Evie," I correct with a forced smile as he reaches us. "So, where is my aunt?"

"Ah, yes, she will be along shortly. So, you like my dresses," he states, as if he can sense how we feel. I mean, damn, he probably can. The devil, an *empath*?

Rosa answers first. "They're beautiful. Thank you. So, did you sew them yourself or…?"

What the fuck kind of conversation is this? Are we really discussing fashion with Satan?

"No," he says with a kind smile. There's not even a hint of condescension in there and I wonder how anyone can think him evil. "It's magic. You are well suited to my Ezra," he tells Rosa. "My demons reported your interactions to me," he admits, answering our unspoken question about how he knows. He extends his hand toward the heavy doors. "Anyway, please enjoy. We shall talk more later."

"Thank you, Lucifer," I say, struggling to find the words on how to describe whatever the fuck this is.

"You can call me Dad if you'd like, as you are my son's intended." My brows shoot halfway up my forehead. I am *not* calling him Dad and I am not Lorcan's intended. What even is an intended? Like his fiancé?

"I don't know what you did," Lucifer continues. "But I could feel my Lorcan's heart more open earlier. He's always been so depressed, even when I let him torture all those demons." His shoulders slump as he huffs out a breath. "Perhaps it's the Fallenmoore charm. I know it well."

Rosa shoots me a wide-eyed stare and I shrug.

Lucifer waves us off, walking ahead of us, and the heavy doors creak open with a motion of his hand.

As soon as he disappears inside, Rosa grabs my hand. "Hell fucking Hell," she exclaims as we walk inside into the large ballroom. "That was insane."

"So is this," I confess as I look around. Flickering, violet candlelight dances over the faces of ghostly spirits gliding around the cold, stone walls. I breathe in the scent of rose, lilies, jasmine, and vanilla, each forming a musk that somehow smells like both sex and death.

Rosa's fingers unclasp from mine as we take in the monochromatic tapestries of angels and demons hanging behind a quintet of violinists and a shiny black piano. A building melancholic serenade whispers from the demon hunched over the piano, his fingers gliding over the keys in rapid succession.

I notice most of the demons have taken on a human form tonight, all of them turning to look at us with stares as dark as charcoal, contrasting their pale, chalky skin.

Rosa shudders, whispering, "This is creepy."

"Yep." The spirits of human souls slip between the demons, their phantasmic forms swirling like smoke. They hover on the edges of the shadows as if they're afraid to bring much notice upon themselves.

The doors open and six out of the seven brothers walk inside, all dressed in fitted, black tuxes, all with different color gemstones on their cufflinks to match their sin.

My heart balloons when I see Lorcan appear behind them, standing tall, draped in a midnight blue tux with his normally disheveled hair slicked back, making him appear more gentlemanly than I thought possible. My smile quickly evaporates when I see *her* on my demon's arm. My brain falters. Evangaline. Rose tattoos cover her body, just as mine do, and her brown gaze sweeps the room. She waltzes inside, clinging to my demon's arm, wearing an ivory dress as if she's his fucking bride.

I'm going to fucking kill her.

Lorcan adjusts the button of this ivory shirt, pausing briefly when he sees me.

Rosa squeezes my arm and pulls me to the side. "Don't do anything rash."

What the fuck are you doing with her? I demand through the bond.

Don't react, he says into my mind, breaking his own rule, then severs our communication.

Rosa's hand is squeezing mine, grounding me as I watch them make their way through the crowd of demons and spirits.

Lorcan towers over them all, draped in a cloak of shadows, his pastel-green eyes glowing when he extends his hand to Evangeline, the same hand that held me. Her palm slips into his, and she smiles at Lucifer across the room, as if a dance with Lorcan is some bullshit peace-making move. But the three of us know she secretly is loving every second of this. As if he she could ever have his heart.

I jolt as a hand lands on my shoulder, the strong hold spinning me on the spot. Samuel's flat-gray psychopath eyes come to life when they bore into mine. "I've been wondering when I would get you to myself, Witch. Can I have this dance?"

His palm is in mine before I can tell him to go fuck himself, and he's dragging me into the center of the room. The last place I want to be is in Samuel's arms, but if it means I can be closer to Lorcan and my aunt and find out what in the unholy Hell is happening, then so be it.

CHAPTER THIRTY-ONE

Evie

Something isn't right.

My instincts scream at me to run as the song begins in a single, eerie note. Lorcan's wide eyes meet mine for a moment before the dance floor is draped with shadows, obscuring my view of him and Evangeline.

His voice grounds me as he breaks his rule for a second time and Lorcan's words echo into my mind. *Get out of here. Now.*

Samuel's hold on me tightens as the music begins like a wisp of an echo, resonating through the cavernous room. My thoughts direct me from the floor, but I am a puppet to the music, remaining glued to Samuel, trapped in this deadly waltz.

My magic sizzles in my fingertips but is quickly quelled as the music picks up.

"This dance is called the Garaud," Samuel explains in an eerie whisper, the shadows shrouding the sea of spirits and demons around us. "It's also known as the dance of death." He glides my leg back with his knee, whispering, "The music is an earworm to the living. Once you start, you can't leave." His long fingers snake lower down my spine, sending a shiver skittling through my bones. "The Garaud once swept through entire towns, and the people in them danced until they died."

I crane my neck, searching for a glimpse of Lorcan amongst the dark fog, but can't see anything beyond the wall of mist. "Well," I say, turning my focus to Samuel, "at least I might die soon and be relieved of the presence of your company."

"You have such a wicked mouth," he intones with a wolfish grin. "It's no wonder my brother is so taken with you."

"So, is this your revenge?" I ask, my body spinning to the music without any instruction from my brain, as if the moves are imprinted in my soul. "To dance me to death?"

Crystals hang from the bone chandelier above, their light refracted into shards, illuminating the reddish hue woven into Samuel's brown hair. "Oh no. Your demise will be far more satisfying, but watching you squirm like this… is…" His eyes close for a second, a satisfied smile curling his thin lips, as if he's tasting my sorrow and it's the most delicious thing ever.

Dark, somber notes resonate from the piano as another song begins, uplifted by the quick sweeps of bows across violins, the melody building into a steady crescendo.

His dead eyes latch onto mine as he moves in inhuman angles, all slow turns, then quick jolts. Quick jabs and off-tones screech together, the deadly rhythm seeping into my ears, ensnaring my senses, and for a moment the world blurs. He spins me once, twice, and I cannot speak no matter how many times I open my mouth in protest.

I want to stop.

My heart rate flutters into uneven beats, rising and falling with the frantic strikes of the instruments..

Masked demons blur in and out of the shadows as my back rises and falls against Samuel's palm, their too-wide grins haunting my swaying twirls. Dizziness encompasses my mind, numbing my inhibitions until all I can feel is the music, my feet aching with the flurried movements as the song descends into a frantic delirium, each chord wildly chasing the next.

I bite my lip, closing my eyes to the spinning world, until I can taste a tang of blood. Entrenched with the music is Samuel's giddy laughter echoing around my ears until tears are spilling from my ducts.

Samuel rotates me outward, but this time lets go as the song ends in a final, heart-jolting chord, followed by a thick, heavy silence.

I collapse onto the floor, my fingers grasping the stone for some sense of stability as the shadows disappear. I blink once, then twice as my vision clears and I see Lorcan standing in front of Samuel. At first, I don't know what I'm looking at until I notice the throbbing, black heart in dripping blood through Lorcan's fingers.

My gaze tracks the rest of the crowd to the musicians, and I gasp.

All eyes are on the bloody, flesh-coated spine hanging over a music stand, and the corpse of a demon crumpled at the bottom.

No wonder the music ended so abruptly.

Lucifer speaks first, his voice deeper than earlier, the command in his tone silencing the room. "Calm down, son."

"There are humans here," Lorcan shouts, and tosses the heart on the ground. "The fucking Garaud, really?"

Lucifer nods slowly and approaches Lorcan on the small stone platform where the other musicians' backs are pressed firmly against the wall. "It was my mistake. It won't happen again."

"It was Samuel's," he spits, pointing at his brother, who watches with a devilish smile, his hand on his hip.

"Come now," Lucifer says, guiding Lorcan from the platform. "Let's continue. It isn't a party without a little murder," he jokes, his voice filled with a mirth that is contradiction with the rest of the room.

Lucifer talks with the musicians, leaving us alone with that bitch. Evangeline smiles, approaching us as the rest of the crowd comes together in rushed whispers, and the musicians step over the demon's entrails and continue playing, a new song this time. She glides in front of me. Unlike many other tortured souls here, her human form isn't lost.

She stops a few feet in front of me. I take in her dark hair that falls in loose curls around her chest, her form tightly bound in ivory fabric, with nary a wrinkle around her eyes. She looks less a great aunt and more like a sister. I suppose she was in her thirties when she died. But, while the family resemblance is undeniable, her square jawline and diamond-shaped face lean more toward her paternal genes, at least from what I could gather in old family photo albums.

"Well, well," Eva says, her eyes darting from me and land on Lorcan, who reaches us, taking a protective stance at my side. "You certainly showed what's really in your heart this evening."

He shakes his head, nostrils flaring. "It was you."

She shrugs and brings a glass of crimson wine to her lips. At least, I hope it's wine. "What can I say? I have always enjoyed the Garaud. I completely forgot that humans were present. Witches too." She tilts her head, and I imagine tearing her throat out.

I guess the ruse is over before it could really begin, I say into his mind as he grips my fingers in his. He blew his cover. For me. I'm so fucking annoyed by that, even if it was an incredibly sweet gesture. *I was okay. You don't need to kill every person who tries to hurt me.*

Yes, I do.

"So, you do have a bond with her," Evangeline spits. "How? You cannot love."

I smirk, forcing a puff of breath through my nose. "You mean he cannot love *you*."

Her expression drops into something akin to a panther eyeing its prey. "Do you think this is going to be a happy ending?" She wags a finger between us. "You'll end up dead like me."

"Lorcan wouldn't hurt me."

"Ha. What makes you think he wouldn't? He's a demon," she continues in a hushed tone, and looks at Lorcan. "Tell her the truth. You cannot love and you know it. Lust, yes. Infatuation, even at a stretch, perhaps. But not love."

I tilt my head and whisper, "Are you jealous?"

"Jealous!" She snorts and taps her long nails against her hip while trailing her glare over me. "Of my namesake, why? You're nothing but a washed-out version of me. What is it you think you have that I don't?"

I tilt my head, offering her my most cloying smile and hold my index finger in the air. "You mean apart from Lorcan?" I almost laugh as I watch her lips fall into a frown and her pupils narrow into slits. I continue to count off things on my fingers. "I'm alive, for one, and I hold the magic of our entire coven while you lost yours, along with your life. And for what, unrequited love? Must you be so cliché?"

She glances around as a few demons come close enough to hear our conversation. "Unrequited love? You must be delusional. I love Lucifer and he very much loves *me*." Flustered, her finger taps against the glass with a clink. "Lucifer would do *anything* for me. Remember that."

As if summoned by his name, Lucifer joins us before things can escalate, but his presence does little to tame the whirlwind of death magic humming in my bone marrow.

Evangeline smiles and drapes her arm over his, running her fingers down his cheek. "I was just telling my niece how sorry we are that the Garaud was played while she was here."

Lucifer brings his hands together, brows pinching, looking actually concerned. Unlike her. "I should have told them not to play it. Such a mistake," he says, shaking his head. "It won't happen again. While you are here in my home, you are safe. All of you are. Come now," he tells Evangeline and grips her waist, "let us dance."

My mouth twists as I watch them leave. "I didn't think it was possible for her to be worse than I imagined."

A low growl rumbles in his chest. "We need to get out of here."

Rosa rolls her hips as she walks to greet us, Ezra bouncing at her side along with Lazarus and Asher. "I wanted to make sure your aunt was gone," she explains and rubs the side of her neck. "How are you?"

"Me? How are *you*?" I ask, realizing she would have been caught in the throes of that dance too.

"Fine," she chirps. "Ezra walked me outside when he realized it was going to start."

She lingers between Lorcan and me as he turns his back to us, grabbing a glass of wine from a passing demon server's tray.

"I'll find you shortly. Stay close," I say as she saunters away with Ezra.

I should have done that instead of playing some part.

I place my palm on his back and speak into his mind, in the softest tone my brain can create. *It's not your fault.*

Before he can answer, Asher pushes between us. "Dad didn't know anything. I thought I was going by his orders so..." Glancing at Evie, he says, "I regret my part in all of this."

Lazarus steps in, too, riding a hand through his blue-black hair. "I am too. I couldn't give a fuck about the humans, but we're brothers."

Lorcan nods, I assume this is about as close to anything sentimental as these three get. Silence hangs between them as the music picks up and I decide to break it. We all should get along, and we might need Lazarus and Asher on our side.

I glance at the spirits lingering nearby, searching for anything to break this awkward silence, and turn to Asher. "Why do they look like that? The spirits? Some appear human."

Asher tips the contents of his glass into his mouth. "Some souls look worse than others." He shrugs. "Don't really know why. Suppose it depends on how long they've been here and how worn down they are."

Lazarus tsks and runs a hand around to the back of his neck. "That's not true. Excuse my brother. He's spent so much time at the crossing that he's forgotten how to observe."

Asher rolls his blue eyes. "With that, I'm leaving. Good evening, Evie, Lorcan." He nods at us both, then shoots a scathing glare at his brother. "Lazarus."

Asher disappears into the crowd, heading toward the nearest exit, and Lazarus turns his attention to me. His neat, slicked back hair doesn't move when he rakes a hand over his head. "When a human soul enters Hell, while they're translucent with their spectral form, they maintain their appearance from the Human

Realm. The more time they spend trapped in their punishment, they forget the essence of who they are and shift into what you see there."

He waves a hand toward two spirits caught in a dance of ghostly smoke, flurrying as they spin to the music, the steps not in time with the symphony, their movements slowing despite the haunting tune lifting into a crescendo. It's as if they're trapped in a memory we cannot see, habitually dancing to a time in the Human Realm that the world has long forgotten.

"Evangeline still has her form," I say, and Lorcan grunts.

"Only because of our dad. Without him, she'd wither here too."

Lazarus's lips quirk upward. "Indeed, she would. I must talk to our father, anyway. Good evening."

I watch Evangeline on the other side of the room now, wrapped in Lucifer's arms, but her gaze is elsewhere—fixed on us.

Let's change the plan, I say into Lorcan's mind. *Evangeline looks as if she's going to combust. Let's make sure she does. Lucifer isn't the only one who can obliterate a soul out of existence. Your brothers hunted me down so I could do it to you, remember?*

Eyes half-closed, long lashes shadowing his lids, and fingers digging into my hips as he tugs me into his embrace. *It won't work here. This is my dad's domain and if you hurt her, I worry what he'll do to you. He needs to see what she's like first.*

Death magic dances in my fingers, shadows coiling around each one like vipers. *Then let's show him. Drive her wild with jealousy and she won't be able to hold back. Look at her, she's already struggling to hold it in.*

A nudge of agreement sears into our bond, but I sense something else has consumed his thoughts over the threat waltzing near us. Bringing his lips to the shell of my ear, his whisper climbing into my brain in a gentle caress. "Did you read my letter?"

Bruising touches linger on my hips as he pulls away, then drifts his fingers up my spine and over my arms, leaving traces of him over every pore in my body. I close my eyes, wanting nothing more than to feel him in every part of me.

I nod, my hand sliding over his chest. "You are my eternity too."

His hand grips the nape of my neck, lips pressing to mine as he holds my face with more urgency than ever before. Breathless, he breaks our kiss and with all that untapped power behind his eyes focused on me, he utters, "I am all yours, Evie. My heart belongs to you, always. I never thought I could love anything or anyone." He brings his hands to my hair, fingers threading the stands as he stares wild-eyed. "It's terrifying, only because I've never truly been afraid, but the thought of losing you tears my soul into shreds." His fingers skate my cheeks, my neck, then down to my chest as if he's needling unseen threads and whispers, "Your mortal heart taunts me with every beat."

Amidst his swirling shadows, my heart quickens. "If I could tear out my heart and give it to you—if it meant I could stay here with you for an eternity, I would."

"*My* Witch." His hand inches down my back and paused at the bottom of my spine with the gentlest touch. "You deserve a life outside of Hell. In the Human Realm. I'm not fit for court life, and you shouldn't be subjected to it."

"I've never much fit into the real world," I say as he spins us to the music, holding me so close to his body, so tightly, as if any gap between us is an insult. "If our plan works, we could stay here. Perhaps it's where we both belong."

He slumps over me, forehead pressing against mine. "I only belong with you, wherever that is."

CHAPTER THIRTY-TWO

Evie

I close the door to our chambers and allow the smile I've repressed for the last hour to spread.

He loves me. I never thought he'd say it. My heart pounds as I replay the memory repeatedly. Lorcan will be back soon, after going to meet with Gideon and Ezra, so I use the time to my advantage.

He tells me he's not suitable for court life and all the politics that come with it, but he has a larger skill set than he realizes.

Even though it's been over a century since he was caged by his brothers, I believe a part of him—even if it's smaller than a grain of sand—still twinges with self-doubt at times. And while that barely noticeable spec is nothing compared to his grandiose personality, it *does* affect him.

I really hope that officially claiming him back, accepting his twisted love, and ensuring him he's my eternity as well, incinerates that black mark entirely. I intend to obliterate it with my claiming shadows.

My footsteps pad quietly against the stone floors as I make my way to the black dresser, open the smallest drawer of the top row, and pluck out the set of silver earrings Lucifer gifted me.

Honestly, I think Lucifer is so relieved and happy to have his sons all back in one place.

I hold an earring in each palm as I stand before the oval mirror above the dresser, watching with fascination and complete acceptance as my darkness bleeds over my brown irises. The once feared evil version of myself stares back.

If Lorcan never forced my magic to the surface, I shudder to think what I would have become.

I infuse the plethora of emotions running through my mind into my soul and focus entirely on the center of my magic.

My death magic stirs first, with no breath of hesitation or pause, swirling from my chest and hovers in the air before me. A soft smile curls my lips as I gaze at it slowly revolving in the air through my reflection. I blink as my shadows stream out next, dancing playfully around my death magic as if trying to provoke it enough to give chase.

I giggle, shaking my head. It still annoys me that I have no idea what was discussed during that conversation Lorcan had with my magic. I make a mental note to bring it up another time.

I snort, like he could tell my magic what to do. It's more like it craves his attention just as much as I do. We don't need it, but we want it.

Shadows split and dart between my hands, swirling circles around them before speeding back to my death magic, moving behind it and trying to push it toward my hands as if it's impatient. My death magic willingly soaks into my closed palms.

A soft, eerie glow surrounds my hands as my dark magic heats the silver earrings and melts them into puddles, a sliver of death magic protecting my palms from injury. Shadows squirm into the cracks between my fingers, prying them up one by one as if it wants a front-row seat to the show.

I tilt my head. Huh, my magic usually isn't this playful... I wonder if it has to do with the fact that this is a gift for my demon.

A pulse of hopefulness lined with arousal heats my blood and balloons my heart.

I will my death magic to form the ten-gauge jewelry I need. My shadows vibrate on the outskirts of my death magic as they form the first of two cylindrical bars with interior threading at each end, then creates four small silver balls with one spoke each to seal the jewelry in his skin.

My death magic hums as shadows leap towards the jewelry, then my black eyes widen as they add embellishments to the jewelry. Shadows form thin horizontal stripes of obsidian, so light that I squint to see them properly. The magic moves onto the securing balls and twirls more. A decorative starburst grows from the top center point to where it connects inside the jewelry on each ball.

Light surges softly from my death magic, the shadows not imbued in the silver pull back, allowing my death magic to coat the barbells once more with a glowing light. Something warm and satisfying curls behind my ribs as my magic works to permanently seal in my essence and the reality of who I truly am into the jewelry.

I am a dark witch seeking to mark and claim her demon.

My shadows swirl lazily around my death magic as I call it back into my body.

It's done.

I throw the last pillow onto the stack piled on the dresser and look up as Lorcan stalks into our chambers, a glower twisting his features.

"Evangeline is still holding it together, apparently. Although she left the ballroom angry, so there is that." Lorcan rubs his temples and presses a kiss to my lips. "We'll get her to do something in front of my dad, though. It just might take more time."

"I have an idea that might help take your mind off everything."

Lorcan tosses his mask aside and arches a brow in response.

"Do you want to play?"

My heart leaps as he embraces me. "I always want to play with you, Baby Girl."

"Interested?"

Lorcan laughs. "Of course, but what about the bat? I'm sure Fluffy Fucker won't appreciate us going at it. Where is he?" He peers around the top of the wardrobe.

"He's in Rosa's room. I wanted to make sure we were alone for this." I step out of his hold, folding my arms over my chest.

"Good. We're going to do this properly. Understand?"

Lorcan growls low, and I admire the growing bulge behind his fly. "Yes, Mistress."

I gasp and clench my thighs together.

Fuck. He did not just call me that. Might as well roll with it.

I swallow. "And you will only address me as Mistress. Take off all your clothes, climb onto the bed, then sit back against the headboard."

Lorcan winks. "Yes, Mistress."

My heart backflips and those pesky butterflies make a reappearance in my belly.

I bite my lip as I stare at him while he removes each article of clothing one by one, his tattooed muscles rippling, then briefly close my eyes as his ass clenches with every step he takes to the bed.

However, Lorcan doesn't just simply climb on the bed. No, of course, not. He raises his knee, plants one foot flat on the top of the mattress, then rises as he lifts himself with one muscular leg.

My lips part and have to remind myself to swallow, less I drool all over my chest.

My demon settles himself in the exact center of the black velvet headboard, his posture straight, and his thick cock jetting up from his groin. "Like what you see, Mistress?"

Fuck. He can't say shit like that or I'll jump him and never get to play out this fantasy.

"Don't speak."

His gaze darkens, a hint of challenge hidden in their depths.

I continue, "That includes in my mind. Actually, there are two phrases you are allowed to say." I pause and raise my chin. "When prompted, you will reply, 'Yes, Mistress,' or 'No, Mistress' through the bond. Do you understand?"

Lorcan's stare narrows. "Evie—"

"No. You're not talking right now, you're listening. If you need to use the color system that we've previously discussed, those are also acceptable words to communicate within the bond." I stroll toward the bed and drop the robe from my shoulders. The silk shimmies over my skin as it drops to a puddle on the floor. "The only thing I want to hear come from these sexy lips are your moans of pleasure."

Lorcan opens his mouth as if to speak, then presses his lips together firmly. My fingertips skim over the muscle feathering in his jaw. "What a good boy. You learn so quickly."

Lorcan's gaze burns into my skin as I retrieve the small ornate wooden box from the wardrobe. The corner of my lip curls up into a smirk, then I bend at the waist and grasp the two thick lengths of chain hidden there. His eyebrows raise and he remains silent, but his cock jerks against his abs.

I use his own words against him. "Like what you see?"

Yes, Mistress.

The words flood my body with searing arousal and a moan sneaks past my lips. "Stretch out your right arm." He does so without complaint. Then I attach the chains to the ring built in behind the headboard.

Manifesting a tendril of shadow, I connect it to the opposite end of the chain not linked to securing the ring, and twist a shadow around his tattooed wrist.

Lorcan inhales sharply, nostrils flaring. I ignore him and take my time gliding to the other side of the bed, trailing a nail along the mattress and repeat the process, then move on and secure his ankles as well.

I reach into the box once more, straightening my spine, and show him the solid metal ball gag swinging on my fingertips. Lorcan growls and his biceps bulge as he tenses against my shadow restraints, his lips pulling into a dark smile that unfurls over his features at a glacial pace.

I crawl onto the bed, then straddle his waist, pinning his cock against his stomach with my body weight.

He snarls a moan, closing his eyes briefly as if struggling to remain a willing submissive.

I push a lock of blue-black hair off his forehead. "Eyes on me. Keep them open."

His eyes glitter with lust, a solid black outlining his pastel green irises. Lorcan's body pulses with his restrained magic, power exuding from every pore, then growls. *Yes, Mistress.*

I arch my back and push my breast onto him as I stretch the two ends of the ball gag around his head and connect it in the back. Sitting back, I run my fingers over the chain, digging the metal into his cheeks.

"Fuck, that's hot."

Lorcan groans and bares his serrated teeth, the sharp points digging into the metal with the ferocity of his desire.

I'm under no illusion that he couldn't simply bite through the metal, but he won't.

He likes this game very much.

My knees slip against the soft sheets as I kneel between his spread legs, willing a shadow to grab the jewelry I made earlier from the box, leaving it empty. My shadow glides back toward me and drops the barbells into my palm.

Lorcan's hips buck and the chains rattle as he eyes what I'm holding.

I squeeze my thighs together as his cock brushes against the bottom of my breast, smearing pre-cum on my skin. *Do you trust me?*

His stare flashes to mine, his pupils rapidly widening. *Yes, Mistress.*

It's laughable to ever call him a submissive, but his compliant response sends bolts of carnal need directly to my clit all the same.

I quickly look away. The bed creaks as I bend toward his lap and lick all the pre-come off the head of his cock with long, wet strokes.

"Ahgh…mmph…" His muffled groan swirls around the ball gag, and his hips rock against my lips.

I shake my head and laugh. "None of that. Settle." My fingers meet flexing muscle as I push a hand against his lower abs, then sit back on my heels.

Thankfully, he requires no more prep than that. It's not like his demon blood would allow an infection to set in.

I purse my lips and blow across the damp, sensitive skin. His abs flex, but his ass stays planted against the mattress. "Good boy."

Lorcan releases a sharp growl and a fresh stream of pre-cum dribbles down his shaft.

I tsk. "That just won't do. We better get this done quickly before you make a mess of yourself."

My shadows manifest into a pair of forceps, and I will them open around his cockhead horizontally, squeezing and holding the position.

Lorcan hisses, but I take in a deep breath and ignore him. If I look at him now… I let the thought float away, intent on my task.

I manifest another tendril of shadow and will it into the shape of a piercing needle. The sharp tip shimmers with magic as my shadows are just as excited about this as I am. I nod to myself, then hold his stare. "Are you ready?"

Yes, Mistress.

"Deep breath," I command, focusing on his cock.

The sharp tip of my shadow needle penetrates the side of his malleable head, a thick stream of dark blue blood runs over the bottom edge of the shadow forceps, his chest rapidly rising and falling. I hold the shadow needle in place and glance up at him under my lashes. *I cannot wait to play with you when this is finished.*

Returning my attention to my shadows, I have to work quickly or his accelerated healing will take over before I have time to install the jewelry.

With my free hand, and help with a shadow, I unscrew one end of a barbell and insert it into the fresh piercing through the tube my shadow provides, then swiftly thread on the tiny ball tightly. Lorcan moans and his skin trembles beneath my touch. I repeat the process, but this time I lineup my shadow needle and pierce it through the opposite side of his cockhead, crossing beneath the other piercing.

My shadows dissolve as I secure the final barbell. I startle and my eyes fly to his wide open, pleasure drunk stare as Lorcan roars and comes all over the fresh piercings.

Holy. Fucking. Shit.

I moan and slap a palm against his tattooed chest as the sight and sound of his climax tears one from me as well. My pussy throbs and clamps on the air, my orgasm violently ripping through me harder and harder the longer I stare at his blood and cum mixing, dripping down his erection.

Lorcan moans again, the tendons in his neck straining with the force of his release, and his hooded gaze darkens as he shivers with ecstasy. His claws grapple against my shadows and their connecting metal restraints, his muffled growling sounds of pleasure mixing with rattling chains.

Oh fuck.

He pants around the mangled metal ball gag, the look on his face hardening into something primal and dangerous. I don't know how much farther I can push him before he snaps.

You know, a girl could get used to this.

He growls. *Making me come?*

"All this power." I skate a black painted nail down the groove between his muscles, humming and biting my lip as goosebumps pop up beneath my touch. "Who knew you could be such a good boy?"

I break our stare and trail my eyes to his cock.

He's such a mess. I could clean him with my tongue. If I taste his blood, will it do anything to me?

My muscles freeze as Lorcan's deep, rumbling chuckle covers my skin in goosebumps.

Shit.

I sent that thought down the bond.

My gaze darts back to him as he digs his sharp teeth into the masticated gag and raises a brow, as if asking permission to answer my accidental question.

You have permission to speak freely.

Lorcan growls into my mind and our bond throbs in time with my pulse as he speaks. *Demon blood in general is an aphrodisiac to other species, especially witches.* He winks, then continues, *"However, because I am Lust, I imagine my blood is much, much more potent.*

You imagine?

I've never willingly shared my blood with anyone.

My pulse thunders in my ears. Oh, gods.

Taste me, Baby Girl. I know you want to.

I stare hungrily at the piercings crowning his delectable cock and moan. Without further hesitation, I lower my mouth around him and swirl my tongue around his shaft from base to tip, collecting every drop of cum and blood. Arousal. No, there's not even a word for the amount of need that slams into me with the first taste of his blood on my tongue. I moan loudly around his cock.

"Mmphm… Ghghuh…" *Evie… Unholy fucking… shit… that's so sexy.*

He jerks between my lips as I voraciously clean him with every lick of my tongue until there's no trace of the liquids. My clit throbs. I need him. *You taste so fucking good.*

Lorcan's breaths skate over the top of my head and he groans down the bond. *Baby…Girl…if you…don't stop, I'm… fuck…going to…Uhghaahhh…*

Going to come? I finish his sentence in his mind, then swallow around him as he rolls his hips upward, his piercings hit the back of my throat. Lorcan's guttural moan shivers over my skin as he orgasms down my throat, his cock twitching and throbbing against my tongue as I pop off him, kissing one of his piercings.

I laugh. *Sensitive?*

My demon pants. *You could say that. Fuck. I can feel how desperate you are for me.*

I moan and straddle his waist, hovering over his cock while holding his heated stare. *What can I say? Your blood is just as potent as you predicted. I. Want. You.*

His strangled half moan, half growl issuing from his throat causes my arousal to pool on his lower abs and prompts me to meet his gaze. The inferno of lust banked in those mesmerizing green depths, torturing my swollen clit.

Release me.

Not yet.

Lorcan rocks his hips upward, grazing my slit with the head of his cock, then leans forward as far as my shadow ropes will allow, his restrained arms testing the strength of my shadow ropes. *I want to be inside you so fucking bad.*

Fuck it, no point in torturing myself too.

I drop onto his thick cock and scream his name. Lorcan tears through what's left of his ball gag, spits out the pieces, then bites down into my shoulder. He rolls his hips with inhuman speed, prodding my G-spot relentlessly, his groans of pleasure blending with mine into a melody of beautiful, debauched sounds.

"Fuuuck... Yes, Baby Girl. Come all over me."

My mind fragments into quivering pieces as the pressure within me explodes and my orgasm consumes me, squirting all over his cock and abs.

Lorcan stiffens beneath me. "Ughnhg... Fuck... I'm co...Ahghghh."

His cum jets into me as my mind-numbing bliss lingers.

Gods, this is the longest orgasm of my life.

Bright and breathtaking, like the corona of a fucking eclipse.

I drop my forehead against his neck and Lorcan sags against my shadow ropes, his chest heaving. "Godsdamn, Little Witch, you can dominate me anytime."

CHAPTER THIRTY-THREE

Lorcan

Warm drops of near scolding water flow from the copper faucet and into the stone tub as my little witch and I step into a bubbling bath. My lips press against her temple in a kiss.

Evie tilts her head back, dunking her long, chocolate tresses into the steaming water, closing her eyes. All the muscles in her body seem to loosen at once, her shoulders slowly lowering as she lowers her chin and rivulets of hot water gushes from her unbound hair. I watch her hungrily, my still erect, freshly pierced cock bobbing as I pour a dollop of soap onto a sponge from the Bitter Sea and scrub it over my skin. "You're so exquisite, Baby Girl, and fucking *mine*."

Her eyes blink open, droplets of water clinging to her dark lashes. "As you are *mine*." The corner of her mouth twitches upward. "This is an incredible tub, by the way. Perks of being royalty?"

I chuckle. "One of the many."

I growl playfully as I bend and suck one of her nipples into my mouth, then nip it and draw away.

My hunger for her strengthens as she soaps her breasts and swirls the bubbles onto her tattooed skin.

Perhaps when we get out of the bath, I'll trace every inch of your tattoos with my tongue. I flood our bond with my never-ending lust for her.

The hair on the back of my neck rises as something crashes in another room of our suite. I growl, "What the fuck?" Gripping Evie's chin, I stare into her eyes. "I know better than to ask you to stay here—"

"Then don't." My witch scoffs, pushes past me, snatching two dark emerald towels from the warming basket and wraps one over her breasts.

I catch the other one before it strikes me in the face. "Didn't fucking think so?" I stride in front of her and stalk out of the bathroom as I secure the towel at my hip.

Steam billows out after us, rising toward the ceiling. My shadows coat the floor in darkness as I follow the sounds of further destruction to the cozy living room. I dodge to the left, then smash an end table with a shadow before it can hit Evie, splintered wood flinging in all directions like miniature missiles. I shift without a thought, pushing my demonic-self free, charging Samuel with a snarl on my lips.

He darts towards the door as I slash a shadow around his torso, then jab him in the windpipe with my fist. I hardly recognize the growl releasing from my throat. "What the fuck are you doing in my chambers?" I don't dare risk a glance over my shoulder to set my eyes on Evie, even though everything within me urges me to see that she's unharmed. Samuel might be younger than me, but he's a quick bastard, and I know better than to take my eyes off the enemy.

He lashes a shadow across my cheek like a whip as he laughs manically, his out of focus, dark gray eyes gleaming with delight. "I know why you're really here, *Lorcan.*" He spits my name like it's an insult. Shadows fly in every direction as he keeps backing toward the door.

"It seems like you have all the answers, so you tell me. Why *am* I here?"

He laughs harder, fisting his reddish-brown hair and yanks. "You want to take her from me!"

I roll my eyes. "I have no idea what the fuck you're talking about, Samuel, nor do I care to. Why don't you go back to whatever hole you crawled out of?"

He growls and reaches for my face with extended claws, but his arms are too short to make contact and he still hasn't used his shadows. "I don't understand why she wants you," he sneers.

"Fine, I'll willingly swallow the bait. Who?"

"My goddess, Evangeline, of course. She kept looking at you and…" The blood in my veins turns to steam. And there's that fucking cunt's name again.

I growl louder and step towards him, claws raised, as I back Samuel into the wall by the open door leading to the rest of the castle, pieces of broken ceramic slicing into the soles of my bare feet. "The only *person* I give a fuck about—"

"Is me." Evie steps up beside me as I stab my claws through his shoulders and into the stone wall behind him, dark blood quickly puddling at his feet. My brother struggles to get free, sheer madness that feels nothing like my own in his narrowed gaze, and tears at my hands with his nails as if he's forgotten he has powers. I disregard the pain, bleeding scratches healing just as quickly as he inflicts them.

Evie folds her arms across her chest, then speaks. "Are you here to *try* and kill me?" My cock jerks, tenting my towel as my witch stares him down, somehow making him look small even though she's several inches shorter than him. "Oh, wait, you tried that once already, and it didn't work out so well for you, *did it?*"

"You fucking bitch," Samuel spits out, shrieking as I twist my claws into the meat of his shoulders.

Remove your claws, Evie orders down the bond.

I don't give it a second thought as I retract my bloody claws and step to the side, Evie gliding into the vacant space. Her death magic swirls from her chest and hovers an inch away from his face as power thickens the air, raising the hair off her neck, and darkness swells over her chocolate irises. "If you even think to come anywhere near this floor of the castle again… Well, you know exactly what I'm capable of. Get. Out."

Samuel bares his teeth but slinks past her and over the threshold, leaving his pool of blood as a parting gift.

I grin at my witch, then squeeze her to my chest. "Fuck, you're sexy when you get blood thirsty."

Evie's shadows slam the door closed and mine twist around the silver handles, providing an additional method of security.

I bend, toss Evie over my shoulder, her towel fluttering to the floor, and spank her ass. "Let's go finish our bath."

Godsdamn, I love my new piercings.

I tuck a hand under my head, then skim the other down Evie's back, her alabaster skin glowing faintly lilac in the candlelight as she sleeps turned toward the opposite side of the bed.

I haven't allowed my cock to soften since my witch pierced me. While I'm aware the actual process of piercing me would have been easier were I not hard, but there was no way in fuck I would have gone soft, even if I tried. Control and desire are not words that pair well when it comes to my feelings for Evie. She has been a challenge to my restraint since the first time I watched her through the Fallenmore Coven's rose bordered mirror.

My tongue darts between my lips as I replay my witch thrusting shadow needles through my cock. A beat of pre-cum trickles from my slit.

"Fuck."

I thought I would miss the Human Realm when we came to Hell, considering the fact that Evie only released me from the Shadow Realm mere days prior, but that's no longer what I want. I want to be wherever she is. Evie is my fucking home. Whether that's in the Human Realm, Hell, or another realm entirely means nothing. We have both been through some awful fucking shit in our lives, defying all the odds weighing against us, and yet, we're alive. All romantic bullshit aside, fate didn't fuck up for once and brought us together.

I mentally scrub my mind of the heavy thoughts, and let it wander, closing my eyes and swallowing thickly. I move a shadow to circle my shaft like it's a cock sleeve. My hand skims down the soft skin of Evie's lower back, gliding it lower and lightly squeeze her ass as I tease myself with my shadow sleeve.

Fuck, that's so damn good.

Part of me wishes she would wake up and catch me jerking off. I can practically smell the flood of arousal that would immediately pool in her needy cunt. With every stroke upward, my shadows suck on the rimmed head. I tighten the column of shadows around me and my magic cross piercings shift. My eyes roll back, and I thrust into my shadows, indescribable pleasure rippling down my cock and into my balls.

I raise a finger to my lips, nick the pad on a sharpened tooth, then reach around Evie's shoulder and smear my deep blue blood onto a nipple. She moans in her sleep and my back arches as an unexpected release takes me hostage. I wrap my hand around my shadow cock sleeve, squeezing tightly as rope after rope of cum shoot over my hand, shadows, abs, and a drop or two strike me in the chin.

I gasp and my cock twitches as I release it with aftershocks, more cum joining the puddle in the dividing lines of my lower abdominals. "Unholy fucking Hell." I drop my hand to my thigh, then glance over at Evie, her breaths slow and even. A quiet chuckle rumbles my chest. *Godsdamn, she really just slept through that. She must be more exhausted than I thought.*

I inhale slowly through my nose, then release the exhale through my mouth. I cannot thank her enough for this gift. Definitely going to have to get a lot of practice in with my witch to tame this sensitivity a bit. My witch sees it as a way to get back at her aunt, but to me, it's so much fucking more than that.

I have never allowed anyone to mark me, let alone permanently. Sure, I could remove the barbells and the holes would close in seconds, but I *never* will.

My eyes slowly open, and I stare up at the sky as seen from the Human Realm, wispy clouds drifting across a full moon. The memory of Dad gifting me the magic projecting the scene across the ceiling to help with my nightmares floats across my mind's eye. And yet, it's still fucking baffles me that he has no idea what my brothers did to me.

I drown the negative thoughts in my subconscious, much more willing to float in my post orgasm bliss rather than flounder in miserable, dead memories. I retract my claws, run my hand over my face, and blow out of breath.

A grin moves across my face as I lean on an elbow and admire my Evie. *How has she not woken up? It's not like I was subtle about masturbating right next to her while she slept.* More delicious thought floats over the latter, obscuring it completely. My baby girl loves when I play with her in her sleep.

I groan, then clean myself up with the rumpled bed sheet and toss it to the floor. The crossed barbells in my cockhead wink in the magic induced moonlight arrowing across the bed as I curl around Evie's back. Sliding my knee between her thighs, gently applying pressure to her clit through her panties. I don't know why she insists on wearing these things. I'm just going to tear them off her body. Although I love stealing them after she's worn them, the scent of her sweet arousal saturating the fabric. I bet it would feel fucking phenomenal to wrap a silky pair around my cock now, gliding my piercings against the soft fabric. A shudder travels through me and I still my rocking hips.

Another time, definitely another time.

I almost wish she would wake and play in the dark with me, but she's not a demon and requires far more sleep than me. I miss her even though she's here in my goddamn arms.

Fuck it. I want to know what she's dreaming about.

I roll Evie onto her back, lowering myself between her thighs, and spreading her lower lips with my tattooed index and middle fingers. Pre-cum leaks against the sheets as I take in my fill of her. *Mmm, my piercing looks good on her.* I smirk as I as I rub the jewelry back and forth with a shadow, the light kiss of the metal teasing over her swollen clit. If I have it my way, her clit will always be swollen like this. Thoughts of me and what I do to her woven into the fabric of her mind so that her every breath aches for me to be inside her.

I kiss and nip along the sensitive skin of her inner thighs as I stroll down the mental pathway linking us and into her unconscious mind. It's peaceful in her thoughts, for once no terrors, or any dreams at all, cloud her mind. I mentally stroll through her brain waves, weaving specific wavelengths together. Evie falls into a much deeper sleep, her breath catching as I play with her mind and strum her clit with the pad of my index finger.

I feel more comfortable within her mind than I do in my own. Her essence soothes something within me. Maybe it's due to my imprint or maybe the bond. Hell it could be for another reason entirely. Her warmth and the warmth of her sleeping mind throbs around me, cocooning me in her unconscious bliss as I weave the last brain waves to keep her unconscious for as long as I wish. A debauched and entirely fucked up dreamscape forms around me as I create a dream for my witch that will leave her desperate and panting for my cock. I dip out of her mind, floating along the bond leisurely as the dream I manufactured pleasures her.

One of my barbells catches on a fold of the fitted sheet beneath me and I grunt, the resulting bite of pleasureful pain squeezing my balls with the need for more.

I press the bridge of my nose to her slit and breathe in her musky, light rose scent. She smells so fucking good. A moan slips past my lips as I suck on her vulva, arousal rapidly leaking directly onto my tongue. Ughgnh. She always tastes so damn delectable— I've been an addict since the first taste. If it were possible, I would never wash her liquid desire from my tongue.

I circle a teasing path around her clit, then catch the jewelry between my teeth and tug on it firmly, all while avoiding the actual bundle of nerves begging for my attention. My groan vibrates around her as it swells further and my mouth fucking waters. *So damn swollen and needy.* I'm desperate to join her in her dreams, but first I need to thank her for my new cock jewelry.

My hand slides against the sheets and beneath my body, growling against her pussy as my thumb glances over the head and gathers a wealth of pre-cum along the pad. I moan as I bring my thumb to my lips, then swirl my tongue around it, tasting myself.

No wonder she craves me. I'm godsdamn delicious.

My hips rock into the mattress, the much-needed friction driving my primal urges higher, but not satiating it.

I want her.

My tongue fucks into her addictive cunt as she moans softly. However, in her dream, I just know she's screaming. The sound of her muted pleasure causes goosebumps to skitter over my arms. My lips move down one side of her opening and up the other, nibbling and teasing the sensitive flesh as I go. Perhaps I made her dream a little too pleasurable. I draw back and cast a shadow around her puckered asshole.

A bought of pleasure filled pain thickens my cock as I harden further and flip her onto her belly. My shadows lift her hips, giving me full access to her ass. Licking my lips, I devour her.

Evie's unconscious body jerks as I lick around the ring of muscle.

"You like that, Baby Girl?" I ask aloud against her skin, knowing she won't respond. The thought of her vulnerability causes my hips to buck involuntarily. "Of course you do, my filthy little slut."

I groan and dip my tongue inside her, then swirl my palm over my pierced cock head, twitching as overly sensitive stimulation shutters down my shaft. "Mmmughnhgn, why haven't we played like this sooner? So fucking good."

Fuck, how am I this close already? At the moment, I don't really fucking care. The puckered muscle beneath my questing lips and tongue quiver. I want to come but I restrain myself, waiting for the perfect moment.

Not yet.

I pull away and slide two fingers into her cunt, Evie's back arching as I fuck them into her feverishly. Her sweet moans join my growling grunts as I grasp her hips and jerking myself off with my other hand, matching the pace of my fingers inside her. My witch's pussy squeezes my fingers, and my teeth sharpen, cutting into my lower as I lip bite down, a trickle of warm blood gliding down my chin and onto my chest.

"Fuck, come for me, Baby Girl. I need it."

My forearm muscle bunches as I thrust into my fist and watch my sleeping witch tremble, rapture seeping into my bones. I grit my teeth.

Not yet.

The tendons in my neck tighten as I restrain myself from coming, teetering on the edge. Evie's heart rate soars and her back arches as she climaxes, her cum leaking onto the sheets.

A roaring growl erupts from my throat as I twist my barbells with a tendril of shadow and orgasm all over her pretty little cunt. "Ugnhnn... Ah... Fuck...Evvvvvie." My gaze locks on her pulsing, cum covered pussy as I stoke myself through my release.

I pant through the aftershocks twitching through me. *Godsdamn. That's a beautiful sight.*

I will a shadow into my jeans pocket, the fabric puddled on the floor, extract my cigarettes and lighter, then proceeded to light a death stick. There is nothing like a cigarette after sex. I inhale that first taste of nicotine, not bothered that the drug does nothing for me. The ritual is enough. I tip my head back, releasing the coiled smoke from my lungs leisurely. Evie continues to moan, her lips parted in a fuckable 'O', twitching on the bed.

My eyes dilate as I smoke and stroke her body with my hungry stare, devouring every single moment of her lusty sounds and pleasure.

I pinch my lips around the end of the cigarette as I position myself at the apex of her thighs, fisting my cock and lubricating the shaft with our combined cum. I suck in a strangled breath and a strangled snarl vibrates my throat.

I need to be inside her. Right the fuck now.

I inhale sharply, the purple cherry eating up half the cigarette, and hold the smoke in my lungs as I toss the remains into the ashtray on the nightstand. My lungs burn with a need to exhale, but I refuse to obey, not until I'm inside my witch.

When she wakes, she won't be able to move any part of her body and without remembering who took her in her sleep. I release the smoke through my nose, the opaque substance trickling slowly from my nostrils as I thrust my cock inside her pretty pussy.

CHAPTER THIRTY-FOUR

Evie

Lorcan grins down at me as he tugs my body across the cream sofa, cushions and drapes my head over the arm rest, my unbound hair swaying against his legs.

Is this my old apartment? I thought everything was destroyed?

I stare at his magic cross piercing as Lorcan slowly pleasures himself above my face and my body rocks back and forth.

Why am I moving when he's above me?

I moan as pressure from an unseen force fills my pussy. "Oh Gods, this is a dream." A flood of arousal soaks the apex of my thighs.

"Good girl. You caught on quickly." Lorcan chuckles then groans. "Right now I'm balls deep inside your pretty cunt, fucking into you while you lay limp with sleep."

My pussy clamps around nothing, yet *I can feel him inside me.*

"Close your eyes, Baby Girl. Wouldn't want you getting dizzy as I fuck your throat."

My eyelids shut and I moan, then open my mouth and stick my tongue out as far as it will go without being asked.

"Good fucking girl," Lorcan praises.

I cannot wait to feel his piercings as I swallow him down. My body rocks forward over the armrest slightly as his phantom thrust from the real-world bucks into my pussy.

Fuck, it feels so damn good.

Loran collars his hand around my upside-down throat, then leans down and sucks my tongue into his mouth. He kisses me hard and deep, his tongue dominating mine in the best way. I thought this position would be awkward for kissing, but it's new and different, and in no way hinders my demon.

This is so, so hot. Fuck my face. Please, I want to taste your cum.

Lorcan groans into my mouth, the sound blending with the constant, simmering growl that's always present whenever we have a sexual encounter, then stands to his full height.

"Hold on to something, Little Witch."

I inhale as much oxygen as my lungs will hold, then cup my breasts.

His rich chuckle shivers over my skin. "Not exactly what I meant, but it'll have to do. I'm tired of waiting."

Lorcan hinges at the waist, covers my wet pussy with his hot mouth, and slides into my throat while fingers press into the side of my neck. *Fuuuuck, I want to feel my cock under your skin as you gag on me.*

I lose track of reality, what is a dream sensation and what is the whispered touch of his actions in real life. My fingers glide into his blue-black hair as he moans and nibbles on my clit.

Do you feel me as I use you in your sleep?

I choke on his cock and mumble incoherent words around it. "Ymmphh."

Lorcan groans, long and deep. *You look so fucking vulnerable right now. Your tits pressed into the mattress as I prep your ass to take my cock.*

My clit throbs, and I nearly come as I focus on breathing around his cock when I can and the distinct, but whispered pressure between my cheeks.

Should I fill this round ass of yours with my cum?

My release screams toward me, so close I could cry. "Ye... Lo...rphmn."

Lorcan thrusts deeper into my throat and gifts me a dizzying hand necklace. "Fuck, Evie! The skin of your throat is stretched so tight under my palm." His lips ghost over my labia as he speaks. "I wish you could see just how fucking magnificent you look right now. Your whispered moans and whimpers in real life are an extreme contrast to how loudly you gag around my cock right now. Godsdamn, it's so fucking sexy."

I push down on the back of his head, urging him to keep fucking licking me as the lighter warm touch on the nerves between my cheeks increases in speed and pressure. I grind against his face, pushing my thought down the bond.

I can feel you everywhere.

My mind melts as a clear picture of my unconscious body screams across my mind's eye. My breasts sway as he stares hungrily at my sleeping face from between my thighs. The authentic version of me parts her lips and a soft, desperate moan slips out.

Fuck. He's using my unconscious body for his pleasure. He can do anything he wants to me, and I wouldn't be able to stop him.

I gasp in a breath as the vision fades and Lorcan pulls out of my throat, leaving his cock on my tongue. "Deep breath, Baby Girl."

I quickly inhale, then he resumes fucking my face, his balls slapping against my nose.

I try to breathe in through my nose instinctively, but between his fat cock, his balls, and the tight constriction of his fingers around my throat restrict all access to oxygen.

My lungs burn as he slides deeper, his piercings rubbing against my full throat, and I scream around his cock. "Oahhg…Go..ds…"

He moans as I swallow around him convulsively as I gag several times in a row.

Lorcan sucks my clit hard between his lips and lashes his tongue against the piercing he marked me with, each flick tapping the jewelry against my bundle of nerves. My lungs burn for a breath I know isn't coming.

My senses buzz with over sensation, and it hardly registers that he stopped licking me, only lightly scraping me with his scruff as his stuttering pants rush over my sensitive skin.

One of his big, tattooed hands lands on my breast and he kneads the sensitive tissue, yet the phantom warmth and pressure between my thighs that was there a moment ago, vanishes and streaks of something warm streaks across my back.

Lorcan's growl shreds his voice to its demonic pitch. "I'm coming... all over your... fucking back... Unholy... godsdamn... Satan's... uugghhhghgg!" Cool air rushes against my slick pussy as he rockets to his full height, rips his cock from my mouth, and comes all over my face. "Fuuuuck...ahhgh...ughgg...Baby, yesss..."

It's too much.

Far too much.

Lorcan's cum continues to spurt against my face in irregular intervals, then my back arches as his palm slaps my clit sharply twice. I reach over my head and grab, digging my nails into his thighs as a sweet, intense release barrels into me.

My demon growls gutturally, "Can you feel my cum coating your back?"

I throw my neck further over the armrest and moan huskily. "Yes! Lorcan... it feels so... so fucking good."

My mind blurs as my climax goes on and on. Lorcan gently lifts the back of my head, lifts it from the awkward angle, then licks a stripe up my cheek, gathering some of his cum, gliding his tongue onto mine, depositing his pleasure directly onto my taste buds.

My eyes open, I stare up at him and swallow everything he gives me, licking my lips slowly.

Lorcan places a fluffy pillow under my head, rounds the armrest, and crawls between my thighs as phantom hands massage my breasts. He cleans off the remainder of his cum with a warm, soft towel, then presses a kiss to my sternum.

His arms dip beneath my body and he wraps his hands around my shoulders, clutching me to him and pressing his forehead deeper between my breasts. We lay there, catching our breaths as he holds me.

Lifting his head, my demon's gaze locks on to mine. "I'm not done with you yet."

My heart flutters. As I absorb his utter devotion and love in the best way he knows how. I'm so turned on. I can hardly pull one clear thought from my mind, but like every time, the thrill of remembering he loves me electrifies my blood.

"Evie," Lorcan whispers against my skin, "tell me what you want me to do to your sleeping body, this one, or both."

My eyes flutter close briefly, "Eat my ass. I want to feel every single lick, not the water down version."

He groans and kisses the hollow of my throat. "I already tasted it once tonight, but once was definitely not enough." His forehead thumbs between my breasts. "You are so fucking perfect for me."

"Lorcan?"

"Hmm?"

"Back in reality… I want you inside me."

He rises and sits back on his heels, the corner of his mouth twitching upward. "Pick a hole."

"I don't fucking care which it is as long as you're inside me. Right. Fucking. Now."

"Spread those pretty thighs wider and lift your hips," he orders.

I do as he commands as his hungry stare rakes over my body with predatory intent.

"Please," I beg as a trickling sensation ghosts between my cheeks. I glanced down, but Lorcan remains unmoving, his gaze focused on the apex of my thighs as he positions my legs. I choke on a moan, a streak of intense arousal buzzing through my clit.

His deep, gravelly whisper shivers over my skin. "Should I describe how I'm pleasuring you right now? Using your body like a fucking toy?"

"Yes, tell me as you fucking taste my ass. I want to feel your tongue so badly."

"As you wish, Little Witch. Close your eyes and focus on the sensations." After a pause, he stretches his massive body out on his stomach.

This dream couch must be extremely long to accommodate him. I giggle at the thought, then press my lips together as Lorcan's gaze darkens.

"Right now, I have you positioned just like this, spread wide for me and completely fucking helpless." A grin unfurls across his face as he nuzzles his stubbled cheek against my inner thigh and runs his knuckles up the other at a glacial pace. "I've already slathered my fingers and your ass in lube, so they'll glide into you easily." As he says the words, a slight burn quickly transforms into beautiful pressure as the real Lorcan plunges his fingers into my ass.

My hips buck into the air.

Lorcan laughs against my skin. "That's my good fucking whore," he praises. The muted pleasure builds within me as his real fingers thrust in and out of me.

The sensation is so good, but not enough. I open my eyes and meet his hard stare. "More. Please… I need more." I don't give a shit that I'm begging so long as he gets his cock inside me, dream or reality. I don't fucking care.

He's taking too long.

Lorcan arches over me, then sucks my lower lip into his mouth and bites down on the digit as he pulls away.

I protest, but a moan cuts me off as he tugs me to his waiting mouth.

"Holy Gods." Wet, hot heat envelopes me as he tastes my ass, swiping broad licks of his tongue over the far too sensitive nerves. My shoulders burn as I hold myself up on my forearms and I scream with pleasure. "Ahgh…Oh, f-fuuc…"

Lorcan attacks me with hungry, primal groaning growls, his mouth vibrating against me as an overwhelming amount of phantom pressure forms inside my ass. My demon praises me, kissing the sensitive puckered hole while as his lips shape the words against me.

"Uggnhg… Baby Girl," Lorcan grunts, "your ass is so fucking tight around my cock… Mmmugghgn… Unholy Gods, you're squeezing me so well, and my piercings—" He moans again, cutting himself off.

I jerk, pleasure electrifying my oversensitive clit as Lorcan rolls it between his forefinger and thumb. His husky groan turns into a laugh. "Mmm, you like that?"

"Gods… Yes! More."

My demon's claws dig into my outer thighs as my body jostles and rocks away from him, sweet, agonizing pleasure decimating me as the real life Lorcan unleashes himself on my ass like a rabid fucking beast.

He grinds his thumb against my clit with tight, quick circles. *You ready to come all over me, Baby Girl?*

I arch my neck and press my head deeper into the pillow. "Yes, yes, gods… yesss," I moan.

Lorcan chuckles against my ass, then thrusts three fingers into my pussy, pumping them furiously. My vision whitens as blinding ecstasy rolls through me and I struggle to absorb the vast amount of things being done to my physical and mental body.

"Fuuuuuuck," Lorcan growls as the last thread of his restraint snaps, and he attacks my ass with his tongue, moaning, biting, and suckling on the tight ring of muscle. The duality of the phantom pressure inside my ass and his rough treatment of it in my dream sends me spiraling into oblivion, orgasming harder than I have in my entire fucking life.

"Ahgn… Baby Girl… Yes, suck me off with your ass… give me more… more of your screams." Pure liquid desire squirts all over his face and I continue coming. The pressure inside my ass streaks higher, but it keeps eating me.

I vibrate on the couch, my head whipping back-and-forth as the pleasure goes on and on like it'll never end.

I don't think I want it to… but it's too much.

My body spasms and twitches as I stare blearily down my body, catching the sight of his tattooed forearm muscles bunching and flexing as he jerks himself off.

"Holy fuck."

His claws bite into my left thigh where he holds me aloft and comes in both realities, inside my ass and all over me at once. I lose track of which cum is real or just an echo.

Lorcan releases a shuttering breath, grinning lazily against my inner thigh where he rests his cheek.

"That was…"

He laughs. "Yes. Yes, it *was*."

Lorcan lifts me into his arms, rolling his body under mine while he embraces me.

I mumble against his chest. "I am so fucking glad I pierced you."

His approving growl vibrates my cheek. "Me too, Little Witch. Me fucking too."

He presses his hand between my shoulders. His finger splayed, and I nearly drool as I admire his flexing abs while he gets into position. Then I crawl over his straining erection and sink over him.

Lorcan moans, his other hand tightens on an ass cheek. I laugh and bite my lip around the smile because I fucking love being able to give him so much pleasure, just as he does for me.

I stretch out over his hard, tattooed body, trailing a finger over his true name tattooed beneath his right eye. My magic comes alive under my skin, simmering where my fingertip skims the letters. Faint wisps of shadows uncoil where we touch, and he stiffens beneath me.

"Evie, what—?"

I didn't think it was possible.

Hope expands in my chest, nearly cracking my ribs with the force of the emotion.

I'm powerful enough. Why didn't I think of trying before?

I close his eyes with my other hand. "Just feel me, My Demon."

Lorcan's chest rises and falls steadily, his muscles relaxing. "Yes, My Witch."

My lungs inflate as I breathe in, focusing all my attention on his true name.

I infuse the skin over the letters with my shadows, willing to take a shape just big enough to fully conceal his name behind the thorned stem of a rose. I lean a forearm on his chest as I work, as one of his hands squeezes my biceps gently, his thumb smoothing against my skin and his even breaths whisper against my throat.

My gaze glides to his closed lids, his lashes appearing more blue than black as they fan his cheeks. I sigh, kissing his forehead. He's so attractive it fucking hurts.

My shadows finish the last petal with a flourish of magic, but just as I lift from Lorcan's skin, my death magic swirls around the tendril of shadow and glows beneath the pad of my finger. I lift my hand away, then my lips part, staring in stunned awe as my death magic burns away the original tattoo and infuses itself into the shadow ink.

"Holy shit."

"What?"

I slap a palm over his thick lips, never taking my eyes off my magic. His gaze narrows, but he doesn't protest further.

My magic is so fucking beautiful.

Purple bleeds into the black shadow ink that forms the delicate petals as my death magic expunges his name from his flesh and leaves only our mark in return. I drag my gaze to Lorcan's and remove my hand. "It's gone."

"What do you mean, it's gone?"

I cup his cheeks, and a fluffy, purely happy puff ball explodes in my chest. "My magic... I removed your true name."

Lorcan sits up so quickly I tip backward, but a strong flat palm spreads between my shoulder blades, catching me. "Fuck, that's..." The shine in his eyes quickly dims and he sighs. "But this is a dream."

"Wake me up."

"Fuck, just give me a minute to process."

I glare at him. "No. Wake me up right now, Lorcan."

My eyes blink open to Lorcan's serious, stony gaze, then I gasp and smile harder than I have in years. I press my lips to the deep

431

purple rose, the same shade and style of my own, tattooed beneath his right eye. "You are mine."

His eyes widen and he vaults off the bed, crashing his palms against the oval mirror over the dresser as he examines his face closely. Lorcan's hand shakes as he traces a finger over my tattooed rose and squeezes his eyes shut.

I sit up and wrap myself in a hug.

I fucking did it.

I claimed my demon in every way possible.

Lorcan whirls to face me, then tackles me onto my back. "Say it again, Evie. Please."

I fling open the doors of our bond and kiss him with each resounding word.

You.

Kiss.

Are.

Kiss.

Mine.

Kiss.

He grins against my lips, but suddenly the firm pressure of his kiss slackens, and the full weight of his body drops onto me, air rushing from my lungs.

What the Hell is happening?

My heart seizes as I shake his muscular shoulder and croak, "Lor?"

My limbs fall limply to my sides as two cloaked figures loom over our prone bodies. One of them speaks but I can't make out the words through the heartbeat filling my ears.

CHAPTER THIRTY-FIVE

Lorcan

Drip.

Drip.

Drip.

My eyes flare open only to be greeted with inky, swirling darkness. Panic squeezes my lungs as I scramble backward on my hands and feet.

This can't be fucking happening.

No.

No, no, no, no!

Pain arrows through my back and slices through my brain matter, the smell of freshly seared flesh jamming up my nostrils.

This cannot be real. I refuse to accept any other outcome.

I struggle to my knees, slapping my palms over my ears as I dig my fingertips into the sides of my head.

It's okay, Lorcan. You'll get through this. It's just a dream. You'll wake up with Evie in your arms. Breathe, just fucking breathe...

But is it really a dream?—Panic swallows all rationality.

This is fucking real. I don't know how I know the horrifying truth, but I do.

Emptiness reigns.

Emptiness reigns.

Emptiness reigns.

The thought bounces against the inside of my skull with spikes as sharp and damaging as a mace.

A shiver pebbles my naked skin as a memory ripples across my mind's eye.

Samuel's face as he laughed and threw me in here, a wide, unhinged smile plastered across his face. He wouldn't stop and fucking listen to me.

Fuck.

This isn't a dream.

I never wanted Evangeline, or the fucking throne for that matter, but now it's clear that his reasons for helping Evangeline have nothing to do with taking the crown for himself. No, it's all about his sick and beyond toxic obsession with Evangeline.

I'm not sure if the witch fabricated his feelings for her or if he genuinely wants her enough to destroy our family. Perhaps I would feel less devastation if that were the case, but I fucking doubt it. Samuel and I never saw eye to eye, even as adolescents. He could not resolve himself to the fact that he would always be the second-born son.

I used to blame his behavior on the fact that he's Envy, but he's so far gone now that my madness wants absolutely nothing to do with his.

When I found Evie, the utter desolate hopelessness that was my constant companion diminished, then disappeared altogether. But there is no denying that the speed at which it returns fucking guts me.

I try to get my thoughts away from this dangerous path, but I can't. I'm too godsdamn weak.

The bars of my cage leached every drop of magic from my bones, my shadows and demon powers completely evaporating.

The cold, damp stones rush to meet my back as I give into gravity.

Absolutely cracked and disturbed laughter looses from my throat as I recognize why one of the many reasons *this stint* in my cage feels so very different.

I no longer fight with my madness.

In the past, I fought against it as it worked to draw my present mind into my subconscious, eviscerating me forever. To lock me in a cage of its own making and bury it beneath the black sands of my most morbid thoughts and dreams.

But now I know the bitter truth—it wanted to protect me. We've come to an understanding and everything about it feels different... as if it actually *is* a positive response to the trauma I've endured.

It's still always present, even in my non-waking hours. However, I don't bear any bitterness towards it or resent its existence. I welcome the blurred, dark oblivion it offers, and willingly sink beneath the sand, no metaphorical cage necessary.

I float here deep under miles of sand manifested by my subconscious, oblivious to my real surroundings even though they claw, and claw, and fucking claw at my psyche, just waiting for the opportunity to slice through it and erase me once and for all.

An emotion that I don't have the energy to decipher swarms like an absolutely pissed off hive of killer Hell-bees. Their black and purple bodies fight for the chance to stab my organs with their jagged toxic barbs, clashing their wings, gnashing their fangs, and decorating my insides with rich violet blood.

I don't fight them.

I lie there, letting the obsidian sand cover my open eyes and worm its way into my ears and mouth. It's almost peaceful here in this numb existence.

An intrusive thought gouges its way into my mind. *Evie.* Is she safe? If anything has happened to her, this is the fate I deserve. Perhaps, the one that I have *always* deserved.

Yes, drowning in sorrow is absofuckinglutely fitting. I welcome the sand pouring into me and filling my body cavity. Pain, desirous raw pain lacerates my guts as the soft, soothing sand transforms into millions of sharp, forgotten puzzle pieces, cutting me open with endless paper cut like lacerations from the inside out.

My mouth opens as I laugh, gagging on the sand that's swiftly clogging my esophagus.

Not too long ago, I thought of Evie as such a puzzle piece, minus the blade-like edges, but perhaps, that's what was missing all along.

Our jagged, sharp, and blood-stained pieces haven't been forced together. No, my little witch's edges carved into mine until she nestled inside my fucking soul, the wounds she inflicted healing and sealing us together for eternity.

I inhale and greedily consume the sand deep into the membranes of my lungs.

How can I protect her when it was so easy for them to toss me away, to lock me in this cage, to be forgotten amongst the memories caked into the bowels of the castle?

I twist and writhe further into the blade-like puzzle pieces, encouraging their honed edges to slice into the outside of my skin as well.

This feels… right.

I gasp and cough as the safety of my madness' hold fades, and scorching agony burns across my chest and thighs where they press against my cage. Any magic that has trickled into me during my spell of delirium seeps from me like it's my life's blood.

Drip.

Drip.

Drip.

My body doesn't bother reacting to the chilling breeze whispering over my naked skin, the source of its creation unknown, just like the motherfucking drips.

I sigh and squeeze my eyes shut as a thought whispers into my mind. I miss my fucking blanket, a constant over the centuries of my initial captivity. Holy and threadbare as it was, at least it was something tangible I could cling to when the manic thoughts overwhelmed me. I looked for it when Samuel and Evangeline shoved me in here but only received bruised knees and burn blistered fingers for my efforts.

While I'm aware it's fucking pathetic, the King of Demons longing for a godsdamn scrap of fabric, I can't be bothered to give a shit.

The ridiculous, binding notion of time holds no sway over me as my mind drifts among the black sands. Perhaps I've dwelled in this expansive, inky void for weeks, or it might only be mere hours. But one truth remains—If I think about how long I've been captive this time, I risk losing myself... permanently.

I hiss and the corners of my cracked, blood caked lips score upward into my taut cheeks as I absorb the euphoric agony my cage inflicts.

Crack.

Crack.

Crack.

I rock back and forth into the bars, slamming the back of my skull against my cage as hard as I can with every backward tilt. And yet, it does nothing to dim the acidic taste at the back of my throat or the twist of the bleeding organ in my chest as it's rung dry.

Sizzling flesh drags against my eardrums as pain crumbles a fraction of my utterly desolate and useless thought loops.

Thoughts of my witch swim to the forefront of my mind and a raw, tortured scream eviscerates my throat, stealing my breath. It's the same every fucking time I accept the inevitable and conjure Evie. I trace her features with wisps of memory, unrepenting yearning swallowing my senses and replacing the throbbing bliss I built rocking into the bars.

This pain?

This soul shredding ache?

Is not one I fucking relish.

I despise it.

When I wrote that letter to Evie and told her she was my eternity, I fucking meant it.

I don't exist without her.

No reason to put in the effort required to live.

Royal demons cannot die, not in the normal sense of the word, but we can fade—Our physical bodies remaining in a stasis, but our minds blank and wholly silent.

Shivers cascade over my body, the frigid floor simultaneously bleeding into my bones and extracting any warmth the trembling has created.

I'm too fucking weak to do anything but lie here… a pathetic, useless heap of a demon.

Pain pulses through my temples as my madness perks up and claws into my brain matter.

If you give in to this feeling and submit to oblivion too soon, all the suffering, both now and in the past will have been for nothing.

My heart hardens into stone. If anyone deigns to inform me that Evie no longer exists on the same plane as myself, I *will* find a way to end it, but only after I have wrought the maximum amount of destruction possible in her name.

My vow echoes inside my mind and lodges between my ribs, etching itself onto the bone.

I swallow thickly, my throat sticking together with the fresh blood seeping through the parched, cracked membranes lining it, then get on my hands and knees and crawl away from my beloved source of pain.

I need to regain all the power that I can while also weakening the wards of my fucking cage. I battle against the persistent craving to harm myself further, then lock my arms around my knees, refusing to give in.

But I acknowledge the necessary evil of grace and allow myself a moment to break, to split open at the seams and pour my blackened misery into the world.

Just.

This.

Once.

I plunge into thoughts of my baby girl, letting everything I hold at bay just to survive, crash over and into me. Memory after memory crash like an angry sea onto the shores of my mind's eye. My vision clouds with wetness, then spills unhindered onto my cheeks. My tongue darts out and catches the last bit of moisture my body possesses as every insufferable emotion trickles down my cheeks as tears.

It's then that I realize music plays along with my thoughts of Evie. I hug my knees tighter to my chest. Not just any music, the playlist I poured every fucking drop of my essence into for her. However, as my voice reverberates around me, I realize the music plays not only in my head.

My voice distorted, raw, and broken, sings along weakly with every fucking song, and for a few precious minutes, drowning out that fucking dripping.

I close my eyes and lay my cheek against my knee, hugging myself tightly, even though I know it will do nothing to keep me in one piece.

My vocal cords burn as I sing through the anguish of my dry, bloody throat. I comfort myself in the only way I know how, other than through pain or Evie's touch.

I open my eyes and blink into the absolute well of darkness surrounding me as I sing my way through The Dark of You by Breaking Benjamin.

Tears are falling harder and I shudder, dropping my control and letting go of everything I've ever felt.

My voice quiets before I stand on quaking legs.

I will do this for my little witch. If Samuel or Evangeline ever deigns to grant me their presence, I'll be ready and fucking waiting.

Time slips by again, unnoticed. My legs no longer shake, but perhaps that is because I cannot feel them.

My stomach launches into my throat as my surroundings drastically alter.

I squint through the darkness and turn toward the faintest spark of lavender. The flickering grows, seeming to draw closer. My eyes burn, unaccustomed to absorbing light after so long forgotten in inky black.

I force my eyelids to stay open, less I blink and the darkness consumes everything once more.

My hands ball into a fist by my sides as my eyelids tremble with the effort to hold their open position, then the slightest scrape of something shuffling against stone annihilates the silence of my solitude.

The lavender light burst into an actual fame as someone rounds what I can now see is a concealed, tightly curved stone staircase. I blink and the bearer of said light source comes into focus, clutching a torch. The hairs on the back of my neck straighten as my mind deciphers our new reality. Then a simmering growl rumbles deep in my chest as Evangeline flounces down the stairs.

My skin tightens. There's another signature close by, but it remains out of sight, higher on the stairs. Samuel, perhaps? I almost call the cunt out on it, but something tells me—urges me—to keep the information to myself.

I bare my teeth as she steps onto the stone floor holding before my cage.

"Don't stop singing on my account, Love. You have such a sexy voice, even if it's rough right now," Evangeline coos as she licks her lips and skims my naked body with her disgusting gaze.

I don't respond, just glare at her with unblinking eyes, absolutely resolute and determined to follow my plan to its conclusion.

She tsks. "What, not even a hello after all we've been through over the years?"

I clear my throat. "My most sincere apology. My memory is spotty right now due to the less than appealing environment." The tone lining my words is hard, but the obsequious nature of my words smooth her ruffled disposition.

Eva laughs and throws a hand against her chest. "Oh, come now. I know you remember. How could you possibly have forgotten *me*?"

I focus on my breathing, working to keep it steady and even. Her gaze hardens and the edge of her upper lip twitches as her true self oozes to the surface.

Good, now we can have a proper conversation.

Eva scoffs.

A flush blotches her skin like welts and her pupils dilate. I desperately want to look away as the gorge rises to the back of my throat.

You can do this, Lorcan. Swallow it down, then launch the attack.

I tap my chin with a forefinger. "You know, now that you mention it, I do recall something." I sigh and shake my head. "Unfortunately, the details are still rather fuzzy. Remind me, won't you, Evangeline?" I intentionally let her name slip and her pulse quickens in response.

She steps closer to the bars and my hands twitch with the need to strangle the fucking life out of her.

The faintest flicker of shadows warms behind my ribs.

Soon.

Almost time.

Just a bit closer.

It's not enough. I need her to fucking break.

I ignore the nausea swirling in my stomach. I cannot let it distract me.

Blood races to my cock as I remember the ecstasy soaring through my body as Evie dominated me.

I quickly halt the rest of the memory from replaying as Evangeline moans and stares hungrily at my now fully erect cock. My skin recoils as if trying to crawl off its skeletal home.

Her expression sours and she hisses, "If you really want me to tell you, remove those disgusting piercings.

I hold her unflinching stare, then shrug, forcing the corner of my mouth to curl. "I would if I could have Eva, you know that. Alas, they're magically pierced, and therefore only the owner of the magic used to place them can remove the jewelry.

She scoffs and stomps a slippered foot. "That explains why every attempt to remove them while you were passed out failed." The bridge of her nose wrinkles. "All you did was bleed and groan. I even made Samuel try, but he was less than enthused about the task."

Revulsion slithers over every inch of my body.

She.

Fucking.

Touched.

Me.

Wrath consumes by body, consuming my veins with sharp, frozen spikes, poking holes into them as they expand and blood leaks into the black cavity of my essence.

Eva inches forward, ugly red blotches coloring her cheeks. I open my mouth to speak, then close it as a signature I'd know even in death sends my heart into cartwheels.

What the fuck is Evie doing here?

Thank fucking Satan and Hellfire, she's alive.

Her essence lingers nearby, but I cannot determine her location. My magic is still too weak to use.

Shoving thoughts of my witch from my mind, I refocus on the evil bitch before me.

An unapproved growl scrapes from my throat and Eva bites her lip. "I have always loved it when you purr for me, Love."

My nostrils flare, but I harness the emotion before she can pick up on it. "Tell me, Eva, what is your favorite memory of us?"

Her mouth parts slightly and lust consumes her stare. "It was the time I used the shackles. Do you remember?"

"Not yet, keep going."

"I had Samuel move you to the bed while you were unconscious from my earlier dose of potion, then secure your arms and legs with magically enhanced shackles. But I knew that wouldn't be enough, so I secured you further with the screws." She flutters her eyelashes like she intends to flirt with me. "Does that help?"

I shrug noncommittally, then lower my voice to a sultry caress. "Tell me more."

Eva giggles and I almost vomit. "Your brother held me as we waited for you to awaken." Her eyes widen so far it would be comical if not for the present circumstances. "Please, you have to believe me. I didn't a-and I still don't want Samuel. It's *always* been you. Everything I've done has been for you, Love."

I cannot describe the utter revulsion and level of loathing I have for this despicable creature.

"So, it was then that I finally took action. I used your brother to show you just how much I love you and make you see you love me too. I sent him away as I formulated a plan." She sighs wistfully, then winks. "And, I might have touched every inch of your skin while I did so."

A shudder ripples over my skin, then I straighten my spine. No.

I fucking refuse to allow her the power to finally ruin me. I curl a wisp of shadows in my palm, ready to strike.

CHAPTER THIRTY-SIX

Evie

My heart withers as I crouch in the shadows of the barely illuminated cold stone chamber. I wish I could look away but I can't.

A small smile curves my lips as a kernel of smugness preens that the plan might actually work. By now Lucifer should be in place, listening to the putrid web of lies and deception his lover spun, and waiting for my signal.

City destroying levels of rage rise beneath my skin the longer I watch, my magic pushing angrily against my confines as Evangeline lusts after Lorcan. My demon held captive in the fucking cage that haunts him like an enthusiastic poltergeist. Power hums from the bars with invisible waves, like heat rippling above pavement.

Not only did she destroy Lorcan's family, she violated him while I was in the same fucking castle.

I will my side of our bond to remain closed and silent, locking away the part of myself that feels everything too intensely, while the remainder—and larger portion—screams into the night for blood.

Evangeline laughs and flaps a hand coyly. "Anyway, it was then that I knew I had to use your other brothers as well if I were to get what I deserve: You and the crown." Eva leans forward, delusion clouding her eyes and unrequited love seeping from her every pore.

And there it is.

The proof we've been waiting for.

I roll back my shoulders, take in a breath, then shed any reticence, unleashing the real me.

My.

True.

Bloodthirsty.

Dark.

Self.

Lorcan growls in pain as I stalk towards Evangeline, my light footsteps lost in the sounds, shadows streaming off me like ribbons. Everything around me sharpens as I glance at Lorcan's broken

448

body, then quickly look away. My fingers curl and my upper lip pulls back.

I can't wait to fucking kill her.

I stab my fingers into her hair, yank her away from the cage, and slam her face into the bars with a resounding crunch. Goosebumps ripple down my tattooed arms and a grin blossoms across my face as blood splatters in every direction.

"Evie," Lorcan croaks, but I resist meeting his eyes.

I hold her against the wards, perhaps enjoying her flailing arms a little too much. While the bitch may not have any magic left, she still houses the essence of a witch, and the wards know it. She screams and thrashes as I lean into her back and shove her harder into the searing magic.

Evangeline struggles against me. "You little bitch. Lorcan is *mine*."

I sigh, then lower my mouth to her ear. "I'll let you in on a little secret. He *loves me* so much that he…" I pause, "Imprinted. On. Me."

"What!?" she screeches. "No! That's not possible." She drags her nails into my forearms and spittle flies with her hurried words. "I hexed him over a century ago. If he wouldn't love me, then I made sure he couldn't love anyone."

I shake my head and tsk. "Unfortunately, your time for scheming and lording power over others has run out." Some of her hair rips free and she hisses as I twist her head around to face me. "Meet your fucking executioner."

"No! No, no, no, please! I'll do anything."

My shadows circle her torso, tossing her to the stone floor. "That's fucking obvious. You're wasting your final breaths; nothing will change my mind."

Evangeline curls into a trembling ball on her side, urine puddling beneath her. "Please, don't do this!"

I laugh hollowly. "You're pathetic."

Lucifer blurs down the stairs, unforgiving malice in his eyes.

My aunt struggles to her knees and reaches for him. "Help me, Luce!

"She's fucking psychotic," Lorcan shouts. "Don't believe anything out of this whore's mouth. She made Samuel believe she's in love with him and used him. Then, under your supposed orders, had me forced into the Shadow Realm for a century because of some made up bullshit that I'm after your throne. All in a sick vengeance because I didn't love her back. I'm sorry, Dad, but she manipulated you too."

His clawed hands curl at his sides, but pain burns behind his silver eyes as they flash to Evangeline, tears gathering along his lower lashes. "How could you, Eva? You told my boys that Lorcan was after my throne?"

"No. I-I didn't do anything! I promise, please believe me," Evangeline blubbers.

Lucifer's gaze drops to the floor, and he shakes his head slowly. "I trusted you."

Evangeline sobs and crawls to him, ugly crocodile tears mixed with snot running down her face. "N-no, please. I would never do anything to h-h-hurt you or your s-sons."

"How could I ever forgive you, when I'll never forgive myself," Lucifer says, slicing into her with words so even and impossibly calm it floods my bloodstream with adrenaline and sends my nervous system into a fight-or-flight frenzy. "You are despicable. I know the truth as I heard every single damming word from your own lips. You believed yourself in love with my son and destroyed him for it. Then you made me believe you loved me, all so you could get close enough to punish him." Lucifer's voice deepens, the sound bitterly cold and hollow, devoid of its usual warmth. That's when I see the devil, the release of that untapped power, come to the surface and, for the first time since meeting Lucifer, I'm afraid.

His eyes blacken to the color of charcoal. "There is only one punishment that will suffice."

Lorcan chuckles. "Fuck, that's really too bad."

His father takes a large step towards my great aunt, then whirls in a movement too quick to track. I blink and find Lucifer across the room, growling at a narrow-eyed Samuel as he pins him to the wall with invisible hands.

Right on schedule. I laugh, then drag my stare leisurely toward Evangeline once more. Evangeline cracks open her poisonous mouth, but I've heard quite enough. My death magic surges past her lips and down her throat as my shadows stringing her up by her wrists.

A scream tears from Samuel but is swiftly muted as Lucifer gags him with a shadow.

Out of my peripheral, smoke rises from Lorcan's hands as he clutches the bars in his fists, an encouraging, growl on his lips. "Fuck yes, Little Witch. End this so we can be rid of her for good."

I grab her square jaw and glare into her hateful brown eyes, the same shade as my own, then shape every bit of suffering caused by her hand into something malicious and dark. My death magic absorbs the offering greedily, then slowly, achingly so, incinerates her organs one by one. Her skin bubbles with blisters as the heat inside her grows so hot I can feel it kiss my skin from a yard away.

Evangeline's cries of anguish trickle over me like soft, soothing rain. Her skin incrementally flushes pink, to red, and dark satisfaction curves my lips as my death magic burns her alive from the inside out.

It's not enough.

I stroll around her immobile form. "You committed countless acts of evil," I pause, "but it's all justified because you were doing it out of love, *right?*"

Evangeline whimpers and chokes on the blood dribbling past her lips.

I will my magic forward, crafting a crown of shadows around her head. I squeeze the band across her brow tighter with each beat of her atrocious heart.

Lorcan's probing stare warms the side of my face as I cross my arms over my chest and a cruel smile tilts my lips. "How does the weight of the monarchy feel now, Evangeline?"

The resounding crack of bone reverberates through my eardrums and slices through her panicked gurgles. My steps halt as I take in her glazed eyes and slack jaw, tilting my head to examine her neck. I nod as I note the pulse thrumming away beneath her skin. "Oh, good, you're still alive."

Lorcan's hoarse laughter floats across me like a caress.

"Can't have you dying just yet." I look over at Lucifer and hold his stare. "Dad, toss me your blade?"

The devil's hard gaze softens, and a genuine smile curls his lips before he lobs the sheathed blade at me.

I snatch it out of the air and turn Evangeline upside down with my shadows, willing my magic to wrangle her limbs. Her arms straighten perpendicularly with the floor, then my shadows pin her legs together vertically.

My head shakes and I cackle. Evangeline exudes the dark energy a sacrifice draws from its victims—a rare true visage in blood, like a fucked up, gory crucifix.

"Shit, I was going to say burn in Hell, but you're already here." I laugh and slash the demonic blade across her throat.

Evangeline's blood sprays my chest in an arc of magnificent carnage. I close my eyes and absorb her last moments, my magic swirling back into me.

I open my eyes as an extended creak of metal hinges shatters the spell death has cast, holding us in its thrall. Lorcan stumbles through the open door of the cage and I hurry over to him, throwing his heavily tattooed arm over my shoulder. His weight nearly knocks me over as we move to the stone stairs, and I help him sit down.

I move to sit beside him, but Lorcan grabs my wrist and tugs me onto his lap instead. Our breaths mingling as reality settles around us. Stubble scrapes my palms as I cup his cheeks and kiss him gently, mindful of his dry, cracked lips.

Lorcan started healing the moment he stepped from the wards of his cage, but his magic was so depleted the process takes far longer than usual.

Evangeline is finally fucking dead. And I was the one to end her.

I look into his consuming eyes and hold his intense gaze. "She's dead."

A sexy, heart-stopping, boyish grin transforms Lorcan's face, those damn dimples bracketing his smile. "Yes, she fucking is." Adjusting me so my side rests against his chest and my legs drape over his thighs, he pulls me to him and buries his face in my hair, heedless of how filthy it is. "Thank you, Evie."

Lucifer snaps and Samuel drops to the stone floor in a heap of limbs, then he literally grabs his son by the nape of his neck and tosses him into the cage. The door slams shut with a final, jarring clank, the bars glow and Lucifer hisses as he pours his magic into the wards and imprisons Samuel.

"Dad! Please, don't leave me down here!"

Lucifer sighs, long and deep, through his nose. "Not only is everything you've done to Lorcan unforgivable, but you tried to tear apart our family. A crime like that cannot be forgiven." He pauses, then eviscerates Samuel with a hard stare and a shake of his head. "I'm so disappointed in you, Samuel."

Evie snorts down the bond. *Fuck. When Satan says he's disappointed in you... just... fuck.*

"You can't do this! I'm your son. Please..." Samuel trails off into hacking sobs.

"A few centuries of solitude is only the beginning of your punishment, My Boy."

I look over my shoulder as we leave what's left of Evangeline's corpse. "Should we do anything with the body?"

Lucifer sighs, his shoulders falling. "No. The stench of her decomposition will only aid in my son's punishment." He glances over at my demon, lips twitching, and waves a hand at his eldest. Joggers manifest on the lower half of Lorcan's body. "I can't have my son walking around, his bits exposed."

Lorcan and I trudge up the stairs until the damn cage is out of sight before his dad pulls him into a bear hug. "I am so sorry, My Lorcan."

"I know, and it's not your fault. I'm just fucking glad the bitch is dead," Lorcan says hoarsely, words breaking in places.

Lucifer offers me a watery smile over my demon's shoulder, then passes the torch to Lorcan and vanishes.

"Just a second, Little Witch," Lorcan says with a smirk, then slowly walks down the stairs and stops before the cage and tucks his hands into his pockets.

I follow but remain a few stairs above him.

"What kind of big brother would I be if I forgot to say goodbye?" Samuel sniffs but doesn't respond. "Do you hear that dripping sound, Envy?

Samuel spits on the ground, then snarls. "Fuck off."

Lorcan chuckles and continues like his brother never spoke, but his deep voice frosts over. "Now that I've pointed it out, it's the only fucking thing you'll ever hear." He pauses, expels a satisfied exhale, and leans closer to the bars. "Drip. Drip. Drip.—That's the sound of your life rotting away."

My demon turns back to me, then I ease us into the In-Between, deep, impenetrable darkness enveloping the cage.

EPILOGUE

Evie

Hell belongs to the damned but is a refuge for the broken. It's here, surrounded by punishment, demons, and ugliness, that I began to heal from my trauma—of a life on the run as an abused, adopted daughter with no one to love me, who believed I didn't deserve love.

I found freedom from mortality and suffering in the darkness, a sense of belonging with a family I chose, and the truest, most fucked up love I could have imagined.

For all my father's words of damnation and injecting the fear of Hell into me, it has become my haven, and it's here where I belong.

If only Lorcan would stay.

My fingers curl over the edge of the stone balcony railing overlooking the layers of Hell, wastelands and trials stretching out seemingly for an eternity, the darkest reaches belonging to the fog. I breathe in the ash-tinted air and allow my eyes to flutter shut.

Death has followed me my entire life, but now I see it for what it is—salvation. There is only so long a mortal can remain in Hell, although time is different here, so my regular lifespan is much longer than it would be in the Human Realm.

How ironic that when my soul passes, I'll never have to leave this place. If Lucifer is merciful, he may preserve me like he did for my aunt. Her soul, however, has been obliterated out of existence. I give little thought to her nowadays. Just like the rest of my biological family and Edward, all of whom were lost to the trials. Some statues, like Edward, Lorcan told me in passing, and a few of them turned into water wraiths or those trees that bleed in the woods.

I could help them if I wanted, but who am I to intervene with divine punishment? Not that I'd want to. Any of the dead who were good in my life, ended up some place else.

I feel Rosa before I hear her footsteps. Her warm, cozy magic a breath of fresh air amongst the grayness. I know why she's come. We've lost ourselves in court life ever since Evangeline was eviscerated and it had to end, eventually.

Her extended sigh grows louder as she closes the gap between us and joins me on the balcony. Wide, brown eyes take in the scenery, her fixed stare absorbing every detail. "You seem happy here."

My lips quirk upward. "I am. Although Lorcan is still intent on me having a human life back in your world."

She purses her thick, rosy lips. "My world? So, I assume that means you're not coming back with us?"

"I'd hoped you'd stay a little longer," I admit and twist my torso to fully face her. "But I get it. You need to get back to your life."

"Well, start again. There's no way I'll be able to get my clients back after this hiatus." She runs her hands through her fading pink ends. "It's no matter. Ezra can walk through shadows, so I'm going to have him rob a bank or something."

I snort-laugh, unsure if she's serious or not. "So, Ezra is going with you."

She drums her long, pink fingernails against the stone ledge. "He won't leave me alone."

My gaze narrows. "You love it."

"I'm not about to get into a relationship with a demon," she says, but the twist of her lips tells me it's something she's contemplated. "He's going to be my first client."

I smile. "So, you do have a plan for a fresh start?"

"Yes." She nods and sucks in a deep breath. "I'm going to treat demons and witches in the Human Realm who need help with their sexual health. It actually opens many new doors."

My brows slide halfway up my forehead. "Well, talk about making lemonade with lemons."

She lands a hand on her tilted hip. "I'm also going to start a line of monster dildos. Ezra agreed to let me make a mold of his in its demonic form."

Her pupils dilate and I shake my head with a grin. "You've seen it."

"A girl can look." Her quirky smile quickly fades as silence hangs between us. This was never a quick stop by to tell me she's leaving soon. This is a goodbye. "Ezra and his little Rupert are waiting by the doors. I didn't know how to tell you... I... I'm going to miss you. Fuck." She grabs me by my shoulders and buries my head in her hair. I commit her scent to memory—raspberries and candy floss. Tears spring unexpectedly into my eyes when she says, "I had no one who really got me. I was always too much for most people and not enough for others. You saw me and I'll always love you for that. I hope we get to see each other again, I mean, before our deaths and all." She pulls me back at arm's length. "I like Lorcan, I mean, for you anyway. He loves you and I already told him if he hurts you, I'll summon him and bind him to a circle and force him to watch reruns of my favorite shows on repeat. He looked positively horrified."

A laugh bubbles from deep within my stomach. "How the Hell am I supposed to manage without you?"

"Oh, you'll be fine, babe. Look, if you get bored here, you can always pop up and see me through one of those visitors' entrances."

We both know that can't happen, at least, not without time catching up on me. I wouldn't be able to come back to Hell. But we hold on to the possibility as we hug again. "Say goodbye to Gomey before you go."

"Of course," she whispers against the top of my head. "I wouldn't leave without giving my baby a cuddle. You take care of him. Give him treats whenever he wants."

"You always did spoil him."

She steps back and winks. "Here's to new adventures, ones without a ton of murder and blood." I watch her walk away, catching the gloss to her eyes as she turns toward the door.

Before she leaves, I call out, "Where's the fun in that?"

The ghost of her laugh lingers in the room after she walks out the door, leaving me alone to say goodbye to Gomez, who's taken up permanent residence in my other room now that I spend most nights in Lorcan's, which is ours now, I suppose. He prefers it that way, to be left to sleep without having to hear any sexcapades, while still spending the days with me. Although, occasionally, when Lorcan is sleeping, I'll shadow walk across the castle and snuggle into bed with my little bat.

A light tapping sounds on the door, and I turn, thinking it's Lorcan back from his meeting with Lucifer, when I'm instead greeted by the devil himself. "Evie, darling," he says, arms wide open. Moving at inhuman speed, he wraps his arms around me, kissing me on the cheek before moving back a foot. "I was hoping I'd find you before you returned to the Human Realm."

"I don't want to go," I admit, and his smile grows, deepening his smile lines.

"Excellent." He presses his hands together, as if in prayer, then turns to look out over the balcony. "Because I do."

My eyes almost bulge out of my head. "You want to go to the Human Realm?" I clarify, figuring I must have misunderstood.

"Yes." He grips the stone and diverts his eyes from the landscape, probably tired of having looked at it in a million different ways. "Hell was my punishment for sins against my father. I was prideful then, and I wanted more from the position he'd given me."

My head spins as he explains his backstory. Lucifer. I still can't wrap my head around this being real sometimes and swear I'm going to wake up from the longest fever dream ever.

"Anyway," he continues casually, as if he's not explaining a story most humans would die to know the truth of, "relieved of my exalted position, I was to begin servitude here until the day my heart was without sin. I know now that no heart is without sin, not even an angel. I don't want to go back to my family up there, not when I have my sons here, and my new daughter." He smiles and tips a finger under my chin. "Which is why I am here. You wear darkness beautifully, better than any mortal I have known. Lorcan is my eldest and always was my most sensitive son."

"Don't let him hear you say that," I tease, and he laughs.

"Lorcan was born to rule. He does it with a level head, and like you, he can handle the crushing darkness. I, however, am tired of it. I don't wish to return to Heaven, even if I could, or stay in Hell. I am looking to retire, to go to the Human Realm and live a human experience. I was there when they were created, after all, but I never got to live amongst them. Punishing souls in Hell means I've been around the worst of them, mostly, but Rosa has told me of all the new and wonderful things there." He pauses.

"Besides, I am hoping to find my cinnamon roll recipe I lost some millennia ago in an old grimoire somewhere."

Excitement brims in his eyes and I don't have the heart to tell him it's probably lost to the ages. Everyone needs hope, even,—especially—the devil.

"Are you saying you want Lorcan to reign over Hell?"

Threads of the universe swirl in the silver fabric of his eyes. "I'm saying I want you both to rule Hell. He, as King of Hell, taking my place and you, as Queen."

My heart palpitates. A million questions caught in my throat as I choke on my response.

"Don't answer now," he says, lifting a finger. "Talk to your beloved first. Lorcan has not accepted the position yet. He believes you want to live out your mortal life." His grin sparkles with knowing. "Although you and I both know that's not true."

"But I am mortal," I splutter, finding my voice. "How can I rule over demons when my body is so vulnerable?"

He taps a finger against the ledge. "I never fully trusted Evangeline. There was something about her I couldn't place, if I am honest, that I didn't want to see. But I could see she was a liar, yet being loved by her was so refreshing and thrilling that I ignored all of that." With a shrug, he says, "I've always had a thing for dominant women."

My nose scrunches. "We all have psycho exes."

He laughs again, and I'm not sure if he's being polite or if he genuinely finds these quips funny. "Well, I could have made her immortal, but I didn't for that reason. However, I do have the ability and have weighed your heart. I know you will not forsake

Lorcan, or me. If you and Lorcan agree, I'll feed you my blood and you won't have to worry about mortality again."

I cough, bringing my hand to my throat as the scratchy words reach my lips. "I want to be with Lorcan for an eternity. I also want to rule Hell," I admit, surprised at how easy it is for me to throw my mortal life away. Then, I never had a good time as one. "I like it here and I see souls that can be saved, with some gentle nudging in the right direction. The ones that are too far gone, too dark? Well, I quite enjoy dishing out punishment to those deserving."

"Wonderful." He spins to leave but stops by Lorcan and my four-post bed, running his hand over the carved expressions in the wood of suffering. "You'll make an excellent Queen, Evie Fallenmoore."

That next evening, Rosa and Ezra decide to stay for the ceremony, and I'm glad to know I'll have a mortal ally here with me. Aiden decided to stay with Gideon for some unknown reason, even after Lorcan removed his mark.

Gomez flaps his wings, a tiny, obsidian crown on his head attached with a little strap as he's given the honorary title of prince of Hell by Lucifer.

Lorcan claps from the dais holding two thrones made of obsidian and bone, surrounded by tall pillars carved from the most intricate cravings. A ghostly mist creeps around the stone steps, thrones, and vaulted ceiling, illuminated by the purple glow of candlelight.

Rosa catches my eye from the intimate crowd swelling at the bottom of the dais. Her smile sparkles amongst the rest and I watch as Ezra stares, a look in his eye I've seen before and wonder: Does Rosa even know that Ezra's falling for her?

Asher leans lazily against a statue of a mortal holding up a pillar, the marble figure appearing crushed under the weight. Beside him, Lazarus glares, arms crossed over his chest. Silas at least looks somewhat happy, or it's an act. Either way, we'll find out soon.

Ezra pushes two fingers in his mouth and whistles as Lorcan takes the center dais, kneeling in front of Lucifer.

I'm proud of you. I push the words through our bond as I watch the crown lower around his black locks. *I'm so happy you admitted to wanting this. You deserve it.*

Pride swells our bond, tightening it as if it's a tangible thing. *You are my eternity, My Little Witch.*

I love you too, My Demon.

He stands, commanding eyes taking ahold of the crowd as Lucifer transfers his powers to Lorcan, the shift invisible to the untrained eye, but I notice a few spectral swirls of smoke dancing from Lucifer's fingers and into Lorcan's. His eyes close in what seems like a peaceful transference.

Silver outlines Lorcan's black pupils, melding with the pastel green in his irises. After a few minutes of silence, Lucifer sucks in a deep breath and smiles at Lorcan, then embraces him. "I love you, Son."

Lorcan's heart balloons in the bond. I walk the few steps as Lucifer descends them, the taste of his blood still potent on my tongue from this morning when he'd kindly mixed his angel blood with a sweet tea.

Suddenly, no one else matters as I stand before my king, my immortal heart racing for his touch.

"Immortality is breathtaking on you." His fingers entwine with mine. "How did I get so lucky to become the demon with everything?"

"To think, this started with you stalking me," I tease, and our conversation falls silent, slipping into our bond instead where our words are all our own.

Even then, he speaks into my mind. *You captivated me. It's why I wanted to hurt you, punish you even. It was never because you were my key to freedom, or your affiliation with Evangeline.*

No?

It was because no one has ever made me hornier. I catch the laugh in my mouth, and he grins. *I always knew you were my salvation, but I didn't understand then that it wasn't just from the Shadow Realm. You were always the key to my happiness, and I could sense it then.*

I could sense it too.

Sense what, exactly? He asks.

That what we had was something epic.

He grabs a crown of obsidian, similar to Gomez's, but full size. "Kneel," he commands. "For it'll be the last time you kneel for anyone, My Queen."

The crown is heavy as it settles around my head. I lift my fingers to touch the cool metal and a smile creeps over my face.

Aiden whistles from the crowd, clapping in tandem with Rosa. "Woo! Bromina!"

I smirk and before I can take in the moment, Lorcan spins me to face him and takes my mouth in his, his tongue meeting mine with the same obsessive word filtering through our bond as he grips me with fervor.

Mine.

Mine.

Mine.

Always mine.

Rebecca writes dark fantasy romance, usually with gothic elements and always with morally gray characters. She loves anything with enemies to lovers, slow burn, and lots of angst.

Christine writes dark gothic paranormal and fantasy romance with epic spice. She enjoys turning the darkness from past trauma into the written word. CM lives on books, coffee, and tattoos.

Check out their Patreon for exclusive paperbacks, artwork and other goodies.

Patreon: https://www.patreon.com/c/huttongarcia

Instagram:
CM Hutton: www.instagram.com/anxioustattooedbookish
Rebecca L. Garcia: www.instagram.com/rebeccalgarciabooks

Printed in Dunstable, United Kingdom

66877596R00272